HIGHLAND
CONQUEST

HIGHLAND CONQUEST

SONS OF SINCLAIR

HEATHER McCOLLUM

Entangled Publishing, LLC
10940 S Parker Road
Suite 327
Parker, CO 80134
Visit our website at www.entangledpublishing.com.

Amara is an imprint of Entangled Publishing, LLC.

Edited by Alethea Spiridon
Cover design by LJ Anderson, Mayhem Cover Creations
Cover art by
VJ Dunraven/PeriodImages.com,
kamchatka/depositphotos,
MRBIG_PHOTOGRAPHY/istockphoto,
Uros Petrovic/Adobestock
Interior design by Toni Kerr

MMP ISBN 978-1-64063-7474
ebook ISBN 978-1-64063-7481

Manufactured in the United States of America

First Edition May 2020

AMARA

ALSO BY HEATHER McCOLLUM

THE CAMPBELLS SERIES

The Scottish Rogue
The Savage Highlander
The Wicked Viscount
The Highland Outlaw

HIGHLAND ISLES SERIES

The Beast of Aros Castle
The Rogue of Islay Isle
The Wolf of Kisimul Castle
The Devil of Dunakin Castle

HIGHLAND HEARTS SERIES

Captured Heart
Tangled Hearts
Crimson Heart

For Braden
You will always be my Highland hero,
one who gives every day.
I love you too.

SCOTS GAELIC AND OLD ENGLISH WORDS USED IN HIGHLAND CONQUEST

a cheannsachadh agus a mharbhadh—conquer and kill

àlainn—lovely

aon, dha, trì—one, two, three

blaigeard—bastard

cac—shite

daingead—damn it

Eun—Bird (name of Cain's falcon)

falbh—go

God's teeth (Old English)—common curse

leasing-monger (Old English)—a habitual liar

magairlean—ballocks

màthair—mother

sarding (Old English)—foking

Seraph—Angel (name of Cain's white horse)

siubhal air—ride on

siuthad—go on

targe—shield, usually made of wood and lined with steel

thoir an aire—watch out

tolla-thon—arsehole

BOOK OF REVELATIONS

1   I watched as the Lamb opened the first of the seven seals. Then I heard one of the four living creatures say in a voice like thunder, "Come!"

2   I looked, and there before me was a white horse! Its rider held a bow, and he was given a crown, and he rode out as a conqueror bent on conquest.

3   When the Lamb opened the second seal, I heard the second living creature say, "Come!"

4   Then another horse came out, a fiery red one. Its rider was given power to take peace from the earth and to make people kill one another. To him was given a large sword.

5   When the Lamb opened the third seal, I heard the third living creature say, "Come!" I looked, and there before me was a black horse! Its rider was holding a pair of scales in his hand.

6   Then I heard what sounded like a voice among the four living creatures, saying, "Two pounds of wheat for a day's wages, and six pounds of barley for a day's wages, and do not damage the oil and the wine!"

7   When the Lamb opened the fourth seal, I heard the voice of the fourth living creature say, "Come!"

8   I looked, and there before me was a pale horse! Its rider was named Death…

CHAPTER ONE

Cain Sinclair surveyed the mist-shrouded battle-field from atop his white charger, standing on the eastern rise of the moor. The field lay like a giant chessboard, his pieces moving according to his perfect strategy. To the north lay the sea. To the southwest lay his prize, Dunrobin Castle, seat of Clan Sutherland.

His gaze swept along the lines of Sinclair cavalry flanking north and south, and the warriors charging through their foes in the valley. He could see his father, the chief of the Sinclairs, down in the middle of it all, slashing away at Sutherland warriors on foot.

Gideon, Cain's younger brother, sat mounted next to him on his black charger. "Put your bloody crown on before Da sees ye've taken it off," Gideon said. "Half the Sutherlands will piss themselves when ye swoop down there wearing God's crown, unleashing your arrows from atop a white steed."

"Bàs is likely doing that already with his sickle and mask on the eastern ridge," Cain said, tipping his head toward the far bluff where his youngest brother rode with his army of pale-colored horses. The plants they rubbed into the horses' gray coats gave Bàs's herd a distinctive green tint, enough to bring the biblical prophecy of the four horsemen to life.

Gideon nodded but didn't break a smile. "Just put the damn crown on, else we must endure Da's wrath afterward."

Cain's gaze caught enemy movement in the west. He raised two fingers to his mouth, whistling. The shrill call brought his falcon, the loyal raptor flapping her black-and-white-lined wings over his head. Leather jesses dangled from her sharp yellow talons as she alighted on his gloved arm. Yanking an orange-dyed scrap of fabric from the back of his targe, Cain held it to his bird's curved beak. She snapped it up and crouched, and he lifted her into the air as she sprang upward to soar low over the field of battling men. The orange flag flapping down would alert his father and two other brothers that the enemy was organizing to advance in the west, opposite from their current positions.

"Let us ride," Cain said, his voice more like a growl, not because of the battle before him, for he'd been raised on battles, but because Gideon was right about their ferocious father. Cain pressed the steel crown, forged in the smithy at Girnigoe Castle, down upon his head. Its familiar pinch around his temples made him curse low.

"Ye go," Gideon said, drawing Cain's gaze. Third in age and trained to pass judgment as well as battle, Gideon was as lethal as the other Sinclair brothers and never stayed back from helping them smash their opponents.

"Blast it, Gideon," Cain said as he spotted blood seeping down from a slash along Gideon's upper arm. Cain hooked his bow and targe onto the back of his horse, Seraph, and jumped down. "Ye are injured." He grabbed a leather satchel and yanked the cord open.

"Just a bit of a slice before I skewered the unlucky bastard." Gideon dismounted to pull his bloodied shirt away from the gaping flesh. "Merida will sew it up back at Girnigoe."

"Aye, but if it gets tainted, Da will have your hide," Cain said, glancing back out at the battle he yearned to join but not before plastering some of his aunt's poultice onto his brother's arm. "We can die in battle with honor, but no horseman from God would die of taint." It was one of their father's favorite bellowing lectures as he schooled them in the biblical promise of victory over their enemies. They'd all heard it repeated thousands of times.

Cain's falcon returned to glide overhead, dropping the orange signal flag onto the ground at her master's boots. Looking toward the battlefield, Cain watched his second brother, Joshua, signal his cavalry, seated on bay horses, to ride west to meet the Sutherland challenge while Bàs drove his smaller army forward to keep guard in the east, along with Cain's white-seated cavalry. Gideon's men, who rode black horses, remained in the middle of the moor, supporting the mighty Sinclair chief.

Their father, George Sinclair, fourth Earl of Caithness, slashed away at the oncoming men on foot from his position in the middle of the summer meadow. Even from the rise, Cain could hear his war cry as he let his wild bloodlust rage against his hated enemy. Spinning to slay foe after foe, his blood-slick sword moved like a familiar dance. The man loved battle and always commanded his sons to give him room to slay his enemy on his own, even now in his advancing years. Some thought him insane. Actually, most thought him insane, but they knew enough to hold their tongues, or the wildness of Chief Sinclair could turn against them.

"Go," Gideon said, adjusting the poultice around his arm. "It will be over too soon, and ye will miss the victory."

He was right. The tide of the battle was turning quickly in their favor. It would be over soon, and they would ride on to conquer the Sutherland Clan's castle, ending the decades-old war that had started when the Sutherland laird divorced Cain's aunt, Merida Sinclair, for not producing a living heir for him.

Cain's muscles contracted with carefully honed strength. He could already taste the sweetness of victory and contentment of conquest. Both were his main responsibilities within their clan, duties given to him by his father when Cain was a boy of nine, the day his fourth brother was born and their angelic mother died.

He hoisted himself onto Seraph's back, the well-trained horse standing as still as a statue carved of white marble. Mist still floated in patches over the land below where men surged and retreated, spun and died around his father, but a breeze coming from off the sea to the east scattered the building heat. A group of Sutherlands fell under the press of Bàs's pale horses, and Cain's white cavalry pushed back a line of enemy on the north side of the field.

Cain inhaled the damp smell of earth mixed with the tang of blood, gathering his reins loosely. Seraph shifted, his eagerness evident as he awaited the press of Cain's heels to surge forward, but movement among the soaring pines on the edge of the opposite slope made him still.

A black horse stepped out into the wide clearing before the forest. Being black, the horse would belong to Gideon once won, but what caught Cain's full focus was the woman who stood straight up on the horse's saddle. Clothed in slim black trousers, the woman balanced while raising a fist into the air. Men emerged from the woods to stand on either side of her.

"What are ye up to?" he asked under his breath. Cain squinted, trying to take in the details of who could only be the daughter of the dead chief of the Sutherland Clan, Arabella Sutherland. He had met her once, a decade ago at a Beltane Festival. She'd been a beauty then, with wide gray eyes, and still too young to do much more than pick wildflowers and dance with the maidens around the maypole. Things had apparently changed, but he wondered if she still favored the prickly Scottish thistles she had carried then. The hood she was said to don in public was missing, leaving her long dark braid free to be seen over her shoulder, but she was wearing a leather half mask to cover the lower part of her face.

"Cain," Gideon said, his voice hard as the men around Arabella raised their bows, arrows nocked, some of them flaming. "They are aiming to fire upon—"

"*Siubhal air!*" Cain yelled. His heels pressed in as he leaned forward over his massive white steed, his targe coming up as they flew like one down the hill toward his father. Hooves churning through the spindly flowers and grass, Seraph leaped over partly hidden gullies and boulders as Cain braced his targe to protect his horse's head and his own. The rest of the noble warhorse was covered in thick leather armor, similar to his own, although without the metal plates lining it.

As the ground leveled out, a hundred arrows sliced downward through the air, hitting men too slow to raise their shields against the onslaught of raining death. Fire caught on some of the sun-dried grasses, but the dew still clung, making the flames sizzle and die. Arrow points thudded against Cain's targe as he raced toward his father.

His youngest brother, Bàs, had broken off from his army and surged forward from the opposite direction. Bàs yelled, his deep voice rising up as he stood in his stirrups, his black armor and skull helmet giving him the appearance of an angel of death. Men scattered from their paths, both Sutherland and Sinclair, as the brothers roared closer to their patriarch and chief.

Whack. The first arrow hit his da's upper chest, followed immediately by three more before he fell, impaling his sword arm, stomach, and lower chest.

"Nay!" Cain yelled. Fury shot lightning through his blood, and he leaped from the slowing horse, smacking Seraph's thigh as he dropped into a crouch to cover his father's prone body. Arrows continued to rain down, piercing the field around him. "Da!"

A short way off, the meadow was clear of the barrage, the circle of arrow-pocked meadow around only his father. "Bloody hell." Every foking arrow fired in that last volley had been pointed directly at George Sinclair.

Cain looked up at the rise and saw her there, still standing on her horse. Aye, every arrow had flown at his father, ordered by the thrust of Arabella Sutherland's raised fist.

Bàs slid off his horse, hitting its flank to get it racing with Cain's horse to safety. The two brothers formed a barrier over their father. Blood soaked up through the laces of his thin battle armor. A thudding horse came from the hill, and Cain lowered his sword to the grass when he saw it was Gideon jumping down. Only Joshua, leading the cavalry of bay horses to the west, was missing. The battle raged, men yelling and steel clanging, but Cain's sole focus was on the mighty man wetting the grasses and yellow flowers with the scarlet flow of his waning life.

"Fok," Gideon swore, his hands trying to dam the welling blood, but it was like holding back an ocean of red.

"Death has come for him," Bàs said, and he pulled his great horned helmet from his head and his skull mask from his face. He kneeled, his sweat-matted hair falling about his shoulders.

Cain yanked off his glove and grabbed his father's hand, but it didn't feel like his da's without the strength that always grabbed back as if trying to prove his superior strength. "Da," he called. "Da."

George Sinclair's eyes squeezed as if pain momentarily robbed him of his courage, but then he blinked, his lids opening to stare up at his boys. Red spittle sat on his lips as blood bubbled up from his pierced lungs. "Cain, bow to no man. Your duty is to conquer. Sinclairs above all else. Ye are God's servant, his weapon against all those who are weak," he said, staring up at him, and he coughed up more blood. Cain felt a shadow of his da's strength squeeze his hand. "Joshua will rule all wars," he continued, a wheeze hissing in his words. "Gideon…"

"I am here, Da," Gideon said, ducking his head to hover before their sire.

"Judge well without mercy. Ye know what is right from wrong. Do not be swayed from your judgment."

George's head lolled to the side, though his eyes remained open as he stared at his youngest son, Bàs. "Ye are named for Death," he said, each word growing weaker. "Ye will bring death to all ye touch. Execute our enemies." He coughed, the lines around his lips stained red as blood filled the tiny cracks in his skin.

Cain yanked off one of the scraps he used for signaling and wiped his father's lips. The movement revived the man enough for his gaze to connect with Cain. "Ye are chief now." His heavy eyes slid up to the crown that sat crooked on Cain's head. "As I have taught ye…the four…sent by God to kill our enemies. Ye are ready to rule together; first my kingdom and then all of Scotland."

The redness that always tinted their father's ruddy cheeks paled until his skin took on the deathly pallor of Bàs's gray-green horse. The corners of his mouth tipped upward. Had Cain ever seen his father smile before? Not since before his mother died. George Sinclair looked up into Cain's face.

"Merida told me I would die this day. 'Tis a good death, this." Staring, locked with the gaze of his eldest son, his eyes stilled as his soul flew elsewhere.

Cain didn't move, couldn't move. His da had been a mountain, spewing energy, conviction, and uncontrolled temper all through his life. Now he was suddenly silent and unmoving with the heavy weight of death. The absence of his bellowing war cry seemed to echo louder than the surprise middle-of-night training sessions he would call to keep his sons ready to fight. George Sinclair had seemed invincible. No matter how many times he bled, there was always more blood pumping through his strong heart.

"Da," Cain said, his hand flat over the man's frozen heart. He bowed his head, his chest tight. His fingers curled into his father's blood-soaked shirt. "Aye, 'twas an honorable death, and we will make ye proud."

Bàs kneeled beside their father, his deep voice rising in a ribbon of prayer, as the discordance of war stormed around them. But there always seemed to be war around them, and they paid it no heed.

The arrows had ceased their rain, and Cain pushed up to stand tall, bow over his back and sword in his bloody hand. His gaze sought his target before the line of pines on the south rise. The woman still stood upright on her horse, her focus toward them. Did she wait to see if the Sinclair chief was dead?

Cain's fist tightened against his thigh, his thumb wrapping around to crack his knuckle. He met her stare, letting her know, without a doubt, that he saw her. "Ye are mine," he murmured, his tone like a low growl.

But first… Cain raised his left arm, still encased in his gauntlet, and his falcon, always hovering overhead during battle, swooped down to alight. Cain pulled the one flag he'd never used before, a black and red woven together. Black for death and red for Sinclair blood. "Fly!" Cain yelled, sending the signal to the one brother who didn't yet know that the day for which their father had prepared them, was here.

The day the four horsemen took over the rule of Clan Sinclair.

• • •

"He is dead," Ella Sutherland said, her words hushed as her heart pounded like the deep beats of a kettledrum.

The warlord who had killed her father, the bastard who had spurred the feud with their clan for decades, the grisly, demented man who had whacked more than a hundred Sutherland heads from their shoulders, was gone. "The madman is dead."

"Are ye certain?" Kenneth Macleod, her father's old advisor, asked. He cupped hands over his eyes to stare across the battle-trodden meadow. "I cannot see."

Ella glanced heavenward. "Of course, you cannot see, because you refuse to wear the spectacles I obtained for you." The man was in his sixty-fifth year and still insisted on riding out to battle, but he wouldn't use the contraptions to help him see better.

He waved off her comment. "If ye see he is dead, then he is dead."

In truth, she couldn't see the crazed leader of Clan Sinclair. "Three of his sons are around him, but their sire is not getting up," she answered, watching the one brother who had risen to stare her way. He was tall and thick with muscle, leather armor tied about his bare chest and upper arms. The sight of the crown on top of his head and bow slung over his back made her breath catch.

There was no mistaking Cain Sinclair, the oldest of the four Sinclair brothers. She'd come face-to-face with him at a festival twelve years ago when she was a young lass and he was a lean-muscled, tall lad. He'd smiled at her until his father whispered in his ear, and Cain's handsome features had pinched in disgust. *Disgust*? And that was before, when her face was unmarked.

Ella tugged on her leather mask, straightening it where it sat under her eyes, and looked away from him. She still stood on top of her mare, Gilla, booted toes secure in the specially made holds on the saddle. Her hand leveled against her damp forehead to block the sun as she surveyed the clashing men in the valley of the moor. "Blast," she murmured, tugging on a wisp of hair that had fallen from her braid. Her army to the west was falling back under the Sinclair cavalry of bay horses.

"If his sons are down there…" Kenneth called up to her, his head snapping back and forth. "Get down," he said, but she didn't have to follow every order now that her father was buried and unable to punish her for her insolence. After all, she was the new chief of Clan Sutherland, at least for the time being.

Kenneth smacked at her boot, but she didn't move as she watched the Sinclair advancement in the west. "I am too far away for their paltry arrows to reach me." Maybe, maybe not.

"But the Sinclair horsemen," Kenneth said, trying to grab one of her booted feet.

"Are only human, like you and I," she said, dodging his hand by standing on one foot, her balance perfected over a lifetime of practice.

Kenneth snorted and dropped his hand. "Those monsters are nothing like you and me."

Ella motioned to Ethan, her captain of archers, to prepare the line of men for another volley. She disliked using the archers at such a distance, because they could hit her own men or the horses from either clan. But releasing their deadly arrows overtop of her men to the west would hopefully stop the push of the Sinclair horde there. It was likely their last chance to divert them—or at least to slow the bastards—while Dunrobin Castle prepared for a siege.

Kenneth squinted out toward the battle. "Can the sons of Sinclair see ye?"

She crouched, landing in her saddle, her gaze sliding back to the meadow before her. Ella's stomach pinched tight, making it hard to swallow. "Cain Sinclair is running this way," she said softly.

"*Magairlean!*" Kenneth yelled. "Ye need to flee. He saw ye order the assault on his sire."

The Sinclair warrior raised his fingers to his mouth. Three short bursts sliced through the deep hum of battle, and his white horse charged down from a rise on his left, dodging men and swords in the melee of battle.

Sinclair's arms pumped on either side of his kilted hips as he ran, using his short sword to slice through a foolhardy Sutherland who got in his way. His features were still distant, but squinting, she could make out the fierce set of his mouth, his teeth showing in a snarl. He wore the promise of death on his face like a mask.

Her heart thumped as the space between them shortened, his long strides eating away the ground like a famished beast. Mesmerized by his grace under all that armor, Ella watched as his steed drew level, slowing to match his pace. The man sheathed his sword and grabbed the side of the saddle, leaping to pull himself up over the horse's back, solely with the strength of his massive arms.

"Holy Mother Mary," she said and twisted in her seat to Ethan, the captain of the archers standing behind her. "To the west. Set them to fire overtop of our front line to strike the Sinclairs giving chase." Ethan rushed off, yelling orders, and his finely trained men followed.

"Get ye the bloody hell out of here," Kenneth hollered, obviously now able to see the fierce warrior galloping toward their rise.

"Hide!" she yelled at him. She pulled Gilla around to race into the thick pine forest at her back. She wouldn't ride west, because he'd follow her to disrupt her archers who must save half her army, so she turned south toward the castle, but she would veer east after fording the shallow river on the other side of the forest. If he followed her, it would give Dunrobin more time to prepare for attack. *Damn.* Without the support of Hew Mackay's clan, she might lose everything. The thought gripped her around the throat, and she fought to swallow.

Leaning over Gilla's neck, she gave the beloved horse her head. The two worked together to tilt and dodge upright and fallen trees and the thick summer growth of bramble as they raced through the woods. They had the advantage here among the Sutherland trees, trees she'd spent days climbing as a child instead of risking an encounter with her father back at Dunrobin Castle.

Blood pounded in Ella's ears with the harsh sound of her breath through the hole cut into her leather mask. Sweat trickled between her bound breasts, and the interior of the mask stuck to her skin.

Several more leaps over the summer-dense bramble and Ella glanced back over her shoulder. She nearly gagged, her stomach twisting into a knot. Cain Sinclair crashed through the trees behind her. *Holy Mother Mary in Heaven.* He was going to catch her. The thought sent prickles along her skin, her chin growing numb with them, and she turned forward.

For several heartbeats, Ella focused entirely on finding the swiftest route through the tangle around her and Gilla. From the sounds behind her, Cain Sinclair's strategy was to leap over and crash through everything. Taking a straight-line route toward his prey, as if his horse was unbreakable.

What would he do if he caught them? Slaughter Gilla? Nay, the Sinclairs were known for honoring horses over people. But he would carry Ella back to Girnigoe Castle to torture her for killing his father, unless he skewered her out here in the dense forest.

She leaned forward, sliding her hands down Gilla's withers to squeeze the mare's strong neck. "Health and long life to you," she called above the rush of wind and then pushed upright in the saddle, searching ahead.

"Please," she whispered, her gaze desperate for a suitable limb. A thick oak stood off to the right, and with a press of Ella's legs, Gilla veered toward it. Ella dropped the reins and tucked her legs to raise into a crouch on the horse's broad back, her body taking the rolling gait of her stride as her fingers anchored her to the saddle. The limb loomed close. With her bow and quiver over one shoulder, she jumped, leaping to grab the branch. Even with her muscles contracted to stop her arms from being torn from her sockets, the tug on her shoulders burned as she caught herself, her leather gloves grasping the rough bark.

"Run home," Ella yelled and gritted her teeth as she strained to lift herself, throwing a leg over to straddle the tree limb. Thank God she'd given up skirts when she'd won the chiefdom.

Reaching to hug the tree trunk, Ella lodged her boots underneath her to stand and hoisted herself onto a higher branch. A thinner bough stuck out level with her chest, and she leaned against it.

"Arabella Sutherland! Ye are mine!" The warrior's deep voice hit her with such force that she clutched the thin bough to stop herself from teetering. She threw her leather-clad leg over the thin limb, pulling herself farther up the tree. A whispered cracking sound made her grab around the tree's thick trunk.

"I belong to no one," she yelled back. The man's words were so like her father's.

"Ye killed my father," the Sinclair yelled.

"And you killed mine." If she could keep him talking, it might give her time to climb higher. But he could still shoot her. Would Kenneth send men to rescue her if she could stay alive?

She peeked down through the branches and broad green leaves. He stared up at her, breathing hard, and lowered his sword. "I have caught ye. Come down," Cain Sinclair called. "I might spare your life."

"Lies, for which I will not fall," she replied.

"Given a few moments, ye *will* fall from your foolish climb onto that branch."

Cac! Holding on, she wasn't even able to give him a rude gesture, the one she'd learned from working with the Sutherland warriors over the last three months. "Get your bloody arse and your men off Sutherland land," she yelled down. "You bastard of a whoring cow." With a tight grip around the tree trunk, Ella lowered her boots to the safer limb under her and turned outward.

Cain Sinclair's brows rose from what she imagined was a persistent furrow, giving him a look of surprise. Dirt and blood smeared his leather armor and his bare arms where she could see the dark lines of tattoos encircling the thick muscle. Blood lay splattered across his bristled cheeks and forehead, where wheat-colored hair hung down around his stony jaw.

"Ye slander my mother and murder my father,"

he said, surprise lifting the ferocious growl from his tone.

She pushed the tightening of guilt down behind the thumping of her heart. "There is no murder in battle, not when both sides are armed and trained," she answered. "And there is no shame in bringing down a foe who is insane with bloodlust, killing hundreds, including my own father." She nocked an arrow in her bow, but the bow was made for distance. Up close it was more cumbersome than effective.

"A father for a father." He narrowed his eyes and rubbed his jaw as he gazed up at her, giving the briefest of nods as if conceding the point. "But my mother was a saint."

"Who gave birth to the Four Horsemen from Hell," she said, trying to hold her bow steady. Damn her shaking.

"We are from God, not Satan," he countered, unstrapping the armor from his arms and chest. The pieces fell away, as if he emerged from leather and steel ice. They thudded onto the bed of moss at the base of the tree. He stood wearing only a thin sleeveless tunic with his green and blue kilt belted around narrow hips.

"So says the man wearing the Devil's crown." She pulled back on the thick bowstring and loosed the arrow.

He dodged it easily by leaning into the tree trunk and yanked the circlet from his head, tossing it to clink against the steel lining his breastplate. Her arrow quivered where it stuck into the ground before the mighty white horse. The trained beast didn't even back away from it but watched his master.

Before Ella could nock another, Cain slid one of his arrows into his bow and held it pointed up directly toward her face. An opening of his fingers would split her skull. "We could spend the morning shooting at each other until ye are dead or out of arrows," he said, his voice as steady as his hand.

Lord, how had it come to this? The day had started off so promising, as she helped young Jamie train with his wooden sword in the glow of the dawning light. The yeasty aroma of baking bread had wafted on the breeze from the kitchens as they'd practiced in the herb garden to the sound of summer finches waking among the trees.

All of that had changed with the thudding of horse hooves across the wooden bridge beyond the wall. Her scout had barreled into the bailey to report that Sinclairs were riding onto Sutherland land, armies of trained warriors led by the maniacal Chief George Sinclair.

And here she was, a few short hours later, about to die.

CHAPTER TWO

Dearest Lord, keep Jamie safe, Ella prayed as she balanced in the branching oak. She stared down the steely tip of Cain Sinclair's arrow, sliding her gaze past the threat to stare into his rare light-blue eyes.

"If the legend of your abilities proves true, you will pierce me dead with one clean shot." With God's grace, he'd be vain enough to dispatch her with mercy. She'd endured pain in her life, and the anticipation of more brought the tingling sensation back to the skin beneath her leather mask.

They stared at each other. Although Ella wouldn't shame herself by looking away, she let her gaze slide along his solid jaw that was covered by a few day's growth of beard, his nose that held a bump where it had once been broken, and his cheekbones where a white line showed a scar from battles past. He had painted blue lines of woad on one side of his face from forehead to jaw to give him the fierce, wild appearance of their Pict ancestors. But he didn't need paint to give him the look of promised death. The intensity of his eyes spoke of slaughter, and the hardness of his muscles preceded pain.

Brows bent and full lips parted, Cain Sinclair looked…curious. He exhaled long and lowered his bow. So unconcerned, he even arched his back and stretched his muscled arms overhead, which only made them look larger. A horse's head was tattooed in curves and spikes of dark pigment on the upper part of one arm, while woven lines encircled both biceps.

She should nock an arrow and fire at that massive chest of his, but instead she balanced on the limb, trying not to disgrace herself with a swoon as her heart pounded. *I am going to die.*

"Remove your mask," he said.

She blinked, her lips curling back in a snarl. "No." She forced herself to breathe evenly to battle against the tingling sensation running along her jaw and lips.

His brows lowered in annoyance. He stripped off his one thick gauntlet and placed his hands on the tree trunk, quickly assessing that the oak was too large and rooted to be shaken. He clicked his tongue, and his horse came closer to stand under the tree. But instead of using the horse to lift himself, Cain bent his knees and jumped, his fingers catching on the first thick branch Ella had grabbed from her horse's back. Biceps bulging, he lifted the weight of his body up through the air.

Cac. She turned toward the other limbs, but none of them were as thick as the two lower ones. Before she could do anything, Cain Sinclair unfolded his huge body into a solid stance on the limb below her, making the leaves quake, his face rising to the same level as hers. Only the thinner bough that had cracked under her weight separated their bodies.

Breathe. Ella pulled in air, glancing down. It was the only direction that afforded an escape. Sinclair's horse stood ready, almost directly below her. Foolish man. All she had to do was take a step out along the limb and drop onto the horse's broad saddle. She'd honed her balance for two decades. Her constant training might save her life this day.

Cain's fingers wrapped around her wrist, anchoring her as if he could read her thoughts. "Take off your mask," he repeated. "I would see the face of my enemy."

How could she break his hold on her? She needed something to shock him into relaxing his grip. Kicking the man in his shin, knee, or if she were lucky, his ballocks, might not be enough to make him release her hand. Ella imagined herself dangling down by her one arm, it being wrenched out of place. "Release my hand, and I will take it off."

His fingers unfolded, only to wind around her other wrist before she could move. He stared into her eyes, a few inches away. She could see the lines and flecks of darker blue in his irises. The fingers of his free hand caught at the back of her mask where ties held it in place over her hair, deftly pulling the knots free.

Very well, let him see her. Let him be shocked, his face pinching in disgust as it had when she was a girl at the festival and he had realized she was a Sutherland. She waited, ready to act. Heart pounding, she forced herself to breathe as he dragged the leather mask free, throwing it below.

The late morning air felt like a splash of cool water against her hot skin, but a flush burned through the relief as he stared at her, his gaze taking in every inch of her face, pausing on the puckered scar. As she fought the urge to turn away, her free hand rose involuntarily to pluck at the loosened hair at her temple. Ella watched for the tight look of revulsion that had haunted her girlhood nightmares after the festival. Time moved forward with the pound of her heart, but his grip only tightened as if anger made his muscles turn to granite. If her hideous scar couldn't shock him into loosening his hold on her, what would?

Her gaze dropped to his full mouth as his lips parted. She'd heard tales of Cain Sinclair's conquests with women, how they gladly crawled into his bed. His prowess and skills as a lover were as much a part of his legend as the lies his father spilled about God sending his sons to conquer the world. Her face grew hotter still as she remembered the foolish stories she'd woven in her head as a girl, stories about him sweeping her away from her cruel life at Dunrobin.

The lines between his brows deepened as he inhaled, fury growing in the clench of his teeth. His voice was deep, like a rumble of advancing thunder over a mountain ridge. "Who is the foking bastard who dared to brand ye?"

• • •

Cain's blood raced with the heat of renewed vengeance. The raven-haired woman standing strong and proud before him had been maimed with a round mark that had been burned into her skin along the left side of her face at the crux of her jaw.

Keeping balance by leaning against the limb separating them, Cain raised his free hand to gently turn her chin with his knuckles so he could better see the mark. It was the size of a large signet ring used to seal parchments with wax. For such a clear picture, she must have been held immobile while the metal seared her flesh. He leaned in closer to spy the shape of a mountain cat. "Bloody hell," he murmured. "'Tis the Sutherland crest."

Arabella Sutherland jerked her face from his touch. "Let me go," she said through her teeth. "I am just a weak, pitiful woman. Let me go, so I can hide away and weep in fear."

There was absolutely nothing weak or pitiful about the Sutherland chief. The fear he'd glimpsed when he'd first caught up to her had faded. Now her angry gray eyes sparked with life and… Determination. Strength. She knew he had every right to crush her. This was war, she was losing, and she had ordered the killing of his father. Her life balanced on his benevolence, yet her gaze and tone held contempt.

"Nay," he said slowly. "Ye will come with me to Girnigoe Castle."

She blinked. Only the slight widening of her eyes hinted at dread. The hand he held lifted, and her free hand landed on his shoulder, the pressure of it almost making him look sideways at it. Her hand slid up to his hair at the back of his head, and she leaned in.

Cain's life froze as her lips pressed into his. She stood there, her mouth against his, her eyes open with inexperience. There was no hesitation or dismay in the kiss. He inhaled her scent, heat and woman with the edge of something floral. It made his heartbeat thud deeply, and a warning flitted through the thickness suddenly clogging his head. What was she doing?

She slanted her face to deepen the kiss, opening her lips against his own. A river of lust surged up inside him to smother the warning, and he released her wrist to cup her face. Her skin was so soft, the strong curve of her jawline the perfect complement to the grace and courage of this warrior woman. The taste of her burrowed into his mind, spurring wild thoughts of them rolling together in the shadows of night under the stars.

She broke the kiss, breathing heavily. His hands curled over the limb separating them, wishing to tear it away to reach the beautifully curved body clothed in black leather. "Arabella," he whispered.

She reached up, touching his cheek. She stared into his eyes, her breath coming deeply as if her heart pounded, too. Her hands slid down to hold his forearms. "I am called Ella," she said, and he felt her breath touch his lips.

"Ella," he repeated, as if tasting it on his tongue.

She stared at him, blinking as if waking from a dream. The unguarded look made her even more beautiful. God in Heaven, he wanted her.

Whack. Ella's braid whipped him across the cheek as she spun away. He reached out to grab her, his hands catching only air. In an instant, she was gone.

"Fok," he yelled, slamming forward against the limb. It let out a sharp crack with his weight as he looked over it. Ella Sutherland crouched on the back of Seraph, her arms out to keep her balance. With a broad smile, she dropped down into the saddle, the largeness of it making her look small.

"*Siuthad*," she yelled for the horse to go. Her

knees clutched around Seraph's girth as she dug her
heels into the horse's side, clicking her tongue. But
the mighty horse didn't move, wouldn't move.

Cain wiped the dampness of her kiss from his
mouth with the back of his arm. She'd tricked him
into letting go of her. He'd purposely given her a
false means of escape in case he had not been able
to grab her arm before she jumped, but the kiss had
robbed him of his senses, something that had never
happened to him before.

"*Siuthad!*" she repeated, not knowing what Cain
knew.

"In his battle armor, my horse will not move for
anyone but me," he said, his words grinding out with
suppressed fury over his foolish reaction. He'd
bloody hell let a lass trick him, a virgin lass, her inexperienced kiss racing like wildfire to burn his
renowned discipline to ash.

Staring down at her, his gaze locked with Ella's
for half a moment before the earlier look of hatred
tightened her face. The kiss had been a complete
farce, tearing through him while she remained
unmoved. *You stupid arse.* One kiss and he was
ready to forget she was the enemy.

"Ye cannot escape me." His words ground out
with wrath, propelling her from Seraph's back.

She swooped down for her bow and quiver,
which she must have dropped while she kissed him.
Obviously, her mind had been clear and unaffected
while muddling his. *Curse the siren.*

Without a backward glance, she ran. Cain jumped
down, his boots thudding against the earth, and took
off after her. She sprinted ahead, leaping over

branches, ducking and weaving around thin pines and white birches. Without his heavy armor to weigh him down, Cain gained on her easily.

Bloody, fiery hell. She'd tricked him, with a blasted kiss. He'd been kissed by dozens of lasses, and none of them had prompted him to abandon a lifetime of training and instincts. Ella Sutherland was the enemy and—*she is mine.*

The muscles in his thighs stretched as his legs pumped, propelling him through the forest, his stare intent on the swinging dark braid. He was closing in on his prey, his strong heart pounding as the air fed his perfectly conditioned lungs. He could sprint like this for hours without tiring, yet he wouldn't need but one more minute to catch her.

He was close enough now to hear her huff as she leaped over a mushroom-covered log, and he reached out to graze her swinging braid. A surge in her speed meant she'd felt his touch. The slightest twitch of her head told him that she would veer to the right. Anticipating the direction, he reached out to grab her, yanking her into his chest as they fell together onto the mossy forest floor.

Taking the jarring impact, he rolled her over, pinning her under him. She twisted, trying to kick out, but his heavy legs caught hers. Damp leaves and twigs caught in her hair as she thrashed, trying to twist out from under him. Grabbing her wrists, he raised them over her head. She paused to glare up at him. Cain leaned forward, both of them breathing hard, until they were as close as they had been in the tree.

"Surrender," he ordered. "Ye are mine." He lifted

slightly off her chest so as not to crush the breath from her. Without it, she could not admit that she had been conquered.

"Death before surrender," she replied, breathless, her beautiful gray eyes narrowing to slits. Damn him for noticing the long, dark lashes encircling them. Och, but she'd grown up into a fierce beauty full of fire.

Submission would be easier, but the challenge fit her better. Nay, Ella Sutherland wouldn't beg for release unless it was another trick like the blasted kiss. He hardened his stare, bringing on the look that promised death. It had intimidated great warriors before; surely it would cow this young female chieftain.

"In truth, there are two outcomes," he said. A new strategy formed rapidly in his mind. He waited for her question, but she just glared, showing her hatred. "Aye," he continued. "Two choices. Death or…ye wed a Sinclair to join our clans peacefully under Sinclair rule."

Her eyes widened, lips falling open for the space of a heartbeat. "Which Sinclair?" she asked.

He frowned at her, feeling the ploy but answering anyway. "Me. With my father dead, I am the chief."

Her mouth relaxed, but it wasn't a grin. Despite her sudden look of apathy, her cheeks bloomed red, and she wet her full lips. "Then I choose death."

His head ached from thirst and dirt. Sweat and blood caked his skin, yet his breath burst from him with one wry chuckle. Cain released her arms, and she yanked them back. He sat on his bent knees over her. What a perfect gift to give his da on the day of his death, the conquest of the Sutherland clan.

Ella dug her heels into the dirt, pushing back-ward, and scowled. She was like a cornered wildcat, ready to spit and scratch if he tried to grab her again. Smooth skin showed above the collar of her black tunic, the fabric in stark contrast to the paleness of the graceful column of her neck. They'd landed in what his aunt would call a fairy ring, a wide circle of purple wildflowers, and one had broken off to dangle in the dark hair framing her face.

"Ye will wed me, and I will rule over both clans." Wedding the Sutherland chief would cement the joining of their clans without slaughter. The conquering of her clan would ensure that his father's sacrifice was not in vain, earn him respect as the new chief, and it would appease his curiosity about the fire that had roared to life within him with her kiss. He could also discover and kill the bastard who'd burned her family crest into her skin. Aye, the union was the right choice.

"Did you not hear me, you big, crown-wearing ox?" She shoved her gloved fist into his chest, making him want to strip it naked to see her delicate hand in the flesh. "I choose death," she said, her bottom lip protruding the smallest amount. "A quick death, befitting a chief."

He caught her hand, turning the palm up to slowly pull the glove off each finger as she tried to tug it away. "Apparently, ye choose very poorly," he said, and tucked her empty glove in his belt. Her delicate fingers tapered to finely shaped nails, calluses built up where they rubbed on the bowstring, like the calluses on his own fingers. Her palm was bruised, the skin torn, likely from her grab onto the tree.

He let her snatch her hand back. "Poorly?" she asked.

"I have a poultice for the scrapes." He pushed up, reaching under her arms to quickly lift her out of the clump of flowers before she could attack.

"I said death," she said, jerking back from his hold once her feet were under her. She stood, her small hands fisted against her legs, teeth clenched. "I choose death."

She was furious. She was beautiful. There among the flowers and trees, he couldn't imagine issuing the order to his brother, Bàs, to execute the brave woman. She was rare, like golden horses from the far east. The thought of her pale and still like his father made his hand itch for his short sword to protect her. *A Sutherland. The enemy.* Not if she wed him. He would force the clans to unite under his rule and be victorious.

Shooting his hand forward, he grabbed her wrist, his fingers becoming a manacle. "Let me go," she demanded, and struggled as he began to walk them back toward the battle.

Aye, the wedding was a good strategy.

"Stop…" she continued, digging her boots into the soft earth, making him drag her. "You said I have a choice."

"I said there are two choices, not that they are *your* two choices." He trudged through the forest, kindly walking around the thick brambles instead of dragging her through them. She didn't seem to appreciate his kindness, as she tried to hold onto any tree she could reach to slow their progress.

"*Mo chreach*," she yelled. "'Tis my capture, 'tis my life. It should be my choice if there are two."

"First of all, prisoners get no choices," he said, glancing back at her. The purple flower still tossed about, tangled in the hair that had come free from her long braid. "And secondly, I have decided there is only one choice." He paused, holding back a low limb so it wouldn't smack her in the face, not that she noticed. "Ye will wed me, and the union will join both our clans under my rule."

She shook her head as she stared directly into his eyes. He watched annoyance pinch her lips, lips that were soft and so incredibly expressive. "I do not care if I am a prisoner or not," she said. "You said there were two choices." Her free hand swung up to show two fingers in a *V*. "When did the first choice disappear?"

Cain leaned in close so that they stared straight into each other's eyes. He let the coldness settle back into his gaze. "The moment ye fooled me with a kiss."

• • •

The horse that had refused to move for her before surged under Ella as Cain clasped her before him, his muscular arm like a steel band around her middle. He'd tricked her out of the tree by placing the horse underneath. She clenched her teeth. They had both tricked each other, but ultimately the man had won. This time. But the next contest would end differently.

Bent over the neck of the white horse, Ella could see the sprawling fortress of Girnigoe Castle where its granite walls clutched the land, keeping it from falling into the North Sea. Massive stables sat on both sides of the road before it, most likely to house the hundreds of horses they kept. Her fingers curled into the fine mane of Cain's horse. Lord help her, she was trapped between the soaring castle before her and the powerful Sinclair monster behind her.

Nothing can hold you if you're smart enough. She repeated Kenneth's words in her mind like she had all her life, especially after her mother died and Ella was left to live in Alec Sutherland's cruel grasp. Ella had learned the ways of escaping from nearly every trap and lock as she grew up, but she'd never been in the clutches of the sons of Sinclair before. *They are only human.* She repeated the words like a prayer, squeezing her eyes shut for a second.

The wooden gates stood open as they neared the outer barbican, a structure with twelve-foot stone walls, the first defense of Girnigoe Castle. Cain slowed his horse to a trot, and Ella bounced. Her eyes scanned the faces of his warriors, each nodding or holding a fist to their hearts as Cain rode through the bailey and under another archway, the horse's hooves clopping hollowly across a wooden drawbridge. Several men even bent on one knee, their eyes cast downward in respect or fear.

Did they wonder why he had not led them on to Dunrobin Castle? Was the death of his father the reason for withdrawal or was the new Chief Sinclair convinced that he could conquer the Sutherland clan by forcing her to wed him? *I will not. I will die instead*. Hadn't she always guessed that she would die young, despite Kenneth's command that she was to live a long life? The thought that she might die today made her heart pound.

Inside the gate, Ella's breath caught, her stomach twisting. Gilla stood with a warrior off to the side. She looked well enough, but did she wonder where her mistress was? "So," she said, "you are a thief of lands, castles, people, *and* horses."

"Unlike Sutherlands, we care for our horses," Cain answered behind her. She didn't bother to tell him that Alec Sutherland had loved his horses much more than his people.

At the end of the drawbridge, the thick points of a portcullis rose up, allowing them entry into the inner bailey, structures encircling it. Beyond the bailey, she saw another drawbridge leading to more buildings. No wonder Girnigoe hadn't been taken by siege. It was built upon the sea for defense with many walls, baileys, and at least two drawbridges.

"Seraph must be walked, watered, rubbed, and fed," Cain said to the lad who ran out to take the reins as he easily jumped down from the tall horse.

"Aye, milord," the lad said, bowing low.

"And check for rain rot along the girth line."

"Aye, milord," the boy said, his face as serious as Jamie's had been when Ella had told him she must ride into battle that morning. Poor Jamie. The twelve-year-old boy must be so worried for her, his kind heart tormenting him with thoughts of her torture. What would he do if she died? Would his nursemaid, Florie, and Kenneth keep him hidden like they had all these years?

Ella watched Cain warily. Would he grab her or perhaps knock her to the ground before his men? He had retrieved her mask but did not give it to her to don. Everyone could see the humiliating brand that marked her as a Sutherland. She stifled a flinch as he pivoted around and grabbed her around the middle. Hand flying in defense, she slapped at him. He moved his face, dodging her strike, and released her where she sat.

"The lad needs my horse," Cain said, looking up at her, his face grim.

"Do not touch me," she said, glancing about before kicking her leg over. She dropped to the pebbled dirt in a crouch and stood, hands fisted and raised.

He considered her stance and then turned away to stride toward a large structure, signaling to several of his men who carried a body wrapped in plaid. She swallowed, lowering her arms. *His father.*

Everyone stared at the body and not at her. Did Cain Sinclair think her coward enough to follow after him without being forced? *Fool.* Without further thought, she took several steps backward and turned, walking briskly back the way they had ridden. The portcullis was still raised. She would grab Gilla and flee.

"Ella Sutherland." The deep voice from behind shot dread through her, kicking her heart into a gallop. She leaped into a run, but no less than six Sinclair warriors slid themselves before the open portcullis, swords drawn. If she continued to run at them, would they slice her through, saving her from torture and rape? Immediate death could be her way out, but the thought of Jamie's worried face flashed through her mind, slowing her steps until she stopped before the wall of warriors and swords. Some frowned; others looked amused.

"Ella Sutherland," Cain repeated from right behind her as she inhaled and exhaled quickly from her run. "Ye are not a guest here to decide when ye leave. We have business in the great hall."

Business? She swallowed down the fear nearly choking her as her heart hammered at her breastbone. Would all four Sinclair horsemen take their vengeance out on her? She turned slowly on her boots, finding her voice. "You think I will walk obediently toward torment and execution?"

His lips pursed as if in thought for a moment, lips that she remembered were deceptively pleasant to kiss. "I plan to wed ye, not kill ye."

Stomach knotted, she forced herself to breathe fully, summoning the anger to beat back her fear. She met his eyes with fire in her own. "Same thing."

He smiled broadly, the action at odds with the blue woad and blood marks still splattered across his face and the coolness in his blue eyes. "Ye are a prisoner without choice in the matter of your life, and I have decided your fate, which does not include death."

She glanced about the perimeter. Certainly there was a blade sitting about that she could fall upon. Her heart pumped like the hard beat of a bird's wings as she contemplated her end.

"This is Lady Ella Sutherland," Cain said, his gaze now on his men behind her. "She is *mine*." He stretched out the last word, his voice as huge as his form. "See that no harm comes to her, even by her own hand, but she is not to leave Girnigoe without me or one of my brothers. Keenan, make sure the others know."

"Aye," one of the guards behind her called out, and Ella turned to glare at him. He had a menacing scar over his brow, and his wry grin made her want to kick his shin.

Ella stood stiffly, wishing she still had a dagger secreted on her. What should she do? Just stand there until someone dragged her away? Because she surely did not want to follow the arrogant clod into his castle. She squeezed her eyes shut like she used to do as a child, wishing to vanish, wishing to blink out of existence to infuriate her tormentor. She heard the crunch of pebbles as he walked closer.

"What are ye doing?" he asked, his words soft and curious.

"Praying to die right here and foil your plans."

With her eyes shut, she waited, listening, and felt his breath touch her ear. Tingles prickled down that side of her body. "Is it working?" he asked.

Her eyes snapped open so he could see the hate in them, but her breath caught at the blueness of his eyes and his nearness, like in the tree. She pulled her lips back, gritting her teeth. "Yes, I have died. Best to toss this stinking corpse out of here."

He leaned in again, and she fought to not back up. Inhaling deeply near her hair, he whispered, "Your corpse smells of fresh Highland air and flowers." His gaze fastened to her eyes until she felt like she could not look away. Like a mouse caught in his falcon's sight. He grinned. "I will keep ye for now."

CHAPTER THREE

The blasted man grabbed Ella around the hips and lifted her up over one of his large shoulders. She kicked her heels to throw him off-balance and shoved against the muscles of his broad back, but the vile man caught her legs, holding them together pressed to his chest, her arse sticking up in the air near his ear. She arched her back, rising to sink her nails into his shoulder to push upright.

"If ye will walk with me without seeking a way to die, I will put ye down."

"Put me down." If she'd been born with the muscles of a man, she'd have beaten him soundly. Of course, she would also likely be dead, but hadn't that been what she wanted when he caught her? Well, not really, only if it was to protect Sutherland Clan from being taken over by Sinclairs. *Death before surrender* was one of her father's favorite bellows.

Cain lowered her, and she yanked her black leather jerkin into place. "Where is my mask?"

"Ye do not need it," he said. "And ye will tell me who branded ye."

"He is dead," she said, frowning over the idea of giving Cain any information at all.

He made a disgusted sound. "A pity." He seemed to shorten his step so she was next to him, and they walked across a second drawbridge designed to slide over the chasm instead of being raised and lowered.

Across another bailey, they entered the tall stone

fortress to step through a darkened entryway. The small antechamber opened up into a large room with a two-story ceiling made of timber and chiseled granite. Glass-paned windows were situated up high in the thick blocks to let in light. Tapestries adorned the walls, and a large cold hearth stood at the far end where another archway led beyond. The largest tapestry was made of bright threads and showed the four biblical horsemen riding down from the illuminated clouds of Heaven on steeds of four different colors: white, red, black, and a pale green.

Ella's gaze slid to two women standing near the table that held the wrapped body of George Sinclair, the sadistic monster of Girnigoe. Her strategy had worked—cut off the head of the snake and the rest of the armies pulled back. But now, instead of readying for the inevitable siege, she was imprisoned in the snake's den with his lethal son.

The room was silent, except for the whispered prayers of the younger of the two women near the head of the table. She was dressed in white, her light-colored hair draped about her shoulders as if she were an angel. An older woman with white hair stood next to her. Was she the Sinclair witch? The woman's sharp gaze crossed over the prone body to squint at Ella. Did she need spectacles like Kenneth or was she casting a spell on her, condemning her for the death of their chief, her brother?

Several other warriors stood about the room, their battle armor streaked with mud and blood. She swallowed against the dryness in her throat when two large men walked out of the alcove. One had a bandaged arm, but it was the other who made her forget to inhale. He wore the dark robes associated with death, and a large human skull covered his face, its white bone polished, his eyes peering from the empty sockets. Hefting a bloody scythe over one shoulder, he was certainly the fourth of the Sinclair brothers. The horseman of death.

"Eun returned your flag," the brother with his arm tied held up a ripped piece of red and black fabric. He was as tall as Cain but not as broad. His gaze slid along her form. Ella crossed her arms before her to ward off the feeling that he was judging her. He finally looked to Cain. "Why did ye not lead us on to smash the Sutherlands completely?" he asked, making a fist. He was either Gideon, the third brother, or Joshua, the second brother.

Cain's voice came out hard as he looked down at the unmoving body of his father. "A strategy to save Dunrobin, its people, and its horses from being smashed and slaughtered."

"We would never slaughter horses," the brother in the skull mask said, his words clear because the jaw of the skull hung lower than his mouth, as if the previous owner had continued to scream when the horseman won his head.

"Who knows what the Sutherlands would do to their herds if they thought we would take them," the other brother said, shooting her a dark frown.

Cain crossed his bare arms over his linen-covered chest, the lines of the horse tattoo prominent along the contours of his muscles. He was a mountain of strength and masculine confidence, his wheat-colored hair tangled from the wind and battle, the blue woad painted down his strong features still marking him as wild. "I would not have my new prizes marred when I have a way of taking them peacefully with a wedding."

Ella's stomach dropped farther down within her. Despite the heat that had flared between them during her distraction kiss in the tree, the thought of being wed to her mortal enemy turned her to ice. She opened her mouth to restate that she would never take the sacred vows with Cain Sinclair, handing her clan over to her enemy.

"Where is he?" boomed a voice from the entryway, stopping her. In strode a warrior with his armor still covering his chest, blood streaked across his bare arms. His hair was darker, and he held a large sword, his arms powerfully built. He stopped before the corpse and yanked back the cloth from George Sinclair's face. "Foking hell," he said. "Da is dead." He looked up, his gaze going to the other three of his brothers. "He is really dead."

He reached out, shaking the corpse's shoulder, and for a brief second, Ella wondered if he might have some mystical power to rouse the madman. He leaned forward. "Wake," he roared in the dead man's face, and everyone watched, but the corpse remained unmoving and pale. He released his father's shoulder. "I did not believe one of us was dead when I saw your bird's flag." He ran a hand through his hair, nodding. "'Tis best that it was Da."

"He said Merida predicted it," the brother with the skull mask said, and they all turned to the elderly woman with thick white hair.

Merida Sinclair. She had been wed to Ella's father years ago, but she hadn't given him a living child, and he accused her of witchery to divorce her. It had started the bloody war between their clans thirty years ago.

The woman's chin tilted up. "Aye, I told my brother his time to die was here." She shook her head and pulled back more of the plaid to look down at him. "Ye never listen to me, ye stubborn goat. See where it's led ye."

Surely to hell.

Merida's eyes had fine lines around them, and her skin was tan but still smooth. Her white hair was loose and long, with one thin braid plaited to hang along her cheek. A mantle of blue linen draped from one shoulder to the other in a regal style that reminded Ella of the ancient Roman's costume that she'd seen painted in her mother's books. Could the crone really see death coming for a person? Maybe her father's claims of witchery held truth. What could Merida see for Ella? There was only one option for her if she couldn't escape.

"Perhaps that is why he battled so fiercely and alone, as if he were beating off death," the brother with the bandaged arm said.

Merida shook her head again as if furious at the dead man. "He always fought like a giant, cornered wildcat. He did not want to strike one of his boys down in his frenzy."

The brother who had yelled leaned closer and pulled the cloth farther down the body. "Arrows?" He turned his head without straightening, his gaze going to Cain.

"The Sutherland chief ordered all her archers to fire straight at him," Cain said. "At least fifty of them."

Fifty of her most skilled warriors, for she had known it would be their best chance to kill the warmonger. Ella swallowed as every set of eyes in the great hall turned to her. *Courage. Stand tall as if you have it, and sometimes it comes.* Kenneth's words reverberated in her mind. What was the worst they could do? Cain didn't want her to die, but pain was worse.

She wet her parched lips, suddenly realizing how badly she thirsted. "It was the best strategy to end the battle and save my people from cruel slaughter," she said, proud of the force behind her words. She met Cain's blue eyes, his longish hair falling around his rugged jaw. "And it worked."

"It is war, then!" the brother yelled.

"It has been war since Alec Sutherland showed no honor by sending me back to Girnigoe, Joshua," Merida said, hands on her ample hips.

"And it ends today," he roared, striding toward Ella, his fists as tight as his scowl. Instinct screamed at her to crouch low and cover her head, but she kept herself straight, drawing on courage and dignity as the only things she still possessed. One hit from the charging man's fist and she might very well have her wish to die. Her heart pounded, giving her legs the power to run, but there was nowhere to go.

In a rush, Cain intercepted his brother, yanking him around in a massive display of strength. He shoved his brother back and continued toward her. A lesser man would have fallen on his arse at the power in Cain's thrust, but Joshua merely took two steps to catch his balance.

Cain caught her to him, holding her before him

with an arm under her breasts. "She is mine," he said, the three simple words filling the room. "No one shall touch Ella Sutherland other than me." And for the moment, she was grateful for it.

"Fok, Cain," Joshua said, walking in a tight circle as if his pent-up energy demanded he stride.

"Da is dead, and I am the chief," Cain said. "We will all play our parts."

Joshua threw his hands up and let them drop, piercing Cain with his gaze where he stopped. "As ye bloody wish," Joshua said, his teeth showing as his mouth pulled back in a snarl-like smile. "But we win this war with slaughter tomorrow."

"We win this war with a formal betrothal and posting of banns," Cain countered.

Ella forced herself to breathe, the feel of Cain's grip like iron against her ribs. Would her wildly thumping heart give away her fear? She steadied herself and opened her dry lips. "I choose death."

Everyone stared at her in a long silence. Did they not think her brave enough to wish for death over wedding her mortal enemy and giving them a solid claim to her castle and clan? "You said there were two choices," she said, turning and tipping her face up to look at Cain. From directly under him, she could see the strong lines of his stubbled jaw and the strength in his neck. Lord, the man was all muscle. She swallowed. "And I choose death."

"Only *two* choices?" the brother with the wrapped arm, who must be Gideon, asked.

"Why Death?" Joshua asked and turned to the fourth brother in the skull mask, the anger on his face dropping away to surprise. "He is still but a boy." A wicked grin surfaced through the hate on his face. "Ye should choose someone with some skill and brawn."

The fourth brother ripped off his cloak, leaving the skull mask still tied to the front of his face. He whipped something through the air. *Whack*. The blade of a *mattucashlass* stuck into the table next to Joshua's hand. The older brother just grinned without moving.

The quiet, ethereal woman with sun-colored hair came around the table. She looked close to Ella's age, her red lips set in a pale face. She stood before her, tipping her head to the side as she studied Ella. "Ye, Arabella Sutherland, wish to marry my fourth brother, Bàs Sinclair?"

• • •

Now that Joshua wasn't charging at her, Cain released Ella. The bending of the woman's brows showed her confusion. "Bàs? I do not under—"

"My youngest brother is named Death," Cain said. Certainly, if she refused to wed him, she would not ask to wed his brother. "Bàs means death in Gaelic, named for the fourth horseman from the Bible."

The woman's mouth dropped open as she looked toward Cain's youngest brother. Even though Bàs was the quietest of the four, he was as large, his strength finally growing into him over the last few years.

Joshua chuckled, but there was no humor in it. "Did ye think his name was short for Sebastian?"

Ella shook her head. "Your mother named you *Death*?"

"Our father did," Cain said. "Since he was the fourth horseman to be born after the third horseman," he pointed to Gideon, "and the second horseman." He pointed to Joshua.

"So, by choosing Death, ye chose him to wed," Joshua said, his maddening grin in place. He looked like he was starting to enjoy the exchange now that the shock of their father's death had waned. Maybe he wouldn't lose his mind and try to kill Ella again.

Ella turned on Joshua. "George Sinclair did not name you 'Start A Bloody Fight,'" she said, jabbing her finger in his direction.

Her cheeks were stained pink, and her voice rose. Aye, she was brave. Even though he'd felt her heart flying, she did not swoon or cry out. She yelled instead. He liked that.

"And you," she said, pointing toward Gideon. "He did not name you 'Starve Your Neighbors.'"

Gideon frowned, and Cain almost smiled. The lass knew exactly where to stab in his brother's most vulnerable spot. "Famine is only one interpretation of the third horseman," Gideon said. "I am to keep track of the food and supplies, but I am also the one to decide what is fair and just." He rolled up the sleeve of his tunic on his uninjured arm to show the tattoo of weighing scales. "I am Justice."

"Fair and just as long as it sways in favor of the sons of Sinclair," Ella finished. The lass had a firm grasp on the beginning of Revelations. He would have to spend time reminding Gideon that they did not think of him as Famine. She spun her gaze toward Cain. "And you are not named 'Spill all the Blood and Replace it with Sinclair Blood.'"

Cain felt his lips twitch with humor, the fire in her voice and her cleverness pulling it out of him despite the grim circumstances. "My mother was not in favor of those particular names. They are a bit lengthy, so she and my father chose biblical names. Joshua was a great leader of battles, and Gideon was a warrior but also a judge. Da felt that Bàs was appropriate for the fourth, and without our mother's influence, since she was dying, he named him so."

"How can naming a newborn bairn Death be appropriate in any way?" she asked, her gaze sliding back to the youngest, who still wore his battle mask.

"My mother was my first execution," Bàs said, his voice an even whisper, his hands fisted.

"She died giving birth to him." Cain finished the explanation. Certainly, she had heard the tale before. Their father had spouted it throughout the Highlands, his grief for his angelic wife turning to rage against the living.

Ella's gaze slid across all the brothers to land on Cain. She cleared her throat. "I was not saying that I choose to wed Death." She glanced toward Bàs. "But that I choose to be executed over being wed to *any* of you."

"Foking harsh, lass," Joshua said. "Choosing death over surrendering to one of us." His grin turned wicked as his gaze drifted over her leisurely, making Cain's fists tighten. "Ye might find being bound to a Sinclair quite…ful*filling*." He arched his brow over his carnal suggestion.

"She is wedding me," Cain said, stepping in front of Ella. "No one else, for I am the chief."

"I said I choose execution," Ella said from behind

him. She stepped back out, giving him a hateful look before turning to the others in the room.

Joshua nodded to the maids who had come to wash their father's body, and turned back to Ella. "Surely, pledging your heart to one of God's warriors would be better than the cold, dark grave."

"The chief of God's warriors," Cain restated.

Ella stared straight at Cain. "Not when wedding means giving Dunrobin Castle and all of Clan Sutherland to the Sinclairs."

"It will happen regardless," Cain said. "Either peacefully through uniting the clans or through smashing your castle walls and slaughtering your people. Would you not sacrifice yourself to save their lives?"

She narrowed her eyes, the hate in them as sharp as a newly hewn blade. "Of course I would if I thought they would accept your rule without a fight. My wedding a Sinclair will not make them lay down their weapons and accept you as their chief. As their chief, their blood will be on my hands either way."

"'Tis the burden of leadership," Cain said, his words a soft grumble. His father had trained him from birth to pick up the reins of Clan Sinclair the moment the old warrior took his last mortal breath. As a woman, had Ella Sutherland been given the same instruction?

Her father, the brutal Alec Sutherland, would have continued to try to beget a boy on his young wife to raise as the next chief while he married Ella off to another clan to form an alliance. In fact, there had been whispers that she was betrothed to Chief Hew Mackay, but that Ella had called it off when her father was killed in battle. Without a living son, Ella had taken the seat. If she'd married Mackay, she'd be giving him control of their clan.

"Is that why ye broke the betrothal contract with Hew Mackay?" Cain asked, remembering his father's poor treatment of the chieftain who currently survived in Girnigoe's dungeon. "Or do ye object to the man?"

"Such a whiny bastard," Gideon said, removing his own armor for one of the young squires to take away to clean and polish. He looked at Cain, well aware that Cain disagreed with his father forcing thirst on the prisoner. When Mackay had been captured after burning one of their crofter's fields on the edge of Sinclair territory, their father had locked him in the dungeon, giving him only salted meat to eat and no water, wine, or ale. After a fortnight, the chief was begging for anything liquid. Even though the dungeon was several floors below, Cain swore he heard the man wailing at night.

Ella's mouth opened with the snap of anger, but it took a moment for anything to come out. "That is nothing with which to concern yourself."

"Actually, it is," his aunt, Merida, said while she pointed out more blood on his father for the maids to wipe. "If ye would not have Hew Mackay because ye think he is a self-righteous, weak-minded, lustful goat, then Cain would be given hope that ye will view him as a better candidate." Merida, even with all her eccentricities and heretical leanings, was exceedingly clever. She could clear away the debris to find the piece of information that was crucial. And she could apparently predict the coming of death, although knowledge of such could weaken a man or make him act foolishly.

Ella turned in a tight circle and sat down in a chair, laying her folded hands in her lap. Cain could imagine her in a royal gown, sitting in pristine fashion. But even in her black trousers and tunic, her hair sticking out haphazardly from their tussle in the woods, dirt smeared across her lovely face, she was bonny. Even if she had ordered his father's death. Hadn't he killed her own father several months ago? War to save herself and her clan was justified. A conviction that even Gideon could not argue against.

"It does not matter," Ella said. "For I choose to die over taking vows of marriage. My neck is thin." She tipped her head back, exposing the slim column of her throat as if Bàs would walk up to her and slice it through right there in the great hall.

"Ye will marry me," Cain said, his voice fierce at the dark thought. Killing the brave, beautiful lass would be akin to slaughtering a sleek, strong, fertile mare. He'd never allow it.

Bàs cursed low and grabbed his dark robe from where he'd thrown it. "If ye decide to execute her, send for me. Otherwise, I will return on the morrow with whisky for Da's wake." Cain's youngest brother lived outside Girnigoe, alone with his grim thoughts, polishing his blades and training by himself. He came up to the castle only when summoned despite all three brothers asking him to remain at Girnigoe.

Bàs stopped to look at Ella, and even though his skull mask made him into a macabre harbinger of death, she raised her head to meet his gaze with strength. "I will sharpen my ax just in case," he said, as he turned and strode away. "For a quick and merciful death," he called from the entryway.

His little brother played his part well. Even though Bàs was Death, he had admitted to Cain once that he abhorred unjustified killing. Slaughtering a whole clan was not something that Cain wanted, either. It was better for Bàs to terrorize the lass into wedding Cain, despite her warning that her clan would still fight them. Surely she could convince her people to accept the alliance. Inside information told him that her clan had grown to respect her and were quite loyal.

"I think decisions should be made after Lady Sutherland has eaten, bathed, and rested," said Merida. Cain's younger sister, Hannah, came forward, seeming to float noiselessly along the floorboards. Sometimes when he saw her walking the halls at night, he thought she might have died years ago and was only a spirit living among them. Was her ethereal demeanor part of her nature or had she learned to keep as invisible as possible around their father? A father who ignored her completely, since she was not part of the horsemen legend.

"Come," she said, beckoning Ella. "I will see ye to one of the guest chambers."

"Nay," Cain said when Ella rose to follow. "Put her in the tower room above Da's chamber for tonight. I will coordinate the cleaning out of his room in the morning before I move my things in there as chief. Once we wed, she will move below."

Ella kept her back to him, speaking to Hannah. "Perhaps you should take me down to the dungeon, then."

"Your rejected suitor is currently stinking up the dungeon," Joshua said and drank from his tankard of ale. He looked at Cain at the same time Ella turned back to him. "I told ye we should add a second cell. Maybe ye can chain her in the bailey."

"I am surprised that he still lives," Ella said, her tone giving nothing away.

Would she have mourned Hew? The thought soured Cain's stomach, and his eyes narrowed, studying her. "Aye," he said. "The only reason that he still lives is that the elderly couple whom he attacked before setting fire to a field of oats did not die. Although, he might argue that he'd rather die after being in our dungeon for a fortnight." He stepped forward, slowly encircling her, his gaze penetrating, as she stood straight. "Perhaps ye wish to be sent to the dungeon to care for him."

"Enough," Merida said, coming around the table. "The girl has had to deal with Alec Sutherland for twenty-some-odd years." She pointed to Ella's face. "And she certainly hasn't come away unscathed." At Merida's words, Ella tipped her face forward, letting her loosened hair fall over the bright scar of her brand. Did she hide it in shame? The thought lit another fire in Cain's gut. Had her *foking* father ordered it? Done it himself? If so, *he* should live in Hell, eternally full of shame for brutalizing someone weaker than him.

Merida pointed up to the ceiling. "There is a bed in the tower room; and a lock." She looked directly at Ella. "To keep people out." The small circular tower room had been created for the chief, above his chambers, to be able to view his kingdom.

Merida curled her finger inward to draw Ella to follow. Cain watched her walk, head held high, with a gentle sway to her hips. Long legs, encased in tight-fitting black trousers, led up over flared hips that curved into a waist perfect for his hands to nestle around. Her braid hung low, a gentle pendulum to swing with her gait, the end swishing against her perfectly shaped—

"Good Lord, that is a lovely arse," Joshua murmured, making Cain turn a glare his way. "I think we should order all the lasses to wear trousers."

Cain's hands balled into fists. "Ye are ogling my future wife, ye bloody *blaigeard*."

Joshua's brows rose. "I think it is quite appropriate to ogle a prisoner, especially one who wears trousers that follow the sweet curves of her legs up to the crux." He looked back to the archway where Ella had disappeared with Merida. "Do ye think she is completely bare underneath? There would be no getting a smock stuffed down between her legs." Joshua was purposely baiting him, but even knowing that did not stop Cain from wanting to punch his onerous face.

Gideon thumped a hand on Cain's chest when he took a purposeful step toward Joshua. "He is always looking for a fight. He is War, after all."

Joshua raised his tankard in salute. "Ye could order me away from Girnigoe, brother."

"Or I could order ye to your bedchamber like a naughty wee lad," Cain said. Joshua had always harbored ire at Cain for being born first, and sometimes Cain did not mind reminding him of the fact.

"Really?" Joshua said. "Your first official order as chief will be to send me to my room?" He seemed pleased and disappointed in Cain at the same time.

Cain glanced to his father's body. Would his ghost rise up and haunt him for ending the torture of a prisoner? So be it. Cain was now the chief of the Sinclairs, even without the clan pledging their lives to him yet.

Nodding to Gideon, Cain walked over to the table to grab a tankard of ale for himself. "My first order is for everyone to stay away from Ella Sutherland." He stared hard at Joshua, who kept his smug grin. "And my second order as The Sinclair…" He looked to Gideon. "Is to send some water and turnips down to the dungeon."

CHAPTER FOUR

"Here is your own key, so ye can bathe in peace," Merida Sinclair said and nodded toward the four buckets of water that the thick-waisted warrior had carried up to the tower room, the whole time huffing, turning bright red, and wiping his brow. "Just heat the water on the fire, and ye will relax your sore muscles."

Ella's hand curled around the heavy iron key, its weight giving substance to Merida's promise that she'd be left alone, but she didn't trust her. No doubt there were more keys on the outside, since she was a prisoner.

"Why would you care about my comfort at all?" Ella asked, and she watched the warrior march out the door, two hands pressing against his lower back as if it pained him.

Merida came forward, her white hair swooped around her head. She stared hard into Ella's eyes as if searching for secrets, and then her gaze moved along Ella's face. "I lived with Alec Sutherland for ten years before driving him mad enough to send me away." The woman was known as an insane witch at Dunrobin. Many older maids passed the sign of the cross before them whenever she was mentioned.

Merida caught her wispy hair together and moved it to one side, turning around. On the nape of her neck was a brand, a wild cat, clan crest of Sutherland. She dropped her hair and turned back, her mouth quirked. "He liked to mark his property, did he not?"

Ella's fingers moved, without thought, to her own scar that marked her as her father's possession. She swallowed hard, remembering the searing pain that came with the burn as his trusted men held her down. She was only seventeen when she'd picked the lock on her bedroom door to find Jamie and flee the brutality that surrounded her at Dunrobin. But she'd been caught, and her father had branded her with the Sutherland crest in punishment. *Ye are mine. Wherever ye go.* His words still haunted her.

"That does not mean you wish me well," Ella said softly.

"True," Merida said, nodding. She tipped her head back and forth as if weighing her words. "Trust needs to be earned, and that takes time. Outward appearances are not always truth." She grinned. "As ye have surely heard about my time at Dunrobin. The masks men and women wear for the world can be quite the opposite of what lies in a person's heart."

"I have no interest in knowing what lies in Sinclair hearts. I will not be at Girnigoe long enough to confirm the evil that lurks here." Either she would escape, die trying, or be executed by Cain's brother, Bàs. But she wasn't planning to stay long.

Merida's grin increased to show her little teeth. "We will see," she said knowingly, and a chill ran up Ella's arms. If the woman truly had the sight to see the future, would she know when and how Ella would try to escape?

The door clicked shut behind her, and Ella heard

a second key turn in the large iron lock. Who else had a key to the room? There was no board to place across the door and nothing of weight enough to shove against it.

She plucked at her dirty shirt. Sweat and dust coated her skin. Bits of leaves tangled in her hair, and the dried scabs on her palms needed cleaning. She sighed. "If I am to die, I want to die clean," she said to the sparsely furnished room that sported three broad, glass-paned windows and several transoms higher up. She grabbed one of the heavy buckets and lugged it to the iron grate over the fire.

• • •

"Mackay is demanding to be released," Gideon said to Cain as he threw himself into a chair opposite him before the cold hearth in the empty great hall.

Even though the stones kept the interior of the keep cool, the summer temperatures made a fire unnecessary. Would Ella be cold in the tower room? He would make sure that Thomas, the loyal warrior who guarded the stairs, had started one for her.

"He wants to come above to argue for his release." Gideon took a haul off his tankard of the fine summer ale Merida brewed.

"As soon as he orders his men to deliver enough oats to make up for the field he burned," Cain said. Clan Mackay had been a thorn in their side, swaying between ally and enemy over the years. Hew Mackay was the young chief who had taken the reins of the clan last year, although it was said that his steward, Randolph Mackay, often acted as leader while Hew was sleeping off his whisky.

The young chief's latest attempt to make trouble was to burn Sinclair fields in hopes they would starve or become dependent on them come winter. But Hew was an incompetent fool. His small band of loyal and misguided warriors had been caught and thus identified, so he couldn't blame it on the Sutherlands. The two Mackays who had survived had been sent back to Varrich Castle, seat of the Mackays, with Sinclair demands for retribution. So far, the only retribution that Cain's father had seen were letters demanding Hew's release. Something George Sinclair would never do, and neither would Cain.

Cain might not tolerate torture under his command, but he wasn't going to release the bastard without recompence. The arse had taken their grain, so he needed to pay for his freedom with grain. If the elderly couple had died, he would have paid with his life.

Gideon pulled his freshly stitched arm around where blood seeped through the wrapping.

"Does it pain ye?" Cain asked. None of his brothers would complain about a battle wound. They'd been trained by their father to brag about their scars as proof of their invincibility in battle.

"A bit," Gideon admitted quietly, trusting Cain not to rib him for it. "But Merida has cleaned it with tinctures and slathered it with salves. I doubt it can become tainted. She is likely brewing feverfew tonight just in case." He smiled.

"Because I need my Justice, especially now that I am the chief," Cain said. He gave him a half grin.

"And I know that ye would feed every starving mouth. Well, as long as they were Scots' mouths."

"Ye make me sound like a foking mother bird." Gideon snorted. "I have never liked that particular part of Revelations. I do *not* want to bring famine."

Cain chuckled, picking up another arrowhead. "Most people do not like any part of Revelations."

"And I would amend feeding every starving mouth, not to include that Mackay fool below," Gideon said. "Shall I schedule a trial for him?"

Cain worked a strong thread around the steel arrowhead, attaching it to a long shaft. "He will lose." Three arrow shafts sat upright in the basket at his feet for him to finish. *An archer must never run out of arrows.* His father's guidance floated through his mind even though he was dead and laid out behind him. The next day they would celebrate his life and bury him in grand style north of the castle, in the churchyard where Cain's mother was resting for eternity. Then his warriors would pledge their lives to Cain as the new leader of Clan Sinclair.

"Aye, he will lose," Gideon said. "All ye have to do is call the farmer and his wife as witnesses, and he will be back in the dungeon until the Mackay oats arrive or ye get tired of his whining and have Bàs silence him with a blade across the neck."

Gideon liked to keep everything as fair as possible. To him, people were either good or bad, and raids were either warranted or crimes. Of all the brothers, he was the most suited to be the third horseman, and Cain was lucky to have him as an advisor.

"Schedule one if ye want," Cain said. "I will leave

it up to Justice." He dropped the completed arrow in the basket and caught another shaft between his fingers, picking a molded tip from a bowl set on the chess table between them.

"What will ye do with the lass?" Gideon glanced toward the archway hiding the tower stairs.

That particular question had bred more and more questions until they buzzed in Cain's head like angry bees. Even the calm that usually came as he wrapped arrows had failed to break through the chaos of too many possibilities. Yet he had no answers, except one. "I am not ordering her executed, no matter what she wants."

"Why?" Gideon asked, moving the bowl of arrowheads from the ancient family chess table before Cain, fixing the few toppled pieces to play.

"Because a peaceful takeover of the Sutherland clan will save property and food they would burn if we lay siege. Their warriors will die when they could be turned to add to our defenses. And although I do not believe they would slaughter their horses, many would die in the battles to take Dunrobin. Ella's death would only make them hate us more, giving them strength to raise arms for her as a martyr."

"What if she were a man?" Gideon asked, moving a pawn two spots forward.

Cain dropped the incomplete arrow into the basket and lifted his arms to cup his head. He frowned. "She would be dead already."

Gideon nodded with a smug smile. His brother could sniff out a lie like no other, so it was no use in uttering one that he would prove false. "So, she is alive simply because ye desire her," Gideon said and indicated the board to make Cain place his pawn.

Cain mimicked his brother's move, his mind full of responses that proved Gideon's statement wrong. "Nay," Cain said. Gideon raised his eyebrow, and Cain glared at him. "Nay," he repeated. "A woman being killed is viewed differently by her people. Their hate for us will make them stronger and delay our victory over them."

"She is their chief who ordered the killing of our father and laird." Gideon moved his bishop.

Cain leaned forward. "Ye know as well as I do that Da took risks as if he wanted to die, especially in battle. Thin armor and no shield, just his sword. And Merida even warned him. I will not punish Ella for Da thinking he was invincible."

"But…" Gideon tipped his head, a grin growing on his lips. "If she were a man, she'd already be dead."

Cain threw himself back in his chair, grabbing his poorly carved king from the board to fist in his hand. The wood was hard, unbreakable, and there was no fire into which to throw it like his father had often done when angered.

"I would not ask her to wed me if she were a man," Cain said. "A siege would be the only way to gain Dunrobin Castle and the Sutherland people. Since their chief is a lass, there is another choice, and I have made it." He tossed the king in the air, catching it to set back on the table. "She will wed me and join the clans under my rule."

"Except that she refuses to say the vows. For it to be a solid union, witnesses must hear her speak the oaths to wed ye."

"I will woo her," Cain said and picked up his ale next to his chair to take a drink.

Gideon laughed. "Woo her? What do ye know of wooing a lass, big brother? All the lasses ye have known fall into your bed with a mere glance."

It was true that he hadn't had to work at swaying a woman into a tryst before, but that didn't mean he was a wet-behind-the-ears lad. "I could say the same about ye," Cain said.

"Ah, but I am not attempting to woo a lass who would rather stab me than kiss me." Gideon moved his rook.

Cain took another drink, moving another pawn. "I will create and employ a strategy like any other conquest."

"Oh?" Gideon said, his brow rising. "How so?"

Cain set the tankard back down by his chair leg. "I will challenge all her reasons for finding me wanting. She will see my charm and strength. I will gentle her like an unruly mare and take her to my bed." Cain crossed his arms over his chest. "I will win her love like I win everything else."

The side of Gideon's mouth turned upward into a lopsided grin. "I do not know much about women," Gideon said, "at least the marrying type. But it seems women do not respond well to gentling. They are not horses."

"True," Cain said, moving his knight. "Then I will treat our interactions like battles, for we *are* at war." He nodded, his mind calming with the familiar set of strategies he used in combat. "I will determine what resources I have to woo her, anticipate her defenses, circumvent them, and press forward."

Gideon stared at him, his mouth open, his smile skewed with humor. "This will be fun to watch."

"I will start by giving her a reason to live." Cain was feeling better with each word he spoke. Aye, this was a battle of a different kind than he'd fought in the past, but it was a battle, nonetheless. "Have the wedding banns posted on the chapel door near Dunrobin and read each Sunday for three weeks in our own. The young pastor, John, can read them at each chapel he visits. I will convince her to wed me before he finishes reading them the third time."

Gideon smiled. "So confident." He raised his tankard, saluting Cain. "As usual, I am in awe."

Cain grinned, too. "'Wooing Ella Sutherland is just another game, and I win every game."

• • •

Ella was in and out of the soaking tub within minutes, washing so quickly that water sloshed over the side. But she was now in the smock that Merida had left for her. The woman had also brought a set of stays, stockings, and a simple blue dress made of soft wool, taking away her trousers, breast bindings, and tunic to be washed.

Ella didn't know what to make of the woman. She'd grown up hearing wild stories of the Sinclair Witch, brewing concoctions and talking to ghosts that no one saw. Could she have been acting the whole time to get Ella's father to release her from the marriage?

"Bloody hell," Ella whispered in the small empty room. She should have acted insane, too, but would

Alec Sutherland have fallen for the same ruse in a daughter, a ruse that he had witnessed before in a barren wife?

The room was warm with the fire and relatively bright despite the deepening darkness outside. No one had bothered to bring her food, but Merida had left a cup and a pitcher of weak ale.

Ella unbraided her hair, running fingers through it, and rolled up her sleeves before tipping her head forward. The ends of her hair skimmed the surface of the water in the tub, and she watched it lie on the top, coiling like grasses in a pond. If she had to, could she drown herself in a bath?

But was death just the easy way out? She would be buried outside the church grounds, shunned for taking her own life. The Sinclairs would then lay siege to Dunrobin, killing all who stood in their way. Her father's strength and keen strategy had kept Cain's father at bay these past years, but now both chiefs were dead, and she bore the responsibility for keeping her people alive, for keeping young Jamie alive.

"*Mo chreach*," she said to the water and sighed. She could do nothing to help her people while locked up in a Girnigoe tower. She must escape. If she died trying, it would not be a sin. But how could she keep her oath to protect Jamie if she was dead? Guilt twisted inside her, and she took a deep breath.

Leaning forward, she submerged the heavy mass of hair in the warm water. Her knees pressed into the damp bathing sheet under her as she worked into her tresses the scented soap Merida had left, her mind still spinning from her capture. Ella's heart squeezed. Kenneth, Jamie, and Florie must be so worried about her. Could she get word to them that she still lived?

She worked through knots and picked pieces of leaves out of the mass. Leaning far over until she was completely upside down, she submerged the hair up to her forehead into the tub for a final rinse.

Rap, rap.

The two short bursts of sound on her door made her jerk partly upright, her soapy hands slipping on the edge of the tub. She lost her balance, falling forward.

Splash.

CHAPTER FIVE

Cain frowned as he tried once again to coax the black and white feline off his head while balancing a tray of food. The large splash on the other side of the door made him lay his ear against it.

"*Cac!*" Ella's voice held fury, and she coughed, cursing further.

"*Mo chreach*," he murmured as the kitten pierced his scalp with her needlelike claws. Perhaps the kitten and her new mistress had things in common, namely a hatred for him.

"I brought ye some food. Are ye well?" Cain called.

"Leave it outside the door," she yelled.

"I also have a gift for ye, Ella." His frown relaxed. "Are ye in need of assistance?"

"No," she said, and he could imagine her snapping gray eyes trying to skewer him through the oak. "What I need is to be released from Girnigoe and for you to leave Clan Sutherland alone."

She may as well have asked to have wings to fly. "I will not bother ye," Cain said. "I want only to deliver my gift and your food." *And for ye to surrender long enough to marry me.* He had boasted to Gideon he could convince her within the three weeks that the banns were posted. And he would see the challenge won.

He had changed into a fresh white tunic and clean kilt after bathing, and the key to the door sat tucked into his sash. As if reading his mind, she yelled again. "Do not pretend that you don't have a key to the door."

What did that mean? Of course he had a key. "Do ye want me to come in with my key?"

"Do what you want, Sinclair. Leave the food and gift or use your key. I will not be letting you into my cage."

Needles pierced his head, startling him so that he bumped his forehead into the frame of the door. "Blast, ye wee beastie."

Enough of this. Leaving the cat to cling to his head, Cain fished the iron key out of his sash and jammed it into the lock. The kitten flexed her other paw, jabbing him with more needles. The key turned, and he pushed the door inward.

Ella stood wrapped in the blanket from her bed, warmth from the fire filling the small room. She watched him warily. "My gift is misbehaving," he said, his teeth clamped together as he tried to force a smile. It felt like a grimace.

Cain bent his knees to lower enough so that he could walk through the small doorway with the kitten hissing on his head. The tray wobbled slightly as he entered, but he kept his gaze on Ella's face.

Her glare melted into a look of surprise. For a long moment, she stared at the two of them. Cain waited, and the kitten pricked his scalp again, making his eye twitch as he tried to hold his smile.

Walking forward, he set the tray on a small table near the hearth. "A gift for ye, Ella. The kitten is the smallest of her litter and has weaned from her mother. The other barn cats are not letting her have as much food, so she needs a protector, someone to make sure she eats."

"I…I suppose I can watch her…while I am here. You said it is a her, a girl?" Ella moved closer, and the smell of the floral soap Merida had given her floated from her wet hair that was twisted up in a bathing sheet.

"Aye, and as ye see, she has spirit."

"And she is scared to death, way up there on top of a giant," Ella said, chastising him with a frown. Tucking the blanket tighter around her, she walked to him, dragging the length behind her like a cumbersome train. "Bend," she demanded and reached high to disentangle the kitten from Cain's head, her arms shaped with slender muscles. "Here sweet thing," she whispered. "Let me take you away from the big bad Sinclair."

Cain bent his knees so she could pull the cat from him, its paws and claws extended wide. "Ye know, the kitten is also a Sinclair," he said, watching her bring the ball of black and white fluff to her face, touching her nose to the cat's little white one.

The heavy blanket around Ella loosened, and she gasped as it fell to the floor. Stepping back, Ella tripped over the wool mass tangled around her feet. Cain's hands shot out, grabbing her arms to keep her from falling backward. The kitten yowled and jumped from her onto the bed.

The feel of him steadying her yanked back a long-ago memory. She had been young and smiling at the festival when he'd bumped into her, making her drop her bouquet of Scottish thistle.

"Thank you," she said and frowned as if she

wished she could pull it back, yanking out of his grasp.

"Ye are all wet." Water drops sat along her collarbone, making him very thirsty. *Och*. What would the lass taste like?

She clutched her arms over her breasts and squatted to grab up the blanket to hold before her. "You startled me when you knocked."

"And…" He looked from her to the tub and back. Water was pooled across the floor. "Ye fell in the tub?"

"No, well…yes. Somewhat. Not all the way."

He took a quick mental inventory of the room. It was small, too small for his bulk, but it suited Ella. "Ye need a robe and another bathing sheet, a rug for the floor, and some rags for the water."

She picked the kitten from the bed to hold before her, but the wee beast wiggled until Ella let her jump down to prowl about. "Do not forget a *sgian dubh* or *mattucashlass*," Ella said and clutched the blanket up to the base of her throat.

Even half drowned, she was bonny and brave. Although she had little defense in being alone and half dressed with him in a small room, she was not cowering or weeping in a corner. Nay, the lass was asking for weapons. The side of his mouth tipped upward. "I will keep your request in mind."

She narrowed her eyes. "Yet you ignore my other request."

His smile faded. He would no more kill her than he would kill the kitten. "I am not going to execute ye, Ella Sutherland."

"Your brother—"

"And I will not let Bàs execute ye, either."

"Then release me," she said. "Because I will not marry you. I will not marry anyone."

"It would be the best outcome for all those involved, both Sinclair and Sutherland," he replied. And he wanted another chance to kiss her. Not like the kiss in the tree, but a real kiss that would make her forget about strategy and escape. His gaze slid along the blanket covering her body.

Mutiny tightened her gaze. "The best outcome would be for the Sinclairs to leave Dunrobin and Sutherlands alone, to live apart but as allies, letting the feud fade away, since both old chiefs are dead."

"Allies can turn against one another, like our allies, the Mackays, who are now trying to weaken us by burning our crops. Uniting under one clan, however, is firm and strong. It would strengthen our herds and increase the number of warriors. I could live at Dunrobin with ye, and Joshua and Gideon would continue to live here at Girnigoe."

It was a sensible plan that would save her people's lives. He would accomplish what his father had not been able to do, taking Dunrobin and Sutherland lands, and he would prove to his brothers and clan that he deserved the highest respect.

Ella shook her head at him. "You think you have it all figured out."

Confusion bent his brows. "I do have it all figured out." He would continue to grow the Sinclair clan, making it the most powerful in Scotland. Maybe one day he could even rule Scotland like his father had hoped.

"How could you without even discovering

anything about the Sutherlands, who we are, and why your plan will not work?"

He crossed his arms to match her stance. "Very well, tell me about your clan, Ella Sutherland, and why my plan will not work."

She exhaled through her teeth, and the cloth she'd wrapped around her hair unraveled, dropping to the floor with a thud. "I cannot."

"Ye cannot?" he repeated. *Or will not.* "'Tis fairly easy, lass. Just open your lips and—"

"I made a promise to someone."

He narrowed his eyes, studying her. "So ye accuse me of not asking about your clan, but ye refuse to tell me anything about it."

She turned away, flipping the end of the blanket around her back. The kitten chased the frayed corner as it dragged across the floorboards. "It is complicated," she said. "And I do not trust you."

"I did not kill or harm ye. Ye have been given clean things, a comfortable room, food, and a gift. Perhaps ye could let go of some of your anger to see the logic behind our union. Even though ye killed my father."

She pivoted toward him. "And you killed my father."

"Aye, but your father was a foking *bastard* who branded ye."

A flush heated Ella's cheeks. "And your father was a foking *lunatic* who thought his sons were the four horsemen of the apocalypse." She kept her blanket gripped with her arms but managed to raise her forearms. She opened her eyes wide and wiggled her fingers upward. "Sent to earth on a heavenly cloud from God."

She mocked him and his brothers. Irritation tightened his jaw. "But…he never raised a hand against a Sinclair, neither person nor horse." Cain crossed his arms over his chest. "Once ye get to know us, ye will see that Sinclairs are actually quite likeable people. Some are a bit eccentric but still likeable."

She huffed, spinning away to pick up the kitten. She looked over her shoulder, her eyes growing wide. "Are you giving me a kitten to make me *like* you?"

He was not sure what to say. His experience with wooing a lass's good opinion of him was completely lacking. As long as he had the respect of his people, he had never cared if they liked him or not. "I would answer truthfully, but I fear ye would make me take the beast away, and it was hard enough to get her up here. She will likely scratch my eyes out if I attempt to carry her down."

"Bloody hell," Ella murmured. She traipsed past him to the open door. "Goodbye, Cain."

He walked slowly across, and as he drew closer, he inhaled the fresh, warm scent of her. What would it be like to have her soft and willing, moaning his name as he shattered her world with pleasure? He stopped before her, staring down into her frowning face over the threshold of the small tower room. "We will wed, Ella, and I will take your clan. It is the way of war for someone to lose. I can make your surrender as peaceful as possible, but that all depends on ye."

Her eyes narrowed into near slits. "Death before surrender," she said and pushed the door shut in his face.

• • •

"Bàs and Joshua are posting the wedding banns, which I wrote out last night," Gideon said, as he sat across from Cain by the cold hearth in the great hall. "The celebration for Da will begin at noon. Hannah and Merida have gone to oversee the cooking and baking to be done this morn. Joshua brought down a stag for the feast before dawn, and I sacrificed a few chickens to be plucked and roasted into pies. Viola Finley and several lasses from town are helping in the kitchens."

Cain's gaze flicked across to the arched alcove where the stairs began. Was Ella awake? It was still early, slightly past dawn. He'd walked up the circular tower steps as far as his father's chamber where he'd stationed a rotating guard last night in case the lass thought she could sneak out. Perhaps, unlike Cain, she had succumbed to sleep immediately and slept deeply all night. He glanced at his brother when he realized Gideon had grown silent.

"She tried to leave only once, before midnight," Gideon said. "Thomas stopped her."

Cain frowned, meeting Gideon's amused gaze. "How?"

"She opened her door, stepped out with her kitten, and took ten st—"

"Ye arse, how did Thomas stop her?"

"Ooooooh," Gideon said, a broad smile irritating Cain. Unlike Joshua, Gideon was the peacemaker, so his teasing had caught him off guard. "He told her that he was stationed there to make certain she did not leave, and that food would be brought to her in the morning. She turned around, without a word, and climbed back up to the tower chamber."

"Has anyone brought her food yet?"

"Merida stopped Joshua from taking it up and said she'd take it up after dawn," Gideon said, his smile thinning out. "I think he has become interested in her."

"He bloody hell better become disinterested fast," Cain said, his hand squeezing into a fist.

The rivalry between the oldest and second oldest had always been fierce, with Cain being the one in charge as the firstborn and Joshua being excellent at starting wars. They would always have each other's backs, though, in and out of battle. Loyalty to one another flowed through their blood.

"I already talked to him," Gideon said. "The last thing we need is a civil war over a lass."

"I would win," Cain said. He always won.

"Speak the devil's name and ye summon him," Gideon said under his breath as Joshua strode briskly into the great hall, saw them, and came directly over.

He smiled and nodded to Gideon before meeting Cain's angry gaze. "Have ye seen the Sutherland lass yet today?" Joshua asked. "She is looking quite lovely in that blue gown Merida found for her. Although I still prefer those tight trousers."

Cain stood, his chair scraping back across the stone floor. Gideon leaped up, ready to break up what was about to escalate. "Ye were told not to go up to her chamber," Cain said. He did not need Joshua interfering in his strategy to gain Ella's trust.

"I have not gone up to her chamber. In fact, I just returned from giving your wedding banns to Pastor John." Joshua made a show of stepping around Cain to flop down into the chair he'd vacated.

Cain spun on his heel. "And yet ye saw Ella this morn? She has not yet come down."

"Ho, she is right now, stuck in the process of coming down," Joshua said, making Cain and Gideon look to the steps. "Not that way." Joshua pointed toward the entryway. "She is climbing down from her window."

"What?" Cain didn't wait for further explanation but ran toward the entryway. He heard Gideon curse as he followed.

"I thought to assist, but ye told me to keep away from her," Joshua yelled from his seat.

Cain grabbed the rough stone of the broad doorway as he rounded the corner, surging out into the morning air and turning immediately to the right where the tower rose four stories straight up. There were a half dozen soldiers underneath staring up, their arms out as if preparing to work together to catch the lass. "Let me through," Cain commanded.

"Joshua said he would tell ye," Keenan said, the men parting.

He looked up the smooth curve of the tower. Ella was halfway down, with what looked like strips from a blanket braided together and wrapped in a crossed hold around her back while her booted feet stepped down the curved granite. The blue gown was tucked around each leg, but part of it still hung down. *Meow*. The kitten was somewhere on her person and quite vexed.

"What the bloody hell are ye doing?" he yelled.

She stopped, one hand at her back where she held the rope as easily as if she sat on a swing. She frowned down at him. "Coming to breakfast."

He stood below her with the rest of the onlookers, heart pounding in his chest. One slip and she could drop to the hard dirt of the bailey below. "We have stairs inside."

She took another step down the wall, and his arms rose as if to catch her. "Stairs that are guarded."

"Merida was about to bring something up."

"I was hungry." She yelled the words succinctly as if rebuking the wall. With a big inhale, she continued to step down while leaning back, letting out the long rope she'd braided as she went. She'd been busy last night.

Each step down seemed to take forever as he waited, his own arms out and ready. But she continued without fault, stubbornly lowering herself until the tips of Cain's fingers could reach her.

Meow, the kitten called, but he still didn't see it. "I will catch ye," he said, his thick arms out and ready.

"I am fine on my own."

He caught her around the waist anyway, pulling her into his arms, her back against his chest. "God's teeth, Ella," he cursed, guiding her feet to the earth and turning her toward him. "What the hell were ye doing?"

Ella's face was flushed with exertion, and mutiny shone in her eyes as she shoved away from him. "Dawn came up faster than I anticipated," she said, her words almost like a snarl, and she yanked her braided hair around to her shoulder. The front of her bodice moved, and the kitten's head popped out the top.

Cain looked up at the open window above and then to her. "Ye wished to escape while it was still dark."

Her hands perched onto the curves of her hips. "I wouldn't have gone to all the trouble of climbing out if I knew everyone was going to see me. I might be a slow climber, and apparently unable to judge the sky, but I am not an idiot," she murmured, her cheeks flushed from exertion or embarrassment. She glanced away. "Well, maybe I am," she added under her breath.

The kitten, its small head popped out of the valley between Ella's breasts, reached a paw out to bat at a stray curl that lay along the curve of her cheek. "I must have fallen asleep for much longer than I thought," she said, not looking at him. "I swore it was closer to three in the morning when I first climbed out. The blasted clouds were blocking the start of the sunrise in the east."

The woman was brave, clever, and strong. She was also used to berating herself. Cain glanced at the men who were still gathered, their expressions somewhere between amused and shocked.

Keenan looked…damn interested. "She is certainly not frightened of high climbs."

"Go on," Cain ordered, and they turned away reluctantly, walking toward the morning training session that Bàs would begin once he returned from the Sutherland chapel.

Cain ignored Gideon and Joshua, who stood at

the keep doors, anger at her risk still strumming through his veins. "Ella," he said and waited until she lifted her gaze to meet his. He wanted to curse at her for risking her life, to demand she promise to not try to escape by insane means, and to threaten that he'd tie her to her bed tonight. The look in her eyes said she expected all of that.

He glanced at the windows way up the tower and then back at her. "Ye are a clever and brave prisoner." He scratched his bristled chin and slid his gaze along the height again. "Most of my men would not have even attempted that climb, let alone with Puss stuffed down their tunic."

"Boudica," she said.

"Boudica?" As dawn flooded the courtyard with misty light, he could see the darker flecks in Ella's gray eyes.

"The puss," she said. "I call her Boo, short for Boudica, the great Celtic warrior woman." She gently pulled the small kitten from her bodice, its round eyes wide as if it knew how lucky it was to still be alive. Ella set her down, and the kitten immediately started stalking a grasshopper, apparently forgetting its fear.

Damn, if the cat had made her lose her focus, Ella could have fallen. He made himself take another deep breath before speaking again. "I will be nailing the tower windows shut today."

She shrugged. "I am very good at finding ways to escape."

Cain's face tightened as his eyes moved to her circular scar. "Is that why ye were branded on your face with the Sutherland crest? So if ye escaped, someone would return ye?"

Ella turned on her boot, traipsing back to the great hall. She looked like she would crash right through Gideon and Joshua, but they parted quickly to let her enter. Cain stopped with them, watching her walk through into the great hall where Merida greeted her.

"Have a guard posted below the tower," Cain said.

Gideon crossed his arms. "I thought ye were nailing the windows shut."

"Aye, but she probably has a way to work nails out."

"Blast, brother," Joshua said. "Ye aren't nearly as furious as I thought ye would be."

He was right. Cain let a grin bend the side of his mouth upward as he looked again at the height. Ella had known nearly as soon as she climbed out that she had miscalculated the timing of dawn. She hadn't the strength to climb back into the room, but she could probably have lifted the kitten over the windowsill. Doing so would have left her dangling four stories up, all alone, knowing that she would be recaptured. If she had let go, she would have died from the fall.

"I just learned something very important about Ella Sutherland."

"That she cannot tell the time," Gideon said, making Joshua chuckle.

Cain rubbed the knot in his chest that was starting to relax with Ella safely on the ground again. "Aye, but also…Ella Sutherland wants to live."

CHAPTER SIX

Cain followed her upstairs to her prison room after gathering some boards. Ella watched the obvious strength in his back as he hammered the nails in, his wavy wheat-colored hair skimming the edge of his tunic. The muscles in his bared calves contracted as he worked to cover every part of the third window. *Bam! Bam! Bam!*

Finished, he turned. His pale blue eyes, legendary to those few who had seen them and lived, stared at her, his jaw firm. She held her breath as he walked past her, leaving the room without a word, the door remaining unlocked.

She dropped her face into her hands. *I am so stupid. Even Jamie would call me a fool.*

Ella paced in her tower chamber, the windows nailed shut, making the air more stagnant. Groggy from waking suddenly to realize that she'd lost a chunk of the night by falling asleep, she hadn't taken the time to determine what time of night it was. With the courtyard below empty, she'd assumed everyone was still asleep.

Damn. She deserved to be captured for her folly, and she should have been reprimanded and ridiculed. Her father would have laughed in her face before knocking her to the ground. Curse Cain Sinclair for doing neither. Instead, the devil of Girnigoe had sought to save her, his classically strong features pinched in what looked like authentic concern for her wellbeing. Even the scars from his brutal past had made him look ruggedly handsome rather than threatening. *Mo chreach.* Surely, his kindness was a trick.

With her view cut off, there was little to do but give in to her lack of sleep. She woke to the sounds of laughter and music filtering up from the great hall below as the celebration around George Sinclair's rigid body began. Ella had been to wakes before where there was more drinking and laughing than tears and mourning. It was a way to work out the sorrow and remember the good about a person rather than their death.

She pushed upright on the small bed, little Boo purring. The kitten yawned and stretched out upon the new cover Merida had brought up with break-fast. In exchange, Ella had to endure a scolding for not being more cautious with her life. Ella still had the key to the room, but she knew there would be a guard somewhere on the steps. Even the one who smiled kindly at her was too large to push by. If she only had a weapon. Of course, Cain hadn't returned her daggers or her bow.

Think. A woman's strength is in her reasoning brain. Her mother's favorite bit of advice still echoed in Ella's memory. She glanced up at the peaked ceiling. *I surely disappointed you with my reasoning brain this dawn.*

She ran fingers through her loosened hair along her scalp as if trying to rid herself of her anger, which was apparently muddling her mind. Where would there be a weapon? Anywhere in this blasted huge castle. Her fingers stopped, and her head popped upward.

"The devil's old bedchamber," she murmured. It was directly below her. If the guard was at the bottom of the stairwell, toasting his old chief, she might be able to sneak into George Sinclair's chamber. The battle-crazed warrior would have weapons everywhere, maybe even a secret tunnel leading out of Girnigoe. Dunrobin had a couple of them.

Ella stood, wishing she had her trousers and tunic back from being laundered. "If I can scale a wall in a gown and stays, I can sneak into a bedchamber," she said to Boo, who batted at a ball of rags Ella had torn the night before.

Tonight would be the perfect time to escape if there was an exit from the room. All the Sinclairs would be well into their whisky, toasting the bastard who had slaughtered so many Sutherlands. It seemed to be early afternoon, the muted light coming in from the small open windows way up high in the tower peak. Reaching under the bed, she dragged out a few ropes she'd abandoned last night because they were too thin to hold her. She tied them tightly around her thighs so the skirt wouldn't rustle or hinder her. She'd learned the art of silence as she grew under her father's suspicious eye.

"You stay here," she whispered to Boo, scratching the playful cat. The kitten blinked at her but went back to chewing on the end of the rag while kicking it with her back paws.

Ella moved to the door and pressed her ear to the oak. Her goal was to arm herself and discover a way out if possible, returning once it grew dark and the Sinclairs were snoring away in their own slobber.

With a fortifying breath, Ella turned the key she'd left in the lock and listened for the slight click of the latch moving within. She could relock it from the outside, but she hoped to be gone for only a few minutes and might need a quick reentry.

The laughter was louder in the stairwell and would hide any stray sounds she might make. The night would be quieter, but she wasn't ready to attempt escape without at least one weapon and Boo. And she would find Gilla in the herd of black horses where Cain's brother, Gideon, had likely put her. That required the cover of darkness and drunken guards.

Ella peeked around the curve of the granite block wall. No guard in sight. Hugging the interior edge, she stepped down slowly, peeking as she went. After three more turns, she spotted the grand inset door that guarded the threshold of the chief's chambers. Her heart pounded hard like when she'd sneak around Dunrobin at night, hiding from her father's guards.

Sliding flat against the door that sported a horse carved into the hard wood, Ella pressed the lever. The latch released, and the door swung inward. *Thank the Mother Mary*. She slipped inside, shutting it with barely a click.

Ella released her breath and turned to face the room, the dusty air heavy with a musty tang. Dwindling daylight from two pairs of large windows illuminated the room, one set on either side of the rectangular space. Even though it was large, or maybe *because* it was large, the room seemed spartan with only a trunk at the end of an oversized bed, a privacy screen with a water basin and jakes, and two sets of bookshelves filled with volumes and various trinkets, which were probably stolen from conquered clans.

A set of padded chairs sat before the cold, brushed hearth sporting a heavy wooden mantel, the only adornment being a small portrait of a lady. A broadsword was mounted above a hanging tapestry. Not only would she struggle to get it down, but the length and weight made it fairly useless against a trained warrior. No, she needed daggers or a bow and quiver full of arrows.

She turned in a tight circle, her eyes scanning everything from the thick double beams above her head to the odd-looking chess game set between the two chairs. Her gaze came full circle back to the tapestry hanging across most of the far wall. It was another scene of the four apocalyptic horsemen riding down from Heaven.

She snorted softly, walking over to the carved chessboard where she sank down to study a knobby piece of wood sitting in the king's spot. Without disturbing it, her gaze followed the uneven grooves carved into the wood to represent a frowning face and crown. She peered next at a tall piece of wood that was perhaps a bishop with a pointy hat. The pawns looked like simple blocks, one set painted white and the other set black. And yet the wooden horses, which represented the knights, were exquisitely formed and carved, nothing like the rest of the set. She stared at the white knight. *Cain.*

A burst of laughter from down below snapped

Ella upright. Curiosity would slow her down. She hurried on the balls of her feet to the chest, finding only folded linens and lengths of woven wool that George Sinclair likely wrapped around his hips. Belts and holsters sat to one side but no knives. *Damn.*

She closed the lid and looked at the large bed, its frame made of whole tree trunks. The size of it could hold six people across. It was luxurious with a multitude of pillows and numerous quilts and several furs. Turning in a tight circle, she frowned. *Where are your weapons?* Her gaze latched onto the thick pillows on the bed. Even with the door locked at Dunrobin, Ella slept with a *sgian dubh* under her pillow. Perhaps George Sinclair did, too, in case enemies got past his drawbridges, walls, and ridiculously lethal sons.

She pulled back the top layers of goose-down pillows to the flat tick, careful not to scatter them. Ella smiled. "Thank you, you rotting devil," she whispered and picked up the two weapons, a six-inch *sgian dubh* and an eight-inch *mattucashlass*, which was more lethal because of its two sharpened edges. Both were well balanced, and with a few practice throws later in her room, Ella should be able to hit her target. Kenneth had spent many years making sure she could use any short blade she encountered.

Fixing the pillows, she hurried back to the chest with the leather holsters. She chose one with thin straps and slid the blades into it, looping it over her shoulder.

She looked back to the hearth. *Now for a way out.* The bookcase or the hearth were the likely places for a secret closet with steps downward. Ella hurried to the bookcase closest to the hearth, her fingers sliding down the leather- and clothbound tomes: books on war, books with odd Greek lettering, several volumes of the Bible. Her palm slid across them, and her finger caught on three books that were pushed outward the smallest amount, as if something might lay behind them. Tipping them out, she found a ring caught into the chiseled stone behind the case.

"Yes," she whispered and looped her finger through the ring and pulled. The sound of a latch lifting clicked in the wall, and a bit of breeze blew under the bookcase as it slid to the left on rollers built behind it. She smiled broadly at her old friend, darkness. There was no way Cain Sinclair could hold her for long.

. . .

"He died a warrior's death, exactly how he wished," Cain said, holding his tankard high.

Gideon grasped his shoulder and jumped onto one of the benches that ran the length of the long table where their father lay. "The greatest defeater of foes."

"War was his game, and he played it well," Joshua yelled, garnering "ayes" and the pounding of fists.

Bàs stood near their father's head. "It was a damn good death," he said, his deep voice softer than most. It was as if guilt and dread weighed his timbre down. Cain couldn't remember a day when his youngest brother had been a carefree, smiling lad. At least Cain had had nine years of a relatively normal upbringing before his mother died and his father had latched completely onto the idea that he had sired the four horsemen. Cain would have to talk further with Bàs about his role in the clan. He would not have any of his brothers living a tortured life to fit into the legend their father had forged around them.

The entire room drank to their tributes, finishing with another song about a siege from long ago. The day had been filled with toasts and stories of his father's greatness. Even George Sinclair's senseless rages and harshness were being commended before the man's corpse. When the sun began to set, he and his brothers would carry their father's wrapped body outside Girnigoe to the dug grave beside Cain's mother, who had died over twenty years ago from fever after giving birth to Bàs. Tomorrow Cain would begin to build the future for Clan Sinclair, a future full of glory and conquest, creating the strongest clan in Scotland.

He glanced toward the steps that led to the tower room. Was Ella catching up on the sleep she missed last night? Would she curl up with her kitten, Boudica? Cain smiled over the name. The fierceness of the wee beastie made it perfect, and the fact Ella had named her and tried to take her with her when she climbed from the window told him much. The little creature needed a champion. Ella had taken on the role immediately, as he knew she would. She was much less likely to request to die when she must remain alive to protect her little Boudica.

Dodging around the warriors laughing near the

steps, Merida hurried over. She and Hannah had spoken fondly of George earlier, before the attendees had started passing the whisky around. They had vacated to work with the kitchen maids shortly after that, leaving only Viola, a wild lass from the village, and a few other maids who did not mind the leers and crude language of the somewhat drunk warriors. They remained mostly sober in case of attack, but the celebration of his father's life would give several of them throbbing heads the next day.

Merida stopped before him, head tipping back to stare up at his face. "I just took a plate of tarts up to Ella."

"I nailed her windows shut," he said. Was it stifling in the room?

"Maybe ye should have nailed over her chimney, too."

"What?"

"Cain, she is not in the tower room."

Daingead. He'd left his guard in the stairwell. "Thomas?"

"Is searching her room and George's chamber right now."

"Bloody hell," he said, setting his tankard down. "Is Da's back stairway open?"

Merida shook her head.

"What is amiss?" Joshua asked, his face turning from laughter to death in the space of heartbeats.

"Ella is missing," Cain said, as Gideon and Bàs came close. Cain didn't wait for a reply but strode through the crowd that opened for him. He took the tower steps two at a time, yelling back over his shoulder.

"Send a guard to the outside door that opens onto the shoreline, in case she found the tunnel." If it was low tide, she might be able to skirt around Girnigoe on the rocks. If it was high tide, she'd have to swim. Could she swim? The thought made him almost turn around, but he'd already reached his father's chamber where Thomas barreled out.

Face red, eyes wide. "I was below this turn on the steps. I did not think—"

"Is she in there?" Cain cut through his sputtered excuse. Thomas shook his head, and Cain continued up to the tower room, throwing the door open. It banged against the wall as he walked in, scanning the small, circular enclosure. He paused. Because the room wasn't empty. Boudica sat on the bed in the dim light of one of the windows up high in the tower's cone. The kitten stared at him from a crouch as if readying to attack if he came closer.

Cain inhaled and rubbed the back of his neck. His muscles relaxed the smallest amount as details pulled together in his mind.

"I will gather a group of men to ride after her," Gideon said, coming up behind him.

Cain turned to leave the room. "First, send Joshua to check if her horse is still in his stables."

"You think she would take it?" Gideon asked.

"I know she would," Cain said. He glanced back toward the tower room. "She did not leave the kitten this morning when she climbed out the window. If an animal is hers, she will not leave it behind."

"But she left the kitten this time?"

Cain smiled. "Exactly." He had studied strategy his whole life, through a multitude of chess games and the wisdom of his father, elderly warriors, and forthcoming chiefs of other clans. He'd read book upon book of battle and how to predict an enemy's movements. If, after all of that, he couldn't figure out the mind of a woman bent on escape, he was indeed a failure to his father and clan.

He walked into the larger bedchamber and inhaled the heaviness of George Sinclair's presence. The tang of the man's sweat mixed with the dust that he refused to have cleaned by the maids. Aye, Cain would see it scrubbed and aired before his own things were brought over. His father had been a warrior through and through, his comfort met with large furnishings of heavy wood. A small portrait of Cain's mother sat on the mantel, but the only other adornments, besides the lopsided chessmen on the board, were the large tapestry and an ornamental long sword.

Walking to the shelves where the books hid the iron ring that would open the tunnel, he turned back to the room. He ignored Gideon who watched from the doorway. "I know ye are in here, lass."

Silence.

"Even if ye did venture down the stairs in the dark, the door at the bottom is locked, and you have left the key hanging here," he said, looking at the key on a wall hook beside Gideon. "And if ye plan to pick the lock at the bottom, there are Sinclairs waiting on the other side."

His boots clicked as he walked to one of the padded chairs by the chessboard, sitting in the one he always took when playing the game each night with his father. "But I know ye have not left. In fact, ye planned to sneak back to your room before Thomas or Merida found ye gone."

Gideon squatted low, looking under the bed. He stood, shaking his head.

Cain's gaze slid evenly about the room. What did he already know about Ella Sutherland? She was brave and agile. She was clever, stubborn, and would champion a kitten, refusing to leave it behind. Cain looked up at the thick beams running the length of the room. And she was definitely *not* afraid of heights. He leveled a glance at Gideon and then at the beams until his brother followed his gaze.

"I cannot imagine that it is clean on those beams," Cain said, standing. "The dust is likely tickling your nose up there, Ella. Why don't ye come down?"

"Damn you to hell," Ella yelled from the ceiling, releasing the rest of the tension sitting in Cain's chest. If she hadn't been up there, he'd have looked like a fool in front of Gideon, and his brother would have told Joshua, and then Cain would have to stab Joshua for bringing it up in every conversation. Not a mortal wound, just somewhere annoyingly painful.

She sneezed and pushed up onto her elbows on the beam to frown down at him, her bent finger rubbing at the tip of her nose, reminding him of her touching her perfect nose to the kitten's. She glared down over the edge of the beam, and Cain fought to keep his grin inside, knowing that would only make it difficult to get her down without climbing up there himself.

Gideon came around, tilting his head back to stare up at her. "How did ye even climb up there?"

"I can fly," she snapped. The effectiveness of her glare was lost when she sneezed again. "Has this room never been dusted?"

"Rarely," Cain said. "And likely never up there."

"If ye can fly, ye would have flown home from your window this morn," Gideon said, which earned him a foul gesture that Cain had never seen a lass use. He glanced down so she wouldn't see the smile that he couldn't hold back.

The beams were high enough that she could not sit upon them, but her legs moved over so her skirt could hang down. "Boudica misses ye and pissed next to your bed," Cain said. "And Merida brought ye another gown and smock that she found and some tarts. Do ye need assistance flying down?"

"Nay," Gideon said earnestly. "I want to see her do it. I have never seen a lass fly before."

"Perhaps I will save you the trouble of ordering Bàs to execute me and dive down headfirst," she said, but she was already inching on her stomach along the beams toward the bed.

"Ye wouldn't die with me down here, but ye might hurt yourself terribly, and then what would poor Boudica do without your care," Cain said.

"*Tolla-thon*," she cursed as she reached the bed post where the thick drapery was hung from a loop of iron cemented into the granite blocks overhead. Cain watched in amazement as she swung her legs down, her skirts tied between them, to wrap around the drapery in such a fashion that she was suspended. She let the drapery slip between her booted ankles until she touched the floor.

"Did ye climb up that way?" Gideon asked,

obviously impressed.

Even as Ella swatted dust from her borrowed blue gown, her hair curling out from her braid and a fierce frown pinching her features, she was a unique beauty. Having glimpsed her in her wet smock when the blanket dropped, Cain knew she was full of curves. Her fingers were slender, almost fragile. She was also strong, and her cleverness made her the most interesting challenge he'd ever come up against. When she lifted her gaze to his, her gray eyes were full of conviction. Had she always had such long, dark lashes? She blinked, and they seemed to touch her cheeks.

"I can escape any room or dungeon," she said, her gaze going to Cain. "You might as well let me, Boo, and my horse go now, and save yourself the trouble."

"I rather like trouble," Cain said. In fact, the last day, thwarting the lass, was the most entertaining day that he could remember.

She shook her head, eyes tipping upward as if beseeching angelic help. "Trouble is all you are about, is it not, Cain Sinclair?" She locked gazes with him again. "You cannot be satisfied with ruling your own huge territory." She spread her arms wide, revealing dust all over the front of her gown. "No, you must conquer and take everything from all your neighbors, too, creating civil war, bringing on bloodshed—"

"And the apocalypse?" Gideon finished. He looked at Cain. "Da would be so proud." His brother was great at debating, poking at his opponent until they exploded and made an error that would tip the argument in Gideon's favor.

Under the smudges of dust, Ella's face was turning crimson with her anger. "Most of Scotland thinks the idea of you four being sent from God, to destroy mankind so we can be judged, is insane." She sucked in a quick breath. "You four are ruthless barbarians, stealing and killing and…and looking at me…at *us* with *disgust* when you should look that way at yourselves every time you see your reflection." By the time she reached the end, her generous bosom was rising with agitation.

Gideon had looked ready to talk over her but stopped when Cain signaled him. Cain tipped his head slightly. "Disgust? When have I looked at ye with disgust?"

She took a step closer to him, her pretty white teeth bared. "Years ago at the Beltane Festival south of our territory."

Cain's eyes widened. She remembered their first meeting?

"You think we are all beneath you, midges to be crushed," she said, fisting her hand in front of his face.

Cain caught her fist. It fit neatly in his palm. He held tight as she tried to jerk it away. "I do not want ye to be crushed, and I am not disgusted by ye. Who has told ye these lies?"

She wet the edge of her lips as if they'd gone dry, the small movement pulling Cain's memory of the way she'd tasted in the tree kissing him. He released her fist, and she yanked it next to her leg but leaned forward like a hissing cat.

"I have *seen* you look on me with disgust, and

you lay siege to any clan who stands against you, taking their castle and lands. What else is that but crushing?"

Conquering was not crushing. In fact, Cain disliked the idea of killing good people who could unite with the Sinclairs, adding to the talents and strength already under his leadership. "I will conquer unequipped and weaker clans, helping them by uniting them with our strength so that we can build a stronger Scotland," he said evenly. "And I do not remember ever looking at ye with disgust."

She crossed her arms under her breasts and straightened. "You did." As if weary of the debate, her voice dropped, and she looked past him toward the hearth. "You, Cain Sinclair, are hollow like that white knight over there on the chessboard, empty of goodness, only a player on a battlefield. Perhaps you were born without a soul or perhaps your crazy father killed it in you with all his bellowing of fanatical ideas." Her gaze came back to him. "But if you do not release me and leave my clan alone, I will know that you are truly hollow of feeling and honor inside."

Gideon shifted, his voice low. "The pieces are actually not hollow, but solid wood, so they won't fall over easily."

Ella spun on her heel, marching out of the chamber, turning right to climb the stairs to her tower room.

Gideon's mouth formed a tight circle as he looked back at Cain with raised eyebrows. "Bloody hell, brother, ye have quite a bit of wooing to do if she is going to marry ye in three weeks. Ye may need

a wagonload of kittens, perhaps some horses." He
sucked in a large breath and grinned. "Isn't that
mare, Ginny, about to foal?"

Cain stood where she'd left him, feeling...guilty?
Of what? Of winning her in a battle and planning to
conquer and unite her clan with his? *I have seen you
look on me with disgust.* She was a young lass at the
festival, perhaps only fourteen, her face smooth
without that foking brand, her hair the same soft
waves of dark silk. He'd bumped her. He remembered
picking up the odd bouquet of purple thistles she'd
dropped when his father came upon them.

Blast it! Cain's stomach tightened, and he inhaled
fully through his nose. His father's breath had been
heavy with whisky, and he'd practically spit his
whisper into Cain's ear. *She is a Sutherland, lad. They
beat their horses, just like their women.*

And the look that had crossed his own face
then...was likely disgust.

Gideon's pinched expression showed he was
weighing the odds of Cain's success.

Cain glanced at the open door and back at
Gideon. "Can a person's view be changed when
they've grown up believing a misunderstanding?"
Cain asked, frowning, his wide hand catching the
back of his head. "Hell, a downright bloody lie?"

Gideon shrugged, but the look in his gaze was
anything but casual. "Are ye talking about a misunderstanding Ella told herself as a fresh lass or the
bloody lie that Da fed us our whole lives?"

Before Cain could even repeat the question in his
head, Gideon turned and walked out the chamber
door.

CHAPTER SEVEN

"Damn bastard," Ella whispered as she recalled Cain's confused expression. Of course he didn't remember her.

He had no idea what his sneer had cost her in childish tears and sleepless nights, nor would he care if he did. It had been a young girl's infatuation, but his look had stuck inside her heart, bolstered by the disappointed sneers from her own father. She shook her head. Why was she even worrying over it? She should be much more concerned about Cain trying to take her clan and castle.

Boo rubbed against her skirt, purring, as Ella sopped up the cat urine and shite left in the room. Cats lived only outdoors, and she would take the kitten there, but the Sinclair chief's wake was still going on below despite darkness falling. She could hear the music and male laughter when she opened the door to toss out the fouled rags.

"We will leave tonight," she whispered, scratching the purring kitten. "If they ever fall asleep." Hopefully, the Sinclairs were drinking lots of whisky, although she had smelled only a hint of it on Cain earlier. Would he post a guard right outside her door? If he did, escape tonight might be impossible. But she must go tonight or tomorrow at the latest if she wanted to use the hidden stairway in the chief's room, because Cain would be moving in there soon.

Rap. Rap. The knock was soft on her door. Ella

slid her hand over the blade that she'd strapped to her leg, the other one secured up her sleeve, the point wedged into the seam of her cuff to keep it from falling out.

"Who is it?"

"Hannah Sinclair. I have some drink for ye to go with the tarts. Cain said ye might be thirsty."

Ella opened the door to the young blond woman. Slight in frame, she was tall like a fragile sapling in the forest and wore a flowing gown that added to her angelic look. She held a tray and had green fabric draped over her arm. "Thank you," Ella said, taking the tray, and Hannah followed her inside. Cain's sister gave a little gasp as she bent to scoop up Boo, nuzzling the kitten against her cheek while Ella set the tray down and washed her hands.

She met Ella's gaze when she came out from the privacy screen. "So…Cain hurt your feelings years ago at the Beltane fair."

Did the Sinclair siblings tell each other *everything*? Ella shrugged. "It was long ago."

"Unresolved hurt never heals properly. Like stitched flesh that does not take. It can break open again and feel like a fresh wound." She set the squirming kitten down and shook out the fabric in her hands. It was another gown, this one in green, and a smock. "I found another set for ye."

"That is…very generous, considering I am a prisoner."

Hannah kept her expression neutral and serious. "Ella, please know that the look my brother gave ye back then was not meant for ye, but for your father. When my aunt, Merida, was divorced by Alec

Sutherland and sent back to Girnigoe in shame, she was quite open about the brutality she endured at Dunrobin under her husband when she could not produce a living child. He wanted nothing more than a male heir."

A bigger truth could not be said. Ella had lived with the stigma of being a female her entire life. Her father would rail against her simply for being a daughter and not a son. She'd spent her early life hiding behind her mother, but when Mary Sutherland died in childbirth when Ella was fourteen years old, Ella had learned to become nearly invisible at Dunrobin to avoid Alec Sutherland.

Hannah squeezed her hand. "That day, my father reminded Cain that ye were the daughter of the devil who beat his horses and his women."

Ella swallowed past the stricture in her throat, her voice coming softly. "Alec Sutherland never beat a horse." The connection between their gazes said the rest.

Hannah breathed in fully. "I cannot imagine the horror of living like that." She glanced away, moving to the window to run a finger down the fresh nails biting into the frame. "My father may have bellowed, but his only crime against me was…" She turned to Ella with a sad smile. "He never looked at me."

"Looked at you?"

"Or said my name, or talked directly to me, as if I was not there. I was treated well, like one of his horses, but when I was born a girl and not the fourth horseman like he'd planned, he basically decided I did not exist. To this day, people are shocked to learn George Sinclair had five children instead of only four boys. As if my presence might make his claim about his sons being the biblical horsemen less believed."

"I do not believe his claim."

Hannah smiled. "Cain says he didn't see any of his brothers coming down from a cloud fully formed, either. But the legend Da spurred makes our enemies quake and gives my brothers a way to organize themselves."

"The legend does not make me quake, either."

"Of course not," Hannah said without hesitation. "Ye are the bravest woman I have ever met. Climbing out the tower window, ordering a battalion of men, standing before Cain without trembling." She shook her head. "And requesting to be executed instead of wedding." She lowered her voice as if someone might hear. "So, the wedding night, ye prefer death to the breeding act?"

"No," Ella said slowly. "I prefer death over surrendering my clan."

The wedding night? What would a wedding night with Cain Sinclair be like? His kiss had nearly wiped all plans of escape from Ella's mind when they'd balanced together in the tree. Her pounding heart had turned from desperation to something else, something like her foolish response when he'd smiled at her years ago.

Hannah's brows lowered. "I do not know how to help ye. Cain was raised to take all he can for our clan. It is his main responsibility." She stepped out into the dark hall and gave her a gentle smile. "Oh, and Cain said that ye must come below in the morn to eat instead of food being carried up here. And I will see if I can find more smocks for ye. Sleep well."

At this rate, Ella would have more clothes at Girnigoe than Dunrobin. "My trousers and tunic?" she asked quickly before Hannah could shut the door.

"Are wonderful," Hannah said, her smiling face popping back in. "I tried them on," she whispered. "I have asked the tanner to make me a pair. I will send yours up to ye right now and a new tunic, because the other one is still being repaired."

Ella watched her slip out, the door clicking into place. She picked up Boo, touching her tiny nose to her own. "I would guess that she knows all the ways in and out of Girnigoe." If only Hannah could be turned away from her brother to help her escape. "No matter," she whispered to the kitten. "I will get us out myself."

• • •

"Ye think Ella will come this way?" Gideon asked Cain as they stood in the darkness, listening to the sea waves rolling the pebbles upon the shoreline. The sliver of moon hid behind the sparse clouds, giving only a dim glow to the ocean stretching out before them.

Cain looked behind him at the door that was nearly obscured by the tenacious trees, their roots clutching to the rocks at the base of Girnigoe. "I told Thomas to sit at the bottom of the steps. She likely heard me mention the key, and she is still angry as hell. Aye, I think she will."

"And ye are just going to wait here?" his brother asked.

"She knows I will be moving into Da's room very soon and that many of the guards have been drinking spirits all day. If she comes this way, it will likely be tonight," Cain said, tossing a rock into the gentle waves coming with the tide. "I have a guard set at her horse and the night watch keeping an eye out for her if she gets past Thomas on the steps." He looked up at the sky and the position of the moon. "But my guess is that she will be along soon."

"What are ye going to do with her once ye catch her out here?"

"First, probably stop her from trying to kill me." Cain felt a grin tug at his mouth. Ella Sutherland definitely had claws. How would they feel scratching down his bare back? "After that I hope she will take a ride with me to Loch Hempriggs," Cain continued.

Gideon chuckled. "Ye are trying to woo her with kittens and stars?"

Cain frowned. He'd never had to worry about garnering the interest of a lass before. They'd been attracted to his build, strength, and position in the clan as soon as he'd started training with real swords. "Do ye have a better strategy for getting a woman who hates ye to agree to wed with ye?"

"Gowns, gold, horses?" Gideon asked.

But what did he know? He'd never wooed a woman, either.

"Passion?" Gideon added.

Now that idea had merit. However, trying to get close to Ella Sutherland again likely meant he would feel a blade between his ribs, one of his father's blades that were no longer stashed under his pillows. Cain turned toward the closed door that he'd left locked, so she wouldn't guess that he knew she was coming until she was already outside.

"Ye could force her," Gideon suggested. "Tell her that ye will wipe out her entire clan and burn Dunrobin to the ground if she does not wed and bed ye."

"Ye say that with all seriousness?" Cain asked, his words heavy with disappointment in the lack of his brother's intelligence. "Passion or kill her entire clan?"

Gideon threw his hands up. "Terrible suggestions."

"And ones that would end any potential of me siring offspring."

"Ye do not need a wife to sire offspring," Gideon said.

The four brothers had been schooled by their father to be very careful not to spread their seed around. He'd warned them any time they paid attention to a lass to spill their seed outside of her body. Claims to the chiefdom through blood relation to the laird was nearly binding in the eyes of King James. No bastards would come from the sons of George Sinclair. And no sons had come from Alec Sutherland, so wedding Ella should not raise the king's ire.

Ella. He glanced up to the slight glow of firelight in the small unnailed windows cut into the peak of her tower room. She was likely plotting his murder right now. Despite her tenuous position, she hadn't cowered or begged for release. Nay, she'd demanded it. Aye, she had claws and acted like no other woman he'd ever met.

He looked to Gideon. "If I were to sire a child

outside my marriage bed, I am fairly certain that my throat would be slit within it if I were wed to Ella Sutherland."

Gideon laughed, the sound of the sea muting most of it. "Da would come back from the grave to kill ye again for dying while on your back, in a bed, without a sword in your bloody hand. Nay, ye are right. Woo away, brother, and may Holy Mother Mary sway the lass's heart." He slapped Cain on the back warmly. "I will check within the stables and head to my bed."

Cain watched Gideon walk along the rocks that lined the coast until he reached the path that would take him to the bailey and stables. He glanced up the length of stone to the tower again. The window had gone dark. She might be going to sleep, or she might be sneaking out of her room to find the key and travel down the steep steps of the secret escape. When his mother was still alive, his father had kept a boat tied here for her and his sons to escape if the walls of Girnigoe were ever breached.

Cain slid through the shadows up against the wall, breathing slowly, listening to the rush and retreat of the ocean. The sound of a key clicking in the iron lock made him grin. He'd been right. He was always right when it came to strategy and winning.

The door swung outward, and Ella stepped out wearing a white tunic and the leather trousers that hugged the curves of her arse, hips, and shapely legs. The kitten was a black blur trotting next to her. Cain lunged toward Ella, knocking the blade from her hand and catching her up in his arms.

"Fok. Dammit, Sinclair!"

"Such foul curses from such a bonny mouth," he said, holding her against his frame, his solid chest to her soft one.

She struggled, her legs sliding against him. "I want to see my horse."

"She is well cared for," he said, her knee grazing close to his jack.

"I would see for myself. Put me down."

He slowly let her slide down his length until her boots found solid footing on the wobbly rocks. She narrowed her eyes and glared up at him. "Does the god of conquest like scaring and grabbing helpless lasses in the dark?" she asked, disgust in her voice.

"First off," he said, his voice rough as he realized how much he wanted to pull her back into his arms, "ye are anything but helpless. Second, we are not gods, we are messengers sent from God."

She snorted softly, which almost sounded like a laugh, and turned to walk along the shoreline where the kitten stumbled, clinging to a large rock. He came up even with her as she rescued Boudica from falling in the water. "We are *all* sent from God," she said, continuing on under the drawbridge.

"Ye know ye cannot escape," he said, walking behind her.

"That is still to be seen, but my intent is to check on my horse and to let Boo out, so she won't foul my room tonight."

The lass had braided her hair so that it ran down her straight back all the way to the gentle slope at the base of her spine. His hand would fit nicely there. Bloody hell, she was enticing with her snapping comments, clever mind, and soft curves. She was unpredictable in a world where most people were as easily maneuvered as pieces on a chessboard.

"The moon is not too bright, and I wish to show ye something. It will require a ride." Although, with her rubbing against him in a saddle, it would prove hard to convince her that he was planning only to show her his favorite constellations.

She glanced at him. "If I can ride Gilla, then I am willing." Problem solved.

He frowned over his reaction to her. His legendary discipline was affected by her nearness. Perhaps he should have Merida give her foul-smelling soap to use.

"This way," he said, reaching under her arm to help her up the slippery rocks while she held the kitten.

She tried to yank away until he saved her from slipping. "Blasted seaweed," she murmured, clutching the kitten close.

He released her arm as they emerged up the slope by the drawbridge. "Your horse is housed with our personal horses within Girnigoe's walls. The rest of our horses reside in stables beyond."

"You separate them by color."

"A strategy set up by my father." Their boots crunched as they walked across the hard-packed ground toward the white-painted building.

Ella lowered the kitten to the ground. "Now that he is gone, will you continue to separate them? It seems unfair to your last brother, since there are not too many green horses in the world." Her words held a hint of ridicule.

"There are *no* green horses in the world," Cain said. "Bàs takes the gray horses and some white horses. Our father had a green paint made from grasses and leaves, with which Bàs's herd is wiped down before battles."

Ella stopped to look at him. "He paints his horses green?"

"Presentation of the legend around the four Sinclair brothers makes our opponents panic enough to flee or, at the very least, undermines their confidence. Victory is often won by those who believe they will win."

"And you always think you will win," she said, looking straight ahead.

"Aye, of course."

"Self-conceit," she murmured.

"Self-confidence," he countered, feeling a smile tug at his mouth.

Cain jogged over to the guard's post where several stood watch, nodding to them as he took up one of their lanterns. Ella crouched at the stable door where she let Boudica run off. Lantern held high, Cain pushed the door to slide along well-oiled rollers. As the light filled the dark stable, Ella ran directly toward her mare, who resided comfortably in the first stall. She unlatched the door and slid inside to wrap her arms around the horse's neck, pressing her face into her. "Gilla, sweet Gilla."

Cain watched Ella stroke the horse lovingly. Not since he was a lad, wishing to gallop away like an untrained stallion to escape his father's wild nature, had he wished to be a horse.

She turned her face to him, and the happiness

there caught his breath. "Thank you," she said. "For not killing her. She has no choice in this war of ours."

High cheekbones accented the lines of her face, and there was a slight shine to her eyes. "No animal has a choice," he said. "Most people do not, either. They fight for whom they are told to fight unless they find themselves in charge."

The mare rested her chin on Ella's shoulder. He wished he could suck the words back into his mouth, because they caused the smile to fade from her face. "You think I am choosing to keep this war going between our clans," she said. It wasn't a question, so he didn't answer. Her eyes narrowed. "You know nothing about me, Sinclair. Not about my family or the oaths I have made to protect it."

"Tell me, then," he said. What promises did her *sarding* father wring from her before he died? "Some oaths are not worth keeping."

"The ones I have made are."

Damn. He wished he could see into her mind to know what was driving her. Her fears and wants for the future. If he knew those, he could strategize on how to…make her happy, make her smile like she did when she saw her horse was safe. Happiness was a prize he had never sought to bring about in another.

Hurried footsteps sounded outside the stables. "Cain?" Gideon's face appeared in the open doorway. "'Tis Ginny. She is foaling, and…'tis difficult."

Mo chreach.

"I have experience with problem foaling," Ella said, sliding out of the stall and hurrying with them from the barn.

The three jogged in a small cluster through the night where the clouds raced off to reveal a slender moon, through the bailey and over the last drawbridge. "Up ahead," Cain said, and they rounded a copse of trees that helped shade the long stable that housed at least twenty-five of his horses. "She is in the birthing paddock at the end."

"Cain!" Bàs yelled, running toward them up the aisle as they entered. "Ginny needs help. *Now*."

CHAPTER EIGHT

Ella ran down the long aisle, barely keeping up with Cain and his brothers. "What is wrong?" she asked Bàs.

"She has been laboring hard, but the foal isn't coming. We see the foal's hind end through the sack that is coming out. No legs," Bàs said.

Cain cursed. "The bairn's legs are stuck forward."

A white horse with light gray speckling on her flanks lay on her side. She breathed heavily, and sweat slicked her coat. "She has been laboring hard," Ella said, dropping down beside her and quickly walking on her knees so she could see the mare's back end. The birthing sack protruded, but no hooves. She looked at Cain. "The foal needs to be guided out." She began to roll up the sleeves of her tunic. "I have done this before."

"As have I," Cain said.

"My arms and hands are smaller and will do less damage to the mare."

This made him pause, and he nodded, his face tight with worry. "We will help pull the foal out once ye position it the best ye can. Ella…" She met his gaze. It was like that of a man clinging to a barrel set adrift in the sea. "We save Ginny over the foal if a choice must be made."

She nodded once and moved down the horse's body to her head. Milk, thick with health for the newborn, was starting to stream from the mare's teats. The thuds of boots running up behind her made Ella glance over her shoulder to see Joshua, all traces of his wry humor replaced with concern.

"She is losing all her first mother's milk. Grab a bucket," Ella said. He ran to the opposite side of the fenced-in area that was half covered, returning with a leather bucket.

Ella lowered her face so she could meet the mare's eyes. "Hello," she said while smiling and talking with a calm voice. "I know you are in pain, and things are not going how you had planned." Did horses plan for their births? Doubtful, but it was the soothing quality of her voice that she wanted the horse to understand.

She raised her palm to the horse's nostrils and breathed relief when they flared to inhale her scent. The mare's big brown eyes were wide.

"No worries now," Ella whispered. "We will help you birth your beautiful bairn." She slid her hand down the horse's neck, feeling the slickness of her sweat.

Cain positioned a bucket of water near the mare's tail. "To wash before and after," he said, handing her a bar of soap.

Ella washed quickly. "This will work better if we get the mare to stand, leaning against the wall. The pressure that is trying to push the foal out will ease up a bit."

"Aye." Cain nodded to his brothers and went to the mare's head. He clicked his tongue. "Up, Ginny." He did that twice, with all three of his brothers against her back to help push her toward her feet, and she rolled. After a few seconds, her hooves went under her, and she rose. "Good, Ginny," Cain said and guided her against the wall of the foaling paddock.

Ella went behind her. Someone had bound the horse's tail with long strips so that it was out of the way. She took a deep breath. "With God's guidance," she whispered, and broke the white membrane with the tip of the blade she'd hidden in her sleeve, tearing it so that she could see the juncture of the foal's tail. Birthing fluid flowed out, the pungent smell filling the air. Flattening her hands and thankful for them being small and strong, Ella slid them inside the mare, following the body of the foal. "Gentle pressure now," she murmured as she guided the foal's body slowly back up into the birth canal.

The horse neighed. "Calm her," she said, and Cain moved around to the front to stroke Ginny's head. He spoke in a deep, peace-filled voice.

"I feel the legs, the back ones," Ella said. "The foal's head is far inside. I have to bring it out backward, so we must work fast to get it into the air once we start."

"Get the ropes," Cain said, and Joshua held them up, already anticipating their need. "I will hold Ginny's head," Cain said. "Joshua and Bàs, be ready to pull the foal out gently. Ella will remove the sack once the head is free. Gideon, be ready to rub the foal down with a towel."

Ella clasped the upper part of the foal's leg, guiding it around toward her. Then the second leg, until they were both facing the opening. Grasping first one and then the other, she worked them down the canal, trying not to pull too much and rip the mother's red sack from the uterine wall. "The legs are coming." She felt one of them try to pull back inside and caught it again. She smiled. "And it is alive."

"There," Bàs said, jumping in to grasp the little hoof and tightening the rope loop around it so it couldn't disappear back into the birth canal.

"And the second," Ella said, prompting Joshua to do the same.

Reaching both of her hands inside the mare, Ella held firmly to the foal's lower half. "Pull gently when I say," she said, waiting for the feel of the mare's contraction pressing inward. Ella held her breath until she felt the start of a contraction against her hands. "Now, slowly pull." The brothers stood directly behind her, Cain at the mare's head. "That's it," she said. "Come on." The little body slid slowly toward the exit, and Ella bent forward, ready to catch it, since Ginny was standing. Inch by inch, the foal moved until the muscles relaxed again.

"We need another contraction like that," she whispered. She glanced over her arm to Cain's brothers. "On my word." They nodded. Another contraction began. "Now. Slowly, steady," she said, guiding the body until the foal slid free. "Yes," Ella cried. The bairn was heavy and slippery. Bàs jumped forward to help her lower the foal onto the hay.

Ella leaped toward the foal's head, tearing away the white sack. "A rag," she cried, and Gideon threw one before her. She wiped at the foal's nose while he rubbed the body, but it had gone still. Had it been too long without air? "You were kicking."

Cain came around to kneel with her in the hay,

wiping his large hands over the small light-colored wet body. "Her breath is gone," he said, his voice solemn.

"Damn," Gideon cursed, dropping to open the foal's eyes one by one.

It was a baby girl. "No," Ella said, not ready to give up. "She was just kicking."

Joshua grabbed the little back legs, working them, trying to wake her up, but she didn't move.

"Rub her with towels again," Cain said, and Gideon began to rub her, jostling the horse. She didn't stir.

"We need to get air into her," Ella said, grabbing her mouth, pulling it open. There was fluid inside that she wiped out with the rag, sliding its tongue side to side to clean the mouth. "You need to breathe," she said and lowered her mouth, blowing into the little horse. She felt air come back out through the nostrils and covered them with her palm. She blew again and again into the baby horse's mouth.

"Ella," Cain said, his hand on her shoulder, but she didn't stop.

"The hoof," Joshua yelled. "The hoof moved!"

Ella rolled back onto her toes, wiping her hands all over the foal's face, tickling the nose and inside her wet ears. "That's it, sweet babe." The newborn's eyes opened to view the world for the first time.

"Aye!" Bàs yelled as the little horse lifted her head.

Ella squeezed her eyes shut, clearing the tears from her sight, and blinked. She looked down when she felt warm fingers cover her sticky hand and turned her face to Cain. He smiled broadly, his eyes alive with joy, the lines and furrows of worry completely gone. He was...splendid. She met his smile with a joyful one of her own.

"Ye did it, Ella," he said. "Bloody hell. Ye brought her to life."

Ella turned her hand to hold Cain's hand back, fingers sliding between fingers to squeeze. "Bringing life to this world is a woman's specialty."

Joshua snorted, making her glance his way. His smile was sharp, almost predatory. "Ye are also damn good at dispatching life from this world, like our father's."

"Joshua, hold your tongue," Gideon said, shoving a hand against his chest.

She looked back to Cain, her smile fading away. Gaze meeting gaze, she slid her fingers away from his strong hand. "And in so doing, how many lives did I save?" She didn't expect an answer and looked down at the foal who struggled to sit up, the hay sticking to her damp body.

"She needs to be near Ginny's head," Cain said and lifted the hundred-pound foal to set her down where the mare could nuzzle her.

"Catch more of her milk," Ella said, the joy in the paddock tainted with the reminder of her status at Girnigoe: killer of the chief, killer of their father, prisoner. "The foal will need all that thick mother's milk to help her recover. The red sack still needs to be birthed and checked that it is complete and not torn." The Sinclair brothers likely knew all of this, having attended horse births over the years.

Everyone watched as Ginny nudged her foal to

stand. Bàs handed Ella a bladder that he'd poured the caught mother's milk into. "Ye can feed this to her after she's had a chance to try to nurse on her own."

Without a word, Joshua retreated down the long stable. He swatted at a hanging rag with enough power to make it fly off its nail to land on the hard-packed dirt floor.

Bàs picked up the ropes, coiling them. "I will let Merida know to prepare some of her foaling brew." He also walked away. Gideon nodded, glancing between them, and then followed Bàs without a word.

"We can wash here," Cain said. "Then return ye to your room for the night. I will stay up with Ginny and the foal to make sure they are both well."

There would be no ride tonight, then. She followed him down the aisle flanked by stalls of dozing horses to the far end where a well was capped. This was a different Cain from the jailor she'd been battling with the last couple days. Such happiness over the birth of the horse and health of the mare contrasted with the brutal killer and strategist she'd known him to be.

Cain lifted the cover and began to wind the chain to raise the bucket from the depths. His muscles bulged as he turned the winch, the coil creaking loudly in the night.

"I would stay, too," she said. "To feed the foal once she has nursed some."

She stepped closer to him, her hand reaching out to rest on his upper arm. The cords of granitelike muscle beneath her palm were hard from training and war. He stopped the cranking to look down where she touched him. "Cain, I would like to stay." He met her gaze, and a little quiver of nervous energy danced through her middle.

"Then we will watch the foal and Ginny. Together."

Together? She had experienced a "together" relationship only once, with her mother before she died. Otherwise, it had mostly been Ella against the world or Ella protecting those weaker than her. Her father's known cruelty had frightened away any friends she tried to make at Dunrobin or in the village. Florie's main charge was Jamie, so Ella ended up protecting them both, keeping Florie hidden until she could claim Jamie as her own baby.

Her father's advisor, Kenneth Macleod, had been a loyal friend to her mother. He had always been near, teaching Ella survival skills and helping her evade her father. He supported her in taking over the chieftainship, remaining loyal to her as well. Ella often wondered if her mother had wrung a promise from him to watch over her. Why else would he have stayed at Dunrobin?

The soap was scented with rosemary and mint, and she rubbed it along her limbs and between her fingers, but her tunic was smeared and wet with birthing fluid.

"There are spare tunics in the stables, although they will be gigantic on ye." He nodded to her legs. "Your trousers are dirty again." Without breaking their gaze, he stripped off his once-white shirt. The dim light of the lantern cast his corded stomach and muscular chest in gold and shadows.

An ache in Ella's chest reminded her to breathe. *He is the enemy. A fierce bloody enemy.* Who had brought her a kitten and loved his horses.

She looked down as if examining her leather trousers until she heard him turn. She peeked up again. The dark lines of his tattoos stood out easily against his tanned skin, following the contours of his well-developed muscles. The sharp lines came together to form the head of a horse on one of his large biceps while Celtic bands encircled both of them. Across his upper back was a tattoo of a horseshoe with a nocked bow lying slanted across it, a crown propped on one side. The sign of the first horseman.

"The leather washes," she said, dipping out water to wipe along each arm, scrubbing hard. "If you let me return to Dunrobin, I have several more pairs."

"We can ride there directly after we share our wedding vows," he said without a pause.

Damn stubborn. Ella plopped the soap into the bucket. Just because they both cared for horses didn't mean that they were like-minded in other ways. She marched back toward the mare who was nudging her foal to rise on spindly legs. A moment later, she heard Cain walk up behind her. Was he still bare and brawny from the waist up?

"I worry Boo will not know where to sleep if not with me," she said, avoiding looking at him.

"I will fetch your kitten if ye stay with Ginny and her foal. There is a stack of clean tunics in the room next to the birthing paddock." He stepped before her so that he could loom down, staring into her eyes. He was bare and so very close, making her stomach flutter. *Good Mother Mary.* She swallowed and gave a stilted nod.

"If ye try to escape tonight, Ella, I will hunt ye down. Wolves roam the woods at night, wolves who crave horseflesh, and I will mount a siege on Dunrobin before dawn, whether ye are there or not."

Threats? Of course. Despite the night, she was still his prisoner, her clan at stake. And damn it all that her thoughts had been about his muscular frame and not about fleeing. The joy of bringing the horse into the world had clouded her focus.

She frowned up at him. "You like to loom over people, don't you? Try to scare them with your grisly frown."

"Ella?"

She huffed. "Very bloody well. I will not leave them if you bring Boo back here."

He nodded and walked away down the long corridor of stalls to the gates at the front. Lord help her. She couldn't look away. Power seemed to radiate off him while he strode with purpose, as if he had so much strength inside that it seeped from his skin. His kilt sat low across his narrow hips, and the muscles in his back moved with an easy grace, the edge of his hair falling just above his shoulders.

He stopped to look over his shoulder toward Ella. "What is her name?"

"Who?"

"The foal," Cain said. She could barely see his expression in the darkness by the barn door. "Aye, Ella Sutherland. Ye gifted the wee filly with life. She is yours to keep."

• • •

"There ye are, ye wee beastie," Cain murmured, shrugging into a clean shirt that he'd retrieved.

He scooped up the black and white kitten who was seated on top of a pile of split logs along the bailey wall, tucking her against his side where she couldn't scratch him as easily.

Kitten under one arm and two wool blankets under the other, Cain strode back out under the portcullis, nodding to the gatekeeper, and continued over the drawbridge. On the far side he saw the familiar bulk of Joshua in the shadows. He didn't bother to stop, and Joshua fell swiftly into stride.

"Ye left her out there alone," Joshua said. "In a barn full of horses." Cain didn't say anything but readjusted the squirming cat. "Let me guess. She promised to stay."

"I have her kitten and her horse."

"Horses are not family to Sutherlands like they are to us."

Cain stopped, his boots crunching hard on the pebbles of the narrow road. "I do not know all Sutherlands, but even ye must consider that Da lied about them after watching Ella save that foal. And no horse that we ever won from them had signs of poor treatment."

Cain began to walk again, Joshua's words plucking at his confidence that Ella would stay even with a new foal to tie her to Girnigoe. Perhaps if he continued gifting animals to her, she would have so many that she couldn't return without assistance,

assistance that he would give only after she married him and peacefully forfeited her family's castle and lands.

Joshua stopped him with a heavy hand on his shoulder, making Cain turn to stare into his brother's eager face. "We need to finish this push to take Dunrobin," Joshua said. "Without their lady chief giving them orders, the clan is likely being governed by Kenneth Macleod, the old laird's advisor. It is only a matter of time before one of the Sutherland warriors seizes the opportunity to take over the leadership of the clan by challenging the old man, since Ella is away." Joshua balled his hand into a fist before Cain's face. "This is the time to strike. Sutherland territory could be ours within days."

Cain kept his voice low. His brother had heard the warning in it too many times to miss it. "With loss of people who could become loyal to Sinclairs."

"Sutherlands will never be loyal to Sinclairs," Joshua said, leaning in as if he welcomed a civil war right there.

"Just because ye have not seen peace between them and us in your lifetime does not mean it is impossible, Joshua. Ye thirst for war, but war for the sake of revenge and blood is not wise."

"Dammit, Cain," Joshua said, dropping his hand. "That woman is a Sutherland. Ye cannot trust her. She will betray ye; mayhap she already has tonight." His brother turned on his heel and strode off down the path that led into the village where there were several lasses who could help him work off his ire.

Cain inhaled and marched on. His instincts told him Joshua was wrong about Ella. If he started distrusting his instincts, his whole foundation would crumble. Joshua had respected their father because of his bloodthirsty ways. Would he ever grow to respect Cain as chief? Not because he was older but because he guided their clan with strength and wisdom?

Cain rounded the corner into the dark barn. Two lanterns still sat at the far end near the birthing paddock. Even steps carried him down the dark aisle between the horse stalls. An occasional snort or whinny came from the dozing animals, as well as the brush of shifting bulks against the wood slats that made up the stalls. At the far end Ginny still stood, but he didn't see the foal or Ella. *Mo chreach.*

Meow. Boudica caught at his side, her tiny nails piercing his shirt to his skin, and made him realize he was squeezing her. He let her jump from his hands.

"Ella?" Cain said, his voice stark in the silent stables. He crouched down and saw her on the other side of Ginny. The air left him, and his shoulders relaxed. Joshua was wrong, and he was right.

Ella leaned against a fence post, holding the bladder of mother's milk with both hands as the foal suckled it. She turned her smile on him, and his gut contracted with…something, something he'd never felt before. Want? Desire? Aye, but something warmer, something more solid than the urgent need that came with lust.

"She was suckling from her mother," Ella whispered. "But came over to me as if she were curious. So I gave her the first milk we saved." The small horse nudged at the bladder as if demanding more, and Ella turned back to her, holding it over her head. "Yes, little one, drink all you can of it."

Cain couldn't look away. Ella was the Celtic goddess of horses, Epona, as she held the bladder so the foal could feed as if suckling from under its mother. She had found a clean tunic, tying the bulk of it in a knot at her waist. Her braid lay over one shoulder, curls framing her face as she watched the foal drink. With her gaze lowered, her dark lashes seemed to lay against the creamy skin of her cheeks. She was completely at ease standing among the muck and hay, caring for a new life that she had brought into the world with her hands and breath.

The kitten wove between Ginny's hooves to find her mistress. The foal stopped drinking to blink large brown eyes at Boudica. "You found her," Ella said, balancing the half-empty bladder on her knee and bending to run a hand through the kitten's fur.

"She was keeping watch for your return on the woodpile," Cain said, stroking his hands down Ginny's neck. She was tired but looked well. He cleared his throat. "Did she birth the sack?" He went around to the mare's tail.

"Yes. I put it in a bucket to be checked."

He went over to inspect it. Amazingly, considering the backward, twisted birth, it was intact. He washed his hands and brought a bucket of fresh water from the well for Ginny. Ginny drank from the bucket and shook her head, swinging it back to look for her foal.

"Luna needs to go back to her mama," Ella said.

"Ye named her after the moon?"

She nodded. "It is a beautiful sliver tonight," she

said, luring the foal back to Ginny with the nearly
empty bladder of milk. Finally, the little filly traded
the empty bottle for her mother's teats. Ella walked
to the edge of the barn and slid down the wall to sit.
Cain lowered himself next to her, their knees bent,
the kitten playing with a blade of hay under Ella's
legs.

"She is perfect," Ella said, her voice soft like a
light breeze. She stared at the mother and foal, and
Cain noticed one of her curls catching in the corner
of her lips. He reached over at the same time Ella
turned to him. Her eyes widened.

"'Tis…'tis caught," he said, using one finger to
pull the hair from her mouth. She remained close to
him. "And ye have a smudge." He slid the back of his
finger along her cheek.

She didn't rear back and slap him. Not even a
frown lurked in the tilt of her soft lips. She studied
him in the dim light as if trying to read his intentions.
What would she find if she could delve into his
mind? That he wanted to kiss her? Aye. That he
wanted to slide his hands along the contours of her
body and discover every little intriguing mark upon
her? Bloody hell, aye. That he wished to make her
moan in his bed? Aye, the image was infiltrating his
thoughts like a stealthy thief trying to steal his
steadfast discipline.

He frowned. Conquest was more important than
pleasure. *Duty above all else*. His father's words still
rang from the grave.

He let his hand fall away, and the action broke
the spell between them. "Have ye done that before?
Blowing into a foal's mouth?"

She leaned back and shook her head. "I have seen it done once. It worked then, too. Sometimes their lungs need a little nudge to start working, especially if it was a hard birth."

"Which Sutherland is such a lover of horses as to breathe life into one?" he asked. "Besides ye."

She folded her fingers together on top of her stained knees. "Alec Sutherland," she said. Just the name made Cain's fist tighten. "My father may have been a cruel devil to people, but he loved horses more than most. He certainly loved them more than…the people in his life."

"And ye had no siblings to share the burden," Cain said.

Her head jerked up, and her gaze slid to his. "No. There was no one else."

"And no one to shield ye from him."

Her gaze dropped to Boudica who bounded off to chase a bug into a corner far from the horses. "I like pity about as much as I am guessing you do, Cain." She met his stare. "I am strong like a sword that has been tempered with fire." Her chin raised. "I have learned to escape any lock and how to be as silent as moving mist. My scars are proof I survived living with a devil, one who is dead and hopefully burning in Hell."

Cain kept his voice even despite the fury welling up inside him. "Ye have more scars?"

"A few lashes on my back and of course the…" She slid a finger up her jawline to the circle brand below her ear.

Damn and blast it. He wanted to… What? Slaughter a dead man or maybe those who stood by and let Alec Sutherland rage against his daughter?

She continued. "I haven't acquired any in battle yet, since I stay out of the heavy fighting. Using physical strength, most warriors can best me, but my skills with the bow and a dagger are far superior."

Lord, how he wanted to run the pad of his finger across each scar on her body. "Ye are a warrior, Ella Sutherland."

"Yes, I am. I am the chief of the Sutherland clan." She turned her eyes toward him, and he pressed his back against the boards so as not to learn forward. "I cannot just give those rights away, the rights I earned," she said.

He didn't want the night to dissolve into anger, and he wanted to know more about the woman who was brave enough to coordinate battle. Brave enough to stand up to him. "Have ye always wanted to lead your clan, or would ye rather have the choice to hand it off? To another Sutherland," he added quickly.

The edge of her mouth tipped upward, and she sniffed with wry humor before she leaned her head back. He watched the long column of her neck. "I did not intend to become the chief of our clan, but someone must do so, and I am a direct descendant of Alec Sutherland. King James is in favor of leadership staying within direct bloodlines."

"No Sutherland challenged ye for it?"

"There were discussions," she said. "But my father's advisor backed me. Kenneth trained most of those men. He helped me pass their tests."

"Tests?"

"With weapons and riding." She leveled her chin

to meet his gaze. "I can hit the center of a target at
fifty yards with my bow while standing on the back
of my moving horse. I can throw the *mattucashlass*
with accuracy, too. And I certainly understand
diplomacy better than most of them."

She had fought for her right to lead the clan. No
wonder she didn't want to surrender it to him, even
if it made sense.

"My warriors look at me with respect now," she
said. "I had the chance to prove my worth, so they
do not look on me with contempt…like some have."
She stared down at the straw she peeled with her
small fingernails.

Did she speak again about when he frowned at
her long ago? He cleared his throat. "That day at the
festival ten years ago, when I came upon ye…"

"It was twelve years ago."

"Twelve, then." He crossed his legs at the ankle
where they sat beside each other. "I did not mean
that look for ye. The one ye interpreted as disgust. It
was not about ye, but about Alec Sutherland and
how he treated women, mainly my Aunt Merida."

Of course, at the time he also believed his father
when he said they beat their horses, but that had
changed.

Ella flicked the stripped piece of straw. "Your
sister said as much."

"And yet ye still hate me," he said. He watched
Ginny nudge the wee foal with her nose.

Ella tipped her head to the side. "Am I still a
prisoner?"

"Until ye agree to wed me." He paused, his voice
softening. "Ye could still lead your clan beside me as

my wife." His words came slow as if the gentle speed could discourage her attack.

Her head rolled against the boards of the wall as she turned her face completely to him, keeping her body straight. "You would let me continue to be in charge of Dunrobin and Sutherland lands?"

"In charge of?" He scratched his chin.

"Yes. Legally, I would retain the Sutherland clan seat, me alone."

He studied her. "Ye want to remain the chief even if we wed."

"That is not an answer."

He could lie. Tell her that he would let her clan remain under their own rule if she married him. Then, once her vows were spoken, he could claim the Sutherland lands and send an official document to King James about the unification. But as much as he'd learned to strategize, war, and conquer, he would not tarnish his honor or the honor of the Sinclairs by lying to win.

He exhaled, knowing the night would not bring them any closer. "Dunrobin and Sutherland lands would be legally held under the domain of the Sinclair clan and me."

Her head rolled back so that she stared straight ahead. "Then my answer is still no, and I will escape from here. Alive or dead depends on you." Without a word, Ella rocked forward and pushed up into a stand, lifting her kitten with her. She walked down the dark corridor toward the double doors at the end.

Cain pushed up and followed at a distance. His stride caught him up to her as they exited. She stared straight ahead, her mind probably already creating a new plan of escape.

"So ye know," Cain said. "Thomas will be stationed on the steps, there are two guards outside your windows in case ye manage to dig the nails out, and another set of guards at the bottom of the back stairs from the chief's room, which I will now be occupying."

She turned her gaze to him, a look of boredom on her face. "I will still escape."

Despite the disappointment of their conversation in the barn, the side of his mouth quirked upward into a half grin in anticipation of her next move. "Challenge accepted."

CHAPTER NINE

Ella tightened the front ties of her stays and slid a green gown over her head. It had a simple bodice of soft, thin wool and curved low to expose the edge of her white smock.

Challenge accepted. Cain's words from the night before slid around in her mind. Getting her to wed him and gaining a solid hold on Dunrobin Castle was only a challenge to the legendary horseman of conquest.

"Damn Sinclair," she murmured. And damn her girlhood memories of his kind smile.

She lifted Boo to her face to stare into her sweet eyes. "Even if I told Cain about Jamie, he wouldn't care. He was raised to conquer lands and people and would still capture Sutherland lands. He is hollow inside," she said. The kitten sniffed, her little white nose scrunching before she meowed as if in agreement. His kindness last night to the horse and foal showed he had enough heart to care for animals, but so had Ella's father, a father who didn't hesitate when exacting brutal punishment on people.

She set Boo down and walked to the window that she'd pried open with one of the daggers she'd taken. The crowd in the bailey below moved in a wide mass to enter the great hall. Today, the clan was coming to swear allegiance to Cain, their new chief.

Rap. Rap. "Ella, the taking of oaths ceremony is going on below." It was Hannah, and Ella opened the door. Boo instantly dodged past her legs to go out.

Ella's stomach growled with disappointment. "From your empty hands, I suppose I need to come below if I do not want to starve."

Hannah smiled. "I think that is Cain's intention."

Ella stepped out and shut the door behind her. "Does your brother actually think that I will join in swearing allegiance to him?"

Hannah walked with her to the top of the dimly lit stairs. "I do not know. All of my brothers are very cunning. It would be best for you not to answer any questions down there then," she whispered as if she conspired with Ella. Maybe she could be turned to help her escape.

"Do you like living here at Girnigoe?" Ella asked as they continued down the steps.

"Aye, although I know nothing else. My father kept me hidden, so I would like to step out, perhaps attend festivals. I hear they are great fun."

The poor girl had never had the freedom to do anything. Where Ella hadn't been able to escape her father's notice, Hannah hadn't been able to escape her father's denial of her existence.

"Do you believe in the legend of the horsemen?" Ella asked as they turned the tight corners, her fingers sliding along the rough granite wall. Hannah was two steps lower than her.

"I certainly did as a girl, with my whole heart. But now that Da has passed, I have room to consider." In the light from a sconce, Ella saw her shrug, the movement somehow ethereal. She glanced back. "My brothers bleed just like other men."

Coming to the bottom of the stairs, they stepped out under the archway into the great hall where rows of silent men stood. With so many inside, it was no wonder that the motionless air held the tang of sweat, horses, and woodsmoke.

Cain stood straight and tall before a throne-like chair by the unlit hearth with the crossed swords of his ancestors and the Sinclair family crest over the mantel. All three brothers stood to the side of him in order of birth, the four of them directly in front of the horsemen tapestry as if to remind everyone who they were.

Joshua held a huge sword and wore an ancient-looking helmet. Gideon held a set of balances, his sword strapped to his side, and Bàs… Bàs wore all black, including his kilt, a great horned helmet, and his human-skull mask. He held his lethal scythe by his side.

Cain wore the polished steel crown and held his bow over one shoulder and a massive sword in his hand. Fierce and royal, the sight made a shiver run through her.

Most of the gazes from around the room shifted to her as she entered. Did the Sinclair warriors hate her for killing their chief? Ella felt a tug on her sleeve and followed Hannah to the back of the crowd where a table held a plate of thick bacon, fragrant bread, and a small slice of butter stamped with the head of a horse.

"I, Gregory Sinclair, swear on my life to battle for and with the sons of Sinclair and pledge my allegiance to Cain Sinclair, fifth Earl of Caithness and chief of Clan Sinclair." The man's voice boomed out as if he wished for the angels in Heaven to hear him. He was bent on his knee before Cain. With his sword in his hand, Cain looked like he might lop off his head. It was as if the man holding the newborn foal last night had been replaced with a darker version, one devoid of softness of any kind. Which was the real Cain?

The man up front remained on his one knee. "My sword is your sword," he said, his voice strong with conviction. He thumped a fist against his chest over his heart as he rose, nodded to all four Sinclair brothers and returned to his place in the crowd as the next warrior stepped forward.

Kenneth had orchestrated a similar oath-taking ceremony for her after she'd passed the tests thrown out to her by various men in the ranks. Her friend and steward must be worried about her. Would Cain let her send word that she was at least alive?

She chewed slowly, as a nervous man came forward to swear his allegiance. Cain gave no indication of softness or care. He was completely the cold-blooded lord of conquest.

Hannah leaned in to her ear. "They are near the end. These things take hours."

"I had the same ceremony as chief of the Sutherlands."

"Oh," Hannah said, her eyes widening a bit. Ella could almost see the questions forming behind her eyes. But for a woman who'd been treated as inferior and invisible, it was no doubt an incomprehensible concept. "I forgot," Hannah said. "It is so odd to think of a woman as the chief."

"How about a queen? Like the powerful one

sitting right now on the throne of England?"

Hannah nodded, her cheeks pink. "Aye, ye are right. It is just so different here at Girnigoe."

Ella ducked her head to meet her downcast eyes. "You can be free of the legend now. Even leave Girnigoe if you wish. Who knows, perhaps all four of your brothers will die in battle, and you will become the chief."

A bubble of laughter came from Hannah, and she held her fingertips over her mouth.

A Sinclair hurried down the narrow aisle to Cain, talking close to his ear. "Aye," Cain answered, and the man hurried away. Cain stood up from his seat, sword in hand. From the doorway came two men, striding in side by side.

Ella nearly dropped her milk and stood. "Kenneth," she whispered. *Good Lord.* Her advisor was walking into the holding of their fiercest enemy, no doubt looking for her.

She blinked back the pressure of tears when she noticed that he wore the spectacles that she'd brought him from Edinburgh after her father's death, having journeyed there to hand deliver the letter about the succession of the Sutherland clan. Kenneth caught her movement, his face snapping her way, a look of relief mixed with anger tightening his weathered face.

The other man was half Kenneth's age and wore the colors favored by the Mackays. Randolph Mackay, Hew's advisor, caused a shiver to tease Ella's nape.

They stopped before Cain. "Chief Sinclair, I am Randolph Mackay, councel to our chief, Hew

Mackay, who is still locked in your dungeon. With the change of power into your hands, I come to request his release."

Cain's gaze was severe. His hard, intelligent eyes seemed to take in everything. The short beard that he'd begun to grow couldn't hide the granite set of his jaw, his mouth hard and unforgiving. At that moment, he looked like he could unleash God's wrath on them all. Ella's heart sped with her worry. Would he kill Kenneth right here? *I won't allow it.* She edged closer to the center aisle.

"Have ye brought the two wagons filled with grain that is the price for his freedom?" Cain asked, his voice deceptively low. "A fair price to pay for the oat field to which he and his men set fire?"

"Our grain has not yet been harvested."

"Then your chief will live in our dungeon until it is."

"Is he even alive?" Randolph asked, contempt in his voice. "We have been told that he is fed only salted beef and no drink."

"He meant to burn our grain, so he deserves no bread," Cain said.

"And nothing to drink?"

"The price one pays for crossing a Sinclair," Cain said, making Ella swallow hard. The quiet cruelty in his words reminded her of her father. Her hands clasped together before her chest as if to ward off the specter.

Joshua crossed his arms. "The bloody thief deserves nothing at all."

"Ye give him only salted beef to prolong his agony," Randolph said.

"Would ye rather he be dead?" Bàs asked, his scythe swinging from one shoulder to the other. The blade caught the air, humming softly, a murmured petition to be unleashed.

Randolph glared. "For all I know, he is. I need to see that he is truly alive."

Cain pointed to one of his warriors, who hurried off.

Ella stood close enough to see the strain in the familiar lines of Kenneth's face. "The Sutherlands have spare grain," her advisor said. "The Mackays have come to us to borrow it to repay their debt to the Sinclairs." Only desperation for her release would make Kenneth work with the Mackays now that her father wasn't demanding she marry Hew, joining their clans to work together against the Sinclairs.

"Very gracious of ye," Cain said, his narrowed gaze sliding to Ella and back to Kenneth. "Is this payment approved by your chief?" Of course not, and Cain knew it. Ella had been locked up at Girnigoe.

"With her absence, I am the acting chief," Kenneth said. "And I have approved it. But only if Arabella Sutherland, chief of the Sutherland Clan, is set free with the chief of the Mackays."

"Ella Sutherland is free to go," Cain said, his gaze centered on Kenneth. "The moment she vows to be my wife until the day she dies and signs a document giving over Dunrobin and Sutherland lands."

Silence enveloped the hall, and her breath sounded loud in her ears. She was merely a pawn in Cain's bloody game. Why would her foolish heart ever think otherwise?

Gazes turned toward her, and a flush rose in her cheeks. Cain continued to stare at Kenneth. "I have agreed to nothing," she said, her voice strong in the stagnant room.

Randolph Mackay turned his little black eyes to her, his face devoid of emotion. She remembered those piercing eyes lurking in the shadows when she visited Varrich Castle with her father during the marriage discussions. "Ye agreed to wed Hew Mackay, a betrothal before God."

A hushed murmur of discontent snaked through the crowd. If she were betrothed to someone else, Cain could not marry her in the eyes of God or the Crown. A betrothal was an official contract. Despite Hew's forceful courtship and bruising kisses, she had managed to escape that noose.

She kept her gaze and voice unwavering. "My father, Alec Sutherland, agreed I should marry your chief," she said. Just looking at Randolph made her fingers clench. "He was killed, and I broke the betrothal contract, paying your clan the betrothal price of ten horses, three wagons of grain, ten sheep, including a pregnant ewe, and three bolts of silk. The price was paid, and the contract was severed, legally and before the eyes of God. Feel free to refresh your memory with Pastor John, who presided over the payment."

Cain stepped forward with the power and might of ice hurtling down from a mountain. He stopped before Randolph Mackay. "We will take those three wagons of grain in payment for your foolish chief's crime."

Randolph's gaze snapped back to him. "Ye said

two wagons of grain."

"It has risen to three. Wait another week, and it will be four. I tire of the man stinking up my dungeon."

"We will pay three wagons of grain for the release of Ella Sutherland," Kenneth called out.

"And Hew Mackay," Randolph added quickly.

Cain's gaze connected with Kenneth. "No amount of grain, horseflesh, or gold will win back Ella Sutherland. She is *my* prize from the battle that took my father's life. The Sinclairs will conquer Sutherland Clan once and for all. It can be done peacefully with a wedding or violently through war. Either way, I will conquer your clan."

Anger shot heat into Ella's cheeks. *His prize? The Sinclairs will conquer Sutherland Clan.* Cain's words slashed through Ella's calm. Her fists clenched as she glared at his profile.

"Then ye thirst for war," Kenneth said, his voice as hard as his eyes, and he drew his sword.

"Here, here!" Joshua rubbed his hands together, a dark grin on his face.

Two of Cain's warriors grabbed Kenneth, quickly disarming him, his sword clattering to the stone floor.

Damn them! Ella ran forward, but Cain's warrior, Keenan, stepped before her. She dodged, but more men slid between her and Kenneth, barring her way.

Gideon's voice rose over the crowd. "We have been at war since Alec Sutherland dishonored our clan by mistreating and divorcing Merida Sinclair." He stepped to the side where Ella could see that he held the scales so that they dipped back and forth on either side, finally leveling out.

Gideon looked toward where Kenneth was restrained. "But if Chief Sutherland weds the new Chief Sinclair, bloodshed can end with the unifying of our clans. Our warriors will train together under the best horsemen and swordsmen in Scotland. And...ye will *not* feel a blade twisting in your middle."

Would Cain impale Kenneth right there in the great hall before his men?

Gideon set a coin on one side of the scales, making the pan dip down. "Tradespeople from both clans will learn from and trade with one another." He added a coin to the other side, making it balance evenly. "The land will become settled, with our Mackay neighbors knowing that we are united and will not tolerate more attacks on our outlying farms." Coin to the first side. "The combination of Sutherland and Sinclair clans will bring peace and balance to Dunrobin Castle and Sutherland lands, perhaps to all of northern Scotland."

The last coin evened out the scales once more, bringing them into perfect balance.

Cain's voice rang out. "I will wed Ella Sutherland and lead both Sutherland and Sinclair clans together. They will act and live as one."

Ella knew Kenneth would not agree. Twelve years of planning and preparation, a journey to Edinburgh to present their case to King James, and the future strength of Sutherland Clan still being guarded by Ella would not allow for the combining of the clans. But Cain knew none of this, because she had sworn to keep her mother's secret.

Kenneth's voice called out with anger. "I would speak with my chief before consenting."

Cain's hard face turned toward her, but before he could deny or consent, Hew Mackay's voice called out. "I declare war on Clan Sinclair."

Ella backed up to better see.

Large and broad, Hew's shorn hair was thick with dirt. His vicious face contorted in anger as he walked into the hall next to the Sinclair warrior who'd gone to collect him. Filth clung to him from living in the dungeon, but he still had his ridiculous swagger as he stomped forward. He didn't look as if he were dying of thirst. "Ella Sutherland and I are betrothed, so her fight is my fight."

Holy Mother Mary. "We have already gone over this, Chief Mackay," Ella said, grabbing her skirt to hurry around the crowd of men to the front where Cain and his brothers stood. She tried not to wrinkle her nose over Hew's horrible odor.

She looked to Cain as she spoke. "As the new chief, I broke the betrothal contract my father had signed without my consent. We have paid the forfeiture price, with Pastor John present." She turned her gaze on Hew. "And I will not wed you."

"But ye will wed him?" Hew threw his thick, dirt-smeared arm out toward Cain, a sneer on his face, a scraggly beard making him look even more like a wild man. The Mackay chief had always been thick and squat, his furrowed brows and piercing eyes giving him a scoundrel's look.

Thank you, God, for saving me from wedding him.

She'd thwarted most of his clumsy advances,

although his brutality had been tempered by his idea of charm, believing she would wed him soon enough and be at his mercy.

"I have not agreed to wed any man," she said, holding firm against the storm of rage growing in his crimson face.

Hew stood taller, his voice ringing out over the hall of men. "Arabella Sutherland and I are already wed in the eyes of God."

A deep murmur rose from the witnesses in the room, their discontent and censure rising into the rafters. Fury shot up inside Ella. Did the idiot think she didn't know what happened between a man and woman to consummate a marriage? Or did he consider her the docile girl he remembered under Alec Sutherland's reign of terror? He was delusional if he thought their few uncomfortable kisses bound them together.

"You lying bastard," she said, her words thick with disgust.

Hew's words rang out. "I challenge the banns that have been posted for their unholy union, for we have joined together carnally if not yet by a cleric."

"Lies," she said, stepping before him. Her nose curled at the smell of human waste wafting off him, and she tugged free the dagger she'd secreted up her sleeve. With an underhand flick of her wrist, she pricked the point into the soft divot between his chin and Adam's apple. "Speak another, and you will speak no more." A drop of blood swelled out to snake down under his torn, filthy tunic.

"If she kills him, the Mackays will war with the Sutherlands and the Sinclairs," Randolph said quickly.

Bàs stepped before Randolph, hefting his scythe. "Or I can kill ye here without a single Mackay learning about your puny threat."

The surprise on Hew's face made her think that she was right about him foolishly wagering that she was docile, even though she'd kneed him in the ballocks when he'd groped her with his meaty paws at Varrich last autumn.

"I have not, in any way, married you, Hew Mackay," Ella said from between clenched teeth. "Despite your brutish tricks to catch me alone, you have won nothing from me but my disdain and several clumsy kisses, you bloody leasing-monger."

His lips pulled back. "Yet ye stand here, a Sutherland, clean, fed, and armed. Are ye whoring for him then? Him or perhaps all four Sinclair brothers?"

"Cain, wait," Gideon said. But he didn't.

Cain surged forward, his fist slamming directly into Hew's face above her dagger. *Crack!*

Ella yanked back her blade as Hew dropped to his knees on the floor, blood gushing from his nose. "Shite," he said, the curse pinched with pain.

"Never," Cain said, his words snapping with rage, "speak of Ella Sutherland that way again. Or in any way to her again." He loomed over the arse. "Drag him back to the dungeon." Cain spun on his heel to stare at Randolph Mackay. "And the price for his release is now the *entire* betrothal price that Ella Sutherland paid for breaking the contract."

Randolph Mackay swore, jerking his vest as if it had become crooked.

"I can execute both Mackays now," Bàs said. His voice matched the lethal promise of the skull helmet, making him look like death incarnate.

"Damn brother," Joshua said, hefting his sword. "Ye get all the fun."

Gideon stepped up beside Cain, who still clenched his hands at his side before Randolph and Kenneth. "Bàs can execute Hew Mackay today," Gideon said to Randolph. "We will consider the Mackay penalty for burning our fields paid with his head."

On cue, Bàs whipped his scythe through the air, the blade humming, his bare arm bulging under the weight. Randolph glanced around him as if contemplating the suggestion. Would he condemn his chief to death before so many witnesses? Word would get back to the Mackay clan. "Damn," he said. "Keep him alive. We will gather the payment."

Randolph pivoted on his heel, pausing to slice his gaze along Ella. His small, dark eyes sent another chill to slither up her spine, but then he strode down the aisle made by the parting Sinclair warriors, leaving Kenneth alone at the front.

Cain's hard gaze moved to her advisor. "Ye may leave, without your chief." Could Cain believe Hew's lies? Hew probably didn't even realize she'd saved his life by denying it. All Cain had to do to release her from a marriage bond was to kill the groom.

"I will petition the king for her release," Kenneth said, no fear in his voice or face, just strength and conviction. "James will see it done or send his five thousand troops to strip the Sinclairs of their lands."

Cain studied Kenneth, seeming to weigh the chances that the man was bluffing. "My instincts, which are always right, tell me that there is more to this refusal than mere stubbornness." His words were lower but still held fury. Ella met his gaze when he turned. Curiosity warred with anger in his eyes, like when he'd stared up at her in the tree, and she kept her emotionless mask in place.

When no one said anything, Cain continued. "My contact at Dunrobin, years ago, did not paint Arabella Sutherland as a young woman determined to rule her clan. Yet now she would rather die than allow me to rule it without bloodshed." *Damn his instincts.*

"Do not kill her!" Kenneth yelled, ferocity in his command.

"I have denied her that choice." Cain's brows narrowed as he looked between them.

Kenneth's shoulders rounded slightly, as if he'd been standing ready to battle his way to her if Cain ordered her execution. Angry tears ached behind Ella's eyes. She hated how her capture was tormenting her loyal friend.

"Escort this Sutherland advisor out of Girnigoe," Cain said. "And the rest of ye are dismissed."

"A word with her first," Kenneth said. "To make certain she is being treated well."

"Quickly," Cain said. The two guards near Kenneth took a step back, but it still wouldn't be a private conversation.

Ella hurried forward, and Kenneth caught her in his arms, holding her tightly. "Tell Jamie I am treated well."

"Listen to me," Kenneth whispered at her ear, his body trembling with controlled rage. She couldn't see his eyes, but she could tell from his voice that they held conviction. "If ye cannot escape with your life or your virtue…wed him."

She held tightly to Kenneth as if giving him a long hug, but it was more to keep herself from falling over. He would have her surrender Dunrobin? "But Cain will take—" Ella started.

Kenneth's words came as a tortured whisper, harsh and succinct in her ear. "Wed him, Ella, and *kill* him."

CHAPTER TEN

Cain watched her advisor pull away from Ella. The man was obviously a friend or more. His gut tightened as she watched him being led away, a hand to her mouth as if she didn't trust herself not to cry out to him. Aye, Kenneth Macleod was important to her.

Cain waited until Kenneth was gone and his men were filing out. It had been a bloody long morning with the ceremony, his men kneeling one at a time to swear allegiance and clanswomen bringing flowers and jams as tribute. Gideon said it must be done to confirm his position as chief in the clan's mind. Through it all, he played his part of unyielding horseman of conquest. It was a role he'd been living for twenty years, a mantle not easily put aside.

He slid the crown from his head. "Arabella Sutherland," he called. "Come before me."

It took her several heartbeats before she turned, sadness still in the bend of her lips. Her sorrow twisted inside him, and he realized that he much preferred her fiery anger. She took a full inhale, her shoulders straightening, and walked to stand before him, once more the proud chief. Even with the hellish Sutherland brand, her face was beautiful, delicate features and pale skin with a touch of freckles across her slender nose and cheeks.

His brothers stood to the side of him, watching for the next step in his strategy to unfold. Cain waited until she met his gaze. "Kenneth Macleod is important to ye?"

The delicate column of her throat showed her swallow, and her lips opened. "He is a friend and wise advisor."

"I will see that he survives any friction between our clans," Cain said, "if ye yield to me."

Her small nostrils flared, her lips tightening into a thin line. "I yield to no man." Shoulders pushing back, she tipped her chin higher, taking on the regal bearing of a warrior queen. "I would, however, accept an offer to save my advisor and clan," she said, her gaze moving past him to stare at the wall beyond. "Although I have yet to be *asked* by you to wed. Seeing as you have posted the banns, I assume you plan to do so soon. When you do, I will say yes in order to prevent as much bloodshed as possible."

"Quite romantic," Joshua said behind Cain.

Ella slid her gaze to center on Cain. "Romance has nothing to do with marriage."

She was yielding to him? What made her bend when she'd continued to thwart him with requests to die instead? Hew's crude words, which showed her how terrible her other prospects were? Doubtful, since she'd said she wouldn't marry anyone. Her compliance must stem from fear her advisor would die.

His gaze raked down her fine form. Despite the dryness of the oath-taking ceremony, and the fury the Mackays had ignited within him, looking at her strong features and courage calmed Cain. She was brave and clever, and her beauty whetted his appetite for another taste of the passionate woman who had been willing to do anything to save those she deemed worthy, whether it was a newborn foal, her advisor, or her clan.

Like last night in the stables, he kept the heat out of his voice. "Arabella Sutherland, chief of the Sutherland clan…" His voice filled the quiet room. "Will ye wed with me?"

"Yes," she said without a smile or emotion of any type. He wasn't sure why that irked him, but he brushed it off, coming closer to her. He bent his face toward hers to seal the promise with a kiss, but she backed up abruptly. "I wish to return to my room to prepare for my ordeal."

Ordeal? What did she think he would do to her? Had another man used his power over her to take more than she wanted to give? "What exactly did that Mackay bastard do to ye when your father signed the betrothal contract?" he asked.

She met his stare without blinking. "He did not bed me, by force nor by my choice."

He'd determined as much, or the man would be dead.

"But he kissed ye, frightened ye."

"Annoyed me." She glanced past him to where his brothers no doubt listened. "And with my hands figuratively tied because of my father, I was not able to skewer him."

"Ye should have let her today," Joshua said. He tapped Bàs on the arm with his fist and tipped his head toward the door. The two began to walk, Joshua swiping up a tankard of ale from the nearest table as he went, walking the rest of the way backward. "I would be happy to take ye down to the

dungeons if ye want a second try at the ogre, lass."
He winked and continued out with his brother.

Cain looked to his future bride. Her face and
neck were flushed, but he knew it had nothing to do
with desire for him. "We should seal the bargain,"
Cain said.

"Shall I bleed on the betrothal contract?" she
asked, turning toward Gideon.

"A kiss will do," Cain said, watching to see if she
would stomp off. Either way, the bargain was made
simply by her word before witnesses.

Ella swung around on her heels, marched over to
him, and grabbed his shoulders. She glared up at him
when he didn't bend. "Shall I find a chair to stand
upon?"

He lowered his face until they stared directly at
each other. Even with her eyes narrowed, he could
pick out the blue flecks in the gray of them, long
lashes splaying out from them to accent their beauty.
Looking at her rosy cheeks and full, lush lips, he felt
himself harden even in the face of her anger. Perhaps it was the sweet smell coming from her hair
that shredded the discipline he kept on his body.

"I, Arabella Sutherland, chief of the Sutherland
Clan of Dunrobin, have agreed to wed you, Cain
Sinclair, chief of the Sinclair monsters of Girnigoe."
With that she pressed her lips to his and backed up
immediately before any warmth or softening could
be detected. She gave him a tight smile and looked
to Gideon who stood mute. "The bargain is sealed."

She spun around, her boots clipping as she strode
to the steps where the much larger Thomas backed
away as if she might slap him on her way by.

"Monsters of Girnigoe?" Gideon stopped next to him, both of them staring after her. He chuckled. "Although… Three days to win her acceptance instead of three weeks. Even I am impressed."

Cain kept his gaze fastened to the now vacant archway where Ella had disappeared. He replayed the words from each character in the room. Something piqued his instincts. There were secrets at play here; he was almost certain.

"Gideon."

"Aye?"

"Take a group of six men with ye to Edinburgh. Gain an audience with King James and see how he feels about the Sutherland Clan being ruled by Alec's only surviving child. See if the crown supports her claim." Aye, something did not fit together in this complicated puzzle that made up Ella Sutherland.

• • •

Wed him and kill him.

The words echoed through her head like a maca-bre chant. Kenneth wanted her to swear before God to cherish and obey Cain, and then, when she found him vulnerable, kill him. She swallowed hard. Could she do that, lie to God to love and cherish a man, and then turn around and end his life? Slice his throat as he slept sated next to her? Would she burn in Hell for doing so?

"This is war," she whispered against the memory of him speaking softly to the mare and cradling the foal last night. "A war that he has brought on himself." He'd shown no mercy to Kenneth as he stood there bravely among men and swords, Cain's brother Death looming before him with his scythe. But did Cain deserve to die through deceit? How many of her people had he killed in battle? A hundred? A thousand? What would he do to her clan if he took it over?

Damn him. Last night in the stables had been a ruse. The harsh look today showed Cain's true heart, hollow and cold. Even when she'd finally agreed to wed him, he'd teased her about the kiss, mocking her helplessness in the situation. Her hands were tied to save Kenneth from future harm.

The door of the laird's room was up ahead, and before Thomas could catch up to guard her, she ducked inside. It was vacant but was obviously in the process of being cleaned and rearranged to accommodate the new chief.

She walked straight to the chess table, picking up the white knight. Too bad there wasn't a fire into which to throw it. She peered at its indifferent features and scrunched up her face like a child. Damn Cain for wanting her land and castle. Damn him for wanting her, too. "You are hollow inside, Cain Sinclair," she whispered, staring at the horse. A flutter in her stomach made her heart pound as she curled her fingers around the chess piece. *But do you deserve to die by your wife's hand?*

"Oh, pardon, milady," Thomas said from where he stood at the open door, his eyes going wide. She tucked the knight in the folds of her skirt and marched toward him. He flattened himself against the curved stone wall as best he could as she brushed past to hike to her small tower room.

· · ·

"And ye told her that no more food would be coming up to her?" Cain asked Merida.

"Aye. The stubborn lass has heard it from Hannah, Thomas, and me. For three days now, she says only thank ye and lets her cat out or back in. The little puss definitely knows where it sleeps."

"She did ask for a bit of parchment and ink," Hannah whispered, her eyes downcast. "I brought her some."

"Did she give ye a letter for us to take to her steward at Dunrobin?" Cain asked.

Hannah shook her head no, her face turning red as she fished something from the folds in her skirts. "She asked me to give ye this."

"When?" Cain asked, holding out his hand.

Hannah dropped a small object wrapped in a scrap of bed linen into his palm. "This morn."

"A gift?" Joshua asked, standing from the table to get a better view. Since Gideon had left for Edinburgh, his second brother was spending more time in the great hall, annoying Cain.

"I do not think ye will like it," Hannah said, her fingernails pinching at her bottom lip.

Cain unwrapped the linen and out tumbled a chess piece. It was the white knight from his father's chessboard above, the one Ella had decided represented him when he'd found her hiding on the ceiling beams. With his chess-playing brother, Gideon, gone to Edinburgh, he hadn't noticed it missing.

The piece had the same markings about it, but it

felt different, lighter. Hannah stood with her hand over her mouth as Joshua and Merida leaned closer.

"Did she maim it?" Joshua asked.

"I do not see anything wrong with it," Merida said.

"Look on the bottom," Hannah squeaked.

Cain turned it over to find the entire bottom of the wooden chess piece gone, as if she had spent hours delicately slicing away the inside of the horse without harming the outside. He held it up to look in the hole and saw a small scrap of parchment folded. Plucking it out, he smoothed the creases to read the one word that she had penned onto it.

"Hollow," Joshua read over his shoulder and chuckled lightly. His hand came down hard on Cain's shoulder. "She is calling ye hollow, dear brother."

Bloody hell. Joshua, as loyal as he was, loved to twist whatever knife was sticking into his older brother. Their rivalry had started when they were lads, wrestling, sparring, and swimming races in the loch. The Horseman of War designation fit him perfectly. Cain breathed through the instant urge to punch him, and Joshua slid his hand off, walking back around to his spot at the table.

Cain held the knight, which from the outside looked regal and commanding as usual. It was the inside that was lacking. *Damnation.* He wasn't hollow inside, was he? What the bloody hell did that even mean?

Merida planted her hands on her hips. "She is angry as a nest of hornets, but that does not mean she should starve herself. I even told her that the Midsummer Fire Festival was coming up in a few days, and she should come to the kitchens to see the tarts being prepared, but she ignored me. Mark my words, we will not see her down here if she is left to her own choices. She will waste away up in that room until ye drag her out."

"If ye drag her anywhere," Joshua said, "ye best disarm her first. She obviously has some type of knife to hollow out the knight." He looked sideways at Cain. "Just looking out for ye."

It had been only three days since the oath ceremony, but Ella had not come down at all. She had a few rolls, dried fish, and wild raspberries from the last meal she took without a word that first night of self-exile, but surely it had given out by now. How long did she plan to stay locked away in the tower room?

"Stop taking her up any drink," Joshua said, pointing at the stairs with a drumstick. "Once she passes out from lack of liquid, ye can bring her down and drip ale into her mouth until she revives."

His brother was an arse and obviously trying to annoy him. Cain frowned, his whole mood heavy and lethargic as if he'd been waiting for a siege for three days. He bent his thumb over his fingers one by one, cracking two of them. His move had been to refuse to bring food up to her. Her move was to refuse to come down for food. What would his move be?

He rolled the hollowed-out knight between his hands. "A game," he murmured.

"I do not think she will be up for a game if she is weak from lack of drink," Joshua said, grinning.

An absolute arse.

Cain rose, grabbing two tarts that sat in a basket on the table and strode toward the steps. He took them rapidly. What if she had already collapsed from hunger? He couldn't go half a day without food before his stomach felt as if it were eating itself from the inside out.

"Oh! Hello, chief," Thomas said as he pushed into a stand on the steps before Cain's new chamber. "No movement from above." He nodded toward the ascending steps.

Cain pushed into his room without a word. The space was all set for him with new curtains and bedding. It had been thoroughly cleaned of dust and his father's clothes. Tonight, he would sleep in it.

Stopping before the carved gameboard, he added the white knight to the chess pieces and picked up the whole game, striding back out the door.

"I will keep guard here, then," Thomas called after him as Cain continued up the steps to the tower room.

Rap, rap. His knuckles banged firmly on the door. He had the heavy key in the leather bag he carried, but he would rather she let him in. Unless she was too weak to stand. *Rap. Rap.* "Ella, 'tis Cain. Are ye well?" *Rap. Rap. Rap.*

"Blast it, Cain!" she yelled through the door. "I am coming. What is the hurry? Are Sutherlands breaching Girnigoe's walls?"

Like that was even possible. He exhaled, realizing that his heart was pumping hard. "I would speak with ye," he said through the door.

"Go ahead," she called.

He huffed. "Where I can see that ye have not

grown too thin from lack of food." Silence. "Ella, open the door. I have a proposition for ye." The iron key turned in the lock. As she opened the door, her kitten dodged out around his legs and disappeared down the steps.

"I am glad to see ye have not resorted to eating your cat," he said.

The simple green gown accented her generous curves, and half of her hair was pinned up on the crown of her head into a bonny swirl. She looked tired and still angry. If he stuffed a tart in her mouth, would she have the strength to fight him off?

"What proposition?"

"A way for your clan to retain their lands and castle," he said and held the board higher.

"A chess game?" Her brow arched high. "To win back Sutherland land? Not that you have it yet."

He wasn't going to argue that point. "May I come in?"

She exhaled and opened the door wider. There were no food scraps around, so she wasn't somehow sneaking past Thomas to get meals from the kitchen. She sat down on the edge of her bed, and Cain set the board on the small table. Ella glanced at it. Did she wonder about the white knight?

"I received your gift just now," Cain said. "Poor Hannah looked quite worried that I might become our father and hurl the piece at her head."

Ella didn't say anything as he moved the table before her and sat opposite in the one chair in the room.

"How do I retain Sutherland lands?" she asked, staring him in the eyes. Her stomach growled slightly, and he set the tarts down next to her on the bed. She did not look at them.

"If I lose," he said, resisting the urge to force feed her, "I let Sutherland clan rule themselves in their own castle."

"And I get to return unmarried?"

He frowned. "Nay. That is not part of the proposition, but Sutherlands can rule their own clan."

She looked mutinous for a moment. "What do I forfeit if I lose? I have little left to give."

Magairlean. He hated to break her spirit by taking everything from her, but he must win at all costs. He stared hard into her eyes. "If ye lose, ye come below to eat a full meal, three times a day at least."

"I do not eat that much normally." She crossed her arms before her.

"And…a kiss."

"One kiss?"

"Aye, but not as fast as the one ye bruised me with to seal our bargain."

She uncrossed her arms. "I highly doubt I managed to bruise you."

"Do ye accept? Sutherland lands against food and a kiss." Would the lure of Dunrobin and independence be enough to entice her to play?

"Set up the board," she said.

Victory. He kept his smile inside and set the pieces out, black to her and white to him, the hollowed-out knight in its spot. "Do ye play?" he asked.

"I have."

Her answer gave him no information about her abilities, but he wasn't worried. He had been playing chess and learning strategy from his father since he could lift a pawn.

"I am surprised you play games instead of training and warring every second your eyes are open." She studied the board.

"'Tis a game of battle, lass," he said. "And all of life is a battle."

She looked at him, her eyes narrowed slightly. "To you, life is one big game."

"Aye. A game of strategy. To keep my people safe and prosperous, I wield them like pieces on the board. It is what I have been trained to do all my life."

"Excuse us," Merida said from the doorway. Hannah stood behind her, face uneasy. His aunt looked to Ella. "I still have the wedding costume that I wore to wed your father. I am thinking ye do not want to wear it."

"Perhaps something not cursed," Cain said.

Merida eyed the tarts on the bed. "They are raspberry. Quite delicious and fresh."

"Whatever gown is fine. I could even wear this," Ella said.

"Eat them," Merida said, hands stacking on her hips. "Ye did not go down the stairs to claim them, so ye have won." Her sharp gaze cut to Cain, and she wagged a finger. "The lass won this round."

"Ye should wear a gown prettier than that," Hannah said, interrupting Merida's scowl. "It is to be your wedding day, after all. We will find something lovely." She linked her arm with Merida's and pulled her away.

"Eat them," Merida called over her shoulder as they left.

"Ye best do it," Cain said, nodding to the tarts. "She may have ye tied to a chair and tarts forced into your mouth. And like she said, ye forfeit nothing by eating them if they were brought up to ye."

Her stomach growled in agreement, and Ella picked up one of the tarts, taking a bite. He swore her eyes floated to the back, but she refocused on the board, chewing quickly. The whole tart was gone in seconds.

"The white side starts," he said, trying not to watch her tongue lick a drop of jam from her finger.

"Which is always you." Her gaze scanned the pieces on the polished squares that made up the battlefield.

"I can be black this time."

She waved him off without looking up, and he studied the swoop of hair she'd wrapped onto her head, held by small pins. "I feel rather dark today," she said. "You go first."

"Are you certain? I would not have ye calling me unfair when I win."

She snorted softly and waved her hand at him to move. "Prideful cock."

"Confident strategist," he countered and moved a middle pawn forward. He preferred to bring his pawns to an inverted *V* formation in the middle of the board to block the straight-moving bishops and rooks. Then his knights could weave between, wreaking damage to her advancement.

She stared at the board with a frown, her gaze moving among the pieces. It was her serious study that revealed that she was a novice, one who very much wanted to win.

"Eat the other tart," he said. He would not play an aggressive battle with her. Perhaps he'd let her feel like she was winning for a bit.

She picked up the other tart and gobbled it down. Unfortunately, she did not smear more jam on her fingers, so there would be no licking this time. He should ask the cook to put excessive jam in all the tarts.

She moved a pawn to mirror his so that they blocked each other. They each took several turns in silence, he building his inverted *V* pattern, and Ella hiding her king in the corner with her rook protecting it, along with the queen. They picked off each other's pawns, but then she made a mistake, and he took her rook.

"Blast," she murmured. She did threaten his bishop, but he moved, hoping she would give chase. She picked up one of her pawns, turning its bulbous, irregularly shaped body in her hands. "Both of Girnigoe's chess sets are odd." She met his gaze, her gray eyes curious. "Most of the pieces are chunks of wood with basic carvings on them."

"Aye," he said.

"Except for the knights." She picked up her black knight and held it out to him as if to show him the intricate carvings on it.

"In chess, if ye pick up a piece, ye must play that piece." He had learned that rule the hard way from his father during his early years of playing, before his discipline had grown. Discipline was like a muscle. It must be worked often to bolster it, and like his strength, Cain's discipline was unmatched.

"Ye must pick it up and move it around in your mind before your fingers go near it."

She rolled her eyes heavenward before coming back to lean slightly forward. "Only the horse heads are from the original set, aren't they?" She ran her hand around the edge of the beautiful wooden board, which was carved with various weapons like swords, maces, and shields. "Did you become so angry at losing that you gnashed your teeth and bit the heads off all the other pieces?"

He snorted a short laugh. "Play." He nodded to the board.

"Tell me," she said. "What happened to all the other fine pieces?" She reached forward, catching his hand. "I would know."

His inhale stopped at the feel of her cool fingers, and he slowly lifted his eyes to hers. It was the first time that she'd touched him voluntarily. Even in the barn, he'd been the one to reach for her hand.

She pulled her fingers back as if realizing what she'd done, but his gaze still held her. Neither of them blinked, and Cain felt as if he were falling toward her, leaning in as her soft lips moved.

"I would know the secret of the mutilated Sinclair chess pieces."

CHAPTER ELEVEN

Cain inhaled softly as Ella sat up straight. Was she merely curious, or was she trying to gain as much knowledge about her opponent as she could? That was what he would do.

Perhaps the touch before was her way of trying to soften him into giving information away. No matter. Learning about him would not win her back her lands.

"As ye likely know, my father had an explosive temper," Cain said, crossing his arms over his chest. "When he became angry, either from me making a poor move or one of us beating him when he was already in a fierce disposition, he would hurl pieces into the fire."

She blinked. "Except for the horses?"

"George Sinclair would slice a man in two without thinking anything of it, but he would never harm a horse, not even a wooden one."

She stared at him for a long moment. Did she wonder what his life had been like here at Girnigoe? If it was as loud as she was imagining with tempers flaring and pawns flying to meet with fiery ends? He glanced toward the door to the room, which stood open. "This is the quietest Girnigoe has ever been."

"So…the clumsy pieces?"

"Were whittled by my brothers and me, some better than others." His mouth twisted into a lopsided grin. "Sometimes we had to use rocks for the pawns when Da was in a rage for weeks."

"Which son inherited his temper?" she asked, and set the knight back in its place.

Cain huffed softly. "All of us and none of us, depending if we are on the battlefield. Although Joshua picks a fight more than the rest."

"I suppose being the God of War he likes to cause fights."

She was trying to provoke him. "Not God, messenger from God," Cain corrected. "And I think Joshua's warring temper as a two-year-old lad started Da thinking about raising us after the horsemen of the Bible."

She tipped her head, and the loose waves of her long hair draped to one side. It shone like a sheet of dark silk where a stray sunbeam hit it from the windows cut up high in the cone of the tower. With half her hair pulled up on top, her delicate jaw was exposed. A curl, pulled from the design, hid the blasted brand.

"Raised you after them?" she asked.

What were they talking about?

He focused on the soft pink of her lips as she continued. "Then you do not believe that you four are actually the four horsemen from the Bible, heralding doom for the world as written in Revelations?"

Cain looked away from her, inhaling. He'd gone around and around about the terminology and philosophy with Gideon many times before. Their father was certain of their biblical origins and had raised them to believe it, too. But George Sinclair had changed so much after his wife died. It was as if she'd kept him sane, and without her guidance and tempering, he'd let his wishes become his reality.

"As far as I know, I was born from my mother, not a cloud. Although Pastor John argues that coming down from a cloud could be an interpretation of one being born from between the thighs of a woman."

Her lips turned up into a small smile. "He really said thighs of a woman?"

Cain nodded. "The image of our mother's inner thighs made Gideon gag."

Her smile remained. It was authentic, like the one he'd seen when she'd hugged her horse or nuzzled the kitten. Her gaze moved to meet his, her features still soft. His chest opened, and he took in a full breath. He'd won another smile from her, but it was a type of win that didn't necessarily translate to giving him anything; yet it had. He felt…lighter.

How joyful would she be if she won the chess game? The thought surfaced through the layers of his determination to win at all costs. It was his armor, and he frowned as if recognizing a chink in it. Of course he couldn't let her win or else he'd have to give up Dunrobin and the surrounding land. He cleared his throat. "Your turn, lass."

She picked up the horse that she had returned to the board, setting it down safely, but his rook took the pawn that was protecting it. At this rate, he would win in three moves. She moved her knight out of the rook's way, but risked it being taken by his queen. If he'd been playing his da, he would've taken it, but instead he moved his bishop to threaten her knight.

She swore softly and lifted the horse again,

letting it hover before setting it back down. She moved a pawn instead. "I did not damage the outside of your knight."

"If ye had, I would have had to replace it with a lump with horsehair tied to it," he said, keeping his voice light.

"You were so…" She rubbed her lips together as if trying to find the right words. "Cold and unmoving the other day, different from helping birth the foal," she said, her eyes down on the board. "Like how my father would care for a horse all night when it was ill and then turn around the next morning and…slap me for bringing his porridge cold."

Cain's hand fisted where it sat on the table. He breathed slowly. "Ella, I would never mistreat ye the way your father did. It is my responsibility to present the strength of Clan Sinclair to all. A man's strength can come across as uncaring when actually I strategize my every move in order to protect my people."

She lifted her eyes to him. "I think all chiefs have two sides to them. One they use before people and one controlled by their hearts." She paused as if taking his measure. "Which man are you? The gentle man who would cradle a newborn foal or the cold killer who will take over a clan or murder thousands trying?"

"In the barn," he said softly. "I still told ye I would take Dunrobin and yer lands. I am the same man as I was then."

"Your heart is made to crave conquest and con-quering only," she said. "Whether it be over a clan or a woman." Ella set the knight down slowly, knowing his bishop had a straight diagonal line to it. Without a pawn to then take his bishop, it was a clean defeat, and he took the beautifully carved black horse to his growing circle of won pieces.

"There is no shame in losing to me," he said, not sure how to respond to her comment. He'd always been praised for focusing on conquest. However, he'd never had a conversation with someone he had conquered before.

She moved her own bishop forward to a protected space and tipped her head. The gentle slope of her neck made his pulse thrum faster. One day he would slide his lips along it and make her shudder with passion.

"What happens if you lose some day?" she asked. "Will you shatter into a million pieces? Impale yourself on your sword for failing? Seek self-exile in shame?"

His brows lowered as he regarded her. "It is not something I contemplate, for if I fail to predict the actions of my opponent in battle, I will likely be dead." He saw that his rook could move to a place that would easily take her bishop, but that would end the game and their conversation quickly. He slid his front pawn forward another space so she could take it.

Her slender fingers tugged and swirled a curl hanging against her cheek. "Did you predict that I would send a volley of arrows toward George Sinclair?" she asked without looking up.

The guilt that sat deep in his gut tightened. "No, and my father's death lies upon my shoulders."

"Because you did not predict my move to use all

my archers to fire at one man?" She took his pawn.

He didn't reply but slid his rook over to threaten her bishop.

She raised her face, her gaze finding his. "People are not chess pieces. They do not always follow rules of logical strategy." She moved her bishop forward on the diagonal, exposing her queen.

"Often they do. They can become as predictable as a piece on a chessboard." He moved a pawn between them instead of taking her queen, giving her a chance to escape.

"Sometimes they try new, risky ideas," she said, sliding her queen all the way across the board to stop before his pawn.

He slid his rook up even with it. "Ye know I can take your queen there," he said.

She shrugged. "Perhaps I am willing to make sacrifices as long as my king is safe," she said and leaned forward, staring him directly in his eyes. The notes of blue in the gray of her irises fascinated him. "And maybe I think my opponent is purposely not acting aggressively so he can extend the game." She leaned back with her palms braced on the bed.

A small grin grew on his mouth. She had deciphered his strategy. "So," he said, "ye have decided to lose a kiss to me."

"Hardly." She slid her queen back diagonally, taking the pawn that protected his knight. He would need to move the knight, or she would take it, but then another pawn would take the queen. "Perhaps my strategy is to sacrifice my queen to take your horses."

"Ye do know the goal of the game is to take my king?"

She narrowed her eyes at him with a wry smile that told him that she knew the goal very well. He found himself moving his knight to a spot that was still vulnerable but where she'd lose her queen. She slid to the other side of the board and took one of his pawns. Two more moves and she could take his white horse with her rook.

"I will add your stallion to my herd," she said, not acknowledging that he then took her rook. Soon only her king, one pawn, and her queen stood in the corner. As he moved closer, she took his rook with her queen, setting herself up to lose it.

"Ye are down to your lowest and highest pieces," he said, seeing the end perfectly in his mind.

"Go ahead," she said, but instead of taking her queen, his queen took her pawn.

She looked up at him, questions in her eyes. "I will take your queen. The most powerful piece on the board."

He shook his head. "Ye are in check." He nodded down to his last rook that was in line with her king at the other end of the board. "Ye have to move to defend your king or move your king. Either way, I will take it in two moves."

She slid her queen in front of her king, and his rook took her. Her king, her only remaining piece took his rook, and his queen took her king. "Checkmate."

He crossed his arms. "'Twas a good game. Ye must play back at Dunrobin."

She imitated his movement. "Some."

"With Kenneth? Ye care for him."

"He taught me chess, along with how to shoot

arrows and throw knives."

"Is he your lover?"

She frowned. "He is three score and five years old, and I am a maid like I said."

One could still be a maid and have a lover, even an elderly lover, but her reaction loosened the tightness in his chest. "A father, then, to make up for your own." He watched her face pinch slightly. "For it was obvious Kenneth Macleod would certainly die for ye."

"Yes, he would." She tried to hide any emotion, but he saw much in the lines of her face.

Cain picked up his king, turning it in his palm. He'd been the one to try to carve it the last time his father lost his temper. "Your man has won his life with his kindness toward ye. I will order my men to spare him, if possible, if he resists our arrival at Dunrobin after we are wed."

She narrowed her eyes. "If I had won, you wouldn't have left us alone anyway, would you?"

"I keep my oaths," he said. "But I never lose."

Her steady gaze seemed to weigh his words. She rose. He followed, so that they stood across from each other over the carnage of their chess battle. She had lost all her pieces, and he had sacrificed many more than he needed to in order to spare some of her feelings.

He raised an eyebrow. "So ye will come down to eat?"

"I would not want to endanger Boo with my returning appetite," she said.

"And the kiss?" he asked. "Ye obviously still have my da's dagger for carving out the knight. And likely the *sgian dubh* that ye held to Mackay's throat. They should give ye courage in case ye fear I would take liberties, although I am not a man who needs to take anything from a lass."

"Except her castle, lands, and freedom."

He crossed his arms before him. "Ella Sutherland, ye owe me a kiss, one that is not disguised as a chicken's peck."

She glanced around the empty room. "Right here, in my bedchamber?"

"Would ye prefer to kiss me in *my* bedchamber?"

She rolled her eyes, making his mouth relax almost into a grin.

"If ye are too frightened—"

"Do not try to goad me into a kiss, Sinclair," she said. "I am not frightened of you, despite all this." She waved her hand at his body. Perhaps she meant to point out his largeness or hardened muscles. "And a Sutherland does not go back on her oath, either, but if someone were to walk in, they would think I have caved to your…demands."

Without turning away, he took two steps backward, his hand shutting the door to the room. "I can lock it, if ye worry."

The slight widening of her eyes showed that she realized her move had put her further at a disadvantage, since they were now alone in a very private place. "No need," she said and took two steps around the edge of the table, a look of resolve on her face.

"Shall I close my eyes?" he asked.

"It is quite stupid to shut your eyes to me while knowing I am armed."

He closed them anyway. "If ye pierce my heart, my soldiers will stop ye from leaving Girnigoe, and ye certainly do not want to end up wed to Joshua. He is an irritating arse."

There was a long pause, but he kept his eyes closed, his ears alert. Would she try to stab him there in her room? He'd be able to overpower her immediately, even if she threw the blade.

He heard something clatter on the table and opened his eyes. She slid a second dagger from her sleeve and dropped it with the first, making his chess pieces quake. "He comes from a family of arses," she said and held up her palms. "I am unarmed, so you do not need to worry."

"Not worried," he said. "Just making my plans."

She walked up before him, tipping her head back. "You even plan your kisses?"

"I plan possible attacks." He leaned down slightly. "And I have learned that ye use kisses to trick your enemy. I will not be tricked twice."

"No?" Her voice took on a lower tone. Her palms flattened on his chest. "Perhaps you will think this kiss means I surrender. Or that I will willingly give you Dunrobin and Sutherland lands."

He stared into her gaze, studying her. "Actually, Ella Sutherland, ye are rather a mystery to me." Should he have admitted as much? "But ye need to know," he said, his brow rising in challenge, "that I win every game I play. As ye saw on the board, I have called checkmate."

The sensation of her light touch through his tunic shot up his chest to his shoulders, and he held completely still. His gaze fell onto her lips. They were perfectly proportioned and full.

She looked up into his eyes. "Cain Sinclair," she said and slid her hands up his chest to curve around his biceps, making his muscles contract in anticipation. "Our game is far from over."

CHAPTER TWELVE

Ella had held her blade in her hand for a long moment when Cain closed his eyes.

Was it true Joshua would take Cain's place to marry her if she killed him? Must she wed Cain first and kill him in a way that made it look like someone else had snuck into the castle to slaughter the great god of Conquest? Then she would kill off each of the brothers.

God's teeth. She needed to consider everything before carrying out Kenneth's whispered… What? Orders, mere suggestions, demands? She wasn't certain. In truth, Ella wasn't sure she could follow his words with actions. She had ordered her armies to kill, but she had never done so herself, and certainly not up close, tricking someone. Making Cain believe she cared for him enough to get around his bloody excellent instincts.

Right now, though, she needed to make Cain trust her. Let him think she was yielding to his marriage request and his handsomely dangerous looks. Let him lose a bit of himself in the same heat Ella had felt when she'd kissed him in the tree.

Ella's fingers twined behind his neck into the soft waves of his wheat-colored hair. *Ye are rather a mystery to me.* Let Cain be surprised by her courage and prowess even though she was a maiden. She wanted to be someone whom he could not easily predict. She wasn't a chess piece, despite his trying to dictate her moves in their game of war.

A small step closed the gap between their bodies, and she boosted onto the toes of her borrowed slippers. The movement brought her into direct contact with his hard body. His thighs were solid tree trunks, and she could feel the largeness of his cod against her. She stiffened, but with an inhale, she tried to relax into the role of seducer, lifting her face up toward his to meet his uniquely beautiful blue eyes. She tugged against his neck. Lord, why must Cain be so handsome? The small white lines where he'd been nicked in battle showed how close he had come to a mortal's death, yet he thwarted his enemy every time, his strength and power so commanding. But right now, she must be in command.

"Once again, you are not making this easy," she said when he didn't tip his head down. "Must I stand on the chair?"

He inhaled, his nostrils flaring slightly, reminding her of a stallion about to charge a mare in season. The thought made her heart pound. His only answer was to slide his hands down her back until he reached the curve of her hips, lifting her slightly. She held her breath as he bent his face to hers, their bodies touching in the most intimate way two could be with their clothes still on. A flush poured through her, making her lips part to draw in breath.

Nose to nose, he stared at her, until she realized he wasn't going to kiss her. It had to be initiated by her to be his prize for winning. His arms were corded limbs of strength on either side of her as he held her there. Ella could feel the whisper of his breath against her lips, the won kiss hanging motionless in the air between them, waiting to be given and taken. The bulge below seemed to grow larger, and the fact that merely holding her had stolen his wry grin fired her confidence.

Ella raised her hands to cup his jaw, the short beard covering his hard jawline rough beneath her palms. She leaned into him and closed her eyes as she pressed, slanting her face so that their mouths slid against each other. His lips were firm yet soft compared to the rest of him. The shape of his mouth fit perfectly against the shape of hers, and her world began to tilt.

As if a powerful dam tore apart under the on-slaught of a raging river, a deep vibration came from him, and he bent forward over her. She braced herself, hands on his shoulders, for the wave she could feel coming. Her heart beat faster as Cain slid his hands up her form to cup her face. The kiss deepened, and Ella was lost in the gentleness of his hands. Lost to heat and sensation and a tipping, giddy world that flooded her until all reason seemed to wash away. No clan names, no secret oaths, no strategies, no disloyalty. Not even games.

She heard another low grumble that vibrated from Cain's chest as he held her, his masculine presence completely engulfing her as he surrounded her with his body. Yet she didn't feel trapped. Oh no. She felt like she soared higher.

Her fingers curled into his massive shoulders as she clung, her mouth opening under his, giving him the freedom to taste her. A mix of chill and heat slid up and down her body as he swept inside, emboldening her to do the same. Her heart beat frantically—not in panic, but in need.

Ella wanted him, and the ache at the juncture of her legs throbbed. She pressed against him, rubbing as his large paw slipped down to cup her backside, helping her find just the right spot. His other hand tangled in her hair, pulling loose the pins holding half of it on top. It fell, adding to the silky curtain of waves about her that he lifted and raked as he cupped the back of her head.

He tasted of honey ale and barely controlled, raw power, the intensity causing her to tremble. Their mouths moved as much as their bodies: sliding, tasting, giving, and taking. Ella's breath ran out, but she barely cared, and she inhaled against him, stealing some of his. Her fingers curled into his arms as she clung, and she moaned softly, pleasure building inside her.

It should scare her, this passion. Cain Sinclair was made of untamable power and lethal strength, someone she had no hopes of controlling. Yet the fire in her swelled up, burning away any concern. The need to draw him into her overrode everything. It was carnal and fierce, an instinct that made her blind to everything else in the world.

"Mayhap we will get some bairns out of this marriage yet." Merida's voice cut through the current of lust enveloping Ella, and she stiffened against Cain.

Cain released her lips, letting her slide down him while still holding her firmly upright, which was fortunate, since she would have plopped down on her arse if he let go. He kept his gaze connected to hers, his thumb coming up to gently touch her damp lower lip. There was no cockiness in his gaze, and she wondered if the ravished look on his face resembled her own.

He inhaled, a soft grin forming over his mouth. "Ye are very good at surprising me, Ella Sutherland," he whispered.

How surprised would he be if she sliced his throat as he slept next to her? The thought made it impossible to swallow, her entire chest caught in tight agony.

Cain turned slowly toward his aunt and sister, one arm keeping Ella against his side. "There is no shame in kissing one's betrothed," he said.

Ella straightened, pulling away, and was finally able to inhale. Her hair was wild and her gown askew. She tugged at the skirt to straighten it around her hips, thankful that the material was wool and not velvet to show exactly what part of her anatomy she had been rubbing against Cain.

Make them believe I care for him, she thought, her stomach hardening into a knot. *Make Cain believe.* To convince him that he could be vulnerable around her, she might have to pretend to fall in love with him. The physical pain in her stomach made her back up to sit on the bed. Her whole life had been a lie. Why did this one bother her so much?

Hannah's face was crimson, and Merida wore a wicked grin. "Aye," Merida said. "Although kissing the lass so fiercely her clothes nearly burned off her requires some teasing."

"And your…" Hannah trailed off as she flapped a

hand toward his kilt, averting her eyes.

Cain reached down and adjusted his cod, although his obvious arousal wasn't something that could be hidden. "Is there something ye wanted?" he asked. "She will be coming below to eat and drink."

"We wanted to show Ella…" Merida nodded to Hannah, who brought forth a rose-colored gown. "It is the gown Cain's mother, Alice Sinclair, wore to wed."

It was beautiful, but all Ella could do was nod. Marrying her son in her gown and then killing him? She would surely go to Hell. Had Kenneth considered her soul with his whispered command?

Cain cleared his throat. "I believe she would like ye, Ella, and would be honored if ye wore it." The kindness in his voice tortured her even more.

Merida smiled broadly. "We will fit it to ye then."

"On the morrow," Cain said. "Ella was about to come below to eat more than tarts."

Ugh. How could she eat with the heaviness of her thoughts?

Both ladies looked to her as if waiting to see if she had conceded. "I lost the chess game, and I keep my promises," Ella said. She stood, walking forward on numb legs.

Hannah and Merida parted to let her out first. Ella stepped lightly down the winding stairway, her head held level as she passed Thomas. She kept a confident expression on her face, as if the very foundation of her world had not just turned on end above in her tiny round room.

Lord help her. He was a Sinclair, her enemy, a

monster she was supposed to kill. And yet her body, mind, and maybe even her soul had forgotten all of that during the kiss. It hadn't been merely a kiss. It had been a carnal tempest that caused her to betray a decade's worth of hating the boy who'd looked upon her with disgust.

The look was about his father's lies.

They reached the bottom where the smell of roasted pheasant penetrated her twisting thoughts, and her nearly empty stomach suddenly didn't care about her inner turmoil. It was definitely time to eat.

Joshua raised his tankard in salute. "Ye managed to get her downstairs without waiting for her to pass out from starvation. Congratulations."

Cain leaned near Ella's ear. "See, an irritating arse. Ye do not want to kill me and be stuck wed to him."

Her breath caught, and she watched him walk toward a maid to whom he spoke. The maid hurried off, and Cain looked to Ella. "She will bring ye some of the last meal, pheasant and turnips with oat bannocks." He looked pointedly at her. "Eat every bit of it." Joshua set his tankard down and followed Cain when he tipped his head toward the entryway.

"I can take ye to the kitchen. It will be faster than waiting for Joan to bring something up," Hannah said.

Would the gentle Hannah hate her for killing her brother? Of course she would. Ella breathed deeply, pushing the thoughts away. "Good," she said and forced her lips into a smile. "I was hoping to see more of Girnigoe." Ella followed her through the archway, but instead of turning up the steps, they continued down a corridor.

Maybe she could poison the brothers all at once so there wouldn't be anyone to avenge them or take over right away. It would certainly throw the clan into chaos. But would the cook be killed if the clan suspected her treachery? Ella's stomach pinched. Obviously, the damning thoughts were not easily put aside.

"I wish to ask ye something," Hannah said softly.

Murder. It would be murder to poison someone or kill them while they slept. But was it murder if she saved her clan by doing so? Would the deaths of the four horsemen really save her clan?

"Hew Mackay…" Hannah started.

Ella blinked, turning to face the woman. "Yes?"

"He did not… Ye were not raped by him, were ye?" she whispered.

"No." Ella shook her head, and the girl's shoulders softened.

"Did he bed ye like he said?"

"No, like *I* said."

"Why did he lie that he had?" Hannah asked, her brows bent inward.

Ella's lips pinched tightly. "I do not know. Perhaps in some misguided attempt to save me from marrying Cain."

"That would be foolish," Hannah said. "Cain would have just killed him, and ye would be free to wed."

"Hew did not think things through." The man was rash and inexperienced. She'd seen it in the way he commanded his warriors to raid and burn fields, not thinking of the consequences or moral taint of random destruction.

Hannah smiled. "But he was gallant to try to save ye."

Ella narrowed her eyes as they stopped before an open room with a fire inside, the smell of baking bread wafting from it, making focus on anything else difficult. But she met Hannah's curious gaze. "His plan had more to do with taking Sutherland lands by forcing me to wed him than gallantly trying to save me from Cain."

"So he does not desire ye?" she asked, her lightly arched eyebrows rising.

Ella frowned. "I have no idea what goes on in Hew Mackay's mind."

The girl pressed her hands together before her as if in prayer and raised the point to gently touch her lips. "He is a handsome man, even after being shut away in the dungeon."

Hew, handsome? Perhaps in a grisly, rough sort of way. Shorter than Cain, wide and given to paunch if he did not train daily, Hew Mackay had never made a single part of Ella ache like she did in Cain's arms. But to a sheltered woman, who'd grown up in the rough company of George Sinclair and her massive brothers, Hew may seem strong enough to be desirable.

She caught Hannah's shoulder lightly. "'Tis not the outer appearance of a man that shows him to be worthy of a woman's notice but the soundness of his mind and honor in his heart. I have never known him to act with honor, Hannah."

"Ye do not look at Cain's appearance?" Hannah

asked, tipping her chin slightly higher.

God's teeth. Cain Sinclair was a heady mix of brawn, masculine splendor, and power ruled by intelligence. With his thick waves of fresh-smelling hair, mesmerizing blue eyes, handsome features, and sculpted muscles, she would dare any woman not to look on Cain's appearance. And he hadn't raped her or tortured her or tormented her with threats, all of which she had expected when first caught. But did that make his heart honorable?

"Just be careful around Hew Mackay," Ella said, warning in her voice. "I have seen him act with deceit and greed more than with honor. He may lie if he catches your ear and try to—"

"No man would dare do anything sordid or dishonorable to me, Ella, not with Heaven's four horsemen as my brothers." She smiled sweetly and tugged Ella's arm toward the warm room. "Let us get ye some of Cook's delicious fare."

• • •

Cain stood in the great hall before the colorful tapestry that his father had commissioned that ran half the length of the wall, depicting the four horsemen. He stared at his own figure riding Seraph, his white horse, as if straight from Heaven.

Through the years, whenever his thoughts or intent swayed from the course of conquest on which his father had set him, he would stare at the tapestry until his soul remembered who he was. No, he did not think he rode down from a cloud as a fully grown man, not when he remembered the pain of watching his mother draw her last breath at Bàs's birth. So, who was he to God?

God, guide me to keep our clan strong. The prayer felt unfamiliar and stilted. Since his mother had died, he rarely prayed.

His mind stopped taking in the colors and textures of the tapestry, turning inward again to the angles of Ella's jaw and cheekbones, and the soft fullness of her arse. The little sounds she had made while they kissed were a cross between the soft purr of a kitten and heavy breathing of a lass who was growing close to finding her pleasure. Her reaction was certainly powerful enough to break his discipline.

He rubbed a hand down his jack, but it had interests other than staying down, mainly the lush woman who stood in the middle of all his strategies, like a boulder on the chessboard that stopped his advance. He'd avoided her since the kiss three days ago, trying to regain control of his thoughts.

"She is to be my wife," he murmured. And a wife should not affect his plans to strengthen his clan. But blast it, Ella Sutherland did affect him with each frown and smile he won from her. She had a power over him, one which he must consider in this game. *Daingead!*

He turned at the sound of footsteps, but it was only his aunt carrying a basket of baked offerings to take outside where the festival was being set up.

"With your father gone, ye will be in charge of the Fire Festival tonight," Merida said.

Cain walked with her to hold the doors. "Aye. I have Bàs reminding the warriors and villagers about the leading of the animals around the flames. Joshua and his men are stacking peat and wood to make three huge bonfires."

Merida shook her head, her white hair swirling around it. "That man loves fire."

Cain stood in the open doorway. Would Ella come down for the festival? They must also celebrate Midsummer at Dunrobin with games, blessings, and treats. But did their celebration veer toward the carnal side once the sun went down and the children put to bed? Just the thought of her dancing with wild abandon around the fire made his jack twitch.

"Is something amiss?" Merida asked, studying him in the light from the open door.

If she could read his tangled thoughts, she'd realize there was a chink in the armor he kept around his strategy to take over northern Scotland. He forced his frown to relax. "All is going according to my plan."

"Hmph. The fates have a way of messing with man-made plans." Merida said, narrowing her wise eyes. "Perhaps Ella will celebrate with us."

"Hannah invited her, but I will leave that up to Ella," he said.

They walked across the bailey and onto the wooden planks of the drawbridge. "It will be your sister's first festival, since my ogre of a brother is not here to lock her inside."

"Joshua, Bàs, and I will watch her," Cain said.

Merida smiled wickedly. "A barrel of my finest whisky is being rolled out here tonight. Give a nip to Ella and see if ye can get another kiss." She laughed. It sounded almost like a cackle, and she wandered off toward the table being topped with delicious offerings.

Would his aunt want Cain to kiss his bride again if she knew what had plagued him since their kiss over the chess table? If she knew that Ella Sutherland had a weapon against him, one that could cause more harm than a newly sharpened dagger?

CHAPTER THIRTEEN

"Is it true that couples wander off into the darkness to fornicate?" Hannah whispered as she stood beside Ella in the warmth of one of three large bonfires. Cain's sister clutched Ella's hand like she worried that some warrior would swoop down and carry her off like a hawk grabbing a field mouse.

Ella patted her hand. "I have never stayed at a Midsummer festival once it grew dark, but I am certain the wandering off would be with the woman's approval. Otherwise, it would be a crime, and I am sure your brothers would prevent it. There is always one of them watching you."

Except for Gideon. Ella hadn't seen the third brother since the day of the oath ceremony. "Where has Gideon gone?" she asked.

Hannah shrugged, her eyes turned to take in the games of strength and agility set up on the moor beyond the fires. "My brothers will ride off for days at a time to patrol our borders or travel to another clan to discuss alliances. Cain would know for certain."

Ella had not talked to or seen Cain since her mind had been taken over by Kenneth's whisper and then their kiss. Was he avoiding her? Could his aunt have warned him about her dangerous thoughts?

The fires crackled, freeing sparks to fly upward into the waning daylight. The smiles all around reminded her of home. Hopefully, despite her absence,

Kenneth had still proclaimed that Dunrobin was to celebrate St. John's Day to bless the animals and people of the clan. He had always been in charge of her mother's favorite festival, escorting Mary Sutherland about on his arm.

"Have ye ever?" Hannah asked, wide-eyed.

"Ever what?" Ella's gaze slid across the leaping flames to the other side, and her breath caught. There he was. *Cain*. Large and commanding. He spoke with Joshua while they watched clansmen jump across the fires to predict how high the crops would grow. His light-colored hair was loose, falling nearly to his shoulders, and he'd taken off his tunic. With his arms crossed and his biceps mounded, the dark lines of the horse tattoo looked wild and tribal. The muscles were evident in his stomach, the ridges running all the way to under his kilt, which sat low on his narrow hips.

Just the sight of him made her heart beat a rapid tempo. The feel of his hands on her and his lips sliding against her own, the taste of him on her tongue, was all branded into her memory. *Wed him and kill him.* The reminder came unbidden. It had never strayed far from her thoughts over the last week.

"Run off from a festival to fornicate," Hannah said, sliding her arm to encircle Ella's.

Ella's mind refocused. "Once again…I am a maiden, Hannah, and I have never run off with anyone to do anything." Truth was that Ella made only an appearance at the festivals, with her father ordering her to retire as soon as the formal ceremonies were over. Not that there was anyone she'd have considered running off with anyway. The warriors at Dunrobin were highly aware that Alec Sutherland would have ordered any man who took an interest in her flogged or killed. She was to remain as pure as fresh milk for whomever he would marry her off to.

Hannah glanced down. "I meant no offense. Ye seem so…worldly wise, like ye are not afraid to do anything." She lifted her face to meet Ella's gaze. "Ye even stand up to Cain."

If he'd beaten her or forced himself upon her, she'd have no trouble with Kenneth's plan, but Cain had done none of the things expected of a brutal Sinclair monster. Ella blinked and looked back over the flames, but Cain was gone. "Most of the time, I am figuring out things as I go along," she murmured, and glanced along the edge where the firelight met the growing shadows. Young and old smiled, toasted, and tipped back tankards of honey ale and whisky, but all the brothers were absent.

"If ye have a horse, go collect it to be blessed," one of the elderly men called from the center of the three fires.

"I have two horses to be blessed," Ella said, glancing toward the stables where the foal had been born. "Luna might be too young to come out."

"Oh?" Hannah said, pointing toward the barn door that was slid open. Cain walked with Ginny tied to a long lead line. The little filly dodged around Ginny's legs, flexing and leaping as if full of joy to be out, but she never wandered from her mother's side.

Cain's strides were confident and unrushed, as if he had all the time in the world despite the chaos that had erupted around them with people scurrying off to find their horses. He stopped before her. "Luna will follow Ginny around the fires," he said, handing her the lead.

"I should find Gilla, too," Ella said.

"She is with Gideon's horses inside the bailey," Hannah said. "I will fetch her along with my own." Excitement lit her face, and she ran toward Girnigoe.

Ella looked left and right. People and horses swarmed down from the hills. "There are so many."

Cain clicked his tongue, and Ginny began to follow him as he walked toward the ring of three fires, spread far apart in the meadow. Ella quickened her step to follow. "Our warriors and stable boys walked ours between the fires," she called up ahead.

Cain looked over his shoulder. "We have too many. 'Tis better to have the whole clan help."

Luna nudged her hand where she walked almost completely under her mother. "Good eve," Ella said, smiling down at the sweet pale horse, her brown eyes thickly lashed. "This is my first blessing, too."

"Ye have never walked around the fires at Midsummer?" Cain asked, turning to stride backward. The three fires had been made in a triangular pattern, the farthest one set slightly off due east. Starting in the east, the animals would walk westward like the circling of the sun through the day.

Ella shook her head, her loose hair keeping her warm in the cooling night air. "I was sent inside as the night came where my mother would bless me by having me walk between lit candles." She shrugged. "I have not done so since she died twelve years ago." Her gaze moved out over the meadow beyond. If she could escape, she would not have to wed Cain or kill him. But he would follow her, striking out at Dunrobin.

"'Tis time ye receive the blessing then." He turned forward to lead them between two of the fires. Dodging others, they came out on the other side as Hannah hurried forward with Gilla and another black horse clopping behind her.

"Joshua already had them haltered. Here is your lady," Hannah said, breathing heavily, and handed her the lead.

Gilla's ear twitched as she took in the chaos growing around them, but she had been trained not to spook. Ella rubbed her palm down Gilla's nose, the mare's lips searching her hand for a carrot or apple that she did not have.

Cain's fingers clasped Ella's. She startled but covered it by pretending to look down at her boot as if her lace was loose. "Ye can walk your horse through," Cain said, taking Ginny's lead line from her. There was a wildness to his deep northern accent, as if he'd been raised on the isles off the coast. His face looked relaxed as if he was enjoying the chaotic festival. "Just listen to Hamish and take your place in the procession." He pointed to the elderly warrior who seemed to be in charge. The corner of his mouth hitched up with a grin. "Try not to get trampled. I have to bring Seraph." He turned and jogged off, the muscles in his bare calves contracting in obvious strength.

"He doesn't smile when he is with other women," Hannah whispered.

Ella's eyes pinched as she looked to Cain's sister.

"Is he with a lot of other women, then?"

"They flock around him. Always have. Some even sneak into his bed," she said, flapping her hand toward Girnigoe, but then dropped it, her eyes going wide. "Do not tell him I said that."

Women sneaking into his bed? Ella frowned at Hannah's panic. "Are you afraid of him, of your brothers?"

"Oh yes, definitely. Everyone is. Are ye not?" she asked, her face full of bewilderment.

"Get moving or pull to the side," one of the farmers said as he brought around a donkey to lead between the fires. The press of people increased as they returned from their stables and fenced paddocks. Pastor John, the young clergyman who visited many of the villages in the northern Highlands, coaxed children into groups to lead them through.

"Two lines," the man whom Cain had called Hamish yelled over the mounting noise, his arms raised high to split the growing group. Children and livestock squealed, horses neighed, and people threw orders and curses around. Gilla waited, her ears flicking as she listened for threats in the throng. She didn't wear her saddle, only a halter without a bit, but Ella had grown up riding bareback, and Gilla knew the feel of her weight.

"Stand back," Ella said and gathered her skirt up high with one hand, grabbing a handful of mane with the other. Bending her knees, she leaped upward, swinging her leg up to catch her heel on Gilla's rump, and pushed against Gilla's shoulder to lift herself onto her back.

Hannah stared up at Ella with an open mouth.

"How did ye do that?"

"Lots of practice." Ella reached down to Hannah. "I will pull you up, and then you can swing across to your horse."

"No one else is riding between the fires."

The people and horses coursed past their group as if Hannah and she were boulders in a stream of humanity. Hamish waded closer, looking up at Ella. "The blessing does no good if ye are sitting."

"Why so?" she asked, and her gaze moved across the sea of people. It would take a very good reason for her to lower herself back into that crowd.

"Ye must have the health to stand to be blessed between the fires. If ye ride, ye are sitting. Even a dead man can sit and be carried between the fires."

She met the man's fierce stare, her mouth tightening into a thin line. "But a dead man cannot stand," Ella said, and pulled her feet under her to pluck the ties of her boots, prying them off her feet, along with her tall stockings. A quick knot caught the boots together, stockings stuffed inside, and she handed them down to Hannah.

"What are ye doing?" Hannah asked.

"Not getting trampled."

Balancing the arches of her feet in the flattest sway of Gilla's back, Ella stood, bracing her legs apart, the tether still in her hand.

Hannah gasped, stepping back. Hamish shook his head and turned to direct a boy leading a young stallion who kept thrashing his head.

Ella huffed. "There is no sense in this." But it was better up above everyone. "I will meet you after our turn through," Ella yelled to Hannah, who held her horse's lead rope and Ella's boots, watching her with a look of awe across her pretty face.

Standing atop Gilla, Ella's head was level with the top of the flames, which undulated as wavering points into the twilight sky. With a slight tug to the right, Ella kept Gilla in line with the others. She used the taut lead lines to steady herself on Gilla's back. Those around her looked up, some shaking their heads as if she were a fool, but most seemed either awestruck or smiled.

As she rounded the last fire, the people before her parted quickly, leaving a man in the middle. Cain stood alone, his gaze resting on Ella. Larger than everyone else, he looked like someone sent from Heaven or Hell, depending from which clan you hailed.

"*Stad*," she called to Gilla, and her horse paused next to Cain. "Hamish said that one must not sit to go between the fires else the blessing does not work, and you said I should avoid being trampled," she said, raising her eyebrows.

"'Tis dangerous to ride standing, especially without your saddle," he called up to her, looking at her toes curled into Gilla's back.

"I have been riding this way since I was a girl of ten."

"And ye have lost your boots?" Cain asked, his gaze sliding back to her face.

"Hannah has them. My toes help me balance." She stood tall, waiting for him to order her down so she could deny him. But instead, he held his arms out from his sides so that the people and animals would give them a wide berth as they flowed around them. A glance behind her showed Joshua doing the same, a wide smile on his face. No one came near to nudging Gilla.

"I have the puss." Cain's youngest brother strode up to them with Boo against his chest. Despite the wild look in the kitten's eyes, she didn't scratch at him.

"I will take her," Ella said, reaching for her.

"Nay! *Thoir an aire!*" someone called from closer to the fires a mere heartbeat before a horse neighed loudly, rearing up to paw the air. People scattered, abandoning their horses to leap out of its way. The young stallion, eyes wild and ears flattened back, dropped into a charge—right toward Ella.

• • •

Cain reached up for Ella's bare ankles. Before he could pull her down, she dropped low, almost sitting upon his hands. Bàs pulled the kitten back in to him and grabbed Hannah to the side.

"*Siuthad!*" Ella yelled, yanking the lead tied to her horse's halter wide to the right. Without a bit, it pulled the mare's face to the side, making the horse snort. Ella's legs and shifting of weight turned the horse with precision, and the tail lashed Cain in the face as it tore off into the night.

"*Daingead!*" Cain swore as he, too, jumped out of the way of the wild young stallion, his gaze snapping to Hannah's horse. He threw his leg up over the mare, hoisting himself into place. The lead rope was useless, and he unhooked it. The horse wasn't as well trained as Seraph, but the four brothers made certain that each Sinclair horse knew basic signals without using a bit. Grabbing onto a clump of coarse mane, Cain pressed his heels into the horse's sides and guided her with his knees.

Reaching the edge of the crowd, he scanned the darkness in the direction Ella had flown. The firelight infiltrated the shadows just enough to show her headed toward the cliff that held Girnigoe out of the sea, a sheer drop to the rocks below.

"*Falbh!*" he yelled, tapping his heels into the horse's flanks, and she took off. "Ella! Stop!" Could she hear him over the wind shooting up the cliff?

He leaned over the horse's neck. "*Falbh, falbh, falbh!*" Would Ella see the edge before it was too late to stop? A vision of her and her horse flying off into emptiness, the wind whipping her glorious hair as she hurtled screaming to the brutal rocks below, clogged his view for a moment. He shook his head. "Ella, the cliff!" he yelled with the strength of a battle cry.

He'd gained some ground, shortening the distance enough to see the black shadow of her horse. Ella's hair streamed out behind her, a dark mass of silk in the night. "The cliff!" he yelled again. As if his voice finally penetrated the wind, she leaned left, and her horse veered along the edge.

He sucked in a large gulp of sea air and turned Hannah's horse to follow Ella where she galloped farther out onto the moor that sloped above the village outside Girnigoe. The direct route cut off some of the ground between them. "Ella."

"Who the bloody hell came up with letting all the horses go at once?" she yelled back.

"My father liked chaos. Slow down."

She raced toward the southwest where Dunrobin sat at least two leagues away. He would stop her before then. Did she really think that he would let her ride away without bringing war on her people?

As she neared the middle of the moor, her horse slowed, turning in a wide circle. Coming to a halt, Ella stared straight ahead over the horse's ears as they both sucked in large pulls of the cool night air. He could see puffs of it in the dim moonlight as he stopped beside her.

That far out from the fires, the sounds of his people were but a whisper. Ella's horse snorted, lifting its head to sniff the salt coming from the sea on the breeze. Ella tipped her head back to look at the vast sky curving above them. "I have nowhere to go," she said, her soft words breaking the silence. "I have too much of a need to live to plunge over the cliff, and I would never harm Gilla."

She brought her chin level and tucked her hair behind her ears, still not looking at him. "I cannot run back to Dunrobin only to bring war to my people. And I will not go to the Mackays for help, because they want Dunrobin as much as you do." She stared out away from him. "I have nowhere to go."

"Ye will have a home at Girnigoe," he said.

A dark bite of laughter broke from her, making her horse's ears flick. "It is impossible to feel at home where one is forced to stay." She sniffed, brushing the hair from her face where the wind sent it flying forward. Silence fell between them as he watched her. He wasn't sure why he waited there, but rushing Ella back to the chaos of the fire wouldn't give him any more insight about what she thought and felt. And somehow those things were important to him.

"I was forced to remain at Dunrobin, too," she said, her words soft against the wind, and he nudged Hannah's mare closer to her. "The one time I tried to leave, my father discovered my plan and had his men hold me down while he branded me." She looked at him. "As you guessed, he did it so that if I ever left, anyone seeing it would return me or suffer his wrath."

That foking lunatic. Jaw clenching as tightly as his fists, Cain stared at her in the thick shadows, wishing he could better see the expression on her face.

"And do you know what he said as he did it?" she asked, leaning toward him over the space separating their horses. "You. Are. Mine."

Bloody hell. How many times had Cain yelled those very words at her as he claimed her as a prize? Each time reinforcing that he was a cruel bastard like her father. "Ella…I would brand every inch of his disgusting body if he were not already dead."

His hands fisted at his sides as he stared hard into her eyes. "Ye have been hurt." His voice was a ragged whisper. "How far have ye been hurt?"

She'd been held down by her father's men. Had any of them, spurred on by her struggles, found her later in a dark corner, trapping her? There were men who felt that women were their playthings with no choice. Is that why Ella had learned to wield a dagger and race like the wind? Why she'd learned how to escape? *Fok!* He would slice the Sutherland bastard's skin from his body and chop off his jack.

"What has been done to ye?"

"The branding," she said, looking out at the night. "Some lashings and bruises. I think his words injured more." She looked at him. "Alec Sutherland loved to rant about my weakness as a girl. Said he did not believe that he'd sired me and not a son. If it were not for my mother and Kenneth, I would have let his words sink in, making me weak." Her voice grew soft. "Sometimes I think his words did."

Her shoulders rounded as she leaned over her horse's neck. Cain released the breath he'd been holding, taking in her truths. They sat in silence, and Cain looked upward, unsure if there were any reassuring words he could say that could wipe away the terror of her upbringing.

He cleared his throat. "I find strength sometimes when I look up at the stars." The words sounded foolish as they broke from his mouth.

She rolled her head to the side as it rested on Gilla's mane. "Cain Sinclair, conqueror of clans, stealer of castles and lands, strategic god of battles... you, Cain Sinclair, gaze at stars?"

He frowned. "Not god, horseman from God. And aye. I know all the constellations."

Ella pushed up to sit and leaned back, slowly lowering to lie flat along her horse, her head on its rump with her bare feet hanging down the sides with her skirt. "Well then," she said. "Let us gaze at the heavens to find some strength."

Cain kept his face turned toward her as he leaned back to match her position. The stars were bright in the black sky, like a million far-off fires or frozen fireflies. He raised his hand to point at a familiar constellation slightly to the south. "Up there. See the square that those bright stars make?" He moved his finger to trace the stars in his sight and heard her shift next to him.

"'Tis a rectangle," she said.

"They call it a square."

"They who?" she asked, but he continued.

"That is the body of Pegasus, the winged horse from mythology. He is one of the largest constellations in the summer sky."

Ella didn't say anything, and he let his arm drop. Even though Cain spent hours staring up at the stars, he'd never brought out any of the lasses who were brave enough to talk to him, preferring to find solitude in the darkness to let his mind work through strategies. He exhaled long, letting his gaze wander. "They are so familiar to me," he whispered, "that if one star was to disappear, I would notice."

She raised a finger as if tracing the outline, and the long line of her arm mesmerized him.

"When I was a boy," he said. "I would lie out under them and wish to capture Pegasus."

"What a mighty warrior you would be if you had a winged horse," she said, a teasing note to her whisper. "Then you could swoop down on your enemies."

He turned his gaze back to the familiar pattern. "I actually dreamed about flying away, especially after my mother died and Da turned wild. First grief took him and then…" He shrugged where he lay on the horse. "He was just wild, warring, and determined to make us into the four horsemen."

Cain turned his face to the side, and their gazes met across the space between their horses.

"He got what he wanted," she said. "His four horsemen, riding down from Heaven to conquer the world for God." She shook her head. "I suppose that would make the rest of us the evil sinners to be killed off. Did George Sinclair have visions from God as to who you should all kill off?"

He frowned at her words and sat upright again. "My father was wild, a mix of vengeance and grief from which he never recovered. I am different. I want to unite with ye, not kill ye." He leaned forward, searching her face in the shadows. "Do ye not want a united Scotland, led by the strongest and most strategic, to keep our country safe from England and France?"

"And if there is opposition to you choosing yourself as the leader, you wipe them off the earth?" she said, also pushing up to sit. The strength in her face made her determined words even harsher, condemning him.

Eyes narrowing, he beat down the defensiveness threatening to come into his tone. "How then, Ella Sutherland, would ye keep Scotland safe?"

CHAPTER FOURTEEN

I would kill you.

The thought surfaced in her mind like the memory of a nightmare.

Cain sat there under the stars next to her, ready to defend her from her dead father, ready to hear her thoughts about making Scotland strong. Was he the monster that Kenneth and all of Sutherland clan thought him to be?

Her lips felt numb in the wind, and she touched her mouth, sliding a hand down to her chin. Kenneth used to clasp her chin when she was a child to hold her attention as he taught her right from wrong. She dropped her hand. "I would unite the clans as allies with a written treaty between them. The clan leaders would work to remain together through quarterly discussions as a group and with King James."

"James is not strong enough to keep the clans together," Cain answered. "Such pacts have fallen apart before."

"It requires honest and respectful listening and discussing to get the clan leaders to agree to stay together. Diplomacy."

"I would be honest and respectful, but I have found that others like to shoot and slash rather than talk," he said.

"Fear makes people attack. Perhaps you should try...I don't know...not growling at people or ordering them around constantly or riding down on them with your crown and bow and three nightmarish brothers."

She sucked in a large breath. "Maybe listen to them for a change. Learn their names and who they are. Other people have ideas, some of them sound. Others, besides you and your brothers, are also clever, but when you roll through clans, taking everything over, killing whomever stands in your way, you silence them."

"I am listening right now to the Sutherland chief, am I not?" He crossed his arms where he sat, the silhouette of a mighty warrior. If he was carved in marble, he could be called The Strength of Scotland.

"Yet you are stripping away my chiefdom," she said. "Trying to change my people into Sinclairs. If you take their name and their pride, no amount of stargazing will make them strong. The strength of Scotland lies in clan pride and loyalty. Conquered warriors will not fight for the Sinclairs, at least not well. If you conquer the pride of our people, Scotland will weaken." She watched his face, his brows lowered. Could she possibly change a mind that had been molded by a madman over a lifetime?

In the distance, a horse neighed, and another round of screams rose up. Cain did not reply to her comments, but at least she'd gotten the chance to say them. No one, besides Kenneth, had ever listened to her ideas about creating a strong Scotland before.

She turned toward the bonfires and leaned forward, making Gilla walk. "I suppose we must return, Gilla," she said. "To the insanity that is the Sinclair clan." Her horse's ears flicked toward her in agreement over her assessment.

"'Twas my father's tradition," Cain called and caught up to her. "He felt that chaos would weed out the weak."

Ella rolled her eyes heavenward. "'Tis a bloody idiotic tradition, and you can change it. You can change a lot of things." She angled her horse across the dark moor and pressed forward into a canter, Gilla's rolling gait making her feel free enough to smile. Cain moved up beside her, the thud of his horse in time with her own. They slowed as they reached the outskirts of the fires. People milled around, most holding onto their horses while Cain's assigned man used sweeping arm movements to try to organize the mass.

Cain held his fingers to his mouth, giving a shrill whistle that sliced through the uproar. Behind the press, a horse neighed, and Cain's massive warhorse pushed through the crowd. Cain waited until his white steed came up to him to dismount Hannah's horse. "Take her to her mistress," Cain asked a lad nearby and held the horse's halter until he grabbed it. He glanced at Ella and then back to the boy. "What is your name, lad?"

The boy's eyes were wide. "Devlin, Chief Sinclair."

Cain nodded to him. "And thank ye."

Shocking. Her mouth dropped open with mock surprise.

He climbed onto his white horse and looked at her. "See," he said. "I can be…not frightening."

She closed her mouth, trying not to smile. *He is still the enemy.* An enemy who had listened to her ideas. *Wed him and kill him.* Her smile faded away.

Cain turned the horse to face the crowd. "*Stad,*" he called out, his voice booming up from his gut to cut through the conversations. It was a vicious growl. Most looked paralyzed in fear, except for the man directing everyone, who lowered his arms in relief.

"Wildness served the Sinclairs in the past," Cain called. "But now we will have order in the walk and save the wildness for the dancing and drinking afterward." Deep chuckles came from most of the men and several ladies.

"Those animals who have already walked or kicked their way between the flames must be taken home now if they haven't already run off into the night."

"Ian's young stallion has been caught," Hamish said. "The rest were ridden down, too."

Cain glanced behind him to Ella. "What order do ye recommend?"

She almost glanced behind herself to see if one of his brothers stood there, but Cain stared directly into her face. Her eyes widened, her lips parting. Before his clan, he was asking a prisoner to organize the blessing?

Ella pressed Gilla forward to come beside him. She cleared her throat and blinked against the smoke that wafted into her eyes. "I would send the wildest horses, one at a time, through first with two strong attendants each and then take them back to their stables to make way for the gentler ones and then the mothers and their foals."

Cain nodded and turned back to the crowd. "This is Lady Ella Sutherland, who will be my wife in a fortnight. Her advice is sound." Cain turned to Hamish, whose frantic look had changed to utter bewilderment, his gaze bouncing between him and Ella.

"Lord of the Beasts," Cain said. "I know that ye, too, have thoughts on making this work smoothly. The two of ye will discuss the order, and ye will see it carried out with the efficiency and masterfulness that ye always employ."

The man's chest puffed up, and he managed to close his mouth and nod. Cain looked to Ella. "Can ye work with Hamish to improve this bloody idiotic tradition?" It was a question, not a command, and Ella nodded.

• • •

Within minutes, Hamish was lining up the stallions with two men each to help hold lead lines. Ella stood with him, pointing, nodding, and listening to Hamish. Whatever she said to him seemed to make the man accept her help. It seemed that she was good at diplomacy.

Cain stood apart, next to Seraph, waiting for their turn to walk between the flames. Joshua sauntered up, a teasing grin on his face. "Very nice, brother." He nodded to where Ella and Hamish stood. Ella said something, and Hamish actually smiled. Well, it wasn't a smile exactly, but his usual frown softened.

"Showing her respect," Joshua continued. "Lasses love it. And before the clan… She will be in your bed before ye know it."

Was that his intent? "She is quite clever," Cain said, thinking over her words on the moor. "And I agree that Da's wild ways need improvement." Cain slid a hand down Seraph's neck.

Joshua came around the horse. "Now to make her jealous."

Cain huffed. "How would that make her more biddable to me?"

Joshua shook his head. "Do ye know nothing about lasses? They can resist carnal temptation much longer than we men, but put another woman in the picture, and they will do anything to keep the man they've decided they want."

"I would not put Ella Sutherland in the category of women who want me," Cain said.

"Ye have declared that she will be your wife," Joshua said. "Therefore, she is already seeing ye as her territory. We have our games of war, and lasses have their own games."

Cain looked over to where Ella stood, her arms up to help Hamish direct a line of horses. Could she possibly think of him as something other than her captor? He'd listened to her sharp mind out on the moor and showed her that he could bend by finding out the lad's name and putting her in charge of the blessing.

Joshua's hand came down on his shoulder, and his brother leaned in as if imparting a secret. "I am telling ye, return some of the glances that soft and curvy Viola tosses ye tonight and see what Ella does."

"Viola Finley?" Cain turned toward the fire to where the voluptuous brown-haired woman stood. She had always been eager to enjoy a night of sport with nearly any warrior. As if the woman could feel his gaze, she raised her eyes to meet it, and her amused smile changed into a seductive grin.

"She has been staring after ye all night." Joshua laughed. "Ye must be struck foolish by Ella not to have noticed. One grin, and Viola will be spreading her legs for ye. Either gain back some of your humor tupping her tonight or at least give Ella a reason to be jealous."

It was said that Joshua knew how to win any lass's heart, or at least her tail, but his advice with Ella sounded too routine, too easy, when nothing about Ella Sutherland was easy.

"Anger and passion are one and the same," Joshua continued. "Poke her temper," he said, nodding toward Ella, "and the fire will follow."

• • •

The log looked incredibly inviting as two men carried it over to lay on one side of the fire for people to sit upon. Ella held Boo in her arms, having returned from carrying her between the fires. She claimed a seat and snuggled the kitten against her chin, watching Hamish finish directing the last animals.

Ella had never even walked around the fires before, and Cain had put her in charge of coordinating the process with Hamish. And he had allowed her to speak out on the moor without interrupting. Her father would have knocked her down for her insolence and called her a fool for desiring a unification of chiefs to make Scotland strong. Yet Cain Sinclair, the fierce demon of conquest, had let her talk. Perhaps it was a Midsummer miracle, or perhaps Cain Sinclair was not the monster she thought him to be.

Ella watched Pastor John say a prayer over a tiny bug that a little lad had accidentally squashed, helping the boy slow his tears. Children toddled through holding fireflies that they'd caught, swearing to their das that their new friends were pets who must be blessed. Ella smiled as one little girl yawned, her father scooping her up to carry her home for bed. What would it feel like to be loved so?

Soon only adults remained, and the musicians started a lively tune. Boo hopped off her lap, trotting back toward the castle. Ella blinked against the smoke and glanced around the darkness on the outside of the fires where men and women laughed.

"Come dance with me!" Hannah said as she ran over. The young woman tugged her arm, making her rise to follow her to a circle of ladies ringing one of the smaller fires.

"What do we do?" Ella asked.

Hannah leaned in to her. "I have no idea."

Ella gave her a comical frown. "You have made it very easy for me to sit back down."

Hannah laughed and clasped her hand while the woman on the other side of her did the same. *Trapped.* "I am Alice," the other woman said. "Just kick your legs and follow the others." *Kick my legs and follow.*

They moved around the fire in a wide circle.

When Alice dropped Ella's hand and began to turn and move her hips, Ella dropped Hannah's hand and turned, too, her hair whipping out. She smiled at the freedom in the movement, her feet leaping and stomping in time with the drum that accompanied the pipes and flute. Around and around they danced until they were out of breath and laughing.

Hannah caught Ella's hands. "I am so happy ye will be my sister," Hannah said. Ella's chest tightened. Would she be happy for a sister with secrets that could hurt the Sinclair clan? A sister who planned to kill all of her brothers, starting with Cain? Ella breathed past the ripple of nausea, pushing the dark thoughts away.

Glancing over Hannah's head, her gaze caught on Cain where he stood watching them with Joshua and Bàs. He was a giant of restrained power, but his hands could move over her ever so gently, his kisses soft and teasing. Ella's stomach clenched again, but this time the feeling was giddy as her rapidly flying heartbeat thudded deeper with the memory of their kiss. The warmth that rose up within Ella dissolved the tortured thoughts of Kenneth's plan.

"I am growing hot," Hannah said above the music.

Ella met Cain's direct gaze. "So am I." Even with merriment all around him, he looked only at her. As if she were important. As if she mattered.

Joshua interrupted him, tipping his head toward the barn. Cain glanced once more toward Ella, said something to Bàs, and then walked away. Ella breathed deeply again, shaking the spell he'd woven over her. *He is my enemy.* The thought felt like a lie.

"Find us a seat," Hannah said, "while I find us something to drink. Maybe a bit of Aunt Merida's whisky."

Ella walked over to take a spot on a log that was vacated by a couple who faded off into the darkness holding hands. Her gaze drifted toward the barn and noticed Joshua striding out. He paused, caught her eye, and walked directly toward her. He jumped over the log to sit down.

"Enjoying the festival?" he asked and held out a flask.

She ignored his offer. "Not the nearly being killed by a wild horse, but yes, the rest has been pleasant."

"Ye dance well." He nodded toward the fire where many of the unclaimed ladies laughed and twirled about.

"Your sister is quite excited to be let outside Girnigoe."

He crossed his legs at the ankles. "Aye." His smile faded somewhat. "Bàs is following her right now. Perhaps I should take her up to her room before things get started."

"Started?" she asked.

He nodded toward the couple on the other side of the fire. "With the wee ones off to bed, the lads and lasses enjoy the evening more and more. A bit of whisky, dark shadows, a lively tune in the background, and the fire in Fire Festival takes on a whole new meaning." He raised his flask as if saluting the carnal tradition.

Ella glanced at several couples kissing in the shadows behind her. "I best be off to the castle, too, then," she said. "I can find Hannah and take her with me." Where was Cain? The clan knew they were betrothed, but would that be enough to keep him away from the ladies imbibing in spirits? From what Hannah had said, Cain had many women vying for his kisses.

"Ye may want to stay out here to keep an eye on Cain," Joshua said as if reading her thoughts.

Her gaze snapped around to him. "Why?"

Joshua shrugged. "Pairing up at Midsummer is a blessing, too, for the couple."

She pinched her lips tight. "I do not care about a blessing for us as a couple. I am still a prisoner here."

"Dear almost-sister." He sighed dramatically. "Whomever ye pair with at Midsummer will warm your heart and bed all winter long. 'Tis a saying, a legend, and pretty much a fact. And I do not take ye as a lass who is willing to share her husband with another." He jerked his thumb over his left shoulder toward the barn.

Blinking to clear the brightness of the flames from her vision, Ella spied into the shadows where the large form of Cain stood…with a woman. Ella's spine stiffened. "That bloody bastard," she murmured before rational thought could remind her that she shouldn't care.

"Ho now," Joshua said, pressing the uncorked flask into her hand. "Cain was checking on that new foal of yours, and Viola Finley caught him there on his way out. She is always up for a bit of fun, especially on Midsummer's Night. But she looks to be pouring on the sweetness with her bodice lower than is proper." He nodded, his brows raised like he was astonished, but then he smiled wickedly. "I would tup her myself tonight, but it seems she has her sights set on the new chief."

Ella's fingers curled into the bladder that Joshua had handed her. She'd never cared about trying to garner or keep a man's attention before, preferring to avoid them all. But the sight of a woman rubbing her breasts across Cain's arm ignited a tempest inside her.

She took a swig from the bladder, the smooth whisky weaving a path of fire down her throat. Her face pinched at the strong brew, and she wiped a hand over her lips, handing the flask back to Joshua. "I have no say over what Cain does with anyone."

Joshua took a swig, too, smiling like a drunken fool. "Just looking out for my soon-to-be sister. If Viola ends up sharing his bed tonight and all winter, ye will lose any influence over my brother."

Ella turned to the cocky arse. "You think I should use my body to control Cain?"

Both of his eyes opened wide, and he placed a hand at his heart. "Did ye not know? A man's mind is often controlled by his cock, dear sister. Control Cain's and ye may control him. Let Viola take hold of it, and she will never let go."

Joshua was crass, but as she looked back toward Cain with Viola draped over him, the woman's knee rising to stroke him through his kilt, Ella glared. What if Cain decided not to wed her? What would that mean for her clan if she had no influence over him at all?

Ella stood, striding away from the fire.

"Claws out," Joshua called. "He likes claws. We

all do." He laughed.

She headed straight toward the situation that, left unchecked, could ruin whatever plans she decided to execute. Laughter and shadows blended the rest of the world away, and the soft tread of her boots over the battered grass was soon eclipsed by the rush of blood in her ears.

"Come now, Cain, just a Midsummer's Night kiss," the woman said, her voice like the purr of a contented puss. "Maybe a quick ride inside the barn to relieve some of this tension I feel in ye." Her hands rubbed along his shoulders, sliding down his tunic-covered biceps. Keeping her elbows in to her sides, her bosom rose up high before him like two puddings on a platter.

"Step away." Ella halted several yards back.

"Ella?" Cain said, trying to turn toward her, but the woman wouldn't let go of him.

"Go away, Sutherland," the woman said with a glance, her pretty face plastered with a fake smile. "I am helping out my old friend now that he is going to be burdened with a wife who despises him."

Did she despise Cain? Of course. He was her captor, her enemy. *He listened to me. He gave me leadership over the fires. He would have saved me from my father.*

"I said, step away." Ella slowly withdrew the *sgian dubh* she had slid up her sleeve.

"'Tis a saying, a legend, and pretty much a fact," the woman said, looking back up into Cain's pinched face, "that a woman who warms a man's heart and bed at Midsummer will do so all winter long. 'Tis good for the clan for the chief to be satisfied." Her face turned back to Ella. "And ye seem incapable of doing it."

The woman's particular wording made Ella pause, and she glanced toward the fire, but Joshua was gone. A sound made her turn back to see Viola on her toes, planting her lips onto Cain's mouth. Anger, regret, and jealousy welled up inside Ella, and she didn't try to restrain any of it. She drew back her arm.

"Ella," Cain said, pushing Viola back from him with two hands, even though she still grasped his. "I was not—"

She cut him off with a step and flick, practiced a million times. She whipped the dagger through the air. Luckily for Viola, Ella's eyesight and aim were perfect. The dagger tip turned forward, breezing by the woman to *thwack* into the wooden beam above her head.

"Shite!" she yelled, ducking and finally releasing Cain's arms. "What the bloody hell are ye doing?"

"Get your talons off him, you witch."

"Ye are a bloody enemy. His bed will be cold as ice with ye in it."

Before Viola could wrap one hand back around Cain's arm, Ella strode up to him, caught his shoulder, and pulled him toward her. He turned without much hesitation, and she grabbed behind his neck to yank his head down to meet her lips in a kiss.

His mouth warmed quickly over hers, and she slanted her face. The mash of emotions that had been churning through Ella all night ignited like pitch within her. His arms slid around to her back until she felt surrounded by his heat, a fire that scorched without pain. The ache of pleasure roared up through her, and she pressed against him. Against Cain Sinclair.

Her enemy. Her betrothed. Her target.

But the fire burned her tormenting thoughts to ash as one of Cain's hands found her hair, his fingers climbing through the mass, guiding her lips into place as if they were meant to meld into one. Ella's body remembered only too well the feel of his power and strength when she'd paid the price of losing the chess game. *More*. She wanted more.

She raked her nails through Cain's hair. Eyes closed, only sensation mattered. Even the sound of Viola cursing didn't pull Ella away from the molten desire raging up like a firestorm through her. She pressed the juncture of her legs against Cain's hard jack, and he fit her intimately along his length.

With a swoop under her knees, he lifted to carry her away from the barn, his lips still on hers. If people watched, she didn't care. None of them mattered. Hot and wet, only the feel of Cain's kiss consumed her. It felt like a promise, a tease of something more, something she had never experienced before. And at the moment, she truly wanted to experience whatever it was that Cain's touch could do to her.

"Shite," someone cursed, and she heard them jump out of the way of Cain's strides. "Sorry, chief."

Cain broke the kiss, his gaze moving ahead of him in the dark. Ella tried to catch her wild breath and realized his breathing was just as ragged.

"Move," Cain ordered, and a group dispersed as he marched them through the crowd. Bloody hell, everyone was seeing this. Did she care? These

weren't her people, and any women like Viola needed to know that Cain Sinclair was soon to be hers.

"Where…where are you taking me?" she asked,
her voice still breathless.

"To my castle," he said, his voice raw with unchecked hunger. He glanced down at her, but his
stride remained constant, eating up the ground between them and a stone fortress of privacy. "But," he
said, and she watched him swallow, "what happens
in my bloody castle is up to ye."

Lifting her higher into his arms, he continued, his
boots thudding across the first drawbridge. Guards
stepped aside to let them pass, shadows falling over
them.

Ella felt the heat radiating off Cain's chest as he
held her against it, her gaze rising to stare at the
solidness of his jaw. His longish hair moved in the
night breeze, giving him a savage look, like the
ancient Vikings, their blood having flowed through
both of their ancestors. With his stern features, it
was almost as if he marched off to war. He growled
low in his throat. "Bloody damn long way to the
keep."

There was a small scar across his cheek. Where
had he earned it? She reached up, her finger
touching his warm skin to slide along it. He glanced
down and then back up at their path.

"What would *you* have happen in your bloody
castle?" she asked, her words soft over the wild
thump of her heart. If she was to die or kill and go
to Hell for it, she wanted to know first what happened if she let the fire in her rage unchecked. She
wanted to know the pleasure Cain's molten kiss

promised before war and death took all pleasure away.

"Cain Sinclair." She waited until he stopped before the keep door and turned his face down to hers again. Her finger dropped down from his cheek. "What will you do to me, if I say yes to…everything?"

CHAPTER FIFTEEN

Cain's breath seemed to stop as Ella watched him stare down into her face, her question making him freeze where he stood outside the keep doors. Sword-wielding warriors could not stop him, and yet her question had turned him to stone.

He shifted, letting her legs lower, and her feet touched down on the stone threshold. She did not move away. *He likes claws.* Her fingers curled into his tunic as she met his gaze with a bold stare. Could she handle the carnal fire she knew must burn within him, all that raw power coiled and ready to strike?

"Ella," he said, his tongue sliding across her name in a way that made the spot between her legs clench. He leaned closer so that their lips were only inches apart. "If ye let me, I promise to bring ye to shattering ecstasy, lass." She shivered at his words. "I will taste your heat and strum and touch every part of ye that aches until ye are whimpering and thrashing in wildness beneath me."

Her lips parted, and she watched his gaze move to them before rising again to her eyes. "Tell me now, Ella, if ye do not want that, and I will…leave ye be."

The pain in his face told her he spoke the truth. This ruler of men and terror to many was leaving her seduction completely up to her. The power that he'd given her was huge and emboldening. She placed her palms over his shoulders and released her breath. With it came all the truth that bubbled up within her.

"I ache, Cain," she whispered. "And I want to know what it feels like to…to shatter."

He inhaled through his nose, his gaze dropping to her lips, and she parted them. "Make me thrash in wildness," she said.

A groan came up from his chest, and he pulled her to him, his mouth descending to cover hers in much more than a mere kiss. It was a ravishment of her mouth. She slanted against him, unleashing her own wildness, and felt him mold her up against his thick length. She pressed higher, feeling his jack rub the ache at the crux of her legs.

He murmured something in ancient Gaelic and slammed his hand into the door, making it fly inward to crack the wall as he lifted her with him to enter. He kicked it shut behind him and strode with her into the great hall. A quick glance showed it to be empty, the shadows from the hearth fire stretching up the stone walls.

He carried her close to the fire, continuing their kiss. When he set her down in the warmth, Ella caught the edge of his kilt, pulling his shirt up until it lay untucked. Reaching under, her fingers slid up over the hot skin and corded muscles of his stomach and chest, stroking over his nipples. He growled in the back of his throat and turned with her, stepping them back until she was pinned against the wall beside the hearth.

Cain broke from her lips, nibbling and kissing over her scar and down her neck, his hands stroking up her sides to cup her breast through her bodice.

She felt him inhale against her skin and felt his tongue tease her before he moved his hungry mouth back to her ear. "I will lick and nibble those hard pebbles I feel beneath your bodice." His hand stroked down between her legs, rubbing against the throbbing there. She moved against his hand. "As well as all your secret places," he whispered. "The ones that ache for me right this moment."

Her breath came fast from parted lips. "Will I survive it?"

He met her heated gaze. "Aye, but barely." His finger lifted to stroke the skin along the edge of her smock, sending a rush of tingling through her as he dipped underneath. "And then," he said, feathering a kiss across her lips, "ye will want me to do it again."

• • •

Was he dreaming? Just this morn, he'd woken with a stiff jack from loving Ella Sutherland in his dreams. And now she was standing before him, asking him to take her to where he longed. All his senses were alert as if he rode into battle. A gentle flower fragrance from her hair mixed with the smokey tang from the bonfire. The dark waves slid through his fingers, and her skin was soft like a doe, making his blood race. Their breaths came quick as he sought the ties at the front of her bodice.

The sound of the door opening behind them barely registered as the softness of her skin under his palm vanquished any other thoughts.

"Ye have the largest bedchamber in the bloody castle just up the stairs," Joshua's voice rang out. If it wouldn't delay him, Cain would have sent his dagger sailing through the air to shut his mouth.

Cain pushed Ella behind him. "Get out!"

Joshua crossed his arms. "The biggest damn bed in Girnigoe and ye are going to f—"

"*Magairlean*," Cain growled over Joshua's asinine words. He turned and lifted Ella against him, his arm under her legs again. Thank the devil or the good Lord or whoever had turned her heart tonight, because she once again let him carry her.

She tucked her face into his neck as his boots hit the stone steps in a near run. He pushed through the door to his new room. Cleaned and decluttered of his father's heavy furnishings, it no longer held the tang of old man.

Damn, he should have thought to make the fire before he left, but he'd had no idea that his luck would turn tonight. Stepping up to it, he let her lower, his arms around her. She looked up, and he did not give her time to reconsider. His lips came down on hers. Hers met his, hot and demanding. When her cool hands stroked under his tunic to his shoulders, he nearly yelled with gratefulness that the flames from below hadn't abated.

Cain grabbed the edge of his tunic and yanked it over his head, leaving him in his kilt and boots. Ella's gaze raked over him, teasing him as if it were her lips delivering tantalizing kisses on his skin. "Och, lass, ye disarm me with a look."

"If that were true, I would not be here right now," she whispered. She was teasing, and he sent out another prayer of thanks.

He caught her face in his hands, his fingers

threading through her soft hair. "Tonight, I am at your command," he said and wondered if she'd ask for her freedom. He was an arse. If she did and he said no, which he must, she would pull away. Before he gave her a chance to think, he swept her up again in his arms, pressing her against him so she could feel how much he hungered for her.

His fingers caught the end of her laces and he pulled, letting her stays loosen to slide down. Perfectly sized, round breasts pressed through the white linen of her smock, perched on the top edge of her stays. Releasing the bow at the lace edge, the smock loosened, too. He kissed her as he worked his hand across her, the heat of her skin filling his palm.

Ella moaned as he lifted the fullness of one breast, her voice loud in the silent room. The sound struck a chord of desire in him so strong that he had to stop himself from throwing up her skirts and plunging into her lushness. But he wanted to tease out her pleasure, build it until she completely shattered in his arms where he could hold her as she experienced such joy. It was the most important goal in his world at the moment.

Cain tweaked his thumb over the tight pearl in the center, plucking gently at it. She raised on her toes to rub herself against his jack, which strained to be released from his kilt. His lips moved from hers to trace a path along her jaw and down her neck, and he heard her heavy exhale. She gasped softly as his mouth closed around her nipple, and he swirled his tongue across it, sucking it between his lips. His teeth grazed it, and then he soothed it with a kiss. Ella arched her back with the exquisite torture. She was everything desirable, and he wanted to bring her pleasure greater than anything she could even imagine. It was his goal, his wish, and his most ardent prayer.

She pulled back, and he lifted his head. Ella stood bare to the waist, her stays catching there with her smock. Straight slender shoulders and arms framed her pale breasts. At that moment, Cain wanted nothing more out of life than to bury his face in their fragrant valley and listen to her sighs of pleasure mixed with the beat of her heart.

Her fingers plucked quickly at her ties until the whole heavy costume slid down her form. He held his breath as inch by inch, her glorious curves were exposed to his sight, her gown and smock sliding past her hips to land in a puddle on the floor.

He walked up to her, not touching her but using his eyes to caress her. "*Àlainn*," he said, his voice raw with hunger. Lowering down before her, he untied her boots. Touching only her fingers, he helped her step out of them. Free of the confines of her costume, Ella stood before him, completely bare and exquisite. "Och, Ella," he said. "Ye are a goddess before me."

He let the fire burn in his gaze as he met hers, and her damp lips opened again as if she needed more air or his air. Stepping in to her, he spanned her back with his hands. She stiffened as his fingers touched the raised marks of scars there. He leaned in, kissing her as he tamped down the rage that rose up instantly within him. Her father was a bastard to beat this clever, brave woman, his own daughter. People whispered about Sinclairs being monsters when Alec Sutherland was worse than one.

Ella lifted fingers to his forehead, rubbing there as if lines of worry had etched into his skin. "They do not pain me any longer," she whispered. "And my tormentor is rotting in Hell. Do not bring him into this room with your anger." She worked the muscles of his shoulders, and he realized that he had stiffened, too. "Make me forget everything except this between us," she whispered, her words like magic, clearing his mind of everything but the beauty of Ella.

Her fingers went to the belt holding up the length of plaid wrapped around his hips. She tugged, and his hand fell over hers, making her pause.

"I have almost lost my mind just holding ye, Ella. Your touch will take what little I have left to stop if—"

She reached up to kiss him, halting his words. "Too late," she whispered. "I have lost mine already. It is Midsummer Night, and I will not share you this winter." She pulled his face back down to hers, kissing him, her mouth opening eagerly.

Damn Joshua. Was she doing this all because she didn't want Viola in his bed? It didn't matter. She was to be his wife anyway.

Ballocks. It did matter.

"Lass," he said against her lips and pulled back again. Bloody hell, his discipline strained at its limits. "Joshua set Viola on me to make ye jealous and then told ye about her."

He stared down at her as he drew a ragged breath. Lips wet, hair raked through, running in wild waves over her bare shoulders. If she sent him away, he'd be in pain for a bloody month.

"Honesty?" she said, her face tilting to the side. Her eyes softened as she studied him. "Not something I expected."

She thought he lied? About what? Surely not his desire for her. He frowned but then lost his thought as she yanked the belt loose at his hips. The heavy wool and leather belt thumped onto the floorboards, but she did not look down. Instead, she gazed up into his eyes, a slight smile on her lips. "And I already guessed that."

• • •

The beard on his jaw was trimmed, and she slid her palm along it. He followed her gentle tug, descending in a swoop much like his falcon, to capture her lips again. For that's what their kiss was, a capture, both of them caught together in the tangle of passion threading them together.

Wrapped up in the fire spreading through her, Ella did not think about anything but Cain and pleasure. It was like the strongest whisky, carrying away all damning strategies and plans for revenge and escape.

Ella's fingers slid over the contours of his muscular chest, sprinkled with hair, so different from her own body. She stroked the ridges of his stomach and grazed the skin of his back. He tasted of honey ale, and his palm cupped her cheek, tilting her face.

He moaned against her lips and lifted her against his jack between them. Hard and insistent, it pressed against her abdomen, making her heart hammer.

She had never been one to run away from the unknown, and the fire within her pulsed, making her even braver. Her fingers slid down his chest as his hands slid over her arse, stroking her curves. Pulling her hips back enough to allow room, she glanced down.

Holy Hell. His jack stood up long and hard. There was no uncertainty about its power to conquer a maiden. But instead of making her shrink away, the fire inside her flooded downward, making her throb.

He tipped her chin up with a finger, his mouth devouring any concern she might have. Their hands and mouths grew frenzied, and she grazed her fingernails across his taut arse. It was as hard and sculpted as the rest of him.

He growled something Gaelic in the back of his throat. "Bloody hell, aye," he said. No clothing stood between them. No barriers forcing them apart. They were together, united in their quest for the pleasure consuming them.

"Touch me, Cain." she whispered. "Touch me everywhere."

Calluses on his palms, from swordplay and training, teased the softness of her skin as he stroked her backside, sliding lower still. She was caught between pressing backward into his hands and rubbing forward against his hardness. But she didn't have time to consider the choice as he lifted her, setting her on the edge of the bed. It was high off the ground, so her legs dangled, spread apart around his hips.

She shivered as his gaze roamed over her bare breasts and stomach, down to the juncture of her legs. The only scrap of covering on her body were her white stockings, tied above her knees. The heat from his bold scrutiny fed her confidence until she cupped under her breasts. Cain's lips parted as he watched her squeeze them, pinching the sensitive nipples.

"Aye, lass," he whispered, the words spoken like a tortured hiss.

She lowered her gaze to his proud jack jutting upward between his rock-hard thighs. He was so large and strong, and she was so small and weak in comparison, but he didn't make her feel that way. His passion, so evident, made her feel powerful and beautiful. She slid her hands along her own body, pressing open her thighs. His gaze dropped as she touched the spot between her legs.

Cain sunk to his knees, sliding his hands up her calves, massaging the muscles as he watched her fingers. She'd never felt so exposed and open before.

"Och, Ella," he said. "So beautiful." He met her eyes. "Can ye trust me?"

And in that moment, she did. He was not The Sinclair, first bloody horseman from God to bring doom to her clan. He was not a man whom she was supposed to lure in and kill. He was Cain, the man who listened to her ideas, the man who had made certain she wanted him with total honesty, the man who teased the flames in her body. She gave a nod, and he lowered his face between her thighs.

Her breath caught in her throat as the wet heat closed around her, his tongue and fingers working together to bring even more delicious heat. She moaned, watching his head of wavy hair as he bent over her, stroking her, teasing her higher and higher. Her toes curled, and she propped one leg on his massive shoulder, feeling his hot skin in the arch of her foot through the fine weave of her stocking.

He growled, the vibration burrowing deep inside her. Working her most sensitive flesh, he spent long moments finding all her hidden pleasures, and her body began to tighten like a bow pulled taut. She lowered flat onto the bed, her fingers digging into the soft quilt.

"Oh God, Cain," she yelled as the pleasure built higher. He moved across her faster until a wave of heat lifted her up and crashed over her. "Oh God." Her moan filled the room as her entire body clenched, the waves of ecstasy rolling over and over within her. She was shattering, but she knew Cain would save her.

He slid up her body, wiping a hand over his parted lips before capturing her mouth again. He lifted them both across the bed sideways. Kneeling next to her, he stroked his hands down her legs to roll off first one, and then the other stocking. "Such beauty." He leaned over her, the size of his form blocking everything else, but Ella needed nothing but Cain. His mouth took hers in another kiss, and she moaned into him as his talented fingers found her again, teasing her sensitive flesh, which still throbbed with her pleasure. She thrust upward against his hand and raked the skin of his shoulders with her nails.

"So much fire," he murmured at her ear, causing more sensation to shoot through her, a tingling that ran all the way to the arches of her feet. She had never felt so alive with need before. If this was losing her mind to passion, she gladly welcomed it, craved it.

Cain's knee nudged her legs apart, and she complied willingly, spreading them wide. His muscles were taut, holding his body ready, every part of him toned and powerful. She lifted her mouth to his as she felt him seek her below and raised her knees on either side of his hips.

With a thrust, he rammed deep inside, splitting her maidenhead and burying himself. A lingering groan came from him as the sharp sting snapped her eyes open to fasten onto his rigid expression. His eyes opened to stare into her own. "I am sorry for the pain," he whispered, the words strained, dampness across his brow.

She shook her head. "A necessary consequence."

He remained still, buried deep, stretching her, allowing her body to adjust. "It will not always be so," he said, inhaling long, his jaw clenched.

"I know." She stared into his eyes, dark in the dim light. "Fire will burn it away." She pulled his face down to hers, her fingers tangling in his hair. She was completely surrounded and filled by Cain, his muscled arms mounded on either side of her head, his body warm against her nakedness. He slid his hand down to thrum her nipple, palming her flesh and kissing her. She squeezed and stroked his taut arse, feeling him inside her, and she lifted her legs to clasp his hips, opening even more as the heat grew again.

He groaned at her shifting. It must be torture for him to remain still. She lifted her hips against him, moving, and deepened her kiss. He slanted across her lips, his fingers trailing down her stomach and lower to find the sensitive spot between them, rubbing his thumb against it. Her breath came shallow, and her core clenched tighter inside her. Ella pushed upward toward the growing pressure, the flood of sensation she knew was coming and craved.

"Ye are well?" he asked against her.

"I am tormented." She cupped his face in both her hands. "Because you are not moving."

Cain needed no more encouragement and slid out and back in. The sting was nearly gone, the rekindled fire replacing it with hot desire. Slowly at first, they began a rhythm, the steadiness of it building faster as their kisses became all-consuming. Ella's fingers dug into his shoulders, and his hands stroked her body, tweaking and teasing, finding all her secret spots that sent more sensations shooting through her.

Ella panted against him, lost in the inferno. His hugeness raked along her, sliding over and inside her as if he was infiltrating her very soul. "Cain, oh God," she yelled out, the shout of her words in the quiet of the room making the passion soar upward until waves of fire toppled her over the edge once more. "Yes!" she yelled and heard Cain growl, his voice rising louder than her own as his body shuddered, ramming into her. His eyes were squeezed shut, his jaw hard as he yelled out his release. Raw, honest passion sat in the lines of his face, and her heart flew along as she watched him.

Cain's eyes opened, and he met her gaze, the waves of ecstasy still rolling through her. "I am yours," he said through gritted teeth. The words were an oath that pulled at her heart even more than the joining of their bodies, even more than the waves of pleasure rolling through her.

"I am yours," she repeated back, because in that moment, with them joined together, honestly giving everything to each other, Ella was his completely.

And she regretted nothing.

CHAPTER SIXTEEN

Cain had never felt such regret in all his life. What in bloody hell had made him ask Ella about her unique riding skills that morning? She stood upon her horse's back as the beast broke into a canter, making her long braid swing across her straight back.

He'd ridden into more battles beside his brothers than he could remember, knowing that there was the slim possibility that one of them wouldn't survive. But watching Ella stand, her knees bent slightly to take the roll of her horse's gait, as she balanced on her specially made saddle, made his breath catch in his tight throat. Fists clenched at his sides, Cain watched for signs of unsteadiness. Someone stepped up next to him, but he didn't take his eyes off her as she somehow signaled the horse to turn in a gentle arc to ride back.

"Impressive," Joshua said, his usual sarcasm absent from the compliment.

Ella kept her balance while slowly pulling her bow around and nocking an arrow along the catgut. Cain couldn't answer or look at his brother while he watched, frozen to the ground. For a moment, she aimed the arrow at him, but tipped it slightly to the side. Her arrow whizzed past him, embedding in the side of the barn at his back. She lowered the bow, a frown on her face, although the shot was very good. His arms came up on their own as if to catch her if she fell but then dropped helplessly back to his sides.

She slowed near them. "It gives me a higher vantage point." Her breath came quickly. Still standing, she wiped her brow.

"It also gives the enemy a bigger target," Cain said. "And if your horse spooks or wobbles, ye are dead."

Her mild frown turned into a glare.

"Well, *I* think it is a hell of a good show," Joshua said. "And if I saw ye in those tight leather trousers riding at me in battle, I would definitely lose my focus enough for ye to pierce my heart straight through." He thumped a hand over his heart and smiled roguishly.

Damn. His brother could turn anything into a stroke of wit. No wonder he had lasses falling into his bed. Cain's teeth clenched together until his jaw hurt.

Ella lowered into the seat, and Cain was able to draw a full breath. She secured her bow and quiver on special hooks worked into the back of the saddle. "I stand so that my men can see my signals clearly," she said. "And if I need to fire at an advancing enemy, I am able." She met Cain's gaze. "It takes honed balance and skill, along with talent that is nearly impossible to imitate."

Joshua laughed loudly and hit Cain's shoulder. "I would love to watch my brothers try and fall on their arses. I am already commanding enough while seated in my saddle, lass." He looked pointedly to Cain. "And from Cain's murderous face here, I am guessing he has some words to trade with ye." Joshua turned and strode off, whistling.

Ella stared at Cain, her head tilting to one side as

she waited.

"'Tis dangerous," Cain said, keeping his voice as light as he could. "I would have ye sitting on a horse so ye cannot fall."

"Gilla will not let me fall."

"Gilla might catch her foot in a hole."

Ella frowned at him, her eyes narrowing. "I have been riding like this my whole life, Cain, and I do not plan to change just because I will be your wife."

He did not retreat from her stare. "There is compromise in a strong marriage."

"I am agreeing to marry the man who was labeled an enemy. 'Tis compromise enough."

Blast it. He would not win this argument right now, and he hated to cause a rift after the night they'd spent together. He walked up to the horse, reaching to pull Ella down into his arms. She was stiff as she reached the ground. "I do not want ye to be hurt, Ella," he said softly, his palm sliding gently along her cheek to catch a few of the curls that had escaped her braid. She still frowned, but even the furrow across her forehead was enticing. He ran a thumb along the lines to smooth them away.

Lord, how he wanted her. The softness of her shape, the tease of her fingers tangling in his hair, the scent of her; it all called to him. He'd thought last night would appease his appetite for her, but the more ways he discovered to make her sigh with pleasure, the more he craved her. He had explored every hill and valley of her body, but he wanted to learn the mysteries of her thoughts, her desires and dreams. It was maddening. It was glorious.

Cain pulled her tighter against him, feeding off

her response. It was the middle of the morning, and he had warriors to train. *Daingead.* "I want nothing more than to carry ye back to our bed and make ye moan my name," he said.

She rubbed her damp lips together. "But you have responsibilities in the light of day."

Was that why she frowned so? "Aye," he answered.

"Chief!" Thomas came running from the open gate out of Girnigoe's first bailey, his short legs seeming to have trouble keeping up with his upper body. The look on his face made Cain reach for his sword. Ella pulled away to run for her horse, grabbing her bow and quiver off the back. Aye, she was a good match for him.

Spotting Thomas running, Bàs jogged out from a group of men he was working with in an adjacent field. He halted next to Ella as Thomas reached them, his face red above his bushy beard. "He is gone, the cell…relocked, but he is not in it," he yelled between pauses to draw breath.

"Hew Mackay is missing?" Cain asked, his gaze scanning the fields above them. "How long?"

"Last meal of turnips and bread was at dusk last night," Thomas said. "I went down just now and saw a lump under his blankets." He stopped to draw in more air. "Made to look like a sleeping man, but I noticed the key was oddly hung on the spike across from the door. The door was locked again when I pushed on it, but I went inside to investigate."

"Good attention to detail," Ella said, making Thomas's shoulders relax, and he finally slowed his breathing.

"Continue," Cain said, and the man's eyes went wide.

"I pulled back the blanket on the bed to see that he was indeed gone," Thomas finished. "His food from last night was eaten, and his piss pot was—"

"Lead a group of ten warriors to Varrich Castle," Cain said to Bàs. "If the bastard shows his face, demand his surrender or the cost I determined for his freedom." He looked to Ella. "The bride price that ye forfeited."

"They will capture or kill your men," Ella said, caution in her voice. It warmed him. Did she no longer see Sinclairs as the enemy? Could one night in Heaven do that?

"Not with Bàs leading them," Cain said, his gaze turning to his lethal brother. Just like himself and his other two brothers, Bàs had been trained from the cradle how to win against all odds. He used perfected skill, intimidation through reputation as the harbinger of death, and clever strategy to predict enemy maneuvers and response.

Bàs gave a nod, and Cain turned back to Ella as his brother jogged toward his practicing men. "He knows not to enter the castle gates without our armies surrounding the place. We need to know if Mackay is hiding or flaunting his escape."

"Maybe he will send out the recompense," Ella said, though the heaviness in her eyes spoke her thought that Hew Mackay wouldn't give in so easily.

"Thomas," Cain said, without taking his gaze off Ella.

"Aye, chief?"

"Determine how Mackay left his cell with a key

that was two yards away."

"Aye," Thomas said and hurried back toward the keep.

Ella's eyes opened larger as she came to the obvious conclusion. "He had help," she said low. "From within Girnigoe."

Her surprise, even without the knowledge that she'd never left his awareness through the festival and all night long in his bed, told him that she wasn't involved. Her fury at her once-betrothed during the oath ceremony had not been an act.

She turned toward the castle, her face pinching. "Have you seen Hannah today?"

"Nay. She usually helps Merida."

Ella nodded absently, her gaze still scanning the grounds. "Are there any horses missing?"

Cain raised his hand to Keenan, who was serving as watchman in the tower that morning. The man disappeared to reappear on the ground, where he jogged out and up to him. Keenan nodded to Ella.

"Hew Mackay has escaped our dungeon," Cain said. "Question the night watch and have the herd leaders get a count of all their horses to see if any are missing. The bastard wouldn't leave on foot if he could ride."

"Aye, chief." Keenan jogged away.

Ella secured her bow over her shoulder. "I will find Hannah."

"Ye are worried about her?"

Ella's lips parted and closed twice before she spoke. "Just something she said that makes me worry that she was developing an unrealistic view of Hew Mackay."

Hannah? Cain couldn't imagine his timid sister going anywhere near a prisoner, but at her words, he felt the prickle of instinct crawl along his muscles. His fists clenched. "Find her."

The men from the training field gathered behind him, and he turned to their grim faces. "Mackay has escaped. Bàs is riding to see if he returned to Varrich. Make certain your swords are sharp and your horses are rubbed down." He looked across the moor where Bàs led his group into the forest to the west. "Prepare for war at my command."

• • •

Ella kept her steps reined in as she strode across the inner bailey and into the keep. Merida would be in the kitchens, since she planned to make more herbal cures this morning.

Ella trotted down the walkway at the back of the great hall, her fingers sliding along the rough stone. The smell of steaming comfrey and garlic grew in the air the closer she got to the kitchen. She practically flew through the archway into the wide room, the far hearth fired up under two black caldrons.

"Merida," she called and stopped to catch her breath as the woman turned toward her. Sweat coated the older woman's face, her hair damp and frizzy like a cloud about her head. She held a wooden paddle like an upraised sword and frowned.

"Lord, girl, ye gave me a start," she said, lowering the makeshift weapon. Before the cauldrons, she did look like a witch making stew from bat wings and infant hearts.

"Have you seen Hannah this morn?"

"Nay."

The word cut through Ella, making her heart squeeze. Had the girl been tricked into thinking Hew Mackay was honorable? Had she not done enough to dissuade Hannah when she mentioned him before? "Where does Hannah spend her mornings?"

Merida shrugged, but her features had sharpened as she picked up on Ella's simmering worry. "Here and there. Stroking her horse, picking wildflowers, helping me with cures for the village. She's never been given an occupation to keep her busy, what with my brother barely acknowledging her existence. Now that he is gone, she is likely dancing about in her freedom." She set the paddle down and wiped her red, moist hands on the apron tied about her middle.

"Hew Mackay has escaped from the dungeon sometime last night or this morn." Ella met Merida's gaze directly. "And he had help from within Girnigoe to do it."

"Bloody hell," Merida murmured, and rubbed her jaw. "Hannah would not have left with him, even if she did give him the key. Her heart does not hold such adventure." She shook her head.

"What if he did not give her a choice?"

Wise, hard eyes met Ella's gaze as they stared at each other. "*Cac*," Merida whispered, her hands curling into fists in the gather of her apron. The two of them turned, hurrying to the corridor out of the kitchens. "Tend the kitchen fire, Esther," Merida called to a passing maid.

"I will check her room and the great hall," Merida yelled as Ella veered off toward the back of Girnigoe.

She ran through a hall adorned with pikes and swords and poked her head into the chapel. The heavy silence halted her, and she gazed at the stained-glass windows. Sun shone through pictures of the birth and death of Christ on the eastern side. Several statues of angels and horses sat behind an inset pulpit where a broad rendering of the four horsemen hung in brilliantly colored glass. Ella hurried down the line of pews, glancing in each as if she might find Hannah dozing. She was not. "Mother Mary, help us," she murmured.

If Hannah was with Hew Mackay, what would he do to her? Force her to marry him to gain a tie to Clan Sinclair? Demand ridiculous riches in exchange for her life? Demand Cain trade Ella for his sister? *I would survive Varrich better than she.*

Ella ran out the other side of the chapel, questioning every warrior she met along the way, but none had seen her. Turning on her heel, Ella strode back through the chapel and armory, boots clipping on the various floors made of wood and stone. "Hannah," she called out, but no answer came from the dark corners and cool granite walls.

He was gallant to try to save ye. Hannah's words repeated in her head, and she surged forward. *Bloody hell!* She should have mentioned the comments to Cain, but she hadn't yet trusted him. Did she now? Dammit. There was so much she should tell Cain. *He is still the enemy.* But after last night... Was he? Guilt nearly made Ella double over. Guilt for enjoying the night more than anything she'd ever experienced. Guilt for not telling Cain what Hannah had said about Hew. Guilt over Kenneth's order. *Wed him and kill him.* How could she?

Ella ran into the great hall and stopped. Cain stood before his brother, Joshua, both of them grim.

"This was neatly tied in loops inside her horse's stall," Joshua said. "It is one of Hannah's. I gave it to her last Christmastide."

Cain snatched the blue ribbon, balling it into his tight fist. "He took her."

Joshua met his gaze. "Or she went willingly."

"She thought him gallant," Ella said, her face heating as both men pivoted around to stare at her. "I warned her that he has no honor, but she did not seem concerned. She has always felt protected here."

Cain shook his head, letting the ribbon drop down, the end pinched between his fingertips. "Hannah would not tie her ribbon. It is a message from Mackay that he took her." Cain grabbed a red scrap from his belt. He tied a knot in it and strode toward the door into the bailey without a word. Ella hurried after Joshua as he followed.

Stepping out into the sunlight, Cain yanked on a thick glove. His whistle pierced the air around them where groups of his men waited to hear his orders. The large falcon that followed his master in every battle swooped upward from its high perch inside the bailey walls to land on Cain's arm. He handed the red scrap and the blue ribbon to the bird and thrust him upward to fly.

"What is he doing?" Ella asked Joshua.

"The bird will circle until he finds our brother, Bàs, riding toward Varrich Castle. The red means that the Mackays are our enemies, and the knot tells Bàs not to act unless absolutely necessary to save his men's lives. Cain will not be made to act rashly. He will strategize first. The ribbon will tell Bàs that Hannah is involved."

Cain strode over to her. "Tell me of Varrich. Where would he keep her?"

"I can tell you on the way," she said, striding toward the gate to find Gilla, who was still saddled.

He caught her arm, pulling her around as if she'd suddenly been tethered to an iron chain. "Nay. Ye will stay at Girnigoe," he said, his face unmoving as granite.

He was stubborn, but he was not plagued by the guilt Ella felt at not warning Hannah further about the dangers of getting too close to Hew. She must help fix this. "Hew wants an alliance, either with Clan Sutherland or Sinclair."

"I will never agree to an alliance with that *blaigeard* wielding the chief's sword," Cain said, his words breaking through the clenching of his teeth.

"If he figures that out, he may kill Hannah in retaliation," she said and stepped up before him to stare into his fierce face. "I can talk him out of harming her. He has listened to me in the past. If you charge in there, Hannah will suffer."

"He hasn't the ballocks," Joshua said, walking up next to Cain, his arms crossed over his chest. Both men stared down at her, the promise of Hew's end etched into their faces. The Mackay chief was a fool. By taking Hannah, he had won himself an early death.

Ella shook her arm loose from Cain's hold. "He is not the true ruler of Clan Mackay. He is a foolish poppet, and the one who pulls the strings might be cocky enough to provoke a war."

"Randolph Mackay?" Cain asked.

She nodded.

"He has eyes like a rat," Joshua said.

She walked backward toward the gate, her gaze still on Cain as he stalked after her. "He whispers in Hew's ear. If Hew doesn't have the vileness to kill an innocent girl, Randolph does."

Hew Mackay may have planted a bruising kiss on her, but it was his advisor who persuaded Alec Sutherland to give his daughter to Hew. She was certain that devious plans lurked behind the advisor's dark eyes.

"Fok," Joshua cursed, his hands going to his hair. "Hannah is an innocent. We should have continued to lock her in Girnigoe for her own good."

Ella stopped, planting hands on her hips. "If Hannah had been given proper instruction from her family on how to spot lies spouted by devious men, she would not have fallen for Hew Mackay. Ignorance breeds folly. Locking someone away does nothing but make them want to escape."

"Enough," Cain said, clearly impatient to leave. He looked at Ella and then beyond her to her horse, his gaze full of warning. "Tell me about Varrich. I will bring her back, and ye can educate her about liars and scoundrels."

"I am coming with you," Ella said.

Cain's rock-hard gaze met her own. There was not a single twitch to show he would back down.

"Hew Mackay wants ye. I will not put ye in danger."

She narrowed her eyes, trying a different tactic. "You would put my safety before that of your own sister?"

Instead of Cain reeling back at the insult, his lips softened the slightest amount, as if he would laugh if things weren't so dire. "Ye have skill with strategy yourself, Arabella Sutherland, but I am not falling prey to it." He turned on his heel, his back broad and muscular as he walked away, holding his heavy sword in one hand. "I have no need of Varrich's details. I will tear it apart stone by stone to reclaim Hannah." He turned to look back at her from the doorway. "And ye will stay safely within the walls of Girnigoe." He snapped his fingers at Thomas, who ran toward the gate, planting his bulk in the middle of the open archway.

As Cain and Joshua left the bailey, Merida flew from the keep's doorway. She panted, shaking her head at not finding Hannah within. Ella turned back to the gate guarded by a nervous-looking Thomas, her temper boiling like the black pitch her father had once poured down upon those trying to breach Dunrobin. "Hew Mackay has her," she said.

"I saw the four herds of the horsemen gathering on the hill from the tower walk," Merida said, catching her breath. She exhaled a rush of air. "They all go to war at Varrich."

"Good," Ella said, yanking her gloves up her arms and narrowing her eyes at Thomas. "Then there will be no one to stop me from following."

CHAPTER SEVENTEEN

Cain leaned low over Seraph's neck as they raced the last league toward the Mackay fortress. In the past, Hew Mackay's father had formed an uneasy alliance with the Sutherlands, trying to combine their strength to attack the Sinclairs. Since the old man's death, a year ago, Hew had continued to court that alliance.

Was he changing tactics? There was no reason for the idiot to believe that wedding Hannah would bring about peace with the Sinclairs. 'Twas true that Cain and his brothers valued and cared for her much more than their father had, but he was a fool to think that Cain could be forced into an alliance by threatening her.

"*A cheannsachadh agus a mharbhadh!*" he yelled, raising his sword high in the air. *To conquer and kill!* His men repeated the war cry at the top of their voices. The thunder of hundreds of horses followed him and Joshua. The rest of Bàs's and Gideon's herds rode, too, divided behind them both. The vibration of power surged up through Seraph, making the horse toss his head in wild anticipation. If it were possible, surely his steed would snort fire.

Cain wore the damn crown that his father had forced upon him, because the look of the horsemen added power to their surge, bringing the biblical warriors of God's wrath to life. He would use every advantage in regaining his sister.

As the bulk of Varrich Castle came into view, Cain raised his arm in the air to halt the armies while Bàs rode toward him with his ten warriors. "She is there," Bàs said with his first breath, his death mask giving him an air of indifference even though Cain knew he must be ravaged inside. When their mother had died giving birth to Bàs, Hannah had taken it upon herself to act like his mother. Although she'd been very young, she had cared for him when he was ill and bandaged his scrapes without alerting their father. George Sinclair would not stand for injuries in his sons and would rail against them when they ailed. Bàs had been weak as a lad, and Hannah hid it, keeping him alive so he could become the unstoppable warrior he was today.

Bàs pulled his horse up beside Cain and Joshua, looking toward the castle. "She stands beside Hew Mackay as he yells down from the wall walk. He says she will wed him, but he does not allow her to speak."

"Does she look…like she wants to be there?" Cain asked.

"Fok no," Joshua said beside him, but Cain needed to know all the truths in this scenario to form a successful strategy.

The skull mask couldn't hide the confusion in Bàs's eyes. "She does not smile or nod. She stands straight like there is a blade lying cold along her spine."

The thought tightened every muscle within Cain's body. Why had God given them women to love? Sisters, mothers, wives who were vulnerable to attack and the rigors of childbirth? How strong and

invincible would he be if he did not care? But he
did.

"We will lay siege to Varrich," Joshua said. "We
have your pale army, too, Bàs, as well as Gideon's
army of black horses." He indicated the hundreds of
horses to the far end of the field. He looked to Cain.
"We but wait for your order to charge and bring war
down on these foking bastards."

Cain scanned the thick walls of Varrich where
Mackays stood along the walkway above. "If we
charge, will he slide that blade straight up her
spine?" he asked out loud. Neither brother answered.

This required a different strategy. One without a
frontal attack. Cain inhaled the cool air that still
lingered across the moor despite the sun burning
through the morning clouds. It funneled down
through him, calming his temper, his blood working
to bring him scenarios of attacks. He stared straight
ahead, but his mind created lists of advantages and
things that could hinder his success.

Chess games with his father were often won by
using a quiet attack to the side of the board. If
Gideon were here, Cain would let him negotiate a
way inside first to read the look in Hannah's eyes.
But his brother was in Edinburgh trying to uncover
any secrets Ella may have. *Damn*.

"We ride forward," Cain said. "The three of us.
And demand we see that she is safe. I must get her
down on the ground before us."

Joshua made a grunting sound that came from
the back of his throat. If it came to all-out war, Cain
would let him decide the movement, but when there

was a chance to win the day without sacrificing their sister, Cain would decide how to conquer this problem.

He raised two fingers high in the air, which brought the second-in-command in each herd forward. "Keep the armies ready for my signal," he said. "We will go forward first. If we cannot talk Hannah out of there, then we attack, pushing through the gates and killing all who stand at the walls so we can breach them."

"And once she is safe?" Joshua asked.

"We kill Hew Mackay, and those who defend him, at the first chance," Cain said, his words solid.

The brothers rode forward until they sat their mounts fifty yards from the wall where Hew stood next to Hannah. Her eyes were round and seemed to glisten, but Cain was too far away to know for certain if she wept. Fury beat at his reserve, but he held it off in order to work out the best plan.

"Hannah Sinclair," Cain called out. "Ye will come forward to greet your brothers."

"She is my betrothed," Hew said. He had bathed and wore a clean white shirt. It would become his death shroud.

"If she desires it," Cain said. "But I must speak with her here before me."

"She fears her brother of death will lop off her head for helping me escape," Hew said.

"An absolute lie," Joshua murmured, for Bàs's sake, since Cain picked out the obvious falsehood immediately. Hannah knew Bàs loved her and would never harm her; none of them would.

Hew leaned over the low wall. "I will consider

the price ye dictated for my freedom to be her dowry. We will be even." He placed his arm around her shoulders. "And we will be united. The three powerful clans of the north: Mackay, Sutherland, and Sinclair. 'Tis a perfect plan."

"Except I have not agreed to the wedding," Cain said, "and I am her guardian." He drew upon all his discipline to keep his voice neutral. To antagonize Hew Mackay further would make him take Hannah inside to horrors unknown.

Hew tilted his head, his eyes wide, which made him look like he'd lost his sanity. "Well, I would not be a very gallant betrothed if I were to let her return to her family who would execute her for her betrayal."

"We kill our enemies, not our family." Cain forced himself to smile.

Hew narrowed his eyes, searching his face, and glanced over his shoulder as if seeking counsel. Where was Randolph?

Cain's jaw felt like it would snap as he held his smile. "Come now, Mackay. I will not harm her here. Come greet us. Bring your men if you are afraid of me."

The easily maneuvered bastard frowned. "I am not afraid of you or the legend that your lunatic father created from his heretical ideas."

"I am going to slice him through," Joshua murmured low.

Cain kept his easy smile and rubbed his jaw to hide his words. "Not until Hannah is safely surrounded by us."

"Aye," Bàs said.

"Keep your archers aimed at us while ye bring her out," Cain advised, and threw his bow and sword to the ground at Seraph's feet. Both Joshua and Bàs dropped their swords, too.

"I will tear him apart with my hands," Joshua muttered.

"Put a damn grin on your face," Cain ordered through clenched teeth. "To lure him out with Hannah, we need to put him at ease."

"With four armies behind us?" Bàs asked.

That was unfortunate. Cain had been so angry that he hadn't thought it through enough to keep the armies back in the forest. He must now work with the way the game was set up. There would either be one death today or many that came with all-out war. For, once Cain let his brothers and his own temper loose, there would be nothing left of the Mackays of Varrich Castle.

Cain held up both of his arms. "See, we are unarmed. Do ye tremble so much that ye cannot come down? You have never struck me as a coward, Mackay."

"Bloody bastard." Hew turned, pulling Hannah with him.

As Hew and Hannah walked out through the archway, all the Mackay warriors along the wall raised their bows. In the middle of them, Cain saw Randolph Mackay step up as if he'd been waiting until now to show himself. He also held a bow, aimed directly at Cain.

Cain waited, taking in all the people and weapons in play. Men with arrows along the wall with Randolph in the middle. Hannah vulnerable with

Hew beside her. Mackay men behind her at the gates on the ground. Had the steward advised Hew to walk out on his own with Hannah? A chill along Cain's nape made him study Randolph. One wrongly aimed arrow, and Hew would be dead, leaving the way open for Randolph to rule. And he could blame it on the Sinclairs or any Mackay firing down.

Movement near the far wall caught his attention. He kept his face toward Hannah, but his breath fell hard into his gut. Ella, dressed in her black mask and black leather armor, stood silently up against the corner, out of view from the Mackays who watched Cain and his armies.

Bloody foking hell. He'd ordered her to stay at Girnigoe. She'd disobeyed him. Blasted woman was going to get herself killed! His fingers bit harder into Seraph's reins.

"Cain," Bàs said.

"I see her," he whispered.

"Fok," Joshua said.

Cain held his gaze forward. "Continue the plan."

Joshua shifted in his saddle. "Which is now…?"

Cain had planned to get close enough to snatch Hannah back, shielding her from arrows with the targe that was easily lifted from off his back. But now he had to worry about Ella getting caught in the crossfire.

"Be prepared to hand Hannah off to ride to Girnigoe when I retrieve her," Cain said, his words low on the breeze. "Then I will save Ella while ye two focus on any guards who are idiot enough to run out." Keeping his face forward, Cain watched her from the corner of his eye. She nocked her bow with an arrow, holding it ready before her but pointed toward the dirt below her boots. Did she see the men above her? They could fire straight down, piercing her skull through the leather hood.

"Hew Mackay is dead," Bàs whispered. "No matter what." The lethal words, coming from behind the skull mask, were not to uphold the legend. They came from Bàs's heart as the three brothers watched Hannah's glistening eyes. She stumbled across the beaten grass, a mix of fear, sorrow, and shame dulling her pretty face.

Hew stopped about five yards before them and met Cain's gaze with a smirk. "Anything happens to me and Randolph will shoot your sister first and my men will shoot all of ye."

"I would think ye would care more for your betrothed than your own life. Or do ye see our sister merely as a pawn to unite two warring clans?" Cain asked.

Hew frowned. "She helped me to escape Girnigoe. I love her for that, and soon she will earn my complete loyalty as my wife. As long as the Sinclairs leave Clan Mackay be, Hannah will remain healthy and happy here with me."

A small sound came from Hannah, and new tears flooded out of her eyes even as she stared straight ahead. Cain held his hand out from his side toward Bàs, stopping him from charging forward. Better her tears than her blood.

"I would speak to her alone," Cain said, slowly dismounting with his targe strapped to his back.

Hew shook his head, a stupid smile turning up his mouth as if he had the upper hand. He pulled her in to him but not quite in front. "Say what ye will to my betrothed here."

Cain needed Hannah completely in front of the idiot to block the arrows from the wall from hitting her back. He was not close enough to cover her before Randolph Mackay's arrow released. Would she know to throw herself out of its path? Damn their father for not giving her basic military training. Damn them all for ignoring her enough that she sought attention from a bastard enemy who could easily trick a naïve lass.

"She is not your betrothed until her brother, her chief, agrees," Joshua said, unable to keep the fury out of his voice.

In response, Hew pulled Hannah a little more before him like a shield. "She is mine," Hew said as if he were a child grabbing a prized toy from another. Hadn't Cain said the same when he'd captured Ella? The thought threatened to crush his neutral look.

Joshua growled under his breath, but he would wait for Cain's signal. Although the three brothers had dropped their swords, they each held no less than three other daggers on their bodies. The daggers could be whipped straight at Hew's heart before anyone above could release a shot, but Cain needed Hew to block Hannah from behind.

Cain allowed his features to coil into a hard look of lethal determination. His father had spread the rumor that Cain's brutal look could drop a hawk from the sky, stopping its heart in fear. At the moment, Cain's rage twisted so tightly within him that if Hew's heart stopped suddenly, it would not have surprised him.

Hew's hand bit tightly into Hannah's upper arm, and she winced but didn't cry out. He took a step back, dragging her, realizing that he was too vulnerable out there before Cain and his brothers.

"If ye drag her back with ye against her will," Cain said slowly. "We will dismantle Varrich stone by stone until we reach ye."

"I will slice your head from your shoulders," Bàs said from behind Cain, his voice controlled.

"And I will spit it on a pike to roast over a fire right here before your gates," Joshua said.

Their words did the trick, pushing panic up within the fool so that he pulled Hannah completely in front of him, using her as a shield before her brothers. The archers didn't have a clear way to shoot her now. But Hew, desperate as he was, revealed his blade, pulling it out to hold under her chin against the pale column of her neck.

"Stay back," he yelled. Hannah said nothing, but more tears leaked from her eyes. She looked at Cain as if beseeching him. Her lips moved. *I am sorry.*

"Ye need to release her now, Mackay," Cain said, but Hew shook his head, his eyes wild.

In Cain's periphery, he saw Ella slip closer to the gate along the wall, but he could not take his gaze off the blade against Hannah's throat.

What the hell was Ella doing? She was putting herself in jeopardy and distracting him from his mission. *Dammit.* Ella Sutherland didn't listen, and she was going to get herself killed, something he would not allow.

He could not even look her way without alerting those above or Hew that someone was creeping flat up against the wall behind him. Even with all his training and strength, Cain felt helpless, unable to act without dooming both women.

Ella slid, step by step, her braid catching on the rough stone. She was near the archway now where guards stood just inside. Did she know they were there?

"Do not move!" Cain yelled, both his hands raised as if to stop time and everyone within his sight. "Do not take Hannah through the archway where your guards stand armed and grinning at your folly. They laugh at their young, untried chief."

Hew hesitated at Cain's words, frowning.

"Come closer so we can discuss the union of our clans," Cain said, willing Hew to come within arm's reach and not look behind him where Ella stood beside the recessed archway.

Her mask covered the bottom half of her face, and her leather armor lay across her chest, but neither would stop a flying arrow nor a sword thrust. Ella slowly drew back her bowstring, raising her arrowhead, and Cain's strategic mind played scenes in rapid succession.

If she hit Hew's hand, sending the blade flying, Cain could hit Hew in the forehead with a thrown dagger. But the thrust to penetrate the skull would cause Hew to fall backward, thus exposing Hannah to Randolph and the archers above. Instead Cain would hit the soft tissue of his throat if Hannah ducked down, pulling Hew on top of her to shield herself. But he couldn't yell to Hannah to drop because Ella might hit her if Hew moved.

There was no time to do anything but react as

Ella let loose her arrow. It flew straight with lethal power. *Thwack!* It hit right into the back of Hew's head with such force that the tip broke through his forehead. Hew was thrown forward as Hannah instinctively pushed the knife away from her throat and buckled under the man's weight. She screamed as they both fell to the ground.

A volley of arrows flew from the wall walk, but Cain had his steel-coated targe, his gaze on Ella by the wall under several archers peering down the granite blocks. His shield before him, Cain scooped up his sword, running to pull Hannah from Hew's twitching body. She sobbed as he shielded her. His brothers ran forward with their swords to stop the two guards running out of the archway. Cain raised his fist, and the silence behind him broke into a roar as their four armies charged forward.

Flat against the wall, Ella held a thin buckler shield over her head. It would be completely ineffective against a crossbow shooting down at her.

"Cover Hannah!" Cain yelled to both of his brothers. As Bàs ran up before them, Cain lunged toward the wall, his boots eating up the distance. He gave three sharp whistles and Seraph ran the other way, out of the line of fire. The full force of the Sinclair armies was hurtling down the slope toward Varrich Castle. Three more Mackays ran out of the gates to swing at Cain.

Ella pierced one with an arrow, and he dropped to the ground as Cain met the downward strike of another guard. He must dispatch them quickly to get to Ella. Meeting the narrowed eyes of the large Mackay warrior, Cain yelled the biblical words his father had quoted daily to him, his lips pulled back in a raving snarl.

"I looked, and there before me was a white horse! Its rider held a bow, and he was given a crown, and he rode out as a conqueror bent on conquest." The man's eyes widened, and his fear cost him strength. Cain pushed him back and impaled him on the end of his mighty sword.

Cain ducked, yanking his sword free to spin in time to slice the arm of the second Mackay clean off. He dropped to the ground, screaming, as Cain ran to Ella. He slid against the wall and angled his own thick targe over them. "What the bloody hell are ye doing here and with a foking puny shield?" he yelled, anger and worry pounding through him.

"It was the only one I could carry with my bow," she shot back. Arrows flew down to pierce the earth around them as the Mackays took aim straight down the wall.

"Run with me," Cain ordered, taking her upper arm. But he didn't have to tug as she hurtled forward from the wall toward his line of seated cavalry. It was easily four hundred against the fifty who could fit along the wall walk. Would other Mackays run in from the village behind? So far none had shown up to defend their chief and castle.

Hannah stood in Bàs's arms, sobbing, as he shielded them behind the first line of cavalry. Joshua remained forward, ready to slice through any Mackay warrior who dared to come out from behind their walls. "Steal away a Sinclair, and find your clan slaughtered," Joshua yelled up from around his own targe, which had one arrow embedded in the front.

Cain pulled Ella behind a row of horses, his men creating a circle around them. He dropped everything, planting his hands on her slender shoulders, and bent to search the parts of her face he could see. Sweat moistened her skin, but he saw no blood. "Take off your mask," he said, and she reached up to pull the ties at the back of her head, letting it slide away from her face. "Ye are whole? Unhurt?" he asked, studying the smoothness of her flushed skin.

"Unhurt," she said.

His chest opened for him to draw a full breath. "Bloody foking hell, Ella! Ye could have been shot through," he bellowed into her face, his hands clenching her shoulders. He needed to lead his armies, his clan, but he couldn't let go of her, not here where she could easily die, her soft body vulnerable to every weapon. Even a horse could trample her.

Her face pinched into a glare. "If you had hit him from the front, he would have fallen back, and Hannah would have been shot from above." She threw her arm out toward the wall where more Mackays gathered. She leaned forward, yelling up into his face. "I had to shoot him dead from behind so he would fall forward. It was the best plan for keeping her alive."

"Dammit," he roared, releasing her to raise his fist to his forehead, rubbing there. His voice lowered to something close to normal. "I deduced the same." He dropped his hand and met her gaze, watching her eyes widen at his words.

His well-trained troops proceeded with lethal efficiency around them, their horses and warriors moving together with practiced precision. Several columns over, he saw the ranks open so that another warrior rode away from the battle with Hannah seated before him. Bàs ran forward, his war cry joining Joshua's as they attacked the now closed gate with axes while Gideon's archers kept up a continued firestorm upon the men at the top so his brothers could hack away large chunks of wood.

"Fire with the others or ride back to Girnigoe," Cain said to Ella. He grabbed her close, staring down into her stormy gray eyes. "But do not die." He held her there until she nodded. Pivoting on his heel, he ran to assist his brothers and his Sinclair warriors who had toppled a tree in the nearby forest to use as a battering ram.

"*Aon, dha, trì*," Joshua counted, and the men slammed the pointed end of the tree against the door. Cain threw his weight into the next hit, and the old oak planks cracked. Another three hits, and the log cut through…into iron bars. The portcullis was on the inside, a design that sacrificed their doors but kept them safe when they needed it most.

Mo chreach! With the added defense, the siege on Varrich would take longer than the day. Varrich was known to have a freshwater well within its grounds, and the Mackays had all of Ella's forfeited marriage recompense to feed them.

Arrows continued to fly overhead both ways as the three brothers and their men held their sturdy targes as a protective roof over their heads.

"Do we burn the village beyond?" Joshua asked, his dark face alive with vengeance.

"Horses and people will die," Bàs said, though his

voice did not lean either way.

Sard it. Would they kill Hannah's mare inside the castle grounds?

"They are Mackays," Joshua said. "And we will take the horses."

"Come," Cain said, and they dropped the ram, moving backward, shields held defensively, past the crumpled body of Hew Mackay to the line of Sinclair men.

Ella stood on the ground by Seraph. Someone had given her another full quiver, and she fired skillfully. Keenan stood on one side of her while another of his elite warriors, Gregory, stood on the other as if they were sentries. Her bowstring twanged powerfully enough to send the steel-tipped arrows all the way up to the men who ducked along the wall.

Cain pointed to the lead archers from the four armies who waited to hear his orders. "I will set fire to the battering ram with pitch-soaked arrows as well as to Hew Mackay's body." He turned to Bàs. "Send the first group from each army to set a ring of fire around the village, but they are not to strike any who flee nor set the structures on fire, only the trees or brush. Take any horses not guarded but leave the rest."

"Ye merely give a warning," Joshua said, his lips pulled back in a fierce grimace. He would obviously rather stomp the village into the earth. His thirst for war made him dangerous and merciless. A good chief needed to use reason and strategy.

Cain's gaze moved back to Ella where she shot her arrows, the rhythm of her pull and release efficient and graceful. "The Mackay people had no say in the actions of their foolish chief. I would punish the one who did." Cain turned to scan the wall and gatehouse, looking for the dark, small eyes of the man who had held the point of his arrow aimed at Hannah's back.

Bloody hell! Where are you, Randolph Mackay?

CHAPTER EIGHTEEN

The burn in Ella's arm felt familiar as she continued to pull and release arrows toward the Mackays. They were enemies now for holding a blade against innocent Hannah's throat.

Guilt sat in the pit of Ella's stomach. Why had she not said more to Hannah about Hew? Or told Cain about his sister's questions?

Because you were thinking about Cain; kissing him and killing him.

"Drink," Cain said, holding a flask across her arm so that she had to cease her constant barrage. She took the flask, tipping it to let spring water wash away the dryness along her throat and tongue.

Ella studied the hard lines of Cain's face. He was still angry at her, but there was no irrational bloodlust or craze in his eyes. There was much more to him than just a warring chief who pretended to be the biblical horseman of conquest. *Yes, he also has deliciously warm skin that tastes of sin*, she thought and forced her gaze back to the battle before her, raising her bow.

Wed him and kill him.

She had killed a vicious scoundrel today. Hew Mackay deserved to die. But could she possibly kill the man who had been honest with her last night, loving her unselfishly with everything he had? The man who risked death and sent his armies to save his foolish sister, obviously forgiving her for helping an enemy escape? Earlier, in the training ring, she had held her arrow briefly pointed at Cain, and the pain of remorse almost made her lose her balance on Gilla.

"Where is your horse?" Cain asked.

"Inside the forest line up the hill," she said, tipping her chin in that direction.

Cain signaled one of his warriors. "Find her mount and take it back to Girnigoe." The man nodded, turning to ride toward the distant hill. Would he make her walk back in punishment or ride with her before him?

Cain nodded to one of his men who held some arrows tipped with black pitch. "I declare war!"

He hadn't taken the time to put on a shirt when he rode from the training field to find his sister. Black lines crisscrossed his upper arm, stretching with the muscles working under his tanned skin as he lifted his arm to raise his bow.

The warrior handed him a pitch-soaked arrow to nock. Cain's massive biceps mounded as he pulled back the catgut, and the warrior lit the arrow. Ella knew that Cain was not sent from the Christian God, but Lord, he looked as if he were chiseled by the Greek gods she had read about. From a block of flesh-colored marble to represent the immortal power of a warrior from ancient lore. The sight of his strength, added to the rush of battle, mixed inside Ella, making her mouth go dry and the fire within her ignite as it had the night before.

Cain's shot flew, hitting the center of the battered door, the pitch flaming up the oak. His second arrow hit the crumpled mass of Hew Mackay.

"It is done," Cain said. "We are at war with the Mackays."

"What makes a better warning," Joshua said, his face still full of wrath, "is tearing through that door and portcullis to rip out their hearts by yanking them up from their screaming throats."

Cain frowned at his brother. "That is not even physically possible."

"Give me a Mackay, and I will see it done," Joshua said, never taking his gaze from the burning castle door.

Cain raised his fist high in the air and moved it in a circle. Within two heartbeats, the entire remainder of the four armies turned. Ella watched them gallop back across the moor toward Girnigoe, one row at a time moving out in precision. With cavalry trained so well, there would be no way her Sutherland warriors could beat them. She was going to lose her clan for certain. But what if she could convince him to follow the plan that she and Kenneth had created twelve years ago? That would require her telling him about Jamie, something she swore she would not do.

Cain looked to Joshua. His hard face was red and condemning. "I will meet ye back at Girnigoe by morning," Cain said. "I will give my strategy for subduing the Mackays then."

Joshua cursed low. "Ye are going to the loch."

"Aye," Cain said without further explanation.

He caught Ella's hand. "Come." Anger weighted the word, and he pulled her behind him to his horse. Without warning, he lifted her into the saddle. Ella's gaze landed on the still-flaming body of Hew Mackay. She grimaced and scanned Varrich's wall. Who would take over the chieftainship of the Mackays? She almost snorted at the absurd question. Randolph Mackay had likely planned this from the start.

Cain's large form mounted behind her, and her backside slipped easily to sit between his rock-hard thighs, his kilt bunched up between them. Those muscular arms, which she'd grown to crave last night, came up on either side of her own. They wheeled around, cantering easily toward the trees. She could smell smoke on the breeze coming from the village as the muted sun shone down, and they cut through the waving wildflowers and blooming thistle. It would take them over an hour to ride back to the northern castle on the sea.

"We do not ride directly to Girnigoe?" she asked as they veered off from the armies.

"Nay," he said, and she could hear the tension in his voice.

Ella turned her face toward the billowing smoke rising over the trees that wove through the village. Hopefully, for the sake of his people, Randolph would take note of it and stay well away from the Sinclairs. If Joshua was to sway his brother to order a full attack, Ella doubted that a single part of Varrich or its village would survive it. Just like Dunrobin if her people chose to fight.

Cain's horse moved like a steady breeze, smooth with a gentle rolling, and he leaned in to Ella's back. With her leather armor thrown over her training shirt, she couldn't feel the heat of his skin, though she imagined she could.

After nearly an hour of riding, they entered a

forest. "To where do we ride?" she asked.

"Loch Hempriggs." His voice was still gruff as if he tried to tame his anger. Ella knew the warning signs of fury, but unlike her father, Cain would not strike her.

Seraph weaved a path through the trees, and Cain passed Ella his water flask. Wiping the grime from her mouth, she spotted the lowering sun through the canopy of leaves. The gold showered them in dappled light. The leaves of the summer forest cast Cain's horse in green so that it looked to be dyed like Bàs's horses before a planned battle.

"Ye did not obey my order to remain at Girnigoe," Cain said, his voice like distant thunder. "Did ye kill Thomas, then?"

She glanced at him to see if he jested, but his gaze remained outward, focusing somewhere over her head. Should she reveal that Merida had helped trick Thomas into the tower room without a key on the inside?

"I did not kill him. He acted valiantly to try to stop me," she said.

Cain snorted. He leaned in to her back, his warm breath near her ear, causing tingles to rush down her skin. "If ye were one of my warriors, ye would be flogged for disobeying."

She pressed her lips together, staring out over his horse's head. "I was responsible for not realizing Hannah's misguided feelings when she spoke to me about Hew."

The horse maneuvered around a wide bramblebush, exposing a small loch of calm water ahead. "Many of us were responsible for Hannah's mistake, but ye put yourself at risk today, something I will not allow."

Allow? The word tightened her jaw. "I am not *allowed* to help save a friend?"

"Hannah is a Sinclair, yet ye consider her a friend?"

"Yes," she snapped back. She shook her head lightly. The line between enemy and friend had blurred completely.

"I will speak with her when we return to Girnigoe." His voice held the faintest edge of torture, its rough tone a combination of checked fury and self-flagellation.

She spoke over her shoulder. "I will first. You might growl and scare her."

"I do not growl."

"You are growling now."

"Because ye bloody almost got killed," he said, his voice erupting as if he could no longer keep the tempest inside.

She threw her arm wide. "You ride out to battle all the time. You could be killed every day as you train and fight."

"Ye are a fragile woman."

She twisted in her seat and glared up into his face. "I might have to stab you for that comment."

He looked over her head. "Not fragile." He huffed. "Women are strong, very strong, but in ways of giving birth, not in slashing through warriors." He looked down at her. "And as for giving birth, perhaps it is too dangerous. My mother died doing it. Maybe we should not have bairns. Plenty will come from my brothers."

Ella's mouth dropped open as she stared at him. She blinked, not believing what she was hearing. His worry over her was making him lose his sanity. "Are you trying to tell me that I am not *allowed* to have a babe? As if you have control of *my* body!" she yelled. Even though the plan to kill him was becoming harder to imagine by the heartbeat, a new plan to kick him in the ballocks was becoming very clear.

"And how exactly will you stop that?" Ella asked. *Pompous ass!* To think he meant to tell her what she could or could not do with her body. No bairns? Her temper emboldened her, and she slid a hand up his kilt. He was already halfway hard. His jack was heavy and long. She grasped it, making it turn to granite under her fingers, and slid up and back down while she watched his jaw tighten.

"Ella."

"What?" she asked, stroking again. "Will you stop me from doing this so as not to risk spilling your seed in me? Will you keep me locked up so I cannot get hurt?" She moved her hand faster and watched him clench his teeth.

Flipping his kilt up, he caught her hand where it lay wrapped around him and leaned his face close to hers. "Ye have a power over me," he whispered, his voice a husky rasp. "I cannot allow ye to rob me of my senses. 'Tis too dangerous."

She yanked her hand away from his hold. "What does that mean? As if you have control over where I am *allowed* to go or what I can do, or touch, or even birth?" Her voice was high, full of indignant seething.

He dismounted, his hand on his rock-hard staff,

rubbing it through the wool to adjust it.

"Your beast will not stay appeased for long." She jumped down and walked closer to him. He took a step back as if the distance might make him better able to deny the passion that flared so easily between them. In her battle clothing of trousers and a small man's tunic, she was able to stalk after him easily. "I never thought to see the brave Cain Sinclair retreat from a fragile woman."

That stopped him. "Ella," he said, bracing his hands against her shoulders as she walked up before him. "Ye bloody hell could die, and…I will not allow that to happen."

He looked up at the trees above them and took a deep breath. "I think…" He swallowed. "If I was to see your pale, lifeless face, your perfect gray eyes still and unseeing…" He leveled his gaze with hers, and she glimpsed pain. "I would go insane like my da did when my mother died."

Ella's heart squeezed, her lips parted as she inhaled and exhaled with shallow breaths. "And I will go insane if you do not allow me to live." She willed him to understand with her eyes. "Cain, I have not spent twenty-six years surviving my father only to be controlled by a husband."

He looked up and away, a curse on his breath. She reached forward, letting her hands slide down his chest. "You forbade me to die when I demanded it, so let me live." She took a step back and unlaced the armor tied around her torso, letting it drop into the bluebells growing at her feet. She grabbed the edge of her tunic, jerking it up out of her trousers.

When she had donned her armor that morning,

she had not bound her breasts. With a lift of one arm, she pulled the tunic off, the summer air cool on her heated skin. As her arm came down, she yanked the tie from her braid and ran fingers through the mass of dark hair until it came down around her shoulders. The feel of Cain's gaze on her made chill bumps speckle her skin and harden her nipples.

"If your mind is running through strategies on what to do and worries about me being harmed, stop it," she said, untying her trousers. Tipping her hips side to side, she slid them down. When she bent to untie her boots, her ample breasts falling forward to hang, she heard him groan.

"Och, lass," he said. "Every bloody inch of ye calls to me." His words made heat wash down through her, a war against the coolness teasing her skin.

"Yet you resist the call because I could be hurt?" Standing straight, she lifted her breasts in her palms, squeezing her nipples, which were already hard pebbles of sensation. Out in the dense forest, she was exposed, but the tortured look on Cain's face and the tenting out of his kilt made her feel deliciously wicked. Her body remembered the peaks of pleasure they had enjoyed and wanted more.

His hand was openly stroking his jack where he stood, his eyes ravishing her so that she nearly felt his caress. Watching his strong hand wrap around himself made an ache grow low in the crux of her legs.

"And if ye get with child?" he asked, his teeth gritted.

"Then we will battle through it all together, Cain.

You cannot tuck me away in a little box. It will become my coffin."

His breath came out ragged. The distance between them that delayed their touching was tantalizing. Standing in the silent forest of greens and golds, naked, her hair sliding against her shoulders and back, the ends teasing the slope of her backside, Ella felt free like she had never felt before. She slid her hands down her body, and his gaze followed her fingers along every curve and valley. She stopped at the juncture of her legs, dipping her fingers there.

"*Daingead!*" The word came as a growl as Cain yanked open his belt, dropping his kilt. Within two strides, he was upon her, grabbing her up against all his hard muscles. His strength thrilled her, and she pressed into him, his massive jack between them. Fueled by their worry and anger, they clutched against each other, limbs entangled, fingers biting gently into each other. His mouth moved on hers, and she met him with her own brutal kiss, her lips already parted as she delved into him. Hands everywhere, stroking and teasing, Ella moaned into his mouth.

Her body was flushed, as was his. "The water," she rasped at his ear as she gently bit upon the lobe. With a lift under her arse, Cain fit her, straddled intimately, around his waist as he walked them to the water's edge. She hugged him tight, his body heat keeping her warm as he walked them into the loch, the cool water lapping at her thighs.

Breaking the kiss, Cain looked down her body as they clasped each other in waist-high water. "Bloody hell, Ella, ye are like a golden water nymph."

She looked down to see that the last rays of sun shone across her skin, casting her in dying sunlight. Her nipples were peaked with the coolness of the water, her pale breasts felt full and heavy under his gaze. She held his shoulders and lifted, bringing herself up so that he could suck a nipple into his hot mouth.

"Oh yes." She arched her back, as he loved first one and then the other. She began to rub the juncture of her legs against him under the water, and his strong fingers found her, opening her as she clutched him with her thighs.

"By the devil," Cain murmured as he moved back to her lips. "I will never be able to resist ye."

She kissed him and pulled back to smile wickedly. "Do not even try, Sinclair."

He sank backward into the lake. The lift of the water flooded around her, and she felt his powerful shaft seek her.

"I do not want to hurt ye after loving ye all night." He palmed the globes of her backside as he held her to him.

She reached down to stroke him where he hovered between her legs, making him groan, his eyes closing. The sound made her feel wild and powerful. She let her tongue slide inside his mouth, tasting and teasing. Trailing kisses to his ear, she touched the rim with her teeth gently. "I ache, Cain. Deep inside." She lifted and lowered herself against him again. "It is a fire." Her lips moved back to his mouth, and she spoke against his lips. She reached for him, guiding him to her. "Touch my fire."

With another deep groan, Cain wrapped his thick arm around her back, kissing her like a wild storm, and he thrust upward into her open body.

She gasped as he filled her, impaling her completely. Full, so incredibly full. She moaned against his mouth as he slid back and plunged inside again. "Cain," she said as he stroked, his fingers finding her sensitive spot to rub, sending lightning spiraling along her limbs. Clenching around him with her thighs and arms in the water, her nails digging into his shoulders, the fire grew within her.

His mouth lowered to suck again on her nipple, pulling it into his hot mouth, swirling his tongue around the sensitive peak, grazing it with his teeth. She gasped as the delicious suction spiraled sensation from their joining up through her entire body, piercing her soul. Panting, she whimpered as he worked on her below, making her body move faster against him as he lifted under her arse. "Yes, Cain! Oh God, yes!"

Head thrown back, Ella's world shattered as the heat erupted within her, her muscles gripping him in waves of flaming passion.

"Ella, I want ye always." His groan ripped through the stillness of the woods as he filled her. Ella wrapped her arms around his shoulders, clinging to his chest as they rode out the firestorm together.

• • •

Ella leaned into the warmth that Cain's body gave off and enjoyed the slow gait of his horse as they rode through the night toward Girnigoe. She could see the torches glowing far off as if they were stars. She sat sidesaddle up against him. "Let me talk to Hannah first," she said. "She respects you immensely. One cruel word will devastate her."

"I do not speak cruel words." The wind blew off the sea, carrying the smell of brine. "And she apparently did not respect me enough to trust my treatment of a prisoner." A bit of hurt edged his words.

Ella patted his fisted hand that rested on her thigh. "People, without a mission or passion in life, often act unwisely. We should help her find something about which to care. She's been told to disappear for so long, she hasn't a reason for existing. Having a reason for living makes one think about consequences before they act."

He caught a strand of her hair that flicked across her cheek, tucking it behind her ear as he looked down at her. "Ye are very wise, Ella Sutherland." His knuckle guided her chin toward him so he could stare into her eyes. "What reason do ye have for living that makes ye so?"

A round face, with laughing blue eyes and freckles from the sun, slid instantly into Ella's mind. She swallowed Jamie's name. "My people. My home." The familiar worry that she felt about keeping Jamie a secret was now awash in guilt. She needed to tell Cain about him, about how she strategized to meet with King James and secure Jamie's future. She opened her mouth, Jamie's name on her tongue.

Cain let her chin go and looked over her head.

"'Twas a terrible home," he said.

She paused and pressed her lips together. *Keep him hidden*. Holy Mother Mary, Ella yearned to speak with Kenneth. To what? Ask him if she could break her oath to her mother? Confess that she had fallen into bed with Cain, seduced the enemy, and in so doing had lost her convictions and would not be killing him? She turned forward again. "Not so much now that my father is dead."

"It can be your home again," Cain said. "I can rule both clans from Dunrobin."

His words tightened in her stomach. "Or…" she drew out. "I can continue to rule over my clan at Dunrobin, and you can lead the Sinclairs of Girnigoe." With Ella still in control of the Sutherland clan, she could pass the chieftainship to another Sutherland chief when the time came.

"I will leave Joshua to run Girnigoe. Or Gideon. Aye, Gideon would be a better steward. Joshua loves war too much."

She frowned, her head tipping slightly. "Where is Gideon? He did not ride to the battle, and I have not seen him since your oath-taking ceremony."

"He is riding south beyond Sutherland territory," he answered.

"Why?"

Hesitation weighted his words. "To obtain grain from the Campbells to make up for the burned crop. There is a distant link between our clans."

Ella watched the clouds move across the growing sliver of moon. Her father had raged once about the Sinclairs having discussions with the Campbells in the south. But something in the drag of Cain's explanation made her wonder if there was more to Gideon's mission.

Her stomach growled, and she reached into the leather satchel tied to his saddle. "I picked these at the loch," she said and held up a raspberry before popping it into her mouth. She found another. "Berry?" He opened his mouth, reminding her of the feel of it surrounding her nipple. The heat of him against her was making her wanton.

"I should return to pick some to bake into raspberry tarts. Do you like tarts?" She shifted in her seat, the tenderness between her legs reminding her of their intense passion. "For someone I am to wed, I know very little about you." *Besides knowing how my little nibbles across the skin of his chest and stomach drive him wild.*

"I like tarts," he said. "But my favorite treat is cake made with crushed hazelnuts and honey." He held his hand out before her. "With spiced pears on top." He made a motion like he was setting a pear down onto a cake by the stem.

"That is quite specific," she said, turning to look up at him.

He smiled. "It was my mother's favorite, so it became mine."

"How old were you when she died?" Bàs was the youngest, but she wasn't sure by how many years.

"Almost nine years. Old enough that I remember her the best. She loved anything baked and sweet. How old were ye when your mother died?"

Ella remembered sitting by Mary Sutherland's bed as she grew weak from giving birth. Her eyes looked like polished glass, round with wildness, as she demanded Ella's promise to do one last thing for her. *Keep him hidden. Do not give him to Alec.* She succumbed to fever while her furious husband drank himself into oblivion when they reported another babe had died right after birth. "I was fourteen."

"Did she die from illness?"

Ella sighed, remembering too well their argument earlier. "My mother was weak from losing many babies after I was born."

"She died from childbirth fever?"

Ella turned in her seat, using her finger to poke him in the chest. "There are many women who do not die during childbirth."

He exhaled long. "Aye." She looked out over Seraph's head.

"I am sorry about your mother," Cain said. She felt his knuckle gently brush down the side of her face. "To leave ye alone with that monster. If I had known, I would have stolen into Dunrobin and taken ye away."

"And I would have likely stuck a *sgian dubh* in your heart," she said. *Wed him and kill him.* Was that how Kenneth thought she should do the deed? With a thrust to the heart? Her eyes squeezed shut at the pain the thought brought.

She sniffed. *Dammit.* She was the chief and did not need to follow Kenneth's orders.

Cain pulled his thick targe to set in front of her. "My shield is not puny like yours. I would have survived."

For a moment she couldn't remember what they were talking about. *Stabbing him.* She inhaled past the lump in her throat. "Tell me more about you, my betrothed," she said as they continued across the moor.

"Hmmm…" he said, pulling her in to his chest. "I have a herd of one hundred and twenty-eight horses, I have never lost a game of chess since I was sixteen years of age, and I hate wearing the crown my father had made for me."

He shifted behind her. "Tell me something about ye."

"I love sweet pies," she said, squinting to make out a few men walking in the pastures up ahead. "My heart hurts for any injured animal, so I tend to have many about my home." She glanced up at him. "I will be bringing a pack of dogs to the marriage."

"Boudica may not suffer that well," he said.

"And I like to carve. Kenneth showed me how."

"So ye can hollow out a knight without harming the outside."

She stared outward. "Yes."

"Perhaps ye could make some better chess pieces than my brothers and me."

Her mouth relaxed. "I likely can."

Looking back out, she saw several guards walking along the perimeter of the castle wall, torches set to light up Girnigoe. "Will your brothers be waiting to talk with you?" There were plans to be made about how to take Varrich Castle.

"Not until the morn," he said.

"Joshua did not seem like he would wait."

"They know I will not see them tonight."

"Why not?"

"I go to the loch to clear my thoughts and devise the best plans. When the stars come out, I watch them above, tracing the shapes. They help me stay calm and wise."

"You learned to stay away because your father bellowed a lot?" she guessed.

He chuckled. "Aye. At first, he would rage that I was not there, thinking I was running away from responsibility. But when I returned, I had plans he could use, strategies he felt were wise. His fury would calm, and it became my way."

"Joshua does not seem to appreciate your way."

"He storms like our father, but he knows I will devise a plan to conquer and find us victory. Every attacking foe has fallen to the Sinclairs. We have taken territory from ye, the Mackays, and the Campbells, expanding our dominion with little loss of life. It is what I was raised to do."

Her smile faded.

Conquering, everything and everyone—it was what he was raised to do.

CHAPTER NINETEEN

"We should still destroy the castle," Joshua said as Cain and his two brothers stood before the cart full of bags of oats and barley.

Cain read over the brief missive again. "Randolph Mackay says Hew acted alone, and that he would never condone the abducting of our sister or any Sinclair. They attacked because they were defending their castle. He's giving the grain that Ella paid in penalty for breaking the marriage contract as payment for the fields that Hew ordered burned, and he's returning Hannah's mare unharmed."

"If we destroy the castle," Bàs said quietly, running a hand down the black horse's long nose, "innocent people will be killed."

"Ye are supposed to want death," Joshua said. "Not talk Cain out of it."

Bàs's gaze narrowed as he turned toward his warring brother. "I do not want death. I but bring it to those who require a meeting with God."

Joshua snorted and turned back to Cain. "Hannah is still weeping."

"Ella is seeing to her, and I have already forgiven her poor judgment in unlocking the cell door." Cain's empty hand fisted. His sister had sobbed as she told him how Hew had asked her to help him make the bed look occupied, telling her how bonny she was. She had snuck him past the guards with her horse only to find herself gagged and abducted. If the man wasn't already dead and burned, Cain would indeed storm Varrich and drag the bastard out by his lying tongue.

"And what will Ella do to calm her down that tearing apart the Mackay castle will not?" Joshua asked.

"Ella had five words to describe her plan when I asked," Cain said, slicing open the first bag of grain. The barley looked dry and fresh without mold.

"A plan to stop Hannah's weeping?" Bàs asked.

"Aye." Cain moved to the next one of oats. They, too, proved to be good quality. The Sutherland fields must be well maintained, and their harvests accomplished with skill if these originally came from Ella's clan.

"Well, brother?" Joshua said. "Let us hear these five magic words that will stop our sister from filling Girnigoe with a flood of tears."

Cain couldn't help a small grin as he looked at Joshua. "Let us plan my wedding."

Joshua stared at him and then at Bàs who shrugged. "How will that cheer Hannah? 'Tis not *her* wedding."

Cain hefted one of the sacks to set against his shoulder. "Apparently, lasses like to plan any woman's wedding, and she was going to ask Hannah to stand as a signing witness along with one of ye."

"The banns are only two weeks old," Joshua said. "It cannot take place for another. What could possibly take that long to plan?" He picked up another sack, as did Bàs, and they followed Cain toward a place in the shade against the wall. His men would take the grain to a dry, cool cellar where it would be stored for use this winter.

"Ye two are already married in the eyes of God anyway," Bàs said, lowering the bag of barley.

"Bloody hell, Bàs," Joshua said with a wry chuckle. "I would be wed to at least half a dozen lasses if tupping tied one up in marriage."

Bàs murmured something that neither of them heard and walked back to the wagon for another bag of grain. Joshua watched him go and turned to Cain. There was a tightness to his brother's eyes. "If Da was here, he would lead us against Mackay now, while they fumble around for a new chief."

"Da is dead," Cain said, meeting his hard gaze.

"Aye, by the order of your bride."

"Nay, Joshua," Cain said, his hand fisting next to him. "He died by the lunacy and wildness that made him a mindless killer, without care for safety or much thought for strategy. And I am most certainly not Da."

Joshua came close, inches apart, to stare him in the eyes. "Ye were raised to conquer our enemies, not compromise and invite them into your bed."

Cain's hand shot out to grip Joshua's tunic tightly in a fist. "Ella is not our enemy, and I do not need to kill and burn our neighbors to ash to conquer them. And 'twas your push at the festival that helped send her to my bed."

Joshua threw his arm up to shove Cain's fist away, his tunic ripping, since Cain's grip was just as strong. "I hold no ire at ye for wedding Ella, but do not start letting a Sutherland rule your head."

"No one rules my head," Cain said, frowning.

"Sinclairs before all else, brother," Joshua said, as

if needing to remind him of his duty. "We must knock down all who dare to stand against us, Mackays to begin with and any Sutherland who tries to block our way when taking Dunrobin."

"Your bloodlust makes ye as thoughtless as Da."

"And your lack of action makes ye nothing like Da," Joshua said, his words full of rage. He pivoted on his heel and strode away, punching one of the sacks sitting in the wagon on his way by. Cain watched him stride out of the gate.

Bàs dropped a grain sack next to the others and straightened. "'Tis God's wisdom that sent ye to be born first, else Joshua would have us murdering all of Scotland," Bàs said and slapped a hand on his shoulder.

Cain's gaze slid along the strong walls of Girnigoe, walls his father and grandfather had built to show the strength of the Sinclairs. In the days when Sinclairs still had to defend themselves from sieges and raids, murdering and striking fear into the hearts of other clans was the way to show strength. But those ways cost many lives, lives that could be used to create a strong Scotland. Cain saw past the petty problems of foolish neighbors to the larger issue of land-greedy countries like England, France, and Spain. If Scotland continued to tear itself apart instead of unifying, there would be no army of Scotland left to defend her borders.

When Cain didn't say anything, Bàs continued. "Ye are nothing like Da," he said. "And I am furiously happy about that. I would wager a guess that Gideon is, too."

Cain looked at his youngest sibling. Bàs, with his

quiet words and deep eyes, as if he felt every strike he laid into another person. He nodded. "I am doing things differently, and Joshua likes the old ways."

"Send him to war in the northern isles while ye create alliances here," Bàs said.

Cain rubbed the back of his neck and turned toward the keep beyond the bailey wall. Day was ending, and he could see candlelight in some of the windows high up. One would be the window of his chamber where Ella took her bath. "Aye. Perhaps I should."

"Because right now," Bàs said, motioning to several of the guards in the bailey to help with the grain, "ye have a lass to see, one that makes ye smile more than I have ever witnessed."

Cain lowered his gaze back to him. "I smile?"

"Aye," Bàs answered. "I never thought ye knew how."

Cain laughed. "Little brother, it is a new world. One where Sinclairs do not massacre innocents, our sister has freedom enough to get herself into terrible trouble, and the chief smiles."

Bàs walked with him toward the keep. Perhaps his youngest brother would stay the night instead of riding off to his cabin alone in the woods. "I did not know our mother," Bàs said as they stepped through the entryway. "But, Cain,"—he stopped to look him in the eye—"I think she would smile, too."

• • •

Ella held the small block of wood in her hand, turning it one way and then another to compare it to the picture she studied in a book on chess she found in the Girnigoe library.

She'd been surprised at the three cases of books in the large room with tables, maps, and what looked like battle plans for taking over all of Scotland. Had Cain's father made him plan a complete takeover of the country as a practice in strategy, or had the lunatic actually thought that King James would allow the Sinclair clan to conquer his entire realm? The more she learned about growing up as a son of George Sinclair, the more she was amazed Cain was as sane as he was. Sane and passionate.

A blush warmed her cheeks as she thought of the last week after their night at the loch. Cain was more man than she ever thought she could handle. His largeness alone should intimidate her, but she had come to trust his gentle touch. He would never hurt her, and the more they explored each other and talked of life and the world, the more Ella could not imagine herself hurting Cain, either.

Wed him and kill him. The words tightened sharp knots in her stomach. "I cannot," she whispered in the room, her hands stopping as she held the wooden block.

There was also her plan to see a Sutherland control Dunrobin. What would happen to Jamie when she married Cain? "I must tell him." Guilt sat heavy in her middle.

What had made her hold her tongue this entire week? Fear? What would Cain do if she revealed the secret that she'd kept all these years? Would he listen like he had when they spoke on the moor under the stars about her ideas on strengthening

Scotland? Would he understand why the Sutherland clan must stay in her command to fulfil her oath to her mother? Her stomach fluttered with nervousness. Would Cain ever turn from his quest to win her land and people at all costs? *It was what I was raised to do.*

Knock. Knock. "Ella," Hannah's voice pierced the door of her chamber, startling her. Even though she spent most nights in Cain's bedchamber, Ella had kept her things in the Tower Room until the official wedding.

"Yes," Ella answered, setting the nearly finished queen down.

Hannah pushed into the room, Merida on her heels. "The gown is complete," Hannah said, smiling brightly.

"And just in time." Merida hurried forward. The wedding was planned for the next morning.

"It is beautiful," Hannah added, laying the rose-colored and burgundy dress on the bed.

The sound of horses clopping over the draw-bridge could be heard from Ella's uncovered windows, making Hannah dash over to look out. "We have more to celebrate," she said, turning to smile broadly. "Gideon has made it home in time for the wedding."

Gideon had been gone for two weeks. Ella strode across. "Does he have grain? He journeyed to Breadalbane to ask the Campbells for some, although it is not needed, since the Mackays paid the price for Hew's raid."

She watched Gideon ride over the bridge with a dozen Sinclairs but no bags of grain. The silence

behind her made an itch tickle her nape, and she
shrugged her shoulders, turning.

Merida frowned, her gaze meeting Ella's.
"Breadalbane, ye say?"

Ella nodded. "That is what Cain said when I asked
him."

Merida's lips formed an *O* before relaxing into a
frown. "I did not know."

Ella pulled Boo up from where she wiped her
face with her licked paw. "Let us take you outdoors,"
Ella said, following the other two ladies from the
room. She carried Boo down the stairs and set her at
the bottom. The little ball of fluff leaped after a leaf
and tumbled into the great hall to run toward the
entryway. Her antics made Ella smile, pushing off
some of the weight of her worry.

The vaulted room was silent as Ella walked in,
and she stopped, because it was not empty. Gideon
stood at the table opposite Joshua, Bàs, and Cain.
Merida and Hannah had stopped before Ella, and all
the brothers raised their gazes to her. All except for
Cain. He leaned forward, his knuckles planted on
the table before him, his broad back bent as if he
labored.

"Ye have returned," Merida said, breaking the
silence.

Despite the tension, Ella forced her lips into a
smile. She nodded to Gideon. He stood covered in
dust from his travels, a frown on his face. "Welcome
back, Gideon. You have made it home in time for
the wedding."

Cain straightened, turning to look at her. His face
had lost the happiness she had seen these past

weeks. It was hard again, like when he'd first brought her to Girnigoe.

Gideon spoke. "King James sends his regards, as does his queen, Anne of Denmark. She also sends her love."

Ella's chest contracted, her hand going to it as if her heart beseeched protection. *Holy Mother Mary.* He'd spoken to both James and Anne. "You did not go to ask for grain from the Campbells," she said. She should be angry about Cain's lie, but it was paltry compared to her secret.

Gideon's hard stare held judgment, his jawline tight. "Were ye planning to tell us after the wedding that Dunrobin and Sutherland lands would be defended by thousands of King James's royal troops in five years, or were ye going to let us find out then?"

Her heart thumped so hard in her chest that Ella wondered if they could hear it. She swallowed, unsure of what to say. Her mouth opened and closed, and her gaze drifted to Cain's hard eyes.

His brows were lowered. "Leave us."

Hannah scurried out of the room as if expecting an explosion. No one else moved.

"I said," Cain's voice grew, "leave me and Chief Sutherland. Now." The last word thundered through the hall.

Ella had been trained by a brutal father not to jump at bellowing, but the fury in Cain's voice as he used her title caused a shudder to run through her. *He will never harm me.* She breathed deeply. But would he harm an innocent boy? No, he had more honor than that.

His three brothers filed out with Merida, who

stopped to shake her finger at Cain. She did not say anything, but her reprimand was evident.

Cain turned to stare at Ella. "Ye have a brother. One who is twelve years old." The words came as if he were instructing her, although she was quite aware of all of it. She clasped her hands together before her as he continued.

"He is named after King James, and your mother was good friends with Queen Anne's mother before she was sent to wed Alec Sutherland." Cain's face relaxed into an apathetic mask as if he were reciting a history lesson.

"When Alec Sutherland died, ye traveled to Edinburgh where ye quickly became friends with Anne. With her help, ye met with James to ask for his assistance in making certain that your brother became chief of the Sutherland Clan. On his seventeenth birthday, James will send his troops to make certain that Dunrobin and Sutherland lands are in Jamie Sutherland's hands, or else he will use the power under his command as king to rout those who have conquered the Sutherlands."

He took two full breaths, and the silence in the hall pressed hard on Ella as she waited. "The full support of the crown," Cain said, "in exchange for Sutherland loyalty and because his wife's mother loved your mother." Cain crossed his arms over his chest and stared at her. "If the boy dies before he turns seventeen, then the clan, its castle, and its vast territory will be managed by whatever clan is strong enough to do so, as long as they are loyal to James."

If the boy dies…? Ella met his gaze with fire in

her stare. "Jamie is a sweet, beautiful boy. Do not kill him."

His narrowed eyes widened before the glare returned. Cain threw his arms wide. "Do not kill him?" he yelled, his words booming through the room. "Ye think I would execute a child, a twelve-year-old lad, who ye apparently have protected his whole life?" His hands went to the top of his head where his fingers grasped his hair, elbows pointed outward. "No one has even heard of Jamie Sutherland. My contact at Dunrobin knows nothing about Alec Sutherland having a son, an heir to his earldom."

Ella swallowed against the dryness of her mouth. "I kept him a secret," she said, her voice coming out hoarse. "My mother... Cain, it was her dying wish for me to keep him hidden until he grew old enough to be chief, strong enough to defeat his father."

"Alec Sutherland never knew he had a son, did he?" Cain asked.

She shook her head. "Kenneth, Florie, and I raised him as Florie's son. To keep him safe so he would not be turned into a monster like our father." She kept his stare, her heart thumping wildly. "She pleaded with me to tell my father that Jamie had died during birth. Kenneth and I buried another newborn who had died in the village."

"Yet ye kept the boy hidden after your father died. Why?"

Ella wet her dry lips and swallowed. "Kenneth thought we should go to King James first to tell him of Alec Sutherland's male heir. Once the king swore to support Sutherland leadership when Jamie turned seventeen, we decided that we should teach Jamie to be a good chief while keeping his identity still a secret. For his safety. Introducing him to the clan a little at a time."

Cain walked across the distance, stopping before her to grab her arms. She let him, her body numb. "And ye fear I will slaughter a child, one of your own blood?"

The ache of unshed tears made her blink. "I very much hope not." Her face pinched as the tension mixed with the relief that he now knew. If he wasn't holding her arms, she would sit before she fell.

"You would marry me with this secret between us?"

"I…I have wanted to tell you. So many times this week, the words have been on my tongue." She breathed fully until her head swam and sparks glittered in her periphery. "I wanted you to meet him first. To see what a thoughtful, intelligent person he is."

Cain turned away from her, releasing her arms, and she wobbled. "Cain, it is a secret I have lived with for twelve years. A promise to my mother. It was not an oath I could easily throw away. You have always said you care only for conquest, winning at all cost."

Anger straightened her spine and gave strength to her tingling limbs. "Dammit, Cain," she said, her voice rising. "I do not know you completely. Before three weeks ago, I have not seen you since that festival years ago. You do not even remember me. I was merely a despised Sutherland. Your face…"

He turned around to study her as one stupid tear leaked out. She slashed a hand across her cheek to rub away the evidence. "Your face…" She shook her head. "You looked on me with disgust because I was a Sutherland. In the darkest of nights, when I helped care for my baby brother, I thought of that look and what it could mean for him if our enemies found him. I couldn't be certain, Cain. If you remember me at all, it is only because I was someone who disgusted you."

The anger in his eyes faded to some emotion she could not name. He rubbed both his hands down his face. "Thistles," he said. "Scottish thistles."

"What?" She shook her head, not understanding.

"At the Beltane Festival. Ye wore a blue dress and held a bouquet of purple thistles. I picked it up when I ran into ye, making ye drop it. I thought…here is a lovely lass who has the heart of a warrior. All the other lasses at the festival picked the weak flowers to tie together, but not ye. Ye bound together thistles, both bonny and a spikey weapon if needed."

He stood before her, but he did not touch her. "The flower suits ye. Prickly in nature, but with the heart and beauty of a Scottish lass."

The tiniest of hope sprang up in her chest. "Will you let Jamie be the chief of Sutherland clan?" she asked.

He towered over her, and his inhale seemed to fill him with more unstoppable power. "I have oaths, too, Ella. To my father, to my brothers, and my clan." He shook his head. "I will not slaughter an innocent boy because he was born to be a Sutherland chief, but I cannot break my oath to conquer the weaker clans, pulling them into our own to make a stronger Scotland."

Turning away, she spotted a chair and sat in it before her legs gave way. "Are we still wedding tomorrow?" she asked, not sure how she wanted him to answer. *Wed him and kill him.* Should she even reveal the plan if she meant never to go through with it? Certainly not right then.

"We have made oaths to each other, too, Ella Sutherland. This wedding is the most peaceful way for me to take over Dunrobin and Sutherland territories."

"What about King James?" She watched his expression harden.

"I will strategize with Gideon about how to handle James."

Would he bring her into the discussions? Or had mistrust replaced anything that had grown between them?

Cain pivoted and strode out of the hall without another word. Ella stood up, watching him walk away, leaving her alone in the massive room.

Alone in the cold great hall of Girnigoe and painfully alone in her heart.

CHAPTER TWENTY

Ella felt numb, except for the twisty ache in her stomach.

"Quickly now," Merida said, beckoning her. "Ye already have the smock on and stays." She nodded her approval at the fresh white smock with lace edging the low neckline, the stays laced to push her breasts upward.

"And the stockings," Hannah said, lifting the lace hem where Ella stood by Cain's large bed. She had tossed and turned there the night before, trying to sleep, but Cain had not come up to join her.

"Now for the gown," Merida said.

"Ye'll be as pretty as a summer rose, but without the thorns." Hannah's eyes went wide. "Ye are not armed, are ye?"

Ella shook her head but couldn't muster a smile to match the excited woman's. Certainly, Gideon had shared the rest of King James's revelations with Cain's sister and aunt, but they continued to act as if all was well.

Hannah dashed to the sunlit window. "The horses from Dunrobin have arrived," she said, and Ella went to see for herself.

Relief lay heavy on her shoulders as she exhaled. Jamie was not with them. Not that she feared Cain hurting her brother, but there was enough emotion swirling around in her that seeing his sweet little face might make her crumble when she needed to remain strong.

Kenneth rode in on his bay horse surrounded by six Sutherland warriors. Had Cain sent word to him about discovering Ella's secret? "I would like to meet with my steward before the ceremony." There was so much she must tell Kenneth.

Merida shook out the burgundy-colored petticoat that was embroidered with roses in white silk thread. "There is no time. We need to have ye dressed and down the steps in less than an hour." She tossed it over Ella's head to float down to her hips where the woman tied it in the back.

Ella huffed but stood still, holding the matching stomacher in place over her stays while Hannah stitched it loosely into place. Merida pinned the elaborate sleeves at her shoulders and added the outer petticoat of a lighter rose-colored silk that matched the sleeves and parted in the front to reveal the undergown.

"'Tis lovely," Merida said with a brisk nod.

"Do ye have a gift for my brother?" Hannah asked. "For his wedding day?"

Along with Dunrobin? Ella nodded the barest amount and swung the wide skirts around to retrieve the piece she'd carved from behind the privacy screen in the corner of the room. She had used a pale ash block and gently cut away the pith into the most powerful piece on the chessboard, a queen. She'd smoothed the wood with a gritty stone, polishing it with wool. With curves and a chiseled crown, she imagined it to look like a true queen. It was white to go with the knight, to go with Cain. Cain was not the king of the chessboard, despite his father making him wear a crown. No, he did not hide away at the back of the board while others protected him. He fought for what he believed in.

Ella sighed softly. Would Cain realize that she was open to truly being his wife when she gave him the queen? If she were just a simple woman and Cain a simple man, she would have told him about her brother. They could wed and face the world, a queen and a knight together.

"I will wrap it in a handkerchief with a ribbon," Hannah said, taking it.

Ella had not seen Cain in the bailey. He had said yesterday that they would still marry. Surely, he would have cancelled the ceremony if he had changed his mind and not trick her into walking down to his absence before his people. The worry added to the tightness that had moved up to Ella's chest.

"Where is Cain now?" she asked.

"He is with his brothers, washing and trying to look less like a barbarian and more like a respectable husband," Merida said.

There was a knock at the door.

"Good," Merida said, turning. "Now to see to your hair. Viola Finlay makes the loveliest weavings."

"Viola?" Ella whispered as the door swung in and the busty woman who had kissed Cain at Midsummer walked inside. She was wearing a crisp plaid dress, and her brown hair flowed around her in gentle curls. She smiled and gave a little curtsy. "Milady."

Merida flapped her hand to bring Ella into a

chair. "Her hair is thick with a natural curl. See what ye can fashion with these summer roses. I have stripped them of their thorns."

"I…" Ella said and hesitated. "I think Cain prefers my hair down."

"Pish," Hannah said, gently pinching Ella's cheeks. Was she as pale as she felt? "He can have it down all he wants after the ceremony, but ye will be the queen of the day, Ella, with your hair up high. Maybe with some curls cascading down from the top."

Ella sat in the chair, which was instantly engulfed by the layers of linen and silk. Viola came up behind her. "I spoke with your steward from Dunrobin," she said near her ear, making Ella turn to her. "He gave me this to give ye." She set a small cloth bag tied tightly on Ella's lap. All three ladies looked at it there, but Ella wasn't foolish enough to open it before them.

"Excuse me," she said, and raised to walk behind the privacy screen before Merida could stop her. She worked the knots out quickly, pulling a small bottle and note from the bag. Kenneth's handwriting scrawled across the bit of paper.

For Cain.

Ella's face and hands went numb, her breath turning to stone lodged in her chest. She didn't need to open the bottle to know it was poison: foxglove, arsenic, nightshade, or some other toxic tincture. Her stomach twisted so hard she nearly heaved. Crumpling the note, she tossed it toward the privy box and set the bottle down on the floor beside it. Taking a shallow breath, she walked back out and sat down again under curious stares.

"Just a note to tell me he supports me…and my
favorite tincture to help me sleep," she said. It wasn't
a complete lie. Kenneth supported her in carrying
out an assassination. From the fullness of the bottle,
there was enough poison for all four brothers and a
tableful of guards to fall into the sleep of death.
Thomas, Keenan, Hamish, Hannah, Merida… The
idea gnawed in her stomach. She wouldn't…she
couldn't kill them all. Not even one.

Viola came around, her hand on Ella's shoulder,
bending forward. The woman's words came quiet, a
whisper with a smile. "My wedding gift to ye,
milady." She leaned in toward Ella's ear. "I will not
chase Cain. Joshua sent me to make ye jealous at the
Fire Festival, 'twas all."

Viola pulled back, giving Ella a nod. "Those
brothers are tricksters, every one of them."

Merida snorted, having heard the last part.
"Tricksters or clever strategists. It depends on which
side ye find yourself."

Viola laughed, a throaty seductive sound.
"Raised from the cradle to win, Cain most of all.
Win and conquer, whether it be a clan or a lass's
heart."

Merida handed her the hair comb. "We have very
little time."

Cain's aunt came around to study Ella and
smiled, making her look lovely. Ella's heart tightened at the thought that the woman had also
endured her father's brutality. The more she grew to
know Cain's family, the more steadfast she was that
she could not harm any of them.

She reached for Merida's hand, squeezing it. "Thank you, Merida. You look beautiful today, and I truly appreciate all you have done to help me." Ella smiled at Hannah. "Both of you."

Merida blinked, her face softening, which made her light eyes sparkle. Hannah leaned in and kissed Ella's cheek. They did not seem to hate her for keeping Jamie a secret. Maybe with Merida and Hannah here at Girnigoe, her life would be a good one even with the breach between Cain and herself. Where there was life there was hope for healing.

As Ella sat still, clasping her hands in her lap, she knew for certain. She breathed deeply over her decision. Neither "Death before surrender" nor "Wed him and kill him" would take up space in her mind or her heart. She exhaled long, trying to relax, as Viola tugged through her long hair. With that conviction, she would turn her focus back to making peace for her clan. Now that Cain knew the king would give back Sutherland lands and castle to Jamie in five years or bring his troops against the Sinclairs, she wasn't sure what Cain's next move would be.

Viola lifted and tucked, curled and pinned Ella's hair into a crown on the top of her head, leaving some waves to fall down her back. Merida attached the roses and ribbons of matching rose-colored silk.

"These were my mother's," Hannah said, laying a necklace of cool white pearls along Ella's neck.

What would Alice Sinclair think of Ella wearing her pearls? "They are lovely," Ella said, running her fingertip over them as Hannah helped her rise from the chair. "Thank you."

Merida indicated the long mirror that Thomas had brought in earlier. "See yourself in the polished glass."

The full skirts belled out, making Ella's waist look small. The tight stays lifted her breasts high so that the swell of them just breached the lace edge of her smock above the square neckline trimmed in gold thread. Beads were sewn along the deep *V* that pointed down to where the overskirt parted. White silk thread was stitched into the shapes of roses, matching the white pearls at her throat.

Hannah crouched to set her shoes before her on the floor. "Even your slippers match, along with the roses and ribbons in your hair."

Ella held back the edge of the petticoat and worked her toes into the slippers. They made her feel dainty and feminine, even if they were not practical like boots. They would surely fly off if she rode in them, and she would feel all the sharp pebbles in the bailey. But they were pretty with the matching silk gathered to fit tightly to the rounded toes.

Ella stared at herself in the polished glass, her lips relaxing into a smile. She felt like a queen in the ensemble. Never before had she worn a gown worthy of court. "I love it. Thank you two for all your hard work putting this wedding and this gown together."

"I thank ye," Hannah said, squeezing her hand. "For letting me help and to show Cain that I am indeed loyal to him." Her eyes teared up. "And to all my brothers." She glanced down.

"They know you are," Ella said, and Hannah lifted her eyes again. "Today will remind them how valuable you are, too, to the clan. You are truly talented."

Hannah smiled. "Wait until ye see how we dressed the great hall." She bounced higher onto the balls of her feet. "Roses and braided wildflowers and ribbons."

"It sounds perfect," Ella said. She turned to Viola. "Thank you for working my hair into such beauty."

Viola's face pinched as if she had bitten down on a tart lemon, but then she smiled tightly and bobbed a curtsy. Merida moved around Ella's skirts, fluffing them. "I think 'tis time. Viola, ye go down first and let Thomas, at the bottom, know we are coming."

Viola strode with purpose out of the room. Hannah walked down before Ella, looking back over her shoulder with an encouraging smile. Merida held up the back of the ensemble from behind. "We will wait in the alcove until I have signaled the pipes to start, and ye will walk down the center with Hannah attending ye. Kenneth Macleod waits halfway down and will escort ye to the front where Pastor Paul waits with Cain and his brothers."

"Where is Pastor John?" Hannah asked.

"Gideon could not find the man this morning. He had to ride all the way to Gunn territory to bring Pastor Paul." Merida *tsk*ed.

They reached the bottom of the steps, and the hum of people came from the great hall. There would be a lot of witnesses to the wedding. Would the Sutherlands accept the union? Had Jamie been revealed to them? Would they support her young brother, or would they choose a new chief and war against Cain when they rode to Dunrobin? Kenneth would have to ferry Jamie and Florie here to Girni-goe to keep them safe. She rubbed a hand across her stomach.

Stopping in the shadow of the alcove before the archway, Ella turned to Merida. The woman's eyes met hers, and they looked wise. "You have the sight," Ella said to her. "To predict outcomes." Merida neither agreed nor disagreed, but Ella continued. "Tell me, will this union bring more death, or will it bring peace to our clans?"

She glanced past Ella toward the people gathered beyond. "No one knows for certain."

Ella frowned. "You told George Sinclair he would die that day, and he did," she whispered.

Merida huffed and leaned in to her. "Child, I told my brother he would die every day of his life, except for church days. Aye, I warned him he would die that day, but it had become our jest."

Ella's chin dropped, her mouth opening. "So, you...cannot see?"

The woman looked closely into her eyes. "I can see that the two of ye are suited for each other, and that Scotland will be stronger if we are united," she said with a brisk nod. "But ye both need to learn to trust each other for anything more to bind ye to-gether."

Hannah ran in through the archway. "The musi-cians are beginning," she said, her smile bright.

Merida squeezed Ella's hand. "Hannah, grab the back of her skirt, and I will go to the front. When I lift my hand in the air, ye can start walking." She hustled down the center, and Ella moved to the open archway.

A murmur rose, and she realized everyone had turned to look at her. She slid a calm smile onto her lips like a mask. Her heart thudded hard, and she exhaled in relief when she saw Cain standing at the end of the aisle. Tall and broad like the perfect Highland warrior, he wore an intense look that was neither happiness nor anger. His bleached shirt stood out white against his tanned skin, his kilt fresh and bright with blue and green and a thin line of red. Her stomach flipped as his mouth relaxed. It wasn't quite a smile, but it was genuine appreciation. Did he see that she wore his mother's pearls?

Ella took a step forward when she felt a small tug on her sleeve. "Cain wishes for ye to carry these," Viola said, shoving a bouquet into her hands. Ella's stomach leaped. Had Cain gathered thistle for her to carry? But when she looked down at the flowers, their stems wrapped loosely with ribbon, she swallowed back disappointment as the cornflowers and daisies bent haphazardly. There wasn't a single thistle in the bunch.

Taking a step forward, she saw a small scrap of parchment caught in the ribbon binding the stems.

I have him. Your secret. If you wed the Sinclair or alert anyone, I will slit his throat. We are watching. Descend the secret stairs to save your brother.

CHAPTER TWENTY-ONE

Cain stood beside his three brothers at the front of the crowded great hall, staring down the aisle made up of clansmen and women and children.

They all wanted to witness the end to the feud that had taken so many lives over the last thirty years. Would this union secure it? Either way, he would wed Ella. Then he would work out a strategy for taking Dunrobin and Sutherland lands without bringing down the forces of the crown upon them.

Those gathered knew nothing of Ella's distrust, because Cain had ordered his brothers to keep Jamie Sutherland a secret for now. He must speak with Kenneth Macleod as soon as possible. Ella's steward waited in the middle with his men nearby.

Cain looked down the path that was cleared for the bride, and his inhale lodged in his throat. *Och.* His heart beat a deep thudding in his chest. Ella was the vision of a young queen, bedecked in pearls and silk, her raven-dark curls woven with flowers and ribbon. He knew her form intimately now, the curves and valleys, and it was accentuated by the lines of the rose-colored gown.

"Those are Mother's pearls," Gideon whispered to Cain.

"I asked Hannah to give them to her to wear," Cain said without taking his eyes from Ella.

Her face was beautiful even with the tension he saw there. She was right. They did not know each other enough yet, but he would fix that. After the ceremony, after he spoke with her steward, Cain would whisk her away to a cabin in the forest, holding her there for as long as it took for them to trust each other. He would win her smile back like he won everything, with a solid strategy and well executed plans. He would also stroke her body to shattering bliss, pulling every little secret from her. Did she have more secrets? No matter. If she did, he would win them from her lips.

Ella took a step toward him and froze, her eyes cast down at the bouquet clasped in her hands. Was she frightened? He couldn't imagine his courageous bride afraid. Even with the full brunt of his anger yesterday, she'd stood with strength as she'd explained. But there, at the back of the aisle, she did not move.

Look at me. See me, lass.

He kept the grin that had grown on his face, willing her to meet his gaze, but she continued to stare down at the bent wildflowers in her hands. Unease slid up his spine, and his hand moved to the hilt of his sword.

When she raised her eyes, they went first to Kenneth, a look of absolute shock on her fine features. Even…panic.

"Something is wrong," Cain murmured.

"Aye," Joshua said softly next to him.

Ella's gaze turned from side to side as if she were searching for someone.

"Ella," Cain called. Her gaze met his, and he saw a glistening in her eyes. Tears? He took a stride toward her, and she held up a hand to stop him, shaking her head. *Bloody hell!* A tear slid from her eye, and she spun around, still grasping the broken bouquet, and grabbed her skirts to race back through the archway.

"She is running out on ye?" Joshua said, his earlier jesting voice deadly serious.

"She is going back upstairs, not leaving the castle," Bàs said. "Perhaps she forgot her handkerchief. Don't lasses always carry a handkerchief?"

Gideon's hand caught Cain's arm. "Something is not right. Her man looks confused. This is unexpected."

Cain yanked away from his brother, striding up the aisle full of rising murmurs. Kenneth fell in line with him. "There was terror in her eyes," was all Cain said.

Before Cain could follow her under the archway, Viola stepped before him, a hand on his chest. "Bridal nervousness," she said. "I saw her run down the corridor that leads to the chapel. Let her alone for a few minutes to gather her courage. She might be thinking that she does not want to be a Sinclair."

"My lady is the Sutherland chief, with too much honor to go back on her commitment," Kenneth said, his voice rough.

Viola's face scrunched, her lips curling in distaste. "Even if she knows her secret has been revealed and her groom may slaughter the only thing standing in the way of his conquest of her castle and lands?" Viola asked, her voice full of vindictiveness.

Cain's gaze snapped away from the corridor to Viola's face. Her eyes narrowed as she stared at Kenneth. The man's mouth dropped open, and he turned to Cain, questions there that he could not speak.

Cain grabbed Viola's arm. "No one knows about that but my close family." His face turned lethal. "And somehow ye."

His brothers now stood behind him, listening. Joshua had drawn his sword, his expression brutal as if he readied for war. War against whom? The Sutherlands? Ella? Viola?

Gideon was the first to speak. "How do ye know about Jamie Sutherland?"

Kenneth turned to him, his eyes wide. "How do *ye* know about Jamie Sutherland?"

Viola's glare turned to panic as if she realized that she'd said too much. Cain shook her, bringing her face back to him. "What evil have ye planned, Viola?"

"Maybe ye should be asking your bride's steward about planned evils," she said, looking to Kenneth. "Did ye think I would not look in the bag ye sent to her, ye fool?"

Kenneth's lips pressed firmly together as he stared at her, but Viola continued. "He sent up a vial of poison to Ella before the wedding," she said. "Was your bride planning to poison the whole wedding party or only her new husband?"

Poison? To kill him. Pain tore through Cain. If not for his brothers there, Bàs and Joshua grabbing Kenneth's arms and taking his sword, Cain would have roared. His nostrils flared as he inhaled. "To arms!" Cain yelled. "Find Ella!"

Down the aisle, his warriors grabbed the other Sutherland clansmen, disarming them as mothers

dragged and shooed their children from the hall as if
a battle was about to break out under the garlands
of flowers. He turned back to the archway where
Ella had run. *Bloody hell.* She wanted him dead?

. . .

Ella grabbed a dagger from her room and flew down
to Cain's bedchamber, sliding it into the hidden
pocket through the inner petticoat of her gown.

In the bottom of the pocket, her knuckle bumped
into the chess piece she had made as a wedding gift
for Cain. She set it, tied in the handkerchief, on the
chess table with a trembling hand where it wobbled
and fell. It hit the white horse, and a small sob
caught in Ella's throat as they both fell over.

Cain distrusted her, and now she had slaughtered
his pride before his entire clan by running away
from the wedding ceremony.

No time. Focus. Jamie. She'd sworn to protect him
from his birth, and she would not stop now. She
loved him, raising him as if he were her own child.
Her mother's dying words filled Ella's ears as she
yanked the ring behind the books to trigger the wall
to move.

"Keep my wee Jamie hidden…"

She had kept her brother hidden from their
father even though she could not understand why
she must hide a perfect son from Alec Sutherland. It
was the man's greatest desire. He would have treated
Jamie like a prince, protecting him with all his
armies. But now the Sutherland clan did not even
know Jamie. Would they support him if he survived

the day? At this point, it didn't even matter if they did, as long as he lived.

Ella hurried down the stone steps as fast as she could, surrounded by all the layers of petticoats. Even the sharp pebbles poking her feet through the silk slippers didn't slow her. At the bottom, she pushed through the door, the iron lock having been cleaved off completely.

The air was cool, feeding her lungs as she took in large inhales, her gaze falling upon men mounted on horses. They stood silent, watching her as one man she knew stepped forward. Randolph Mackay grinned at her, bowing his head. "Thank ye for joining our party, milady."

"Jamie?" His name came out on a heavy exhale.

"Back at Varrich, waiting to stand witness for his sister's wedding."

"My wedding is here at Girnigoe." She stared hard into his black eyes.

"Not your wedding to Cain Sinclair," Randolph said. "To the chief of Clan Mackay like your father always intended."

"Hew is dead. I killed him," she said, her words rushing from her clenched mouth, the tension grasping along her jaw and neck.

"Aye," Randolph said, a pleasant look on his face that his men behind him could not see. The look, more than any word, confirmed her suspicion that Randolph Mackay had wanted his chief dead all along. "Ye will wed the new chief of Clan Mackay."

He took a step closer to her, his hand coming up to her face where curls hid the Sutherland brand near her temple. She jerked her head back so he couldn't touch her, but he reached forward to catch the back of her head, his fingers curling in to rip away at the curls pinned and woven into a beautiful design.

"Today ye will wed me, the new chief, the chief who will rule both the Mackay and the Sutherland clans."

Ella kept her footing, refusing to bend down under Randolph's painful yanking in her hair. She forced herself to relax in his hold, but her eyes pierced him with fury. She could snatch out her *sgian dubh*, but then how would she get to Jamie? "Jamie Sutherland is backed by King James to lead Sutherland Clan," she said.

"Aye." Randolph's thin lips twitched up into a smile. "And I will serve as regent until he comes of age. If he comes of age." He shook his head. "But children die so easily."

"No!" she yelled, struggling. Two of Randolph's men dismounted and grabbed her, their hands grazing her breasts and waist without care. One wrapped both of his thick arms around her, pinning her own to her sides.

"Perhaps we can work something out," Randolph said, bending to look into her face, her hair tumbling free to hang before her eyes. "If you behave and your brother asks King James to let me unite his clan and mine, then Jamie might live a long life unburdened by the weight of leadership." He straightened and flapped his fingers toward the horses. The man lifted Ella forward. With a flick of her wrist, she dropped the bouquet of flowers that she had been clutching.

The man carrying her hoisted her and the many layers of her costume into the arms of a large Mackay warrior who smelled of sweat and smoke. Randolph mounted his own horse, bringing it near her. "We will discuss it tomorrow, for today we have our wedding to celebrate."

• • •

Cain crashed through the open door at the bottom of the hidden steps, the smoothly polished wooden queen that he'd unwrapped, toppled on the chessboard above, still clutched in one hand, the bottle of poison in the other.

Had she planned to use it on him? The note saying that it was for him had been crumpled, and she'd obviously spent hours making the queen, a perfect match for his knight. It was enough hope for him to hold onto while everything else fell apart.

"Ella!" But the only answer was the sound of the waves hitting the rocks edging the land. "Bloody foking hell!" He ran first to the water's edge, his heart thumping with the fear that she could have drowned, but she wasn't there. "Ella!" he roared, hurling the vial of poison into the waves. His fingers raked his scalp as he drew in deep breaths. Even if she refused to wed him, she would not kill herself or she would have drunk the poison when it was delivered.

Damn it all! She *had* sworn to die before wedding him, but that was before. Before they had spent two weeks loving each other. The time spent together could not have been all lies. Could it have?

He turned back, his gaze dropping to the damp ground where at least five horses had stood not too long ago. Joshua ran up behind him. "Someone met her here. Sutherlands?"

"Nay," Kenneth said as he stumbled out of the door at the bottom of the steps, his hands already bound. Bàs's grip pinched his shoulder. "I would know, and she had no plans other than wedding ye."

Cain turned to him. "No plans to kill me, then?"

"Maybe she decided to run away rather than do that," Bàs said. His young brother, despite all the executions he delivered, still held onto hope that people were good. Could Cain?

Kenneth stared at Cain, swallowing hard. "I gave her the poison in case she could not live wed to ye." The man exhaled through gritted teeth, anger and worry ravaging his face, making him look much older. "Ye carried her away, locked her up in your fortress." He sneered at Cain. "Not in your dungeon but in your bedroom. Did ye rape her? Beat her?"

Cain stepped up to him. "Never," he said, not caring if he spit on the man.

"Her life is worth more than bringing the clans together," Kenneth yelled. "I gave her a way out that did not include killing *herself*. I raised her and will always protect Ella as best I know how. I gave her a weapon to use if marriage to ye was nothing but pain and torture."

Fury and anguish smashed against worry inside Cain, creating a storm that threatened thunder and lightning. His calm, strategic mind churned in chaos, all the years of discipline and training crushed under the thought that Ella was gone.

Gideon stood at the door. "The lock was cleaved with a blade," he said and dropped the heavy lock back onto the ground.

"It was not the Sutherlands," Kenneth hissed, fury still etched on his face. "Ethan would not have ordered this without my knowledge."

Cain's fists clenched as he stared at Ella's steward, searching his haggard face for truth.

"I am telling ye, dammit, I did not order this," Kenneth said. "Whoever did…" He raised his bound hands to his forehead, rubbing it. "They could harm her." The man looked completely stricken.

Cain turned to Gideon. "Ye have Viola Finley."

"Keenan has her above," Joshua said as he walked along, his gaze trained on the ground. He crouched, touching the dirt. "They left not too long ago."

Cain clutched the beautifully carved queen in his fist. If it was not Sutherlands, then she was taken by force. Tears in her eyes. A look of regret and panic. "She went with them."

"With whom?" Kenneth asked.

"We will follow the tracks," Bàs said, but Cain knew.

He looked to Kenneth. "The Mackays have your Jamie."

Kenneth's eyes closed as if pain, too, radiated through him. He truly loved Ella, loved her enough to give her a way out of her marriage if it were worse than Hell. A weapon so she did not have to kill herself to escape.

Joshua straightened. "If we leave now, we can overtake them."

"Prepare the horses and men," Cain said. Joshua ran off toward the bailey.

Cain's eyes scanned the seaweed-slick rocks and spied the blue ribbon that held the stems of Ella's bouquet. He snatched it out of the incoming tide and turned the thin stalks in his hand, stopping at the sight of the small paper tied there.

Gideon came up to read over his shoulder as Cain read the words out loud. "I have him, your secret. If you wed the Sinclair or alert anyone, I will slit his throat. Descend the back stairs to save your brother."

Kenneth swore. "Randolph will kill them both."

"Cain," Gideon said, his face hard, his voice low. "If the boy dies at Mackay's hand, the contract with King James will be null. The Sinclairs can take Dunrobin and Sutherland Clan without royal interference. Mackay will be blamed, and ye might win Varrich and the Mackay lands, too, if ye tell James of their involvement."

"Ye would let the boy die?" Bàs asked. "And Ella?"

"Nay," Kenneth yelled, his face going ashen. "What type of monster are ye to let them be slaughtered?"

"Not a monster," Gideon said, turning to the elderly steward. "A chief and conqueror who can see that the sacrifice of two people could unite three clans and strengthen all of Scotland."

Kenneth struggled in vain against the thick rope binding his wrists. "But Ella—"

"Was planning to kill Cain," Gideon said, his hand going to his own sword.

"That was me!" Kenneth yelled. "Not Ella. She never agreed."

The tearing inside Cain was almost a physical pain. Gideon was right. If Mackay killed the boy, Cain could take Dunrobin and Sutherland lands. Right now. Today. He could turn the four Sinclair armies to ride south to Dunrobin instead of west to Varrich. He could win what his father had fought for most of his life without worrying about King James's wrath. He would win the respect of his brothers and his clan. He would strengthen Scotland.

"Listen to me, Cain," Kenneth said, his voice lower as he struggled to keep his composure. "If ye save Ella, the Sutherland Clan will see ye as an ally. Ye can still take Dunrobin peacefully. As before, if ye let her die and try to take it by force, without her as your wife, blood will soak the halls ye wish to claim. Good people and horses will die, and hate will fester in the hearts of your new subjects."

Cain breathed, trying to clear his mind, setting all the pieces on his mental game board. Jamie Sutherland, King James, Randolph Mackay, Dunrobin, his brothers, and…Ella. The beautiful, courageous, intelligent woman who surprised and challenged him daily, the queen to his knight. If he did not ride to Varrich now, he would surely lose her. He could feel it like he could feel the hard hammering of his heart. The threat of loss.

Loss. He had no real experience with it. He loathed it. Cain always won, and he would do so again today. He looked at Gideon, his face as hard as his determination. "Gather the four armies. Today we go to war."

CHAPTER TWENTY-TWO

Ella yanked her arm free from the meaty hand of Randolph's henchman as he pulled her in through the entryway of Varrich Castle. The vile guard had pawed her body, locating her hidden dagger. Her stomach still clenched with nausea as she watched the ogre adjust his cod, obviously enjoying the order Randolph had given him.

"Tsk, a knife on a lady," Randolph said, following them, tipping her *sgian dubh* to catch the light from the high windows cut into the great hall's stone walls. "Although ye are something of a warrior lady." With a downward thrust, Randolph stabbed the small dagger into the wooden table. "I trust that ye found all of her secret weapons, Iain?"

"I would be glad to strip her out of them fine clothes and search further," Iain said, leering. "From her toes to the curls on her head and everywhere in between."

Ella looked away to quell her stomach. Would vomiting all over him squelch his lust?

Her gaze fastened onto movement toward the back of the hall. "Jamie!" Picking the voluminous petticoats up, she ran to him, pulling him into a hug against her. *He is alive. He is whole and alive.*

Even though he was already twelve, with all the reticence of a boy wanting to prove that he was almost a man, Jamie clung to her for several long seconds. When she felt him drop his arms, she let him pull back and searched his face. Dirt smudged his cheeks where smears showed that there had been tears at some point. His blue eyes shone with them, though he bravely blinked them away.

"I will get you out of this," she said, her voice low.

He sniffed, his mouth firm. "But how will *I* get *ye* out of this?"

"Cain will come," she said.

Jamie's gaze lifted over her shoulder.

"Are ye certain about that?" Randolph asked, his voice strong and directly behind her.

She straightened, turning to him. "Of course he will, he and his four armies, to tear Varrich to the ground."

Randolph shrugged. "Perhaps he will see this opportunity to take Sutherland lands."

"He cannot," she said, her face full of unchecked anger. "King James will support Jamie Sutherland as chief," she said, grabbing Jamie's hand. He held tightly back. "Cain knows that. If you or Cain try to take Dunrobin, King James will bring his massive armies down upon you."

The blank look that Randolph held gave nothing of his thoughts away. He batted his hand through the air. "If Cain Sinclair decides not to ride against the Sutherlands today, coming here instead, ye will turn him away by telling him that ye have wed."

"I will not," she said.

He smiled, his grin toothy. "Ye will, to save your brother, of course. A brother that no one even knew about. Not even your father."

"How did you discover him?" Ella asked. She had kept him a secret for twelve years.

The natural tilt of Randolph's dark brows made him look evil. "A bit of investigative work spurred by an ill woman in the Sutherland village who said that her bairn had died twelve years back. She said that she had been called to Dunrobin to nurse a boy bairn without its mother. She went on and on in her delirium, wishing to be buried by the remains of Alec Sutherland's dead son as it was actually her own."

Randolph chuckled. "The information made it to Viola, who passed it to me. I sent a maid to work at Dunrobin, and she followed the tales to a boy born to Florie Sutherland. With a jug of whisky poured down your nursemaid's throat, she told all to keep her life." He *tsk*ed.

Was sweet, loyal Florie dead? Ella swallowed down the question, keeping her brother at her back. He was growing so fast, but she was still taller than him. "You will accomplish nothing by wedding me," she said. "King James supports Jamie, his namesake. He prefers bloodlines over battles to secure leadership and has sworn to back Jamie's claim to my father's earldom and to lead the Sutherland clan."

Randolph stepped up closer to her. "The boy is young and untried. I will but do what Cain Sinclair would have done had he known about him. I will become regent."

"You are not even a Sutherland," Ella said.

"Ah, but I am half Sutherland." Randolph's smile faded. "My mother was from your clan and found herself with child by a Mackay warrior. My father wed her, but he was a cruel man." Randolph rubbed hard against the back of his hand as if scrubbing away at a pain. "When my mother tried to take me and my sister back to her home in the Sutherland village outside Dunrobin, your father refused to let us stay. He said we were exiled, since we were the spawn of a Mackay enemy." Randolph's face pinched with obvious hatred.

Damn Alec Sutherland. How many lives had he torn apart with his cruelty?

Randolph pushed a smile onto his thin lips. "So ye see, I am a Sutherland, and once I wed ye, your clan will accept me to act as regent until the boy comes of age." The slight narrowing of his eyes, along with a hitch in his smile, made chill bumps rise along her arms.

Her hand slid behind to pull Jamie closer into her back, as if she could hide him away inside her. It was obvious from Randolph's smirk that he did not plan for Jamie to live five more years to take over the leadership of his clan. If Jamie died in war or by some illness or accident, which could be a hidden assassination, whoever was wed to Ella and acting as regent would be in a strong position to lead the clan. Why hadn't she told Cain before? She had been so foolish not allowing herself to trust him. He would not hurt Jamie.

Randolph shrugged and gestured to the priest who could not be found that morning. "Pastor John, your services are now required."

Ella shook her head. "Our banns. They have not been posted for three weeks."

Randolph tipped his hand in the air as if that meant nothing. "The Sinclairs saved me the trouble of doing so. Banns are pinned to the chapel doors so that anyone who might have an issue with your marriage could come forward to declare a previously made agreement. No one has come forward, so the pastor may proceed." Pastor John looked small standing between two large Mackay warriors.

Randolph slid his gaze down her dress, a grin making him look eager. The man obviously did not plan to leave her alone once they were wed. "Ye are even attired for such a special event," he said.

"I will not wed you, Randolph," she said. The thought of him touching her made bile rise, and she swallowed.

Randolph came to stand before her, his face closing in until she could smell his breath. Beer and rot. It reminded her of her father and made the muscles in her shoulders tighten and ache. "Then I will slit his throat now."

Ella felt Jamie's fingers curl into her dress as his body pushed against the wide flare of her petticoats. "And then King James will take all of Mackay lands," she said. "He knows that Jamie is the rightful leader of Clan Sutherland."

Randolph's grin made her skin pock with another wave of chills. "He will think it was done by Cain Sinclair or one of his brothers. Gideon was already there asking him about leadership of your clan. And I have a man in Edinburgh who is, right now, telling James how the Sinclairs are bold enough to eliminate the boy to take over the clan. If Cain rides today to conquer Dunrobin, the king will believe every word my Mackay emissary has said."

"And if I tell the king the truth?" she whispered.

"Ye will lose your tongue and maybe your head

before that happens. James will believe that Cain Sinclair was so outraged with ye and your secrets that he went crazy like his own father and killed you in his fury. The legends around the Sons of Sinclair will easily back up the story." Randolph walked over to the table where two goblets sat and picked them up. He turned back to her, his face relaxed as if they were talking casually at a celebration. "So ye see, Lady Sutherland, we will be wed this day." He brought her the goblet. "A toast to our union."

Would he drug her? Not before she took her vows before the pastor and witnesses. She should have grabbed the poison Kenneth had sent. She looked to the pastor, his pale face showing that he was clever enough to know his own life was forfeit after hearing Randolph's plans.

He was another whose life depended on her cleverness today, along with her brother's and all the lives of the Sinclairs. Surely the king would send troops to subdue them if Randolph made him believe that her brother's blood was on Sinclair hands.

Would Cain ride against her people instead of coming to find her? The thought churned tightly in her chest until she felt she might sob. *He will come. He must come.* Surely there was feeling for her after what they had shared. *He will come.*

"Pastor John!" Randolph yelled, and the men practically carried the clergyman closer.

"I am heartily sorry," he said, staring at Ella as he righted his robes, cutting a frown to the guards. "God in Heaven will sort this out."

Ella preferred to save them from attending that

particular meeting, at least until they were old and withered. If she agreed to wed Randolph, she could save Jamie for a while, maybe long enough to secret him away. Either way, though, the young pastor's breaths were numbered.

"No reason to be sorry," Randolph said. "Today Arabella Sutherland honors her sire's proposal to bind the Mackay and Sutherland Clans together to form a strong union against the bloodthirsty Sinclairs. We will feast tonight and plan our return to Dunrobin tomorrow once your steward shows up to congratulate us."

The man was insane, and Ella needed to delay. "What of Viola Finley?" Ella asked. "Who is she to betray the Sinclairs?" There were more playing pieces in this mad game of conquest. Could Cain guess them all and find a way to call checkmate on Randolph?

"Ah, Viola," he said and shoved the goblet into her hand. "My dearest sister is right now on her way here."

"Sister?" Ella asked, noticing the similar set of small eyes and tipped noses in them both. "How did she come to live at Girnigoe?"

"My mother sent her to live with a Sutherland friend who had wed into the Sinclair clan. Vi was ten and old enough to attract my father's rather base attention, so my mother packed her off."

What horrors Randolph, Viola, and their poor mother must have endured. "Randolph," Ella said, holding the goblet before her like a shield. "I am sorry that my father did not take you and your family in. Alec Sutherland was a cruel man. I lived under him, so I know. But forcing me to wed you and harming an innocent boy will make you the same as he. Do not be my father. Do not be *your* father. Be your own man."

Randolph's face contorted, turning red as his lips rolled back. He threw the goblet, where it smashed against the wall, making Ella jump at the sudden explosion. Red wine sprayed out against the stone to stain it like blood. "I am my own man, Arabella." He held up his arm, which was thinner than most of the warriors with whom she'd grown up. "I was born without the bulk and physical strength of my father and without the foolish sentiment of my mother."

Tall, dark, and slender, Randolph Mackay could have been handsome if his heart hadn't decayed with wrath.

He tapped the side of his head. "But I have a cunning mind, one that I am pitting against the strategic planning of Cain Sinclair." His nostrils flared as he inhaled, shaking slightly as if ridding himself of his fury, and his leer-like smile crept back across his face. "Hew was easy enough to control like a child's poppet, and ye finished him off quite nicely while saving that foolish sister of Cain's. Cain Sinclair has a much brighter mind, but I have had a lifetime of planning my rise to power. I but waited until someone slaughtered your father. I would have done it myself if I had not been implementing my plan."

Ella glanced at the few men around the room, Iain being the largest. Grim and formidable, were they loyal to this lunatic? They stood frozen, as if cut from marble, their faces impassive, all except Iain who continued to watch her like a predator stalking his kill. Had Randolph promised her to him for helping him? The thought made her legs feel weak.

Randolph stretched his empty hands over his head to cup the back of it. "If all goes according to my plan, I will end up the chief of Clans Mackay, Sutherland, and eventually Sinclair with the royal backing of the Scottish throne." He laughed. "I could be king."

He crossed his arms over his chest and cocked his head to the side. "Ye can either keep your brother and yourself alive by wedding me now, or ye will be responsible for young Jamie's immediate death. Ye will then eventually die yourself, probably painfully and after my men and I have had our fill of ye." He motioned behind him, where Iain smiled broadly. Even the ones flanking the door grinned.

"Ye see," he said, holding his arms wide and then letting them drop as if surrendering to the brilliance of his plan. "There really is no other choice than to take your vows as my wife."

Ella's heart pounded hard, her breathing quick. If she swooned, would it give her time? Time for what? Escape? There didn't seem to be any.

The pastor closed his eyes, his lips moving soundlessly. *Yes, pray for us all. Pray that Cain found the ragged bouquet I threw. Let him forgive me enough to come.* But what could he do? Even storming the castle would take too long to stop Jamie from dying. No, she must do something herself.

Ella's gaze snapped back to Randolph. "Very well," she said. "If you…swear to release the pastor unharmed after the oathtaking, and keep Jamie and me alive…I will take the vows with you now."

Behind her, Jamie wrapped his arms around her waist and buried his face in her back. The space between Randolph's brows tightened for a moment before his face relaxed into a smile, one that looked genuine. "I am very glad ye have chosen the wisest and least bloody option."

"The pastor?"

"Aye." He waved his hand. "He will stand as witness that ye took your oaths willingly."

"And Jamie will be right by my side, always."

Randolph's brow raised. "Certainly, although I take objection with him sleeping next to us in our wedding bed." Several of the men chuckled. "But when ye have clothing on and are not pleasuring me, the lad may stay by your side. Anything else?"

"I would have a word alone with my brother before I take my vows."

Randolph huffed. "Very well, but only for a minute. In the unlikely event that Cain comes here instead of conquering Dunrobin, he must see that ye have wed me."

Ella took Jamie's hand, leading him to a corner away from the men. His palm was damp and cold, and she looked down into his eyes.

"'Tis because of me," he said. "Ye have to wed that greedy, brutal rat. I would not have ye do that for me. Ye have given up so much of your life already."

"Jamie," she said, stifling a sob. She pulled him in for a hug, her heart clenching. "I would do it all again to keep you safe. Even if our mother had not asked." Her lips went to his ear. "Stay close to me and the pastor."

She pulled away and waited for his nod. "I love ye, Ella," he whispered.

"I have always loved you, my sweet brother." Ella clasped Jamie's hand, turning quickly as another Mackay guard barreled into the great hall.

"The Sinclair armies are riding across the moor."

"How many?"

"Horses of gray," he said and shook his head. "Or pale green, I cannot tell. And a second army of black."

"Green and black," Randolph said. "That would be the youngest brother and third eldest. They have split forces, with Cain riding to Dunrobin."

Ella's heart pounded with rapid fire. Had Cain sent Bàs and Gideon for her even after she ran out of the wedding? Her breath came quickly with the thinnest renewal of hope. "He sent them for me."

Randolph's gaze snapped to her, his face pinched. "He wants ye only to gain Sutherland territory and Dunrobin. It is what he wanted in the first place, to avenge his father, to conquer as he was raised to do. Half his men ride here while he rides to Dunrobin. He thinks to win ye and Jamie as well as your lands today. Cocky bastard."

Ella's chest tightened. The pressure of tears built in her eyes, but she would never let them fall. Cain had not come himself even if he sent his armies to Varrich. There had been no words of love between them, but she had grown to know him. Cain was not the brutal conqueror his father had raised him to be. What would make him abandon her to ride on Dunrobin today?

"We will go to the wall walk," Randolph said, grabbing Ella's hand. The goblet dropped from her fingers, the red wine splashing across the beautiful silk of the bodice and skirt that had belonged to Cain's mother, ruining it. He yanked her behind him as they went through an archway to the castle steps, his fingers digging into her flesh as if punishing her. Jamie clung to her other hand. The lecherous Iain followed behind.

"I want the Sinclairs to see ye have chosen me," Randolph said. "Let them tell Cain that ye spoke the vows without me holding a knife against ye."

"But you are," she said.

"They do not know that." He laughed, the edge of insanity in the inflection.

Even if she was to profess her love of Randolph Mackay, Cain would never believe it. But she would not persuade the madman with that.

Randolph paused, glancing down the darkened stairwell past them. "Bring the pastor," he yelled and then continued.

"Are you not worried about your sister?" Ella asked as her own plan began to take shape in her mind. She trudged up the curving stone steps. She could not yank away from him here, or he would pull her and Jamie down with him.

"Viola is a smart lass. She will have fled as soon as she delivered the note to ye." What about the poison? Had that been part of Randolph's plan? No, the note was penned in Kenneth's slanted script.

A crash funneled up from below. Randolph looked back, his eyes sliding over her head down the stairwell. "Little man is putting up a fight," he murmured. "Get that pastor up here," he yelled.

"Aye," came a voice. "Your sister has arrived."

Randolph smiled back at Ella. "See, she is a bright lass and had a plan to escape."

"She left all the family that she made at Girnigoe? Without a backward glance?"

"She thirsts for revenge, too, for not being welcomed by our mother's Sutherland clan."

"But the Sinclairs have been only good to her," Ella said.

Randolph yanked her through the outer door. "Stop talking."

Ella and Jamie followed Randolph onto the stone walkway that rose above the walls of Varrich, Iain bringing up the rear.

Ella's breath caught at the display of force. Sinclairs were mounted and stretched across the moor and crest before the castle. She had fought with them before but had never seen them spread out before her. Pale green and black horses numbered over two hundred.

"I am here," the pastor said, coming up, his breathing labored. Glancing back over his shoulder, he slid a shaking hand across his face and wiped it on his dark robes. Had the guards frightened him below?

"Should we not wait for your sister to come up?" Ella asked. "Milord, you should go check on her."

The pastor shook his head and swallowed hard. "She…" His brows rose as if trying to act casually, and his head wobbled slightly as he glanced over his shoulder at the door. "She said she must refresh herself and would rejoice in the union after it is… um…complete."

Randolph narrowed his eyes as if the pastor was a simpleton, but then smiled at Ella. "Come, my love." Randolph pinched her elbow hard enough it would bruise and pulled her toward the wall that reached to his middle. He clutched her hand and raised it overhead. "Sinclairs," he called, his voice carrying down. "Today we wed, joining Sutherland and Mackay clans."

Ella's gaze fastened onto Gideon and Bàs seated on their mighty warhorses in front. Bàs wore his skull mask and horned helmet and carried his scythe. Gideon frowned up, his gaze searching her out.

From the side of the castle, a bird soared up and over the armies. It was Cain's hawk, its yellow beak clutching a scrap of material. Why wasn't it with him at Dunrobin?

"Kill it," Randolph ordered as it flew overhead, but Iain had no bow, only his sword. He withdrew it, swinging wildly, but the bird was too high. Over their heads, it dropped the piece of fabric to fall down the wall away from them. Jamie ran for it while Randolph cursed, watching the bird fly away.

Randolph grabbed it from Jamie. "A love note?" He held it in two hands, and Ella could see the piece of rose-colored silk, a scrap from the extra fabric of the gown. Randolph slid his thin fingers along it, stopping at a single knot tied in the middle.

The colors mean different things. The knot tells them not to act unless absolutely necessary to save their lives.

Cain didn't want her to act. Did he know that Randolph was forcing her to wed and wanted her not to do it? But Cain didn't understand what was at stake, the lethal retribution Randolph would bring down on Jamie, the pastor, and herself. She must say the vows. *And I will keep them.*

"What is this?" Randolph stared at it. "A bit of your gown." He stared at Ella. "What does this mean? Tell me!" he yelled, spittle flying.

"Just…that he wants me back. 'Tis my dress." Ella pressed Jamie behind her again.

"He is not even here for ye," Randolph said. He threw it over the low wall. "Like I said before, Arabella Sutherland, he wants Dunrobin and your clan, not ye, unless it is to ride ye like his beasts." He grabbed between his own legs as if to see if he was hard. He smiled. "Aye, while Sinclairs are blasting away at our gates, we will be consummating our vows in the great hall where the good pastor can witness." He flipped his hand. "Or perhaps right here on the wall walk for Clan Sinclair to witness."

"We would talk with Ella Sutherland." It was Bàs's voice from below.

Randolph extended his hand toward her. "Speak to her here."

Some words passed between Bàs and Gideon, but they were too far for her to hear them. Gideon raised his gaze to her. "Ella Sutherland," he called. "Did ye plan to poison Cain Sinclair, our chief and the man that ye were about to swear to love before God?"

All the air in Ella's chest turned to stone, her body frozen. Cain had found the vial. She hadn't had time to dispose of it before the ceremony. Was that why he wasn't there himself? Had he given the chore to his brothers and ridden with Joshua to bring slaughter to Dunrobin? He had not turned against her when Gideon exposed her secret, but now he thought she was planning to kill him. The condemnation on Gideon's face showed that they all felt that way.

Randolph chuckled. "Well now," he said, turning to look at her with a wide, surprised expression. "Maybe I should have waited for ye to kill him and then taken ye as my bride." He shrugged. "But who knew ye to be so vicious."

Ella stared at Gideon, blinking back the sting in her eyes. "No," she yelled. "I would not do that."

"The evidence shows your words to be a lie," Gideon said, scorn in his voice.

"Perhaps ye should be thanking me for taking Cain's bride away today," Randolph called down. "He is in my debt for saving his life." He laughed and nodded to Iain who pushed Pastor John to the wall next to them.

"The Lord is my shepherd…" the pastor murmured.

Randolph frowned. "Wrong prayer. But we hardly need ye." He turned back to look out on the throng. "Ye all stand as witness along with Pastor John and God." He grabbed up Ella's hand, holding it to his chest over his heart. She was surprised she could feel it beating knowing how decayed it was.

"I, Randolph Mackay Sutherland, chief of Clan Mackay, take ye, Arabella Sutherland, from this moment forward, as my wife in the eyes of God and the Protestant Church, till death us do part, according to God's holy ordinance. This is my solemn vow."

He looked at Ella. "Ye say the same," he

whispered. "Now." He looked at Iain, and the man strode over to Jamie. Jamie pulled back but didn't cry out. Terror sat in his eyes as Iain pulled out his short sword, holding it to Jamie's thin neck. Even a slice would kill him.

Ella's breath came fast along with her words. "I, Arabella Sutherland—"

"Face front and speak loudly," Randolph instructed without moving his lips.

She tore her gaze from Jamie. Nothing mattered now, nothing but saving her brother. Cain thought she wanted him dead. He'd abandoned her to ride against her clan. "I, Arabella Sutherland, take ye, Randolph Mackay—"

"Mackay Sutherland, chief of Clan Mackay," Randolph said.

Ella swallowed past the lump and cleared her throat. "Randolph Mackay Sutherland, chief of Clan Mackay, from this moment forward, as my…husband in the eyes of God and the Protestant Church. Till death us do part, according to God's holy ordinance."

Randolph reached over and pinched the back of her hand that lay below the wall. "This is my solemn vow," he said, his words like a hiss. "Say it or he dies now."

Jaw tight, she forced her lips to open. Behind her, the door swung open, slamming into the wall, and she tried to turn to look. Randolph yanked her forward, wrenching her arm. "Say it now!"

God forgive me. "This is my solemn vow," she said.

CHAPTER TWENTY-THREE

Cain's arm held the heavy door aside.

This is my solemn vow? This is my solemn vow! Ella's words bellowed in his head. "Ella!" He charged forward.

"No!" she yelled.

He followed her line of sight to the back wall where a Mackay warrior clutched a boy to his chest, a blade pressing against the lad's neck until a line of red released several drops of fresh blood. The boy stared straight out, his eyes calm as if he accepted his death.

Cain's gaze snapped back to Ella who now stood the same way clutched before Randolph Mackay.

"She is my wife now," Mackay yelled. "Leave here or face King James's wrath. He knows ye are bent on killing Arabella and her brother and will stop at nothing to avenge their deaths."

"Wait," the pastor called out, his hands clutched together before him. "Wait, I must bless the union for it to be binding."

"What? That is not—" Randolph started.

"Quickly," the pastor said, coming forward while passing the sign of the cross before him and speaking in Latin. Randolph turned Ella before the clergyman, the knife still at her throat above the line of Cain's mother's pearls. The red that stained the front of her gown looked like blood, and it almost made Cain lose his mind. Was she hurt underneath, bleeding through the layers of fabric? He would tear Randolph Mackay limb from limb.

Cain's jaw ached with pressure as he clenched his teeth. His short sword was drawn and bloody from the work he and Joshua had done below. Cain could hear his brother charging up the stairs, having barred the doors and locked Viola away. Cain braced himself to block him.

"*Stad*," Cain said evenly as Joshua reached the top.

Joshua grasped his shoulder that barred the way, looking over at the scene before them. "Fok!" Joshua yelled.

"Blessed in the name of our holy Christ, Amen," the pastor said. "And I must give the bride the kiss of Christ."

"Do it, then!" Randolph yelled, his eyes bulging as he watched Cain and his brother.

Trembling, the pastor moved closer, staring straight into Ella's eyes. His long robes blocked Cain's view for a moment as he caught her hand below and kissed her cheek before retreating to his place on the wall.

A wild look contorted Randolph Mackay's face, and he smiled. "All done and official before a hundred witnesses."

"More like five hundred, ye arse," Joshua said. Without looking, Cain knew that the other two armies of white and bay horses had advanced from where he'd ordered them to wait on the other side of the hill. "Five hundred who will be smashing every stone of this castle and every Mackay head into the ground."

"Not unless ye want Arabella and her precious brother killed right here before ye," Randolph said.

"Enough," Cain said. "What do ye want?"

"For ye all to withdraw to leave my bride and me alone to raise her brother to be the chief of the Sutherland clan."

Cain knew that would never happen. The boy would die by Mackay's hand, if not today, then another day under the bastard's regency. And what of Ella? He had signaled her not to act, but she had no other choice to keep her brother's blood within his thin body.

"Ye will release Ella and her brother to me," Cain said. "And I will not destroy your castle and village."

"Bloody hell, Cain," Joshua said.

"Otherwise, ye will be responsible for the deaths of hundreds of Mackays." He paused as the emotionless guise of certain slaughter hardened his face. He stared Randolph Mackay dead in the eyes. "And I will cut your randy cod off and shove it down your throat so that ye will choke on it."

"Quite a picture," Randolph said, adjusting himself. Obviously, the promise of violence against Ella and her brother had inflamed the *tolla-thon*.

"A promise," Cain replied.

The quiet conviction in his tone muted Randolph's foolish smile. "If I die, she dies," he said.

"Ye die either way, Mackay," Cain replied. He took a step forward.

"No!" Ella called. "Stop!"

He heard nothing from the boy but did not turn to look at him. His first target was Randolph and freeing Ella, even if that was not what she wanted.

"Stop," Ella repeated. "Cain, I swore just now to be wed to Randolph Mackay, and I will honor my oath."

"Ella—"

"No," she said, and Cain could see that her words made Randolph relax his blade so that it did not sit against her neck but hovered before it.

"I will stay with Randolph Mackay as his wife, from this day forward…" she said, her voice dropping and her hand slowly rising next to her. Her eyes stared at Cain, and he could see so much in them. *Goodbye. Hope. Determination.* And maybe something that he never actually believed in. "From this day forward," she repeated. "until *death* do us part."

Death.

With the last word she slammed her hand into Randolph's arm enough to dislodge it, dropping down, her right hand whipping from the side to let loose a dagger. Before Cain could draw breath, the blade thrust point first directly into the forehead of the Mackay guard who held her brother.

"Go!" Cain yelled the order, knowing Joshua would leap past him to the boy.

Cain's muscles contracted, time seeming to move slowly as he threw all his power behind the thrust that sent his short sword flying across the distance. It was like an arrow, his arm a bow. *Thwack.* The steel cut through the flesh and bone of the devil's chest. Randolph Mackay's eyes went wide, the blade he held that was edged with Ella's blood clattering to the stone walkway next to where she crouched.

With her gaze centered on her young brother, she

did not see the shock turn to vengeance on Randolph's face. Blood reddened the man's lips with a cough, and one hand reached out to grab Ella by the tangle of hair that had fallen to the side, yanking her against the low wall.

"Let go!" She struggled to use her feet to brace herself, but her slippers slid impotently against the stone.

"Together into death then, my bride," Randolph said, glancing over the wall.

Cain rushed forward, but the pastor reached them first, his arms going around Ella's middle to hold her from tipping over as she clawed Randolph's arm away. Cain's hand caught hold of Ella's arm as his other palm slammed into the end of the short sword embedded in Randolph's chest with such power that it threw him out over the wall. A sputtering scream descended as the evil bastard dropped, thudding below on the hard-packed dirt of the bailey.

"Ella!" the boy yelled, running toward her. Ella caught her brother in her arms, clutching him tight even with Cain's hand still wrapped around her wrist.

Her gaze went over the boy's head to Cain. "You came," she said.

He gave a brief nod, his heart pounding with… fear. For the first time in his life, the feeling had nearly crippled him. He swallowed it down. "Aye, I came."

Tears leaked from her eyes, her words a whisper. "I…I could not kill you. I was going to throw the poison away."

Kenneth had yelled continuously that she hadn't accepted his suggestion, but watching the pain on Ella's face, her crumbled strength as she waited for his verdict, brought the truth into focus. Cain nodded. "We will talk."

• • •

Ella turned in the warmth of the softness enveloping her, not willing to let go of the pleasant dream of riding across the moor on Gilla's back.

She could hear a cat purring not too far off. She stretched, feeling aches across her back and in her neck. Her fingers rose to the line that extended across the skin of her throat, and her eyes opened. *Where am I? Who…?*

Pushing up from the covers, she jerked around, her breath flying out of her in a gust of relief. Jamie lay sleeping next to her in Cain's massive bed. They were at Girnigoe. Little Boo raised her head from the pillow set between them, but then lowered it, her eyes staying open, watching her.

Ella bent down to check the similar but deeper cut along Jamie's throat, but it had not reopened after Joshua had held a rag to it as he carried her brother before him on the ride back to Girnigoe. She raised her hand to run her fingers through Jamie's shaggy hair, but stopped, not wanting to wake him. Boo stood, stretching in an arch as her paws flexed, extending her tiny claws to dig, one at a time, into the pillow.

Ella glanced at the windows with the curtains parted enough for her to see it was just past dawn.

The remnants of supper sat on the tray near the hearth where she had left it last evening after she had tucked Jamie into bed and taken her own bath to rid herself of the feel of Iain's hands and Randolph's dark promises.

Where was Cain? She perched on the edge of the bed. They had not spoken as he held her against him, riding them home, but his warmth had enveloped her. As he lowered her in the bailey, he had met her gaze, repeating his earlier words. *We will talk.*

She had time only to nod before Merida and Hannah whisked her and Jamie away, leaving Cain issuing orders in his military voice on how to fully conquer the Mackay clan. Was he laying siege to Varrich this morning? The thought of him riding through the night to fight knotted her stomach. She wished to be with him, guarding his back.

Perhaps Kenneth rode with him. She hadn't seen him at all after fleeing the wedding.

Pastor John had explained to her in breathless excitement, as they waited for Cain to retrieve Seraph, that two Sinclair warriors had snuck into Varrich Castle with Cain and Joshua. They had forced Viola to say she must see her brother. When they had brought Viola into the keep, the pastor had to tie down and gag her in the great hall while Cain and his brother dispatched the remaining guards. The clergyman had deep scratches under his robes from the she-demon and had hidden Ella's dagger there before climbing up the tower stairs to the wall walk. He'd passed it to her with his contrived kiss of Christ.

Rap. Rap. Rap.

The light tapping on the door brought Ella out of the bed to pad across the floor. She cracked it to see Hannah's broad smile, Merida behind her.

"Does she look well?" Merida asked, standing high on the balls of her feet and bobbing her head around Hannah to see. "Are ye well, lass?"

Ella held a finger to her lips but nodded. "Yes. Jamie is still asleep." She opened the door wide for the two ladies, and Boo ran out past them, likely headed outside to start her day. Had they heard about the poison? It was no longer anywhere in the room.

Merida held another tray of food and drink. She set it down near the first one and turned to study Ella. "Sleep terrors?"

Ella shook her head. Actually, she had slept quite well, with none of the usual dreams of hiding Jamie and herself.

"Well, she *is* a warrior," Hannah said, signaling for Ella to sit. As soon as Ella lowered, Hannah gently pulled her hair back and started to comb through the mess of curls. "Let us get these snags smoothed out."

Merida bent to look closer at the line across Ella's throat and nodded. "A shallow cut. It may even heal without a scar." She glanced at Jamie. "Although the boy will likely have one to boast over."

"Has anyone seen to Florie Sutherland?" Ella asked, her hands fisting in her lap.

"Aye, she is well enough after being filled with whisky and tied up," Merida said. "An achy head, troubled stomach, and rope burns will heal quick enough, especially now that she knows ye are well."

Merida held out a small clay jar of ointment. "Use this on the cut. I sent some to your lady last eve for the burns."

Thank goodness. Sweet Florie would have no defense against such wickedness. "Did Kenneth take it?" Ella asked.

A glance passed between Merida and Hannah before Hannah smiled weakly. "Nay. Your steward remained here through the night."

Ella twisted in her seat, catching Hannah's arm. "Is he well?"

She nodded. "My brothers…well…Cain needed to question him."

Ella's eyes widened. Did Cain know Kenneth brought the poison for her to use? "Where is Kenneth now?" Another glance passed between them. "Stop that," Ella said louder than she'd intended, but Jamie didn't rouse from his exhaustion. "Just tell me," she whispered.

Merida folded her hands before her, her face serious. "He spent the night in the dungeon for admitting that he brought the poison for ye to use on Cain."

Ella's heart hammered against her breastbone, and she swallowed, shaking her head slowly. "I was not going to use it," she said, her gaze meeting Merida's with truth. "On any of you. Kenneth does not know you like I do now. To him, Sinclairs are all monsters bent on rape and killing."

Merida's lips were pinched tight, but she nodded. "There have been many untruths believed between our clans."

Ella stood. "I need to tell Cain."

Merida gently pushed her back into the chair. "He is not here right now, and I believe that your steward already told him as much."

Merida stood before Ella while Hannah worked quietly on her hair. "And Cain must have decided that he acted to save ye, or Kenneth would still be locked up in the dungeon," Hannah said. "Which he is not."

Relief pressed like a heavy blanket across Ella's chest, and she gave in to the support of the chair. Kenneth wasn't cold and hungry, but she still needed to find him.

So," Merida said, glancing at Jamie, "that bastard father of yours actually sired a son. And ye kept the lad hidden from him." A wicked smile cracked her frown. "He died never knowing." Alec Sutherland had banished the woman from Dunrobin and divorced her because she could not give him a son, so the smile was genuine. But it made Ella sad for her. To be tormented with such anger inside was not how she wanted to live.

Ella laced her fingers together to lay in her lap. "My mother begged me to hide him when he was born and she lay dying. I swore to see it done," Ella ended with a whisper.

"Denying the bastard the one thing he wanted in the world." Merida shook her head. "A perfect revenge."

"I suppose," Ella said, glancing back at Jamie, who had their mother's light-colored hair and blue eyes. He had both of his parents' coloring, unlike Ella. She studied him as she thought back to their kind, docile mother. Mary Sutherland was light and happy most of the time, keeping Ella away from Alec Sutherland. Never had she spoken an ill word of anyone. Revenge was not within her.

"Lots of beautiful curls after your bath last night," Hannah said. "Let us get ye dressed in one of the other gowns we brought ye before. There is much to do today."

"Much?" Ella asked. "Are the brothers still battling?"

"Heavens no," Merida said. "Once the warriors loyal to Randolph Mackay were killed, the others surrendered. None of the townspeople wanted him as their chief to begin with."

"What of Viola? She is not a Sinclair but half Mackay and half Sutherland like Randolph."

Hannah's face pinched inward with sadness. "The Sinclair family who took her in years ago are petitioning Cain to let her live even though she acted the traitor. There is no immediate family member left on her Mackay side, and those who knew her Sutherland mother have never known Viola."

"Where is she?" Ella asked.

"Being guarded by Mackays at Varrich," Merida said. "Gideon is still deciding her fate."

Hannah pulled part of Ella's hair up and secured it with a small silver hair brooch on top. "All my brothers have their parts. Gideon is judge, Bàs executioner, Joshua makes war—"

"Quite easily and with great delight," Merida said with a snort.

"And Cain—he is the leader, the one who was born to conquer," Hannah finished. "He has won Varrich Castle."

Her words tightened into a ball in Ella's stomach. And now he would take Dunrobin as he always said he would. Regardless of his feelings for her.

"Cain has ridden out to talk with the warriors in your clan this morn," Merida said.

Ella swallowed past the tightness constricting her throat. She raised her hand to the bruising there, but it was her own guilt that made it difficult to draw air. The confusion on his face when she'd stopped her march toward him in the great hall, when she'd read the note, crushed against her heart. She had hurt him when he found out her secret from Gideon. By turning away at the wedding, she had hurt his pride before nearly his entire clan. And then he'd found the poison meant for him.

Would he ever trust her again?

• • •

"Ye are head of the Sutherland army then?" Cain asked the man standing across from him outside Dunrobin's walls.

The castle was grander than Girnigoe, with turrets and flags, but its defenses were nothing compared to the many layers of impenetrable walls, baileys, and guard towers around the seat of the Sinclair Clan. The streets of the village that sat before Dunrobin were completely empty, the people likely hidden within Dunrobin's walls or barred in their cottages.

"Aye," the man said, his face drawn into veiled fury. Even though Ella's kin outnumbered Cain and the twenty-five Sinclair warriors he had brought that morn, the man was bright enough to know that numbers wouldn't defeat his lethal band.

"I am Ethan Sutherland. Where is Kenneth Macleod, and Ella and Jamie Sutherland? Have ye slaughtered them?"

Joshua snorted where he sat upon his charger. "We do not slaughter children and women."

"All three are safely at Girnigoe after we saved them from the Mackays yesterday," Gideon said on his black horse.

The muscles around Ethan's eyes twitched, the only change in his face. "I had heard that Randolph Mackay was killed by ye," he said, keeping his gaze on Cain.

"After he tortured a Sutherland woman named Florie and abducted Jamie Sutherland from Dunrobin and then Ella from Girnigoe," Cain said.

Ethan's brows rose. "Someone breached the mighty Girnigoe to take her?"

Cain didn't have the time to let the fool provoke him. He had a mission to finish, one that would see his father revenged and his clan stronger. "Ye and whoever ye feel rules and protects Sutherland lands are to meet on the moor north of here, the one directly between Dunrobin and Girnigoe."

"The moor where we shot down your father?" Ethan asked. Was the fool trying to get himself slaughtered this morn? Behind Cain, Joshua growled. Cain raised his fist to still him.

"Aye, and where Alec Sutherland drew his final breath around my arrow buried in his black heart," Cain answered. For branding Ella, the bastard certainly deserved more: entrails stretched across the moor, eyes plucked from his skull, his whole face branded with a molten horseshoe.

"Why would we be meeting ye there?" Ethan asked, crossing his arms, his gaze fanning out to take in the two dozen Sinclair warriors seated and ready behind the brothers.

"That is your choice. Ye can either peacefully relinquish control of Dunrobin and unite with Clan Sinclair as I wed Ella Sutherland there, or ye will fight until every Sutherland standing against us is dead."

Cain pointed one finger toward the sky where Eun circled. "When the sun is high, all four Sinclair armies will return. Bring the Sutherland chief's sword to surrender. If ye are not on the moor, we will assume ye wish to fight, and we will ride on to Dunrobin."

By warning them, Cain was giving the Sutherland Clan time to ready for a siege. He knew that and had argued for it with Gideon and Joshua on the way. Dunrobin would still fall, but he wished to give them a chance to think things through instead of just reacting. Surrendering and uniting would be best for them, best for Ella.

The thought of her twisted in his stomach, and he clenched his jaw. They still needed to talk. Kenneth had sworn over and over that she never agreed to carry out his plan to poison Cain and likely his brothers. The crumpled note seemed to support his claim, as well as Ella's words at Varrich.

He needed to hear it again from her own lips, but there was no time right now. To lose the momentum after securing Varrich would make taking Dunrobin harder, and he intended to conquer it no matter the issues with King James. Gideon would work the diplomacy required to untangle that mess. And the conquering and taking of Sutherland lands would unite them, something he had always pledged to do.

Cain curved his arm, creating a perch, and the massive falcon dove, pulling up enough at the last moment to sink his talons into Cain's gauntlet. With the pressure of his heels, he turned Seraph from the gathered Sutherlands, and they trotted away from Dunrobin, their shields slid across their backs in case the Sutherlands decided to strike.

Hopefully, they would come to the moor. Otherwise, Ella would see the attack of her childhood home. As terrible as it had been there for her, he would still be taking it violently from her people.

"They will come," Gideon said beside him.

"They do not even know the lad." Joshua's frown was harsh. "Would they go to war for him?"

From the information Cain had gleaned from the maid who'd been living within the Sutherland village, everyone thought Jamie was Florie's boy, raised within the servants' quarters of Dunrobin. It wasn't until a village woman who was dying pleaded to be buried beside her lost bairn in the chief's plot that the twelve-year-old secret was slowly uncovered.

"The Sutherlands will surrender," Gideon said. "There is no other choice if they want to survive and their leaders to be spared." The coldness of Gideon's words made the ache in the back of Cain's head throb.

"I am not ordering anyone to be executed," Cain said, his tone low.

Gideon glanced over his shoulder. "They do not

know that." He turned to Cain. "Perhaps ye should go to the loch alone to strategize." There was only the tiniest edge of insolence in his words, as if he hinted that Cain was not planning this conquest and victory properly.

"Hold your foking tongue," Cain said, the iciness of his words making Seraph's ears twitch as if detecting a possible battle.

Joshua chuckled. "Ho now, I am usually the one Cain swears at."

Cain exhaled slowly and pushed Seraph to ride ahead so as not to be in line with either of his brothers. Ella didn't fear that he was a threat to her brother anymore, did she? He'd held her as they rode from Varrich the day before, cradling her against him. She had assured him that the stain on her gown was wine and not blood, but still he listened for her breath, making sure it was not labored.

They hadn't spoken further.

There was too much to say and no privacy surrounded by armies of men. He had left her safely with his sister and aunt and gone below to bear Gideon's lectures, Joshua's ranting about crushing the Mackay defenses, and Kenneth Macleod's heated explanations. Bàs had remained quiet as usual, his dark expression giving away little.

Cain looked out across the moor and lifted Eun up into the sky to soar again. The summer grasses and wildflowers stretched out before him, but he paid little attention to the wind making them bow. Instead, his mind moved the players about in the game of strategy he always had laid out in his head. Four armies of horse, a newly acquired Varrich

Castle, a boy chief, an experienced Sutherland advisor who had wanted him poisoned, the future of Sutherland clan in his grasp. And Ella.

The polished wooden queen sat in the satchel strapped to Seraph, and he pulled it out, wrapping his fist around it. The queen in his mental game was in jeopardy. He could conquer her and take Sutherland lands, with or without a vow to King James. It was what he was taught to do and raised to believe was his destiny.

Conquest above all else.

And that meant conquering Ella, Jamie, and the Sutherlands. He tucked the queen inside his tunic, the sash of tartan across it keeping it snug against his heart.

As his gaze lowered to the field before him, crops of Scottish thistle sat upright in the breeze even though the fragile wildflowers whipped in the wind around them. He halted Seraph and leaped down to pinch off one spiky flower head.

Joshua halted beside him, his brow rising. Cain remounted and looked forward across the moor. "The thistle is good luck and strong, like our clan and all of Scotland once we unite."

CHAPTER TWENTY-FOUR

Ella hurried down the tower steps toward the great hall.

Where was Cain?

She had watched him return from the south an hour ago, but he had not come up to his chamber where she had waited with Jamie. Her pacing had become too much to bear, and she'd asked Hannah to stay with Jamie while she left the room.

Dressed in a simple blue petticoat and bodice, she stopped in the archway at the bottom of the steps. Her gaze moved about the great hall that had been filled with Sinclairs the day before. A few tankards and platters sat on the long table that had been moved back into its usual place. Garlands of wilted summer flowers still lay draped around the two iron chandeliers and across the mantel of the cold hearth.

Gideon was the only soul in the room. He had turned cold toward her after his trip to Edinburgh, but she didn't blame him. She exhaled, her brows lowered, and walked in. Gideon turned from some parchments he was staring down at on the table. His normally superior smile had vanished, and he studied her as she approached. "Lady Ella," he said, nodding. "Good day."

She returned the gesture. "Have you seen Cain? I have not spoken to him since we arrived last eve."

His eyes narrowed slightly, and he moved closer,

his gaze shifting along her face. He tilted his head. "Aye. We returned not too long ago from Dunrobin."

Her breath hitched, and she forced a deep inhale. "For what reason?"

"To summon Ethan Sutherland and his warriors out to the moor between our lands when the sun is high."

She swallowed hard. "And what will happen there?"

Gideon crossed his arms. He was as large as his brothers but seemed to keep himself more contained. "That is up to your people. They can witness the union of our two clans as ye and Cain speak vows of marriage before Pastor John, with ye surrendering control of Dunrobin and the Sutherland Clan to our leadership or..." He met her gaze without blinking. "If they do not come to the moor, we will ride on to lay siege to Dunrobin and declare war upon Sutherland Clan."

Cain had said that was his plan from the start. He was born and raised to conquer lands and people, and he'd never hidden that fact or apologized for it. But she had hoped...

His brother seemed to wait for her to say something. She wet her dry lips, her head held level, and her voice came strong. "Jamie should take his rightful place as chief of Sutherland Clan, the way my mother wished."

Gideon frowned deeply as if the statement irked him. "He is an untried boy. Cain would never put part of his holdings into the hands of a child."

"I could stand as regent at Dunrobin and guide Jamie until he comes of age."

Gideon smiled as if instructing a child. "I may not know exactly what is going on inside my brother's head, but I do know for certain that he is not going to let ye escape him to go live at Dunrobin." His eyes narrowed. "It is like ye hold an enchantment over him."

Ella crossed her own arms, her hands sitting loosely at her elbows. Although his words made her sound like Cain's prisoner still, the truth that she had come to as she had been dragged away from Girnigoe was that she truly wanted to be by Cain's side, Sinclair or not.

"If I could enchant people, I would see Jamie as head of Clan Sutherland," she said, dropping her arms. Her heart heavy, she turned to walk the length of the hall to the entryway, her fingers catching a long garland of wilted cornflowers that had broken to dangle down the wall. Holding it, she kept walking out the massive doors of the keep, looking across the inner bailey.

Sinclairs strode with intent, in and out of buildings, accomplishing their individual missions. Only a few wore bandages from the early morning battle at Varrich. Her gaze landed on Kenneth as he walked out of one of the barracks inside Girnigoe's inner wall.

Exhaling, she ran to him. "Kenneth! You are well?" she asked. He'd even retained his spectacles.

He pulled her into a hug. Through her often-lonely life, Kenneth had been one of the only people who gave instead of trying to take something from her. *Even Cain wants something from me. Everything from me.*

"I am well," he said and kissed her forehead. His gaze dropped to the line at her throat, and his smile turned into a grim frown.

"It will heal," she said. "And Jamie is well. Rested, clean, and fed." She shook her head slightly. "I am so sorry that they found out about Jamie. Gideon went to King James weeks ago. I did not know, or I would have gotten word to you."

He shook his head, his hands warm on her shoulders. "I am the one to apologize, Ella." He lowered his voice as he glanced past her. "I should not have sent the poison without talking with ye about it first. If Cain had been convinced that ye wished to kill him, he may not have gone to Varrich to save ye." Pain sat heavily in his eyes. "I have wanted only to protect ye, and I almost cost ye your life yesterday."

Tears pressed hard against the backs of her eyes. "We have survived. Thank you for all you have done to keep me and Jamie safe. Even if I failed to keep my oath to my mother to protect Jamie, you did not. Thank you."

Kenneth's brows bent inward, and he gave a small shake of his head. He squeezed her hands in his. "Ye did not fail your mother."

She stared into his kind gray eyes.

"Ella," Kenneth started and stopped. "Your mother did not make ye promise to keep Jamie a secret to protect the lad. Keeping him a secret was to protect *ye*."

"I…" She shook her head. "I do not understand."

"Mary Sutherland…" he started, and she saw the shine of unshed tears behind his spectacles. He looked upward toward the heavens. "I loved her," he said, his voice dropping into a whisper. "Such kindness and beauty." His gaze lowered back to Ella. "And she loved me. I tried to protect her from Alec as much as I could without making him suspicious, but that became harder once she...became with child. My child."

Ella's heart began to beat faster. Kenneth's eyes softened, his lips tightening for a moment. "We celebrated in secret when our beautiful daughter came into this world, even as Alec raged that ye were not a son. And as ye grew, looking not like either he or Mary, his suspicions grew."

Ella's lips parted as she stood rooted to the dirt. Men and horses and the rest of the world sat at her back, but it all faded to nothingness as she stared at the man who had helped raise her, the man who had wiped her tears, picked her up off the ground, taught her to shoot a bow and throw a dagger.

Ye cannot escape me. Ye are mine. Alec Sutherland's furious words pressed through her mind. "He —" She drew in a thin breath. "He branded me to mark me as his because he was not sure."

Color drained from Kenneth's face, his strength seeming to fall away. He leaned back against the wall as if it was what held his large frame up. Ella grabbed his hands. "But you helped me heal from it, you and Florie."

Kenneth's words came faster then, as if once started he couldn't stop until all was spoken. "Alec started searching for your true father, Ella. He pressured Mary continuously, stopping only each time she was with child so as not to cause her to lose it. When Jamie was born alive, Mary knew she was dying. She also knew if Alec had his legitimate son, he would have absolutely no need for a daughter who may or may not be his."

"He would have…killed me?" She dropped his hands as memories came back to her. How Alec Sutherland hid her away much of the time. How he wanted to use her only to marry away as if she were a commodity to be sold. How he would stare at her as if doing so would give him some answers to questions she knew nothing about.

"Mary knew she would not be there to protect ye. I could have secreted ye away, but where could I take ye where Alec Sutherland could not reach? And then I would not be at Dunrobin to protect Jamie until he could become the Sutherland chief." He rubbed his hands down his face. "I agreed to every promise Mary asked. Especially the one to keep ye as safe as I could, which meant keeping Jamie a secret."

"Is Jamie your son?" she asked.

He shook his head. "Nay. He is the true son of Alec Sutherland, the only child of his to survive."

Ella's gaze had dropped to her hands clasped in her skirts, but she raised it back to Kenneth. "You… are my father."

"I would have told ye when Alec died, but for the clan to accept ye as the new chief, they also needed to think ye had his blood running through your veins. I didn't want to risk it." His words came rapid and soft, as if he'd run out of breath from all his revelations. He took a full inhale. "Aye, Ella, ye are a child from the love your mother and I shared."

The bubble of tightness in her chest seemed to burst. With a little hitch of breath, Ella threw herself into Kenneth's arms.

• • •

Cain walked from the barn where he had left Seraph to be washed and fed, alerting the men to tell the others that those not still at Varrich would ride with him at noon to the moor between Dunrobin and Girnigoe.

Contested for decades, it was the battlefield where many on both sides had died. The memory of blood soaking the dirt and the lifeless bodies crushing the tall grasses would hopefully help the Sutherlands remember what was at stake. *If they come.*

As he rounded the inner wall, walking under the spikes of the raised portcullis, he stopped. The blue of Ella's dress caught his eye, and he watched her hugging Kenneth in the corner of the bailey. Was she afraid, her courage finally leaving her with the thought of her clan being conquered?

His chest tightened, but then she backed up, and he saw a smile on her face. She wiped a finger under an eye to catch a tear, but the smile contradicted it. Had she feared that Cain would have executed Kenneth Macleod?

Gideon stopped beside him, following his gaze. "Da would have executed him or at least left him to rot in the dungeon."

"I am not Da," Cain said, turning to walk the

opposite way along the wall. He had no words to give Ella yet. For that matter, he had no words for his brother, either.

Gideon fell in step as they circumvented the bailey and trod across the wooden drawbridge. "I have drawn up both the marriage papers and the surrender of Dunrobin and Sutherland lands," Gideon said. "In truth, Ella could sign both and be done with it here if ye do not want to bring her out on the field. She is still the current chief of Sutherland Clan. If ye want, we can have her brother also sign the surrender. Macleod says the boy can write."

Cain's jawline hardened as he frowned, his gaze before him. "I would have her clan see her sign and that she and her brother are unharmed." He saw a bird fly up from a tree growing alongside the wall and watched it climb higher into the gray sky. "I would have Ella take her vows before them, so they know that it is what she wants."

Was it what she wanted? To marry him? He had told her that there were only two choices and that he had taken away her choice to die.

Hands fisted at his sides, Cain glanced at Gideon. Always the brother with level-headed answers, he stared at him. "She will take the vows with me?"

Gideon's brows rose. "Joshua says that she has lain with ye, more than once. Tell her that no other man would have her."

Anger, already ignited by the incessant questions tangling his thoughts, grew rapidly with every word from his brother's mouth. Cain stopped, centering his fierce gaze on Gideon. "I will not let any other man touch her." It was all he could do not to punch him. Why the bloody hell was he talking to him anyway?

Gideon spied Cain's fist and met the challenge in his eyes. "Well, tell her that, too. She might be flattered by it."

Why had he ever thought that Gideon knew anything about women?

Cain whirled away from him, but Gideon stopped him with a hand on his arm. Cain almost slammed his fist into him, but his brother stepped away when Cain turned back with murder in his eyes.

Gideon sighed. "Cain...I am only looking out for our clan and for ye. Ye have seemed...distracted." Gideon clenched his fists as if preparing to defend himself. "And Joshua worries ye might not go to war against the Sutherlands because ye have..." He unclenched one hand, lifting and flipping it as if trying to find the right word. "Because ye have grown soft for Ella."

Cain walked straight up to him and pressed his closed fist hard against Gideon's chest. "Joshua can fok off, and so can ye. If either of ye think that I am not the chief of the Sinclairs, feel free to draw your swords."

"Neither of us are saying that, Cain. We were all raised knowing ye would lead our clan to victory, making us and Scotland strong. With our armies growing, ye could even be king someday. Joshua, Bàs, and I would see it done, putting ye on James's throne.

"Today is another step forward in making Clan Sinclair the strongest in the land." Gideon smiled, which was at odds with the worry in his eyes, and backed up so that Cain dropped his fist. "Ye win every game ye play, brother. Ye could win all of Scotland."

Cain stared at him, his hand sliding up to his sash that hid the queen that Ella had carved. He won every game. Aye, he could just take it all. Call checkmate and put a bloody crown on his head.

He looked at Gideon. "Whatever the Sutherlands decide today, I want Ella, Jamie, and Kenneth Macleod to be kept safe."

Gideon frowned. "He sent her poison to use."

Cain met his gaze with unbending strength. "He protected Ella against Alec Sutherland all those years, and he sought the only way he could protect Ella while she was in my grasp. He deserves to live." Before Gideon could argue, Cain turned on his heel. "If ye follow me, ye will find yourself in a lot of pain," he yelled back and strode along the wall of Girnigoe, his strides eating up the ground as his fists swung at his sides. His thoughts spun around and around as if all the pieces on the chessboard had been scattered.

When he looked up, he realized he'd entered the castle's corridor and stood before the small chapel that his father had erected for Cain's mother. He walked inside the vaulted room, the stained-glass images looking down on him. Behind the altar was the image of the four horsemen, Cain and his brothers riding down from Heaven on their steeds.

Your duty is to conquer. Sinclairs above all else. You are God's servant, his weapon against all those who are weak. His father's last words echoed in his brain as if his ghost had risen up to support Gideon's damning words.

*Ye are ready to rule together; first my kingdom
and then all of Scotland.*

Cain looked at the pictures of angels, their
watery eyes seeming to mock him. Did God want
him to be a weapon against the weak, rolling across
Scotland in a tempest of slaughter? He sneered at
the watching angels. "What do ye want from me?"
he yelled, but only silence answered.

He grasped his mouth, sliding his hand down his
chin as if he could slide his skin from his skull.
"Ella," he whispered in the room stuffed with silence
as if all the saints and images were judging him.
"Ella." He wanted Ella.

He exhaled, seeing her face in his mind, the
contentedness of her smile as she looked back at
him when they rode home from Loch Hempriggs.
The mischievous spark to her voice as she laughed
while they galloped across the moor. The depth of
her beautiful gray eyes as she stared into his, seeing
him, really seeing him, not the conqueror, not the
chief of the mighty Sinclairs. Just Cain.

He could bind her to him forever, never let her
go. Like his falcon, she could have a bit of freedom
but always come back to him.

"Nay," he said, his voice echoing off the smooth
granite. She was not a pet. Ella was a woman, a
clever, beautiful, passionate woman. To tame her
would be to crush her spirit. He would be no better
than her father. Cain would not brand her with fiery
iron, but he would brand her with his name.

"I cannot lose her." He looked up at the image of
the horsemen. In the past, the image had always

helped him focus, but not now. Now it only fanned the rage leaping wildly inside him. *Free her.*

"Nay!" he yelled, his voice a ferocious growl to crush the silence in the room. "I will not!" So much fury welled up inside Cain that he strode to the altar, hefting up one of the marble horses, the one with a rider wearing a crown. Pulling back, he hurled it at the four horsemen. It shattered through the stained-glass image, exploding it, shards and pieces of soldered metal crashing down over the white table-cloths below.

The door swung inward, and Cain spun around, his sword singing as it slid free. Seething, he breathed heavily, welcoming anyone who might want to fight.

His aunt, Merida, stood there, her sharp gaze taking in the empty room and broken glass below the huge jagged hole, finally stopping on Cain. She tipped her head, her face calm. "I thought perhaps your da had come back to life to rage at the heavens for not welcoming him there." Her brow rose in question.

Cain sucked in air through his nose like a demonic horse bent on violence. Slowly he lowered his sword. "I am the bloody first horseman. And…" He took a deep breath. "I do *not* want to conquer." He exhaled long, the admission rolling from him like a boulder he had carried…since he was nine years old.

Merida planted hands on her hips. "Yes, ye do. Ye always like to win. It is part of who ye are."

He shook his head. "Some things…cannot be won."

Her lips pinched inward for a moment before she

relaxed them, and she folded her hands to lay in front of her skirt. "Winning is not always taking, Cain." She looked hard at him, scrunching her nose. "Take, take, take. There is a difference between that and winning."

He stretched his hands behind his head. "Taking the prize is what it has always been about."

She smiled, but her eyes looked sad. "Your da would be proud of ye. Taking over the clan he despised, taking the daughter of his sworn enemy and the power away from his only son. Aye, my brother would toast ye with the finest whisky for taking all the prizes."

He stared at her, and she finally walked down the short aisle. "What have ye to gain by taking today?"

He turned to look at the shattered glass. "A clan, a castle, hundreds of horses, warriors, and…a wife."

She stopped in front of him to lean against the granite altar, making some of the shards clink on the stone floor. "Ye already have all those things… except a wife."

"But by bringing the Sutherlands under the Sinclairs, we will be the strongest clan in the Highlands."

She leaned closer, her words intense as she met his gaze with hard eyes. "Sinclairs are *already* the strongest clan in the Highlands."

"Then what would ye have me do? I am the first of the horsemen."

Merida smiled. "First of all, it is not the end of days, as far as I know. God does not need ye to ride down slicing through everyone *yet*." She slashed her arm as if she wielded a sword. "My brother thought it was the end of days after your mother died." She lowered her arm, shaking her head. "But it was not. And if ye read anything of the Bible besides the bloody end, ye would see that the plan is all about love, which has absolutely nothing to do with conquering."

Love? "I do not understand."

Her smile remained, and she closed her eyes, opening them again with a shake of her head. "No, ye do not, but I was rather hoping that ye were learning about it."

After a moment of silence between them, Merida crossed her arms. "I may not have found a love in this world, but I have been alive long enough to have seen it." She swatted her hand in the air. "Love messes up things, turns logical men and women into fools, changes perfect strategies." She plopped her hands back in their usual place on her hips, leaning toward him. "And it definitely has nothing to do with taking." She shook her head. "Conquest is about *taking*. Love is all about *giving*."

She straightened. "Ye must decide if it is worth… well, everything." After a moment, she tipped her head toward the front of the chapel. "And this mess is going to have to be cleaned up," she said, arching a brow at him. "After ye come to your senses and talk to Ella." She turned, her heels crunching on the glass, and walked out of the chapel.

Love? He knew nothing about it. The only time he had witnessed the emotion was when it had crippled his father as he clung to Cain's mother while she released her last exhale. Gideon and Joshua felt Ella weakened him, but when she smiled at him or looked out at the world by his side, he felt strength like he never had before. Was that love too?

Cain sat down in a pew and bowed his head. How long had it been since he really prayed? Since before his mother died. "What do I do?" he whispered in the hollow silence of the chapel.

When he had seen the stain on Ella's gown and the knife at her throat, all Cain could think about was her, that he might lose her like his father lost his mother.

Ella made him vulnerable, and yet, as they came together, he felt strong and more importantly, at peace. The frenzy of always having to be right, always having to plan the perfect strategy to win at all costs—it calmed under her touch, under her smile. Contentment was such a foreign feeling for someone raised to never be content with what he had but to always be searching for more to take.

With an exhale, he let his hands slide down his face. *Love gives.*

"What do I do?" he murmured again, his eyes closed.

Let her go. He looked up at the picture of Christ on the cross as if He or an angel or perhaps his mother had spoken inside his head. *Let her go.*

His chest clenched at the horrendous thought as if his heart might be physically torn away. "Never," he said, and stood up from the pew to stalk out of the chapel.

• • •

Ella sat straight on Gilla as the horse walked through the wildflowers bending in the breeze across the moor. The last time she had been there, she had stood on the rise at the far end, ordering Ethan to have his archers fire at George Sinclair, the madman leading the fearsome Sinclairs. And Cain had charged up the hill toward her like a madman himself.

Then she'd kissed him, and she had known she was in jeopardy—not just because his horse would not move under her when she'd jumped on Seraph's back, but because in that kiss, she had lost herself for a moment. The restrained power in his gentleness had pulled her toward him.

Everything with Cain had been like that. She felt constantly drawn to him but also needing to escape. She had known him only as a coldblooded killer, but after that kiss, after helping him birth a twisted foal, after watching the care he used around Hannah and the respect he had for his aunt, the mercy he'd shown with Kenneth, she realized Cain Sinclair was so much more.

She had not been able to find him before Kenneth said they must ride to meet her clan for the wedding ceremony and surrender. Hannah and Merida rode horses next to Ella, insisting that they wanted to be there for the wedding. Pastor John, seemingly recovered from the ordeal at Varrich, rode one of Cain's horses, too, Kenneth and Jamie on their mounts beside him. Overhead, a large falcon circled, laces on one talon. Eun. Ella glanced around for Cain.

Turning in her seat, she saw him behind her with his three brothers, all of them riding in a line on their colored horses. Cain had his bow but not the crown. His gaze was centered on her, but his features remained still and serious. Lord, what would today bring? He would take her lands, castle, and her people's pride, and she would have to return with him before all the Sutherlands.

Her hands fisted around the reins. Would they think her a traitor? Or worse, would they not show up, making Cain and his armies lay siege to Dunrobin?

She turned forward again, her heart thumping in time with Gilla's quick step. They rode across the empty moor. There were no Sutherland men or horses yet. *Holy Mother Mary.* She glanced overhead at the glow behind the heavy clouds. The sun was high, and the Sutherlands were nowhere to be seen.

The Sinclair army advanced across the field, surrounding Ella as she rode Gilla. She raised her gaze to the rise where she had ordered the last battle. Her breath caught, and relief tightened through her as she sucked in air. Sutherlands slowly emerged from the forest at the top of the rise.

The Sinclair armies broke into a canter, surging past her, eating up the ground, as the Sutherlands rode down the slope to the base. Hundreds of horses sounded like thunder, vibrating under her, and she pressed Gilla to follow.

"We will stop here," Kenneth yelled across to her as they watched Ethan Sutherland lead the group out to meet them. Kenneth sat his own horse, and Jamie rode on one of Cain's white horses next to him. Pride filled Ella as she watched her brother sit so straight, his face full of the strength into which his young body must still grow. At least he would not die. No, Cain would not let harm come to him or to her. Of that she was certain, even if everything else was unclear. Even if she was to rage at him over the wrongness of this day, he would not harm her body. But what of her heart?

Ethan and his loyal warriors came forward, stopping in a line fifty feet away. There were at least one hundred, nearly her whole army, behind them. Ethan nodded to her and Kenneth, his gaze sliding to Jamie. He'd known Jamie only as a maid's son, never realizing that Kenneth and Ella had been teaching him about archery, battle, and diplomatic strategy.

Ella slid a hand across Gilla's soft coat, needing the feel of her strong, sweet mare to steady her. Cain, Joshua, and Bàs rode forward toward Ethan and his men, stopping halfway between them. Off to the side, the pastor approached with Gideon, who held rolled parchments under one arm.

When Cain stopped, his voice came loud and booming like thunder. "I, Cain Sinclair, the fifth Earl of Caithness and chief of the mighty Sinclair Clan, call this assembly together to secure a peaceful change of leadership within our clans."

Ella's heart beat hard as she watched Ethan's frown deepen, but he did not say anything, and he did not draw his weapon. What could she do? Ride away and refuse to wed? Without a blood tie to Alec Sutherland, wedding her would not help Cain justify taking over the clan, but with his power he did not need a justification anyway.

Cain continued. "Pastor John will make these proceedings official, our oaths before God."

Gideon came forward with the rolls of parchment. "Ethan Sutherland, come forward," Gideon called out. Ella's head archer and three of his men guided their horses across the narrow chasm to sit directly across from Cain and his brothers.

"Kenneth Macleod and Jamie Sutherland, come forward," Joshua called out without looking behind him. Both Kenneth and Jamie moved their horses forward.

Ella watched Cain's back. He wore a white tunic with his plaid wrapped around him, the end slung over his chest. His bow sat tied to the back of Seraph, and a sheathed sword lay strapped to his side. No leather armor, not even his shield, although the armies at his back were completely dressed for war.

"Arabella Sutherland, come forward," Cain's voice rang out.

Ella swallowed past the wild thumping of her heart and pressed her heels gently into Gilla's sides. He would make her wed him. She wanted to be with him, but...the scene was so similar to the one at Varrich that her stomach clenched, and anger straightened her spine. This would be no joyous wedding with smiles and congratulations. This would be a forced surrender.

Ella moved forward, once again without a choice.

CHAPTER TWENTY-FIVE

Cain didn't dare look at Ella or he might weaken in his resolve. The same with his brothers to the right of him. Gideon held the rolled parchments for him to take, but he ignored the wide sheaves with his brother's neat script outlining the surrender of Ella to him and the Sutherland lands to Clan Sinclair.

Ella moved her horse up to the line next to Jamie, the lad being quite brave there among the deadliest warriors in Scotland.

"We are here, Sinclair," Ethan called across. "We know ye have the strength to conquer or kill. Be done with the conquering then." His tone showed begrudging surrender. It would be an easy conquest, one without much bloodshed, if any.

Cain drew his sword and moved into the center. He raised it high in the air and inhaled to fill his words with force. "From this day on, the Sinclair and Sutherland clans will be united as allies." He turned his gaze to Ella. She sat regally in her blue gown on her horse, lovely curls blowing in the breeze, her face tense and brows furrowed.

"Clan Sinclair under my leadership," Cain continued. "And Clan Sutherland under the leadership of…Jamie Sutherland, thirteenth Earl of Sutherland. Until he comes of age, Kenneth Macleod will act as regent."

He heard one of his brothers curse behind him, likely Joshua. But Cain watched only Ella's face. Her beautiful gray eyes blinked as her lush lips parted. Hands clenching together before her, she shut her eyes, bowing her head.

"What are ye about?" Ethan asked, making Cain drag his gaze from her.

He looked across at the frowning man. "The full force of the Sinclairs supports Jamie Sutherland as chief with Kenneth Macleod acting as regent, and any act to dissuade or hinder this will be met with deadly force from Girnigoe."

Cain looked to Jamie. "Advance," he said. Kenneth nodded to the lad, and he tapped his mount to stand before Cain's horse.

"Bring the chief's sword," Cain said to Ethan. The man pushed his mount closer, drawing out the Sutherland sword that Cain had asked him to bring. Cain held out his open hand, and after a pause, Ethan passed the hilt to him.

He looked to Jamie. The lad kept a straight spine and a serious squint to his eyes. Cain nodded to him. "This sword rightfully belongs to ye. Kenneth Macleod, Ethan Sutherland, and I will teach ye to wield it well. May ye take the advice of wise men and women and rule with keen strategy and an unselfish heart."

The lad pressed his horse forward, and Cain laid the blade of the sword across his other palm to hand it over to him. Jamie's arms were thin, but he would grow muscle. Cain would make certain of it.

Kenneth nodded to Cain and moved closer to Jamie, who wasn't quite certain where to put the massive weapon. Kenneth pulled a short length of plaid off the back of his saddle and passed it to the lad. "Wrap the blade in this for now and balance it in your saddle," he said quietly. "We will get ye the scabbard for it from Dunrobin." Aye, the man would be a wise advisor for the new chief.

Jamie turned to meet Cain's gaze. There was maturity in his eyes. "I do not know why ye have done this," Jamie said, "but I am grateful there will be no bloodshed for my people and yours."

Spoken like a chief already. Cain felt his frown relax. Jamie turned his face toward the Sutherland Clan. "Clan Sutherland will call Clan Sinclair our ally from this day forward," the boy said, each word rising in volume.

Bow to no man. His father's words echoed in Cain's mind, but the rules of the game had changed. To win, he must give. Cain brought his fist to his chest and bowed his head briefly. Jamie did the same, as did Kenneth.

Kenneth glanced over his shoulder at Ella and then looked to Cain. "And what of Arabella Sutherland?"

Cain swallowed hard. Even with his brothers' stares boring into him, it was Ella he worried over. He turned to her. The breeze blew her curls about her shoulders, the muted sun shining down on them. She had risen again to sit straight, her expressive eyes narrowing.

"And for me?" she asked, guiding her horse forward.

Ye are mine. The words fought to come out of his chest as if they were buried blades anxious to slice through his sinew and skin.

Conquest takes. Love gives. Merida's wise words

overrode his selfish dictate, a dictate that had always ruled Ella's life. But he would not be Ella's cruel father, demanding ownership over her. He was a conqueror, but he would never have Ella's love by taking it.

Cain moved Seraph alongside Gilla so that Ella and he sat only feet apart as she waited for his demands. "I was wrong," he said, meeting her gaze. "There are not just two choices, Ella, one of which I took away for good." He released a deep exhale. "Apart from death, all the other choices in the world are yours."

He pulled the queen from his sash, along with the other piece he had retrieved after leaving the chapel. "Ye have never had your own choices. Your bastard of a father—"

"Actually, Kenneth is my father," she said, interrupting. "I did not know until an hour ago," she said swiftly. "I would have told you—"

"That is…good," Cain said. He glanced at Kenneth and then back to her.

"Go on," she whispered.

His mind stumbled over the words he had planned. He always had a strategy when playing a game, but this was not a game. In a game, the winner took the prize. The only way he could win with Ella was to give away the one thing he wanted above all else.

He cleared his throat. "Ye have never had choices, Ella, and now…ye do. Ye always should have had them."

He held the two carved chess pieces in his hand, the queen she had made and the white knight that she had hollowed out earlier in her fury. "And ye were right. I was hollow without knowing I was." He set the knight in her palm and tucked her queen back in his sash. "And I do not want to be only about conquest and war and taking. *Love* requires giving. I have never had the need before."

Ella's eyes had gone wide with the word, her hand closing around the white knight.

"Is…is this a game?"

"Nay, lass. No game." Cain inhaled deeply. He must finish his words and leave before his discipline deserted him and he grabbed her up to carry her back to Girnigoe.

"I want ye, Ella, more than land and horses and castles. If this is a game, I forfeit it all." He stared hard into her eyes, gray with little flecks of blue, and his throat constricted. He kept his hands fisted so he would not reach for her. "I want ye in my life for now and always. I could carry ye away right now." He watched her lips part, their softness drawing him in. But he held back and shook his head. "But my whole life has been about taking. I will not take ye. The choice, Ella, is yours to make."

His chest felt tight enough to burst, and he inhaled to prevent himself from flying apart as he stared into the depths of her eyes. "Do ye understand?"

"Cain," Gideon yelled, his voice full of barely contained fury. No doubt both of them would end up needing stitches by the end of the night. Right now, Cain welcomed the promise of physical pain as his heart struggled to beat in his clenched chest.

With one last look into Ella's wide eyes, he

turned Seraph and touched his heels to the horse's sides. The horse moved forward in his usual gait, and Cain closed his eyes, every muscle in his body tense.

Thunder rumbled over the sea in the distance as if his father bellowed down from the heavens. His brothers came up to ride alongside him in their birth order as they had always done. Horses all around him pivoted in tight circles to leave the moor, parting the clans as allies instead of conquered and conquerors. His warriors closed in behind him while he rode through their lines, bridles jingling, ready to follow him back to Girnigoe.

He was encircled, and yet he had never felt so alone.

• • •

Ella watched Cain's broad back until his warriors surrounded him.

The choice, Ella, is yours to make. Do ye understand?

A small sob escaped her as she repeated his words in her head and in her heart. Yes, she understood. Cain Sinclair was showing her he *loved* her.

Heart thudding, she looked down at her fisted hand. One by one, she uncurled her fingers to look at the beautiful white knight. It was the one she had carved out when she'd accused Cain of being hollow inside, caring only about conquest and the material spoils of war.

Turning the knight over to see the space beneath, she saw that something filled it. Pinching her fingers, she plucked out a flower, a crumpled thistle. A purple Scottish thistle.

Her other hand fisted against her mouth. *Prickly in nature, but with the heart and beauty of a Scottish lass*. In that moment she knew what her choice was. She snapped her gaze back up to the mass of Sinclairs riding away. "Cain!" Her voice was loud, but he could not possibly hear her over the sound of hundreds of horses. "Cain!" she yelled again.

"Ella, what?" Jamie asked, his gaze going back and forth between her and the Sinclairs riding away.

"I need to get to Cain."

"But he is letting ye go home," Jamie said.

Kenneth sat beside him on his own horse. "Aye, Ella," he said, drawing her gaze. Her father smiled warmly at her. "He is letting ye go home, lass. Ye need to figure out where home is."

"That is at Dunrobin," Jamie said, frowning. "The Sinclairs captured her, and then their chief said she could go."

"Come along, Chief Sutherland," Kenneth said. "Your sister has to think without anyone jabbering in her ear."

Ella looked across the field laid out before her, hundreds of mounted Sinclairs moving across in their color divisions: white, bay, black, and the smaller group of pale green horses. She leaned left and right but could not see Cain's back anymore. He must be up in front with his brothers. Pushing up higher in the saddle, she still couldn't see him. "Cain," she whispered, her heart full.

Her fingers wrapped around the knight in her hand as she leaned over Gilla's neck. "*Falbh!* Go!" Gilla leaped forward, barely needing Ella to guide her, which was good, because the field was flooded with trotting warhorses. She strained to see Cain up ahead, but the front of the four armies had begun to enter the forest, making the mass halt as the front horses slowed to weave around the trees and summer-thick bramblebushes. Gilla was forced to slow and finally stop.

Ella's feet went under her, boots slipping into the toeholds, and she pushed up into a stand. Men were all around her as she tried to see the front of the mass. "Cain Sinclair!" She tucked the knight into the top of her bodice and cupped her hands around her mouth. "Cain Sinclair!"

Faces turned in her direction, but her words did not penetrate the crowd or the trees. She could see Hannah and Merida riding off to the side. "Cain," Hannah yelled, but her voice hardly moved through the heavy air that smelled of rain and sea. Keenan, who rode partway to the trees, cupped his hands, standing in his stirrups. "Cain Sinclair," he repeated, facing forward.

Hamish, the elderly man whom she had helped guide the horses at Midsummer, pushed up in his stirrups. He cupped a hand and faced the forest. "Cain Sinclair!"

Thomas waved to Ella from the other side, a grin on his round face. He looked toward the forest. "Cain Sinclair!" Next to him, several of the guards who had stood below her when she'd foolishly climbed out her window did the same.

The wind blew and thunder rumbled. Would their words be blown away? Cain had gone against everything he had been taught. Conquest was his world, and yet he had given. *Love requires giving*. Ella's heart thudded, and her knees felt weak as they held her there above her saddle. Gilla knew the feel of her standing and kept still, and Ella cupped her hands again. "Cain Sinclair!"

As one massive unit, the warriors before her cupped their hands around their mouths and yelled. "Cain Sinclair!" His name crashed through the air like the thunder overhead, making her breath catch in her throat. She blinked back tears of gratitude and watched the tree line. Horses began to spread out, filling all the space between them as the warriors opened a path.

"Cain," she whispered as he emerged from the darkness of the forest, the sun having been covered by fast-moving clouds. Sitting straight and proud on his white stallion, even without the crown, he looked like a mighty messenger from God. Strength evident in the set of his shoulders and the lines of his face, he moved closer, his three brothers following.

"Come along," she heard Merida yell as she beckoned to Hannah to maneuver closer to Ella. "Move aside," she ordered the men.

Ella continued to stand on Gilla's back, frozen by her hope, her breaths shallow as he approached. Cain stopped Seraph and swung down off his back to stride through the crowd of mounted warriors. She was reminded of the first time she'd seen the ferocity in his face. She'd been standing on Gilla's back to order her men to fire upon the Sinclair armies in the west, and then he'd charged across the field and up the bank after her. She'd been desperate then to escape. Now…she was desperate for him to reach her.

Cain stopped beside her horse, his face tipping back to look up at her. "Ella?"

She wet her dry lips and swallowed, standing high above all four armies, who sat silent. "You said I have a choice."

"Ye have all the choices," he answered.

She stared down at him, their gazes connected, and the rest of the world around them meant nothing. The thunder overhead, threatening rain, hundreds of warriors seated and watching, the scowls of his brothers as they sat their mounts directly behind Cain. All of it disappeared. Only the piercing blue of Cain's eyes remained. She inhaled. "I choose you, Cain Sinclair."

His lips closed, and he took two steps closer. "Ye have all the choices in the world."

"So I have been told," she said, a hopeful grin spreading across her face. "And I choose…you."

In three powerful strides he stood directly below her, his face tense with a mix of disbelief and joy. She lowered into a squat on Gilla's back. "Will you catch me?" she asked, putting her arms out toward him.

He stepped up to her, a smile finally sweeping across his face, his strong arms reaching. "Always and forever."

Her feet touched the trampled grass of the moor, and Cain's hands cupped her face as he gazed down into her eyes. "I love ye, Ella. I give ye all of me."

Ella blinked as tears of joy broke from her eyes. "I love you, too, Cain." She caught the back of his neck as he bent over her, his lips covering hers to seal their declarations. A warmth spread through

Ella as he held her, kissing her with gentle thoroughness.

Caught in the joy that bubbled up inside her, Ella did not hear the roar around them at first. But as Cain raised his face to look again into her eyes, the full force of Clan Sinclair cheered around them.

Ella's heart overflowed with such happiness.

Cain wrapped her up again, enveloping her in his strength and love, right where she belonged.

EPILOGUE

"If Gideon rules against ye, do I get to cut off your head?" Bàs asked, his grin wide as he met Cain's gaze. Cain snorted softly as he attached his polished Sinclair sword to his side.

Gideon huffed. "I am not ruling against Cain. We are brothers, and I swore an oath to follow ye," he said, raising a finger to touch the stitches above his eye. He shook his head. "Although I still do not understand why ye gave up *everything*. It was in the palm of your bloody hand. All ye had to do was close your fist around the Sutherlands, and we would have their clan right now."

His brother was correct, but then Cain would not be standing in the forest by Loch Hempriggs waiting for his beautiful bride to walk to him. "Nay," Cain said. "I suppose ye don't understand, Gideon." He looked to his brother. "I hope someday ye do."

Gideon opened his mouth, but whatever he wanted to say was cut off by the billowing swell of the bagpipes that Thomas played across the glassy water.

Bàs leaned in to Cain. "Where is Joshua?"

"Perhaps he already left," Cain said, frowning as his gaze slid across the crowd of Sutherlands and Sinclairs that had gathered. Hannah and Merida waited near the flower-covered archway at the end of the small dock they had built into the loch, but there was no sign of his second brother.

Joshua had requested to journey north into the

islands where the people warred without distinct clans. His frustration with Cain's decision to let Sutherlands rule themselves had made Joshua even more hostile. Cain had given Gideon the task of bringing the Mackays at Varrich to heel, because Joshua seemed to spur more conflict with their conquered neighbors. So Cain had granted his request to leave. Had he done so without farewells or seeing his brother wed?

Pastor John stepped with confidence along a path that Bàs had helped Cain clear earlier. Cain's breath caught in his throat as Ella walked out from the summer trees behind the pastor, Kenneth at her side. Her hair was a cascade of soft brown curls down her back with part of it pulled up high to encircle her head like a crown. She wore a blue dress, simple and crisp. He smiled broadly, for in her hands she held a bouquet of Scottish thistle.

He remembered the girl from long ago who'd caught his eye. Lasses had been a shallow game then. But love had changed his life into something much more than a game. He had risked everything, and in so doing, he and Ella were winning the greatest prize of all.

Kenneth bowed to Cain, presenting his daughter, and stepped back next to her brother, Jamie. Cain met Ella's eyes. "Beautiful and prickly," he said, glancing at her flowers.

Her lush lips turned up with happiness. "A true Scottish lass."

They turned toward the pastor, who had positioned himself at the end of the dock, and walked together to stand before him.

In the forest on the other side of the water, a large bay-colored warhorse emerged from the thick foliage. Joshua looked across to Cain, catching his gaze, and nodded to him. A grin played along Joshua's mouth, and he raised his sword high in the air. His voice rang out, traveling across the water. "All hail, Cain Sinclair, chief of the Sutherland Clan, fifth Earl of Caithness." The warriors around the pond raised their swords and repeated his declaration.

Joshua kept his sword high. "All hail, Arabella Macleod Sutherland Sinclair, lady of Girnigoe Castle." The rumble of voices shook the woods as everyone again repeated his words.

Joshua sheathed his sword and bowed his head to Cain from on top of his horse. With a press of his legs, Cain's brother turned around, riding away.

"He leaves?" Ella asked.

"Aye," Cain answered, taking a full breath. "He yearns for war, and I rule for peace."

Pastor John lifted his Bible in the air. "We stand here before your people and before God to hear the oaths that will bind these two together forever."

"Forever and always," Cain whispered, staring into Ella's storm-gray eyes that sparked with the fire that lay within her.

"Forever and always," Ella whispered back.

Smiling, they both turned to speak the vows for the pastor and their people, the vows that they had already taken into their hearts.

Follow the epic adventure of the second Son of Sinclair, *Joshua, Horseman of War*, as he journeys up into the turbulent Orkney Isles off the north coast of Scotland in the second SONS OF SINCLAIR book releasing in winter 2021!

A BIT OF HISTORY

The Sinclair clan was established in Scotland in 1057 when Sir William St. Clair of Rosin near Edinburgh married Isabella, daughter and heiress of Malise, Earl of Caithness. The castle of Girnigoe, situated on the east coast of northern Scotland, was built around 1480 by William Sinclair, the Second Earl of Caithness as a tower house defensive structure. An addition to the castle was built in 1606 and connected to the original tower by a drawbridge over a ravine.

The 16th century was rife with disputes and battles between the Sinclairs and their neighbors, the Sutherlands. When Alexander Gordon, Twelfth Earl of Sutherland, divorced his annoying Sinclair wife in 1573, he started a war with her father, culminating in a battle outside Wick, Scotland in 1588. More than a hundred Sinclair warriors were killed in this battle along the shoreline, but the Sinclairs withstood a siege of Girnigoe Castle. In 1589, in retaliation, George Sinclair, Fourth Earl of Caithness, invaded and laid waste to Sutherland lands.

In the 17th century, George Sinclair, the Sixth Earl of Caithness, had accumulated a huge debt with the Campbells of Glenorchy. To pay the debt, the Campbells claimed the earldom and lands from George Sinclair. In 1679 the castle was besieged and captured back from the Campbells by George Sinclair of Keiss. The ensuing battle over the earldom and lands was at Altimarlach, where the Sinclairs were "slaughtered in such numbers that the Campbells reportedly could cross the river without getting their feet wet."

In 1681, the Privy Council of Scotland settled the feud by giving the Sinclairs back the earldom, while the Campbells were made Earls of Breadalbane. Girnigoe Castle was so damaged by Sinclairs, who had strived to make it uninhabitable for the Campbells in 1680, that it was never reused.

After being owned by several families through the centuries, it was sold back to the Sinclairs in 1950 and now sits in a historical trust. Today the castle ruins are open to visitors, although the cliffs and structure can be dangerous. I plan to visit it in 2020!

ACKNOWLEDGMENTS

A huge thank-you goes out to all of you wonderful readers! Your support of historical romance and the authors, who work for months to create these adventures, is as rich and valuable as gold. *Slàinte!*

And to my family who give such amazing, constant encouragement. Braden, Skye, Logan, Kyrra, and Mom—thank you for all your love and words of support. Thank you for making your own dinners, doing your own laundry, and living in a messy house during deadline weeks. And for not teasing me too much when I stare off into space or put the butter in the dishwasher while I'm listening to the voices in my head. You all are an integral part of me being able to achieve my dreams. I love you so very much!

A special thank you to Lisa Kim and her horse, Chloe, for letting me visit and learn so much about these grand creatures. Large, patient, and kind, Chloe let me look in her big brown eyes and pet all the contours of her face for as long as I wanted. She is the inspiration for the gentle giants, full of beauty and majesty, in my books.

Thank you to my fabulous agent, Kevan Lyon, for always being in my corner. To my wonderful editor, Alethea Spiridon, for helping me create the best stories I can. And to my whole team at Entangled Publishing and Liz Pelletier for giving me the opportunity to release my stories out into the world.

Thank you all for helping to make my happily-ever-after come true.

Also…

At the end of each of my books, I ask that you, my awesome readers, please remind yourselves of the whispered symptoms of ovarian cancer. I am now a nine-year survivor, one of the lucky ones. Please don't rely on luck. If you experience any of these symptoms consistently for three weeks or more, go see your GYN.

- Bloating
- Eating less and feeling full faster
- Abdominal pain
- Trouble with your bladder

Other symptoms may include: indigestion, back pain, pain with intercourse, constipation, fatigue, and menstrual irregularities.

Beauty and the Beast meets *Taming of the Shrew* in this laugh-out-loud Regency romance that *New York Times* bestselling author Sarah MacLean calls "smart and sexy."

THE BEAST OF BESWICK

AMALIE HOWARD

Lord Nathaniel Harte, the disagreeable Duke of Beswick, spends his days smashing porcelain, antagonizing his servants, and snarling at anyone who gets too close. With a ruined face like his, it's hard to like much about the world. *Especially* smart-mouthed harpies—with lips better suited to kissing than speaking—who brave his castle with indecent proposals.

But Lady Astrid Everleigh will stop at nothing to see her younger sister safe from a notorious scoundrel, even if it means offering herself up on a silver platter to the forbidding Beast of Beswick himself. And by offer, she means what no highborn lady of sound and sensible mind would ever dream of—a tender of marriage with *her* as his bride.

AMARA
an imprint of Entangled Publishing LLC